Singing Creek

A Nathan Wolf Novel

Books by James Duermeyer

Nathan Wolf *series*
Trail of the Outlaw
Singing Creek

Novels
Flint Bluff
Market Time Conspiracy

Nonfiction Books
Heroes in Obscurity
The Capture of the USS Pueblo; the Incident, the Aftermath, and the
Motives of North Korea

Singing Creek

A Nathan Wolf Novel

James Duermeyer

SPEAKING VOLUMES, LLC
NAPLES, FLORIDA
2021

Singing Creek

Cover design by Hannah Linder

ISBN 978-1-64540-479-8

Introduction

Singing Creek is a work of historical fiction. As such, the larger events shaping the United States during the time depicted in the book are accurate, but local events and characters are fictitious. In addition, I offer the following to provide the context and setting of the story.

The 1860 census indicated that nearly four million Africans were enslaved in the United States. The thirteenth amendment to the U.S. Constitution was adopted on December 6, 1865, and with the approval of a sufficient number of states, it abolished "that peculiar institution" known as slavery within the United States.

On its face, the thirteenth amendment seems straightforward, but a system of agricultural production using the labors of nearly four million enslaved men and women throughout the United States for over one hundred years does not disappear with the stroke of a pen in a belea-guered nation's capital. At the time of the passage of emancipation law, most slaves knew no boundaries other than those external to their owners' property. Thus, many remained on the land with which they were familiar and on which they had toiled for years without remuner-ation. Other more adventurous souls struck out on their own to expe-rience freedom and a sense of self-worth.

Those subjugated Americans leaving slavery did so in one of three ways: they were manumitted (freed by their owners), they ran away during slavery, or they were freed by the Emancipation Proclamation in 1863. The executive order freeing the slaves in the rebellion states was instituted with little resistance in the North but was often ignored in the South.

Historians often disagree on the exact dates of the start and end of Reconstruction, but generally it is considered to be the time from the end of the Civil War in 1865 until approximately 1877. Most historians contend that Reconstruction was only partially successful due to post-war conditions such as a downturn in the nation's economy, high unemployment, and the continuing attempt to repress ex-slave liberties by the southern Democratic Party. These factors led to the migration of great numbers of former slaves from the South.

In 1879, the state of Kansas was flooded with emancipated former slaves moving from Missouri and from the southern states of Louisiana, Mississippi, Texas, and Tennessee. They moved to Kansas because the state was formed as, and remained, a free state throughout the Civil War. A second reason for the black migration was the state's implementation of the Federal Homestead Act in 1862, which provided to any settler, regardless of sex or race, 160 acres of land if the settler remained on the property for five years. Between the months of March and May of 1879, over thirty thousand former slaves utilized the act and migrated to Kansas. Following the Civil War and during reconstruction, the total number of freedmen immigrants to Kansas approached forty thousand.

Beginning in 1854 and continuing well after the Civil War, battles were waged across the prairies of Kansas between pro and anti-slavery factions. While Kansas had been a free state during the war, hostile contingencies within the state did not passively agree with the wishes of Washington and the beliefs of a majority of the state's populace. Disagreements ranged from healthy debate to outright killing of the opposition by lawless vigilantes. The frequency and ferocity of these acts of terror earned Kansas the infamous nickname of "Bloody (or Bleeding) Kansas." For years following the Civil War, and after the influx of free black men and women, murderous slavery/antislavery skirmishes, which often masqueraded the true motive of racial hatred, continued and were led by misguided miscreants intent on ridding the territory of its black immigrants by use of unbridled terror, including murder. It was the job of a small number of overworked and underpaid lawmen to valiantly attempt to rein in those outlaws. And so, our story begins.

Part One

Men of Evil

Outside of Chanute, Kansas

Far in the night-shrouded distance, occasional muffled thunder could be heard, sounds that were diminished in the low, black, drizzle of fog. Sounds of moisture droplets falling on the men and their horses from the surrounding overhanging tree branches and the chirping of a few nearby crickets added to the natural sounds of the foggy night. Disturbing the quiet sounds were the rhythmic and steady sloshing of the horses' hooves falling into and lifting from the wet, slightly muddy roadbed, and the occasional creaking sounds of saddle trees rubbing against leather, as well as the punctuated metallic clink of harness trappings. The pungent smell of wet horses and men in dirty clothing permeated the thick air.

At nearly two a.m., the darkness was all-enveloping. Making their way in the light cool drizzle, the horsemen all wore white knee-length tunics over their coats. Unseen in the dark, the white robes were decorated with various dull-colored symbols and belted at the waist by their individual gun belts, each laden with a holstered pistol and spare cartridges. Moisture ran from the men's hair and faces as they wore no hats, but a folded conical white hood hung from the belt of each man. At the appropriate time, they would don those hoods, covering their cowardly faces, leaving only their eyes visible through openings in the hood.

Their leader rode at the rear of the line of horses. He preferred to leave the more distasteful "work" to other men within the group. Like the other riders, he was cold and wet. He, too, was hatless, leaving his dark hair plastered to his scalp by the rain. Chilling rivulets of water ran from the nape of his neck, past his shirt collar, and down his back.

To make matters worse, he was riding a skittish two-year-old horse he had recently acquired in a trade. The gelding was just past green-broke and was a handful for the rider to keep under control. For the past hour, the leader had rued his decision to accompany the group this evening. He was a relatively young man and beneath his tunic, he wore finer clothing than that of his cohorts. A mud-flecked dull sheen still shown on his black leather boots in spite of the falling mist.

Normally, he did not ride with the group on an outing, and at this moment, he was thinking of the warm companionship of his house-keeper mistress and the bed he was missing this night. Even though younger than most of the men he accompanied, he held intimidating, economic power over the men in this unscrupulous group and other members of the same Ku Klux Klan chapter to which they claimed membership. Because of his position, he could choose to lead or follow in the generally distasteful business of the Klan. He preferred to lead from behind and leave the intimidation and violence to the enforcers in his group of Klansmen. Cold and miserable, with water droplets find-ing their way into his shirt collar, he had twice thought of turning back to town to leave the others in the group to carry out their ugly mission, but the group was now nearing the cabin and it was too late to turn back. Along with the other men, he stopped his horse momentarily and donned his hood. And once again, the green horse took advantage of the slack rein to wheel around skittishly. After gaining control of the horse, the leader finished donning his hood. Two of the men in the group drew their horses next to each other, huddled while pouring the liquid from a short spouted can, and managed to light their kerosene-soaked torches in spite of the mist. The flames revealed seven riders dressed in identical white robes. In addition to their pistols, two of the group carried shotguns and two others carried rifles.

In the distance, a dog at the cabin had heard them and began to bark, the noise somewhat muffled in the damp fog. The group moved toward the sound.

While the Ku Klux Klan had nearly died out by 1879, isolated chapters, such as this Kansas group, remained clinging to their outmoded beliefs, persistently carrying out their nefarious and hateful raids against Southern sympathizers and the former slaves who had peacefully settled in the northern states during and following reconstruction. Such was the purpose of these men on this dark night.

The muffled barking of the dog became clearer and louder, and through the dark mist, the men could just now make out the faint outline of the cabin. As the group neared the cabin, they heard the wood-framed screen-cloth door slam. After a half minute they heard the door again bang into its frame. It was not until they were only a few yards from the cabin that they heard the voice.

"That's far enough, you men. You need to get off my property. Ya'll are not welcome here."

The slowly moving mist became somewhat lighter, and the torches stretched fingers of light to pierce the darkness. The horsemen could now see the black man on the cabin's small, covered porch. He was shirtless, clad only in his trousers, and he was holding a twin-barreled shotgun. A woman dressed in a nondescript night shirt stood by his side. She was visibly shaking, whether from the chill of the night air or from fear, and she clung tightly to the arm of her husband. A lean tri-colored dog with black, white, and brown markings stood next to the black couple and continued to bark, its hackles raised in challenge.

A horseman at the front of the group spoke. "Shut your mouth, boy. It's you and your people that ain't welcome here. You're trespassing on Kansas territory. You know damn well we've had this conversation with you before and you're too damn stupid to listen. Remember, we warned you."

The man on the porch responded, "Yeah, you warned me, but that don't mean nothing. Mr. Lincoln gave me this land, fair and square. Now you need to be leaving."

The Klan leader nodded his head to one of the men who held a burning torch. The man brought his arm back and heaved the fire-brand. It flew from his hand in a spark-filled tight arc and crashed through the only window in the front of the house. The remaining glass in the window frame fell to the porch floor, and the dog yelped in fear. Inside the window frame, flames danced in the darkness. The small wood cabin would soon be engulfed in flame and smoke. The woman's scream hung in the damp night air as her husband raised his shotgun.

As the farmer's shotgun moved toward level, several shots rang out. The riders had drawn pistols and fired at the man and woman standing on the cabin porch at the same time that the shotgun of the man on the porch threw its deadly pattern of hot buckshot into the night. A horse screamed and lurched as buckshot peppered its side and the leg of the rider on its back.

When the gunfire finally stopped, the couple lay dying and con-torted on the porch of the cabin, their clothing and bodies torn by the bullets. A piercing continual yelp of pain came from the dog that had also suffered a gunshot wound, contorted on its side next to the inert human bodies. At their back, the flames from the interior of the cabin danced ever higher in the window opening. The fusillade of shooting by the mounted men had been so furious that splatters of blood and flesh bespeckled the porch floor and wall of the cabin.

The gang's leader cursed while looking down at his right leg. "The son of a bitch hit me," he said. Already, in the dim light, his trousered leg began to glisten from the blood-soaked wetness. "God dammit. Let's get out of here," he said.

The horseman who had been holding the other burning torch now tossed it, and sparks jumped from the torch as it landed on the porch next to the immobile couple. A muffled, deep roll of thunder announced that the rainy mist would not stop soon, as the men slowly wheeled their horses and trotted away.

As they rode toward town, one of the riders came abreast of the leader and spoke. "Say, didn't them niggers have a kid and another woman living there with 'em? Do you s'pose they were in that cabin?"

The leader was silent for a few seconds. "It doesn't matter. Even if they were in the cabin, they aren't our concern anymore. I don't go after kids and old women. If they died, so what?" He gave a half-hearted kick to the horse, but his leg was in pain, and he grimaced each time the horse jostled him in the saddle. He had already pushed the gruesome image of the dead couple out of his mind. Now, he only wanted to get to town and wake up the doctor to look at the wound and dig out the burning buckshot. He gave little thought to his horse, which was seeping blood from numerous buckshot wounds to its side. With later medical attention, the horse would survive its wounds, and the leg of the rider of that horse would be saved, but he would forever walk with a slight limp.

Moments later, the roar of the fire, accompanied by popping and crackling from the flame-engulfed cabin were the only sounds heard after the withdrawal of the Klansmen. Twenty yards from the burning cabin and a few yards from the near-vertical bank of the creek was the family's weathered outhouse. From their hiding place, down the steep creek bank, a woman and young boy peered over the edge of the bank and around the side of the outhouse, watching the cabin burn, its flames lighting the darkness. The boy trembled and sobbed quietly while his grandmother snuggled him to her side with an arm tightly around the boy. She was silent, but tears trickled down her cheeks. She whispered, "Daniel, they done killed 'em. They killed your momma and papa. Satan's evil done had its way this night."

When she felt certain that the riders in the white garb had left the farm, she led the still-crying boy to the small tool shed behind the smoldering cabin, opened its door, and sat on a few discarded rags on the floor with the boy on her lap to avoid the drizzly night air. The odor of wet dirt, tempered by the smell of dry grain, mingled with the smell of the woman and boy's wet, soiled clothing. They remained there through the night, the boy sleeping fitfully on her lap. He awoke periodically, stared up at his grandmother's face, and quietly asked her about his mother and father, and the reasons why evil men had killed them. He would then begin to cry again, quietly sobbing until he would once again fall asleep.

The morning dawned clear with the fresh scent of the prior evening's rain mixed with the odor of burnt wood. Dew glistened off the grass and shrubbery. Meezie Jones roused her five-year-old grandson, Daniel Chambers, and took him back to the creek to wash in the clear cold water. They walked back to the smoking rubble and ashes of the cabin. Meezie could see that the prior evening's rainy mist had saved some of the cabin timbers from complete destruction, but she shuddered at the thought of trying to rebuild a home for herself and the boy.

In addition to the storage shed at the rear of the cabin, there was also a chicken house. A tethered milk cow behind the shed raised its head, continuing to chew the only-partially green grass as it gazed at Meezie and the boy. The woman went back to the shed and found the fishing poles, handed one of them to Daniel, and told him to go back to the creek, lovingly caressing his smooth face while giving him instructions that he would need to catch fish for their breakfast.

"But I want to stay here with you, Gramma," said Daniel.

"I know you do, child, but I have some work to do here while you fish," said Meezie.

She watched him walk away carrying his fishing pole. More tears fell from her eyes as she turned and walked to the shed, where she retrieved the worn, iron-wheeled wheelbarrow, a large grain shovel, and a smaller shovel. She placed the shovels in the wheelbarrow and rolled toward the cabin. She stopped a few feet from the rear of the cabin where a small ground-level wooden door remained unscathed by the fire. It led to a half basement that held preserved foodstuffs, painstakingly set aside after each growing season. She slowly pulled the door upward, and peering into the dim light, she could glimpse the rows of dried and canned vegetables from the most recent summer. She was satisfied that their meager food reserves were untouched by the fire's heat. She closed the door, knowing that she and the boy would not immediately go hungry, then pushed the wheelbarrow to the front of the cabin. She stood just in front of where the front porch had been. The gruesome remains of the charred bodies of her daughter and son-in-law were easily seen where they had fallen on the front porch. She carefully gathered the remains in the larger shovel and reverently placed them in the wheelbarrow. She made multiple trips with the wheelbarrow, pushing it to the edge of the creek bank, well away from where the boy was fishing. In the soft, moist earth overlooking the creek, she dug a hole using her shovels and solemnly placed the human remains into the hole. She then carefully covered the hole with water-soaked dirt, all the while silent tears fell from her cheeks. She said to herself that later she would make a marker for the grave. After standing a moment at the gravesite, she carefully climbed down the creek bank, washed her hands and the two shovels, and removed her grimy apron and washed it in the cold water. She stood next to the water for several minutes, head bowed, speaking to her God. Turning to climb the creek bank, she glanced upstream and saw the boy staring at her, fishing pole in his hands. She forced herself to smile and managed a small wave of her hand. The boy was now her primary responsibility.

Resignedly, Meezie knew that she would need help to put order back in her and Daniel's lives, but she also knew that her only help would come from nearby exodusters who had settled on claims not far away. She would make the long walk to see them in the next few days to explain her situation and ask for assistance in rebuilding the cabin. Meezie felt better, knowing that other exodusters had experienced tragedies of their own and were always willing to help one another as best they could in times of hardship.

When she thought about justice for the heinous killing of her daughter and son-in-law, Meezie knew there would be no retribution. Having previously lived as a slave, subject to the whims and laws of the white men to whom she had belonged, and knowing that this same group of men had previously visited the cabin, she knew that there was little to be gained by walking into town and reporting the murder of her daughter and son-in-law. It was simply the way it was.

While still relatively young at forty-three years of age, the responsibility of raising her grandson and eking out a living on the small farm was daunting to Meezie. The thought occurred to her that perhaps she was simply not up to the task, and she felt overwhelmed by the thought of the heavy burden. The horrid scene of last night's killing unfolded in her mind again, and she fought back nausea. In the next moment, she gave thought to the hard work and decisions that had brought her to this small farm three years ago.

Part Two

The Exodusters

Nueces County, Texas
January

Some might contend that at times, one could hear the singing on all four adjoining farms, and no doubt, when it came to praising the Lord in song, there were no shy singers in the small congregation. The joyful, melodic sound rose and filtered through the rough board siding and roof of the building and made its way through the surrounding trees, floating skyward as the people sang in earnest to praise God.

Most would say it was not much of a church. It had been built from scrap rough-sawn lumber by the sweat of the parishioners. It was just a sad looking, hand-built shack in the midst of an overgrown grove of post oaks. Those stunted trees were covered with greenbrier vines, and the short but tenacious thorns on those vines threatened to choke the life out of the struggling oaks and slowly absorb the ramshackle church. The shack was on a useless and nearly inaccessible piece of stony ground, which was so dense with trees and brush that it thwarted any attempt to put it under cultivation. In a rare appeasement of their respective slaves, the owners of the properties had consented to allow the negroes to build the shack to be used as a gathering place for worship. The location was where the edges of four adjoining farms came together, making it convenient for the working families on those farms to all meet together. Dirt paths lined on each side by dense, wild vegetation, meandered from four different directions leading to the door of the small church.

They met twice each week and sometimes even three times if the parson and deacons called them together for a special gathering. Tonight, was one of those unscheduled, specially called meetings on a

Sunday evening at the African Episcopal Methodist Church at four corners. The parishioners had named the church using terms they had heard while serving their white slave owners.

It was cool and drafty in the shack on this chilly winter evening. The attendees kept their coats on in the unheated room. A score or more of homemade tallow candles lined the walls of the church creating sufficient light to carry out the meeting but radiating scant heat. On this night there was no church service aside from the opening prayer of the faithful gatherers. Instead, there was other business to discuss; however, prayers and a closing song of praise would conclude the meeting.

Raising his hands and clearing his throat, Pastor Jed Starnes offered words to the Lord. Following his prayer and a chorus of heartfelt amens, the church became quiet. The candles created a multitude of wispy smoke plumes and dancing shadows around the sparsely furnished room. The congregation was seated on the hard, rough-hewn wooden benches and all eyes were locked on the salt-and-pepper bearded pastor and the man standing at his side at the front of the room, where a plain hand-made wooden table served as an altar. At a signal from the pastor, four men left the building to stand watch outdoors.

Even though everyone in this meeting was a freedman following the Civil War, it was not uncommon for a white overseer from one of the farms to ride unannounced into the small clearing when meetings were being held, just to "keep tabs" on the activities of what they still mistakenly considered their "live" property. Nothing could be farther from the truth, because as freemen, the former slaves working on these farms were no longer the property of anyone and could walk away from the farms at any time. In fact, the only thing holding them to the farms was habit and the paltry subsistence provided for their labor.

But church members cherished their privacy and that was the reason for posting men outside the church. An approaching horseman could always be heard plodding and scraping his way along the path and through the thorny greenbrier vegetation by the men outdoors, who would quickly warn the congregation of the approaching foreman. If there were such an occurrence, a rousing song of praise would be initiated until the intruder departed. Fortunately, on this night, they would have no such interruption.

The attendees of this meeting knew why they had come together this evening. Unlike other plantations and farms in the South, the farms on which these former slaves worked had access to much more timely news and information from around the nation. The reason was because the farms were close to the seaport of Corpus Christi, Texas. Each year, the entire harvested cotton crop of these four farms and others in the area was laboriously taken overland to Corpus Christi to be sold and loaded on boats bound for New Orleans and Mobile. From New Orleans, a portion of the cotton moved up the Mississippi, while other shipments moved across the Atlantic to British and French manufacturers, and from Mobile, the cotton moved overland to gins and manufacturers in the North. When the cotton crop was transported to Corpus Christi, the laborers who accompanied the cotton shipment, or who made other trips to the coast, intermingled with the crews who manned the boats and/or worked in the coastal city. In the course of their travels, the men working on the boats knew the latest news from eastern cities and shared it with the city laborers and the farm crews. When the workers returned to their farms, they shared the news and information with the families who lived in the vicinity. Even so, the news of the legislated freedom of negroes in the South was not received until well after the same news had been absorbed by cities in the North.

Aside from the news of having gained their freedom from slavery some years prior, most recently the single news item of highest interest to the families who attended the small church, and the item that had caused an unquenchable excitement, was the story associated with former slaves travelling to the state of Kansas to claim homesteads. All of their lives, they had toiled as slaves for masters who, in many cases, cared little for their general welfare. Some former slaves carried the residual scars of cruelty on their backs, the results of even the slightest disciplinary infractions. The very thought of striking out on their own and the heretofore impossible dream of actually owning their own land lit a fire in the very souls of these people.

The attendees watched the two men standing at the front of the room. Everyone knew and respected Pastor Jed, who until emancipation had spent his entire life as a slave. His white hair and beard, his slightly stooped carriage, and his large, callused hands were testament to his life of manual labor. Next to him stood a stranger to the group. This gentleman had a lesser dusting of white in his hair, but in contrast to the pastor and the audience, he wore a neat, but well-worn suit of store-bought clothes. In a few moments, he would address the audience.

The pastor's deep resonant voice broke the silence in the church. "My friends, as I promised, tonight we are joined by our brother from Tennessee. He is an acquaintance of Mr. Pap Singleton, whose ventures we have all recently heard about. As y'all know, Mr. Singleton is asking for brothers and sisters to join him in forming negro communities up north in the state of Kansas. This here is Mr. Jonathon Abner. He works with Mr. Singleton and is come here to tell us all some exciting news." The pastor looked to his side, and with a slight smile, stepped back to allow Mr. Abner to receive the attention of the audience, while the gathering responded with polite applause.

"My Texas friends," said Abner, as he held up his hands palms outward to the audience. "It is a great blessing from the Lord that I am able to come and talk with you tonight. It is a great honor because I know of the years of struggle you have endured by the grace of God. Yes, I know of your struggles to work at your never-ending tasks, all the while fearing the wrath of the white men who were your masters through no choice of your own." He paused until the murmuring of the audience subsided.

"But today, we are all free men and women. Through the grace of our past savior, President Abraham Lincoln and the good men in our nation's congress, we now walk without the weight of chains on our souls."

The gathering erupted in loud shouts of joy and amens.

Abner continued. "Yes, indeed. Amen. In addition, we are now able to travel anywhere we like in this United States." He paused, then continued.

"Many of you have heard about our brothers and sisters moving to the state of Kansas. Why, there are so many of our brothers moving there that they are being called 'the exodusters.' Just like them folks in the Bible, our brothers and sisters are making an exodus from their old homes where they were slaves. But why are so many folks moving north? They are moving to Kansas because the United States government is making it possible for us to own our own land." The murmuring of the small group grew.

Abner held up his hands to regain their attention. "Think of it. The government has got this law called the Homestead Act, which was passed some years back. That law says that the government is going to let you have your own land. Just imagine, if you will! Mr. Lincoln, God rest his soul, has made it possible for us to be given some land of our own, or to buy property at a fair price."

Abner had to hold up his hands again to quiet the room. "Mr. Singleton sent me here to tell you that this is all true. In fact, glorious little towns have been born in Kansas. Those towns all have people like us, former slaves and freedmen. And Mr. Singleton wants you to join in this wonderful adventure and opportunity. Our brothers and sisters who are moving into Kansas have earned the nickname of exodusters, and Mr. Singleton wants you to become part of those folks and come to Kansas and claim your own farms. Why, there are already two fine towns named Nicodemus and Dunlap in Kansas, and all the folks in those towns are colored."

This news was nearly unbelievable to the congregation, and Abner was forced to pause once again until the talk and murmuring from the audience subsided.

"Yes, it's true. If you move to Kansas, you will be given free, one hundred and sixty acres of good Kansas farmland of your very own. You will also be able to buy additional land at a reasonable price."

Again, Abner stopped as the level of talking and questions rose in volume and began to be directed to him from the audience. Abner continued speaking and answering questions for the next hour and a half. And after the formal meeting concluded, those members of the gathering who had further questions remained to continue discussing those questions with Abner. It was late in the evening before the little church was once again quiet and dark.

*****

After leaving the church, the couple walked closely together, following the winding foot path back to their quarters on the Chambers farm, a farm owned by Frederick Chambers. Jonah Chambers and his wife Dehlia had been born on this farm, born as slaves at birth. As children, they had each been raised by their mothers. Jonah had been given the last name of his master, Frederick Chambers, with his first name, Jonah, given by his mother. Dehlia had been given the last name of Jones, the previous owner of her mother who while pregnant, had been sold to Frederick Chambers and moved to the Chambers' farm, where Dehlia was born. Dehlia changed her last name to that of her husband, Jonah Chambers, when they were married a few years ago. Together, they had one child, Daniel, scarcely two years old.

"Jonah, I'm scared," said Dehlia. "I just don't see how the words that man spoke could be true. I've never heard of anyone giving away land," she said. "I'm afraid to believe him, and plum scared to set off on our own."

With those few words, Dehlia had expressed the paradox facing an entire race in the United States at the time. Most Africans had entered the young nation as salable cargo on a slave trading ship and had been sold into bondage, expectedly for the remainder of their lives. But the Civil War had made monumental changes in the nation. Oh, certainly, the eventual emancipation had set the black race free from slavery. Yet life on their respective farms and plantations remained very much like it had before slaves were granted their freedom. A few slaves wandered away from the farms in an attempt to start a new life of freedom, but the bulk remained on their respective owners' farms, simply because they knew no other home or work, and were, therefore, strongly attached to their farms and families at those locations. In addition, many of the slaves who left their employers' farms to strike out on their own soon found that work was difficult to find, often forcing them to return to the farms they had optimistically left a short time ago.

Yet now, Jonah and Dehlia Chambers and the others at the evening church gathering had heard a most wonderful story, a story alleging that the state of Kansas would welcome freedmen to come and claim one hundred and sixty acres of free farmland. How could this be true? It was almost unbelievable to the black couple as they walked back to the Chambers farm.

"I know why you're scared," said Jonah. "We ain't never had any good words in all our years working for marse Chambers. And why should it be any different now?"

A quiet, sighing, "uh huh" came from Dehlia.

For the next few moments, they continued walking in silence until they reached one of the squat, flat-roofed buildings that had formerly served as slave quarters and was now their home. The living space, consisting of only one room, was dimly lit by one hand-made tallow candle. Dehlia's mother, Meesha Jones, whom everyone called Meezie, sat on one of the two rough-hewn chairs in the room, nodding her head as she dozed. She raised her head when the couple closed the ill-fitting outer door. The older woman's wooden cot, covered with a wool blanket, occupied one dark corner of the room. The couple slept on the opposite side of the room on a larger wooden platform, also covered with a woolen blanket. Cloth bags that had once held dried beans, and which had been sewn together to form a larger curtain, hung from the ceiling next to Jonah and Dehlia's sleeping platform, giving the couple a semblance of privacy. At the foot of their bed was a smaller bed with built up sides in which their son Daniel slept peacefully.

Meezie watched as her daughter leaned over the toddler's bed and gently touched the child on the cheek with her fingers. Daniel remained motionless in sleep except for his lips, which puckered and moved slightly in response to his mother's touch. Dehlia smiled at her sleeping son and whispered quietly, "Thank you, Lord."

When the candle had been extinguished and after the family had settled on their beds, Jonah and Dehlia quietly whispered, relating the events of the evening church meeting. For the next few days, at every available opportunity, the discussion regarding the opportunity in Kansas continued. More than anything else, fear of the unknown and apprehension regarding the veracity of the stories told by Jonathon Abner at the church meeting dampened the couple's fervor toward making a drastic change in their lives.

The next day, Meezie was brought into the discussion, but the mother's wisdom, born of experience, kept her from voicing a definitive opinion. She knew it was best that she allow her daughter and son-in-law to make the final decision. She had condescendingly resigned herself to their judgment. Inwardly, the fact that she had been a slave for a great portion of her life had instilled an innate fear of change and physical relocation from a situation she had grown accustomed to.

Impromptu meetings among church congregation members, who had been friends and neighbors for many years, took place after church services for the next three weeks. For the most part these discussions were quiet and thoughtful as men and women continued to weigh the arguments for staying on their farms or making a move, yet there were some members who were excitedly outspoken, and who had firmly decided that they would take their chances in Kansas. After serious soul searching and prayers, Jonah and Dehlia joined the group who had decided to leave. This would be a chance for them to better their lives and to give Daniel a better life. They were to become exodusters, with a goal of reaching Nicodemus, Kansas.

*****

Encampment on the Nueces River, Texas
Late February

No one in the group had a clock, and even if they had, it would make no difference. The scrawny rooster with the missing tail feathers set up a racket every morning as the first light visited the eastern horizon, and that proud, squawking fowl was their alarm clock. As they had every morning as slaves and freedmen laborers, they woke to the rhythm of nature, roosters crowing, dogs barking, or first light. It was the time to rise, put fresh kindling on the campfires and begin another day. But instead of walking to the farm fields to work, they would now spend the daylight hours walking on the trail that stretched northward. They were on their way to Kansas. To the surprise of nearly everyone who had attended the ramshackle church back in the woods of south Texas, Pastor Jed Starnes and his family were among the travelers. Because of the respect he had earned from his congregants, he also served as a pseudo leader for the group.

Ten families as a group, nearly fifty persons in all, had started out walking three days ago. As the travelers departed, their procession had been watched by their former owner/employers. While a few white men had begrudgingly wished them well, others had been so bold as to place bets among themselves as to when the travelers would be forced to return.

It could justifiably be said that the group as a whole presented a most unlikely picture of travel readiness. No one in the group owned horses. Hence, all of the travelers, with the exception of the very young or very old, would be walking, no small feat considering that it would be over four hundred miles just to get to the Red River at the border of Texas, and several hundred more miles to reach destinations in Kansas.

The travelers had pooled their money to buy one mule. That animal would pull the single larger wagon crammed with a variety of heavier possessions of the families, mostly tools and farm utensils that would be used on their individual plots of land. There were two milk cows with respective calves, and one of the cows was owned by Jonah and Dehlia. The cows were invaluable, as they provided milk for the infants and children. There was a large pen of chickens perched on the larger wagon, holding enough noisy hens and a few roosters so that each of the families would be able to start their own flocks upon reaching their destination. It was a particularly vocal fowl among those roosters that woke everyone each morning.

Each family had constructed its own crude, hand-built two-wheeled cart that held their personal goods. The stronger men from each family provided the muscle necessary to propel the carts. On these carts, each family carried clothing, food, mementos, and other items felt to be necessary to be taken to their new homes. Within those personal goods and well hidden at the time of their departure from their farms was an assortment of firearms that families had either honestly purchased or deviously purloined from unsuspecting overseers, the justification being that the workers had never been adequately paid for their labors. The guns were retrieved at their first stop for the night and then kept in the possession of the men in each family.

The carts had large wheels, meant to roll easily, and were moved by either one or two men standing behind and pushing a cross bar that extended forward from the body of the cart and across the width of the single-axle cart. It was hard work rolling the family carts, as well as the mule-drawn wagon, especially in hilly terrain and high prairie grass. When necessary, families would assist one another with the carts by either pushing on upgrades and in tall prairie grass or holding the cart back on downhill descents, back-breaking labor for all involved. Yet, only the most inclement weather would be cause for the caravan to pause temporarily and continue with the passing of storms.

It was no wonder that some of their previous owners/employers were certain that members of the travelling group would turn back. But those same men would be proven wrong, as none of the families gave up. This is not to say that the journey was not strenuously difficult and hazardous; it meant that the desire to secure their own personal property was overwhelmingly stronger, strong enough to prevail over the difficulties of the journey.

*****

Several established cattle trails led north across Texas in the 1800s. The Chisholm Trail and the Shawnee Trail extended from near the Mexican border to the northern border of Texas. Ranchers were still driving Texas longhorns to rail hubs in the north, but by the time the group began their travels, railroads had expanded and now took cattle to northern markets. Therefore, the cattle trails were much less traveled by the cattle drovers, and in some instances might have grown over or been washed out, which made the group's travel more difficult. Therefore, the group of exodusters would follow whichever of the two trails was most easily travelled, as they were nearly parallel to each other. North of Waco, Texas, the Chisholm trail split with the eastern trail becoming known as the Sedalia and Baxter Springs Trail. The group of former slaves would follow the course of that trail to Baxter Springs in southeast Kansas. After that, they would turn to the northwest to make their way to Nicodemus.

*****

In the not-too-distant past, but prior to the time of the journey of these former slaves, several events had occurred that forever changed the character of the Great Plains. For centuries, the Comanches, the Cheyenne, the Kiowa, and other native Americans had dominated the prairie. To defend their homeland, the Indian tribes had attacked buffalo hunters, dishonest traders, and settlers, and for the most part, had held onto their hunting lands.

Eastern traders, and more specifically, the United States Government carried out a continuing pattern of creating and subsequently breaking treaties and agreements with Native American tribes. Under the guise of Manifest Destiny, Indians were relegated to sub-human roles in the expansion of the West. In 1874, the Red River War began in earnest, with the U.S. Army relentlessly pursuing the Indians, driving them to starvation and eventual relocation to reservations in Oklahoma. In 1875, the Comanche war chief, Kwahada, along with Quanah Parker, surrendered at Fort Sill, Oklahoma. America's long conflict with Native Americans was, for the most part, over.

A second event in the Great Plains was still transpiring as the former slaves moved northward. Buffalo hunters were destroying the bison of the Great Plains at an alarming rate. To meet the eastern demand for buffalo hides, hunters killed millions of the animals indiscriminately, chasing and killing the buffalo while on horseback, skinning out the hides, and leaving the meat to carrion and to rot in the prairie sun.

By the time the ex-slaves were making their journey to Kansas, there was no longer a large-scale threat from Indians. Only a few small groups of Native Americans surreptitiously remained on the prairie to eke out an existence, posing no great threat to the travelers. Additionally, the travelers would see considerably fewer native bison.

*****

As the sun cleared the eastern horizon, the last of the cooking utensils were restowed on the wagons, and the group began to break camp. Some of the men wore pistol belts, and others had rifles or shotguns easily accessible in their respective carts. From their small clearing near the river where they had camped, the group of wagons moved back to the trail, walking slowly northward. Still considered part of the southern great plains, the area they were leaving was more humid, with more frequent rain. As they slowly moved to the north, they entered the much drier area of central Texas. But many years prior, when the early cattle drovers had scouted and plotted the cattle trails to the best of their ability, they had ensured that the course of the cattle trails would remain within reasonable distance to water, a key necessity for the cattle, drovers, and for the travelers.

Some days later, the group found shade in a post oak grove and were eating a meager lunch of coffee, wild onions, pork jerky, and hard biscuits while resting and talking with one another. Their discussion centered on the condition of their equipment and their diminishing supply of food. None of the men were skilled hunters, and hunger was becoming a problem. Breakfast had consisted only of coffee, wild onions, and more hard biscuits. They talked quietly as mockingbirds scolded them from tree branches above their heads. The soothing sounds of the nearby flowing river could be heard and the mothers in the group carefully watched the children playing. They feared the children getting too close to the river as none of the youngsters knew how to swim.

As silently as a soft breeze, the Indians appeared. No one saw them until one of the Indians shouted at them, and the four-man hunting party began talking loudly among themselves. They rode ponies with minimal trappings. Only a hackamore guided their horses, two paints, a roan, and a black. The men were dressed in hunting attire; loin clothes, leggings, a thick leather shirt to ward off the chill, and moccasins. They were not dressed for ceremony. They were obviously hunters, as two of the Indians each had a recently killed white-tail doe draped across the back of their horses, while a third man had a small mule deer on his horse. They continued to talk loudly, using a great deal of hand gestures.

Most of the travelers had never seen Indians. They had heard many stories about them, of course, and had seen some of the results of Indians stealing food crops on the farms where they had worked. They were greatly afraid of these strange men. Yet, they did not flee and kept a hand on their pistols, mindful that they had not yet taken the time to practice and become proficient in the use of the firearms. The women and children remained behind the wagons, while the men stood in the open. Except for Dehlia. She held Daniel in her arms and stood just to the rear of Jonah.

"Get back behind the wagon, Dehlia. I don't want you hurt!" said Jonah.

"No, I won't. I don't think these savages mean to hurt us. After all, there are more of us than them," she said, and stood firmly in place. Daniel squirmed in her arms, turning to see the strange men on horses.

The Indians were Caddos, a tribe that had been forced by the government into Indian Territory (Oklahoma). But Oklahoma territory could not contain nomadic hunters, and many Indian tribes continued to follow game while hunting, no matter where the game migrated. These horsemen had been hunting for a small band that had not yet made a permanent move to Indian Territory and was camped two miles away.

In truth, the Indians were nearly as afraid of the black men and women as the travelers were of them. They had seen many white people, dressed in a similar fashion to these people, but a person with ebony skin was beyond their comprehension. Yet, their curiosity was strong enough that they moved their horses forward slowly so that they could more clearly see the dark-skinned people.

The Indians' language and gestures meant nothing to the travelers, and the men talked quietly to one another, contemplating whether to shoot at the Indians or wait to see what would happen. They did not have to wait long. The horseman without dead game on his horse dismounted. He walked very slowly toward the men, then turned to his companions and uttered a few words, then turned back to face the dark faces. His eyes moved from person to person and then to the wagons, then back to the travelers. His head and eyes moved to the two milk cows and their calves. But four men of the travelers, their hands resting on the handles of their pistols, slowly moved to stand in front of the cows. The Indian watched this, and a slight scowl crossed his face. He stared at the four men for a short time. He then broke off the stare, moved his head, and seemed to focus on a woman who was holding a brightly colored quilt on which she had been sitting only moments before. She stood behind her family wagon, but the quilt was still visible. The Indian had also seen something in the wagon, and he stepped closer to it. From the wagon, he lifted a decorated porcelain bowl, which only moments before had held the wild onions the family had been eating. He turned the bowl in his hands, examining the floral designs on the sides of the bowl. He made a low utterance of words, then lifted his eyes back to the woman holding the quilt. The Indian's staring eyes terrified the woman, and she could not help making a small gasp. As it happened, the wagon on which the Indian was so intent belonged to Pastor Jed and his wife. Jed moved toward his wife and faced the Indian. The Indian locked his eyes on those of the black man. The two men stood in that position for several seconds, neither showing any fear. Every eye in the group of travelers was focused on the two men as they faced each other.

Ever so slowly, the Indian reached out his hand, palm up and then touched the quilt being held by the woman. His fingers moved over the pattern of the quilt and then he drew his hand back, but not to his body. He then moved his hand very slowly to the arm of the man standing by his wife. He touched the skin of Jed's arm and looked into his eyes. He then pinched Jed's skin between his fingers. Pastor Jed did not move. Slowly the Indian withdrew his hand, grunted, and turned back to face his companions, while still holding the bowl. He uttered several loud words to them, and the three other Indians slowly walked their horses closer to the dismounted Indian who then turned again to speak to the couple. His words were completely unintelligible to the pastor. After pausing, and realizing that his words had not been understood, the Indian's voice became louder and he now placed his free hand on the quilt once more. He motioned to one of the men on horseback, who then tugged at the small mule deer on his horse and let it drop to the ground. The Indian motioned toward the deer, and then to the quilt the woman was holding. The meaning became clear to Jed and the travelers. The Indian was offering to trade the recently killed deer for the bowl and quilt.

One of the travelers said, "I think he wants to trade with you, Pastor Jed."

Jed knowingly nodded his head. He also knew that the group was in desperate need of meat. He slowly turned to his wife, and as if reading his mind, she reluctantly passed the quilt to her husband. Jed handed the quilt to the Indian and then very slowly walked to where the deer lay on the ground. He simply stood over the deer and looked at the Indian. It was over as quickly as it had begun. Leaping to the back of his horse and placing the quilt in front of him, the Indian gazed at the colorful bowl in his hand, raised it above his head in a primitive form of departure salute, wheeled his horse, and the four Indians trotted their horses away from the encampment.

No one spoke, but hands were released from pistol belts and shoulders relaxed as travelers again breathed easier. They watched as Pastor Jed removed his hat and bowed his head. He quietly spoke to the Lord, replaced his hat, and said, "We'll dress out this here deer tonight when we camp and have a nice piece of venison, but right now I guess it's time we get to moving again."

As the days passed, the former slaves became more proficient in their hunting skills. They quickly learned that not all the buffalo were gone, and small scattered herds were often sighted. Using the thick prairie grass as cover to remain hidden, men in the traveling group learned to quietly approach passing buffalo, usually resulting in the killing of a straggler in the herd. They augmented their diets with fish, wild onions, wild asparagus, rhubarb, and anything else they knew to be edible, and as the nights became slowly warmer, they were certain they would not go hungry.

*****

North of Chanute, Kansas
April

Many days back, the travelers had left Fort Gibson behind after making rough repairs to equipment and purchasing meager foodstuffs. Their funds would not allow more refined repairs or extravagance on unnecessary food. As a result, many of the carts were showing signs of needing more extensive repair.

As they moved northward, they remained within territory covered with prairie grass, with trees lining the creeks and rivers. The tall, dense grass, which threatened to take over the cattle trail, made pushing the travelers' carts difficult and was a strain on the men and equipment.

Hasty repairs to carts that had been made miles back, were now beginning to show their unfortunate results.

Near noon time, a light spring rain was falling on the day that Jonah and Dehlia's cart broke its axle. The cart's two wheels canted inward at their tops and would roll no further. The travelers carried no spare axles and only a limited number of assorted parts for repair of equipment. Jed Starnes and Jonah Chambers lay on their backs on the wet trail peering up under the raised rear of the Chambers' cart.

"I'm afraid your cart is not going to go any further, Jonah," said Pastor Jed.

"It appears you're right, Pastor," replied Jonah. Anguish was reflected on his face and in his voice.

The men gathered to discuss the situation. Initially, no one suggested that the Chambers be left behind, but it became apparent that there might not be a viable alternative, other than loading Jonah and Dehlia's belongings onto the carts of other travelers. Everyone knew that none of the carts had any spare room and loading more goods on them would make the burden that much more difficult for the men to move the carts. Yet, no one wanted to leave the Chambers family behind. In the end, it was Jonah who resolved the problem.

"The Lord provides, but sometimes we don't even know it," he said. "I think it's God's plan that we simply make our homestead in this area. Look over yonder, there's a nice creek, with trees lining both sides of it, and I'm sure the game will be plentiful. I believe the Lord has provided for us right here. I'm going to file a land claim back in Chanute, and Dehlia and I will make our home here. So the rest of you continue on your way." A short time later, tears fell silently from Dehlia's eyes as she watched the wagon and carts of her friends move northward into the distance. Jonah had already begun removing canvas tarps from the wagon in order to build the temporary tent shelter for the family, which he then constructed within the stand of trees in order to provide further shelter, and to hide their camp. Dehlia and Meezie joined him and by carrying smooth rocks from the creek bed, they soon had constructed a fire ring for cooking. They were now settlers on the Kansas prairie.

Part Three

Jonah and Dehlia

Two days later, after making sure that the women and Daniel would be all right, Jonah set off for Chanute to submit a claim for his homestead. He carried a bedroll tied over his shoulder. In addition to his blanket, the bedroll contained hard tack biscuits and pork jerky, meager rations for a ten mile walk each way, but Jonah also had money, which he and Dehlia had saved for several years. The money was carefully folded and carried in a cloth money belt he wore under his trousers. In addition, he carried a few bills folded into the band of his hat. In earlier years, when he and Dehlia had toiled in servitude, they had managed to set aside money from selling hand-made items such as baskets and wooden toys and performing side labor for others when their former boss had allowed it. Over those years, Jonah and Dehlia had saved what they considered a respectable amount of money. But until they came to the meeting at their church, they had no idea that they would be using their savings to establish their own farm. They still worried that they may not have sufficient funds to buy the materials needed to begin farming.

As Jonah walked into town after spending the night sleeping on the ground at the edge of town, he noticed a few black faces among the people walking the main street of Chanute. What also caught his attention were a few unfriendly stares from the white faces of men who gathered on the wood-plank sidewalk of one of the taverns. He pulled his glance away from these men and continued walking toward the territorial recorder's office where he entered the small rough-hewn building. In the dimly lit office, a spectacled, balding man stood behind a small counter. Surprisingly, he was burly in stature, with broad shoulders and beefy hands, a physique appearing to be more suited to hand labor. His face did not hold a friendly countenance. Behind him on shelves, were rows of ledger books that contained filed deeds and other governmental recordings.

The recording clerk eyed Jonah, finally asking, "What do you need, mister?"

"I aim to register a piece of land under the homesteaders' act. I'm hoping you can help me with that," said Jonah.

The clerk continued to eye Jonah, to the point that Jonah was afraid the man would take no action. But after hesitating, the man turned and retrieved a worn book from the shelf. "I reckon I can," he said. "But most of the land hereabouts is already claimed. Where 'bouts is this land you're talking about?" The clerk had pulled a map from the book he had opened and spread the map on the counter. "Show me where it is on this map," he said.

Jonah had seen a few maps before but did not know how to read them. Therefore, he hesitated, looked at the map, and told the clerk that to the best of his knowledge, the land was approximately eight miles north and west of town. The clerk just looked at Jonah and said, "That doesn't tell me enough about it. What else can you tell me?" Jonah then told him that the land was about a mile west of the main trail and had a creek running alongside the property. The clerk studied the map.

"Hmm. Well, I believe you might be in luck," said the clerk. "There is a piece of property right here that is still unclaimed, but the thing is, it isn't a hundred and sixty acres." His finger was pointing to a place on the map. "The way that trail runs north and because of the farms already claimed around it, the property is only about a hundred and twenty acres. You still want to claim that land?" After he said it, a sneering slight grin appeared on the face of the recorder.

Jonah looked down at the floor and unconsciously scratched his ear while he measured his options. He felt that he was stuck and thought that it did not seem fair, but he had no choice. He and Dehlia had no means to continue northward to find another homestead. He looked up at the clerk and said, "Yes sir, I believe I will claim that land if it's all the same to you."

"Mister, it doesn't matter what I think," said the clerk, sarcasm registering in his voice. "The government says you have the right to claim a homestead. I'm just here to register the deed."

The clerk looked up, and Jonah turned slightly when they heard the office door open. Jonah could not help but notice that the man who had entered was one of the idle men he had seen in front of the tavern. Standing closer to the man now, Jonah could see that he was young, probably no more than twenty years old. The stranger said nothing and placed one worn boot against the wall as he leaned against the front wall by the door. The clerk seemed to recognize the man, and ever so slightly nodded, but said nothing.

"Mister, you need to fill out these papers to claim the land. Do you know how to read and write?" asked the clerk.

Reading and writing were skills that were forbidden to be passed on to the slaves at the old Chambers farm, as it was at most all farms and plantations where former slaves worked. Consequently, Jonah answered, "No sir, I surely don't know how to read and write."

"Well, damn," said the clerk. "Anyhow, no matter. The government says I have to help you, so I will. But I surely get tired of filling out all these papers. Oh, and it will cost you two dollars to register the deed. You got two dollars?" Jonah couldn't help but see the slight sneer on the face of the recorder.

"Yes sir," said Jonah. And while the clerk filled out the forms, Jonah furtively removed his hat and drew a five dollar bill out of the inside band. But the action by Jonah was not missed by the stranger leaning against the back wall, who slowly opened the office door and departed.

With his three dollars in change and a copy of the homestead deed in his pocket, Jonah then walked down the street to the livery stable. The sign over the entrance to the stable was lettered, *Mullins and Son Livery.* Next to the smithy's shop was a corral that contained several mules. Farther out to the side of the livery stable was a large pasture where a half dozen horses and other mules grazed. Jonah stopped at the corral and studied the livestock, making a mental assessment of each animal. After making a decision, he entered the smithy's shop. A rhythmic clanging sound resonated from the large anvil where a muscular, yet thin, white man was shaping a horseshoe. A glowing pit of red embers next to the anvil gave off a dim light as the man continued shaping the shoe. After placing the glowing shoe in a large vat of water to harden it, the smithy looked up at Jonah. He then pulled the shoe from the water, locked the tongs holding the shoe, and placed it in the bed of hot coals. Then, looking at Jonah and not recognizing his face, he said, "Name's Mullins, Dwight Mullins. Whatcha need, mister?"

"I seen you got some mules out there in your corral. Any of them for sale?" asked Jonah.

"I reckon they're all for sale. Those are army mules that I bought at auction. Seems the army doesn't need quite so many mules to haul cannon around now that we ain't at war with nobody. You got any money?" asked the smithy.

"Yes, sir, I got money," Jonah answered. "But how much you gonna charge for a mule?"

Mullins looked at Jonah, then stepped over to the water vat, leaned over, and put both his hands in the dirty water. He then stood up, shook the water off his hands, and wiped them on his trousers behind his leather apron. He then extended his right hand. "Told you my name. What's yours?" he asked.

"My name's Jonah Chambers," said Jonah. The two men talked for a few minutes as Jonah explained to the blacksmith that he was just getting started with his farm, and that he would need some livestock for farm work.

"Let's go take a look at 'em," said Mullins, and the two men walked outside to the corral. As they approached the enclosure, the smithy said, "I didn't pay too much for the mules, 'cause nobody wants to ride one of 'em. So, I can let you have one of them for twenty dollars."

Jonah's work experience included working with farming livestock and attending livestock auctions when the plantation needed to replenish stock. Hence, Jonah knew that twenty dollars was too much to pay for a mule, but he didn't say anything. Even though he saw no malice in the white blacksmith, he had learned long ago to be cautious in business dealings with white people. He bent over and entered the corral between the fence rails and walked over to the animals. He slowly moved among them, examined them more closely, ran his hands down their legs, and gently pulled the lips up on several mules to judge their ages. When he was satisfied, he walked back to the corral rail. "Mister Mullins, I'll give you thirteen dollars for that gray over there," said Jonah.

The blacksmith chuckled while looking at Jonah. It was as if he was sizing up the black stranger. "Naw, you know I can't do that. I still need twenty dollars for a mule." He turned his head and spat in the dirt.

Jonah didn't answer him right away. He looked back into the corral, biding his time. After a few minutes of silence, the blacksmith spoke.

"All right, you're wasting my time, but I'll sell you the gray for fourteen dollars."

Again, Jonah took his time answering. "Well sir. I'm of the opinion that none of those mules are worth twenty dollars. And for what I need them for, there's a good chance I'll have to harness break them for farmin'." Jonah looked back into the corral. "But mister, I'll give you your twenty dollars, if you throw in the dun over yonder, and you need to shoe both mules 'fore I go." So, Jonah's offer was twenty dollars for two mules, and they were to be shod by the smithy.

At this, the blacksmith guffawed. "Sir, you offend me," said the blacksmith. "Whatever gave you the idea that them two mules was only worth twenty dollars? Why, those are fine animals and worth every penny," he said.

"Yes, sir, they appear to be good stock," said Jonah. "But I've worked around horses and mules all my life, and I know what they are worth. Twenty dollars for the pair is a fair price."

The blacksmith was no fool. He had been feeding those army mules for several weeks without any interested buyers. People seemed to have no use for the animals, and he knew that getting rid of two hungry mules would help his feed expenses. Plus, he had taken a bit of a liking to the brash young man. It was not often that he chanced upon a knowledgeable black man, but he could not give in quite yet. "I don't know," he said. "That seems to be a bit on the low side for money. I may need to think some about it."

Jonah now took a gamble. He came back through the corral rails and stuck out his hand to shake with the smithy. "Well, Mister Mullins, my offer stands," he said as they shook hands. He then turned to walk away, hoping he had not underestimated the smithy. He soon knew the result.

"Now hold on there mister," said the smithy, and Jonah stopped and turned back to look at the man. "All right, I'll let you have them for twenty dollars, but it's only because I have too many of 'em right now. Come back in an hour or so, and I'll have 'em shod and ready."

Jonah walked back and again shook the smithy's hand. "I'd like a bill of sale to go with them too," he said.

The smithy grinned and held up his hands in mock surrender. "All right, all right, come back in a bit, and I'll have them all ready to go."

Jonah's next stop was the general hardware store. But as he walked to the store, he passed the tavern again and once more saw the man who had been standing in the territorial recorder's office. Jonah was now convinced that the man was intentionally watching him, but he kept walking. He entered an alleyway between two stores and entered an outhouse behind the buildings. The crude toilet behind the main street businesses was used by the public when the necessity arose. The stench of the outhouse nearly made Jonah turn around, but instead, he entered. Flies soon harassed his face with their insistent buzzing and landing. Safe from view, he loosened his trousers and retrieved the money belt from around his waist. He then retrieved some bills from the belt, carefully folded them and put them in his hat band. After re-securing the belt and his trousers, he walked back to the street where he saw that the man who had been watching him had moved closer to the alleyway. Jonah entered the hardware store, where he soon had the hardware owner scurrying around the store to retrieve supplies, which were then placed in a pile on the floor. The supplies included basic foodstuffs such as flour, corn meal, and beans, along with hardware items. An axe, an adze, a draw blade, harness, chain, rope, a one-bottom plow, and other assorted tools were added to the pile, as well as canvas tarps. After the hardware owner added the total, Jonah paid him from the bills in his hatband. "I'll be back in a bit to load all these goods," said Jonah.

"Take your time. I ain't going anywhere," said the store owner.

He had not heard the man come into the store, but as Jonah turned to leave, he saw the man who had been watching him standing just inside the door of the store leaning against the wall. He partially blocked the doorway. As Jonah attempted to walk out, the man spoke. "Where'd a dumb nigger get the money to buy all that stuff? You some kind of thief?" The stench of the man's breath caused by several decayed teeth in his mouth reached Jonah's nostrils, causing him to slightly pucker his lips.

Jonah was a half head taller and considerably more muscular than the skinny white man he was facing. He wasn't afraid, even though the white man wore a pistol low on his hip. Jonah faced the man for a few seconds and could see the bully's lack of real confidence in the man's eyes. Jonah stepped around him and went out the door.

Jonah was a bit upset by the meeting with the man who had been following him, and a small thread of worry crossed his mind. He quickly forced it out of his thoughts, because more than anything else, Jonah was hungry. While sleeping on the hard, rough ground outside of town last night, he had dreamed of a stack of pancakes. Dreams are funny that way, and he could not figure why he had dreamt of that particular food. He walked into the street and made a straight line to the small cafe he had seen earlier and stepped through the door, where he was hit by the aroma of fresh coffee and food cooking. His mouth watered in response. He looked around the cafe and saw only one other black fellow who was sitting at the very back of the room, near the door to the kitchen. All the other customers in the cafe were white. He knew where he would be sitting if he was served. He watched as a waitress came up by him and filled a mug of coffee at one of the tables. She then looked at him and said, "If you're going to eat you need to sit back there at the table with Clarence," as she nodded in the direction of the only other black person in the cafe. Jonah walked past the tables where white patrons looked up at him as he passed.

After sitting down at the back table, the two men introduced themselves. It turned out that Clarence had always been a freeman, and he raised and sold chickens to make a living, selling dressed-out birds to the cafes in town. The men continued to make small talk after Jonah had ordered pancakes. When the pancakes arrived, there was a small sliver of ham next to the cakes, and a mug of coffee steamed next to the plate. It was not long before the plate was empty. Jonah laid a few coins on the table and got up to leave. Before parting, Clarence said, "If you ever need chickens, come see me. My place is just a little bit north of town." This information jogged Jonah's memory. He remembered walking past a ramshackle cabin set back from the road and hearing the low clucking of chickens, but it had been near dusk when Jonah had passed Clarence's, and he had been looking for a place to bed down out of sight so had kept walking.

Jonah soon left the cafe, and as he walked back to the livery stable, he noticed that his constant observer was sitting on a bench in front of the tavern. When he got to the livery stable the two mules were tied to the top rail of the corral. Immediately, he could see that both animals were bitted and saddled. The smithy walked out of the shop to meet him.

"Mister, I can't pay you for the harness and saddles," said Jonah.

"You don't need to do that," said the blacksmith. "When the army auctioned them mules off, they all had saddles and other tack with 'em, and I can't sell any of them damn army saddles. They're too uncomfortable, so nobody wants 'em. They're yours, no charge."

"Well, I'm grateful to you, mister," said Jonah. "Say, would you have a double tree harness? I need collars and leather strapping too. I'm going to need to make a plow harness."

43

"Three dollars," said the smithy after he returned from the shop carrying the collars and strapping. In addition, the smithy put a bill of sale in Jonah's hand. Jonah paid him, the men shook hands, and Jonah led the mules up the street to the hardware store where after much lashing and tying, all of Jonah's purchases were stacked on the saddles and the backs of the mules. The collars were hung over the necks of the mules and tied to the front of the saddles. With no room left on the saddles for him to ride, Jonah thanked the hardware owner and walked out of town leading his mules in single file, heading for home. Leaving town late in the day, he knew he would be walking well into the night and would most likely be sleeping on the ground again tonight.

While it was still light, Jonah made camp by a small rivulet, its water quiet as it gently made its way downstream. He hobbled and tethered the mules to a nearby tree and made his way to the creek to wash up. As he splashed the water on his head and face, he had been pleasantly surprised to find the water teeming with crawfish which he painstakingly caught and skewered on a thin tree branch for roasting over his small campfire. The crawfishes' unique, aquatic taste was a real treat, and he savored the chewy "mud bugs." Later, as Jonah lay on his back staring at the blanket of stars edged by a half-moon, he bent his knees and rubbed his tired feet, and it was not long before he drifted off to sleep.

The low muffled bray of one of the mules woke him. He knew that sound. It was not a full bray; it was lower in volume and duration. It was meant as a greeting, a hello to a visitor. Jonah knew that someone was approaching the camp. He rose, grabbed the ax that had been by his side, and quickly stepped out of sight behind a coppice of scrub cottonwoods.

A mounted rider slowly approached the glowing campfire coals, swung down from his saddle, and drew a revolver. "I know you're here, boy. Come out where I can see you."

Jonah could see in the dim moonlight that it was the same man who had been following him in town. Jonah did not move. The man shouted again for Jonah to show himself, with no result. The outlaw slowly moved around the campfire to where Johan had been sleeping and kicked Jonah's bedroll with his boot. But then he saw what he was looking for. Jonah's flop-brimmed hat was lying near the bedroll. The man bent down and picked up the hat. He then looked inside the hat, peeled back the headband, and saw the folded bills. He holstered the pistol to use both his hands on the hat. His full attention was on retrieving the money from the hat, and that was his mistake.

From the shadows, Jonah had moved closer behind the outlaw. Silently, he raised the ax and before the outlaw had seen him, he swung the ax striking the outlaw in the hand. The man screamed in pain and dropped to his knees. An angry red slice extended from his wrist through the thumb web on the hand, nearly severing the thumb. Blood flowed freely from the wound. Quickly, Jonah leaned down and pulled the man's pistol from its holster. The outlaw was gripping his right hand with his left and moaning. He screeched, "Damn you boy, look what you've done to me."

"Consider yourself lucky, cracker," said Jonah. "I could have gone ahead and killed you and nobody would know the difference. Now stand up." Jonah grabbed the man's arm and helped lift him to his feet. He then reached in and unbuckled the man's gun belt and let it drop to the ground. "Now get on your horse and skedaddle. I don't ever want to see you again."

The outlaw struggled to get on the horse using his good hand. Blood continued to drip freely from the wound on his other hand. "You ain't seen the last of me, boy. I'll see you in hell!" He then spurred his horse into a trot and the rider faded into the dark.

When the man was gone, Jonah reached down and picked up the pistol and gun belt. He walked over and tossed them into the creek, knowing that if they were found in his possession, it could lead to further trouble, trouble that a black man did not want any part of. He kicked dirt on his dying fire, unhobbled the mules, checked all the rope ties on the goods on the mules' backs, and began walking toward home in the dim light.

*****

In the ensuing weeks, shelter for the family was the first priority. The fastest shelter to construct was a dug-out, a hole dug into the ground, with the earth serving as walls, and covered with a log roof with grass and mud chinking the spaces between the logs. Even building this minimal shelter was difficult work for one man and Jonah struggled, felling each tree and stripping it of branches. He then used the mules to pull the logs to the build site where a hole had already been dug in the tough sod. By the first snow of the year, their sod house was finished, and the family would be sheltered from the harsh forthcoming winter.

In the following year, Jonah would start on an above-ground cabin, but tilling the soil to make a livelihood became the primary work of the couple. While their son Daniel played nearby, Dehlia's mother, Meezie, Jonah and Dehlia broke the stubborn sod, planted corn, laboriously turned the tough sod for a vegetable garden, and built the small cabin. They toiled to eke out a meager livelihood, selling part of their produce and preserving and drying a portion for their own use. While the work was backbreaking and the rewards small, they found peace and satisfaction from owning their own piece of the prairie. The unforeseen broken axle of their cart had determined where Jonah and Dehlia had settled in Kansas, and where they would later meet their untimely deaths.

Part Four

The Wedding

Summer Prairie Ranch
Two Miles Northwest of Chanute, Kansas

It was four o'clock in the afternoon. From their vantage point the couple could look down on the ranch house, and they watched as the last two dark-colored canopied buggies each made a wide turn in front of the covered front porch, the individual drivers urging their horses into a trot down the ranch house lane as the last guests headed toward the country road. Shep, the mixed-breed ranch dog followed each buggy to the end of the lane and trotted back to the ranch house porch wagging his tail and waiting for the next buggy to depart.

The small, raised, lush glade where the couple sat on a blanket watching the departing visitors was a beautiful spot. Claire May believed that it was the most peaceful place on the entire ranch, and maybe the whole world as far as she knew. As children, she, and her older brother, Will, had spent many hours playing in this very spot, making up all sorts of children's games and having imaginary adventures. They had favored this glade because the interior of the green clearing was not readily seen from the ranch house below, but the occupants of the glade could keep a covert watch on the comings and goings below them. In their childish imaginations, the children had believed that they were hiding from all the adults at the ranch house. In reality, their mother and father, Robert and Virginia Summers had known exactly where they were, never worrying for the children as they were not far away. Those years of child's play were now well in the past, and presently Claire May sat on a blanket in the glade as a beautiful young woman with a different man beside her.

One hour ago, Claire May and Nathan slipped away from the crowd of visitors, changed from their formal wedding attire, and took the large pre-packed picnic basket from the kitchen as they quietly left the house, walked to the stable, and mounted their waiting saddled horses. To avoid being observed from the house, the couple had taken a rounda-bout path to arrive at the glade where they unsaddled and hobbled their horses, laid out their blankets, and sat quietly watching the guests leave the ranch house. They each held a squat, pedestalled wine glass in their hands. The champagne bubbles still formed and rose in their respective glasses.

Toasting each other, their glasses made a tiny musical ting as the couple touched them together.

"To my beautiful bride," said Nathan Wolf as he intently looked at his wife. "May our love last forever."

"And to you, dear husband, I love you so very much," whispered Claire May. She looked intently at her new husband. Nathan was a handsome man. His brown wavy hair was parted at the side and sloped across his forehead, forming a wavy line above his clear blue eyes. A faint smile curved his lips on each side of his face. Nathan's shoulders were broad, and he had a thick body, giving him the appearance of be-ing taller than he was. In truth, he was only a bit over average height, but he was a good half foot taller than Claire May. She marveled at how peaceful his face seemed, but she had seen that countenance change into a ruddy ferocity when dealing with law breakers. And when that happened, the outlaw in Nathan's focus did not stand a chance. She had heard the stories of Nathan's treatment of criminals who were uncooperative. He put up with no nonsense or lies from law breakers. But she also knew him to be kind, with a loving soul. She considered herself to be very lucky to have found such a man.

Nathan returned the gaze. He recalled the first time he had seen beautiful Claire May. They had met quite by accident a year ago when they had boarded a train in St. Joseph, Missouri. It turned out that Nathan and Claire May's family were in pursuit of an outlaw who had stolen horses from the Summer Prairie Ranch, as well as committing other heinous crimes including a train robbery. During the ensuing days, the couple had fallen in love while chasing the desperado, Henry Vogler. Their chase ended in Iowa with the death of the outlaw. But before the Summers returned to their ranch in Kansas, Nathan had promised to come calling later, and he had subsequently made good on his promise and arrived with the gift of a wedding dress for Claire May. His visit was extended when he accepted the U.S. Marshal position for southeast Kansas, and their beautiful wedding had taken place only hours before.

Under the green, treed canopy of their glade, as they gazed lovingly at each other, they each took a sip from their glasses. Claire May giggled quietly. "The bubbles tickle my mouth," she said. Nathan smiled, and they both turned their gaze back to look at the ranch house.

Five hours ago, on this very warm late summer day with a house full of visitors, and after the old, seldom-used harpsichord had played out a traditional wedding song administered by an equally ancient piano player borrowed from a church in town, Nathan Wolf and Claire May Summers had stood on the wide front porch of the ranch house. As the guests crowded around, the couple had faced the travelling parson, tightly clung to each other, and repeated the vows first stated by the minister. Claire May's mother, Virginia, stood on one side next to Claire May, while the young woman's brother, Will, stood to the side of Nathan. Before a crowd of ranch hands and guests, the couple reached the end of the vows. At the conclusion of the rites, they tenderly embraced and enjoyed a rather lengthy kiss. So lengthy, in fact, that polite chuckles from the observant ranch hands and guests could be heard. As the couple parted, they looked at each other and smiled as a tear escaped from the corner of one of Claire May's eyes. They were now Mr. and Mrs. Nathan Wolf.

In a few minutes, the music began anew, this time played by lively ranch hands with a few real musicians who comprised a small band of guitars, harmonicas, and a fiddle. As they played, guests began to move to tables laden with food so plentiful that no one would leave the ranch hungry. Shep wandered beneath the tables hoping for an accidental drop from a guest's plate. Nathan and Claire May slowly made the rounds, greeting the guests and thanking all of them for coming to the wedding. They expressed their gratitude as they knew that many of the visitors had travelled a considerable distance to reach the Summers' ranch.

With their hunger sated, many of the guests began to gather together and form two couple squares for dancing in the front yard. Claire May and Nathan soon joined the dancing couples and listened while an impromptu caller began a sing-song square dance cadence, accompanied by the musicians. The dancing, twirling couples laughed and talked happily with fellow dancers as they followed the caller's lead, and Claire May held a handful of her skirt in order to avoid tripping over her beautiful white dress.

A bit winded but smiling broadly, Claire May and Nathan left the dancing couples and continued to mingle with the guests. As is the custom of ranchers and farmers who lived in the country, and of whom Claire May had come to know through the years, Nathan was properly introduced to all of the guests whom he would also come to know better as the U.S. Marshal of the southeast Kansas Territory. It was important for these people to meet their Marshal face to face so that they could briefly appraise the man who would serve them to keep the peace, and perhaps more importantly, to get a close look at the man who had just married the daughter of one of the territory's most prominent ranchers. Nathan knew that he would not remember each neighbor and friend of the Summers, but he also knew that he was subtly being critically examined for suitability, and that it was important to curry the favor of these hard-working ranch folks. So, he kept a smile on his face while shaking hands with the people who would soon become his friends.

Tiredly finishing the greetings, and after a proper interval of time spent meeting new friends, renewing friendships, partaking of the sumptuous food, and catching up on news from other areas of the territory, the couple had inconspicuously left the revelers and met in the kitchen of the ranch house, preparing to make good their clandestine escape. They then climbed the back stairs of the house, changed their clothes, and returned to the kitchen just before departing.

In the shady glen, Nathan set his wine glass aside next to the picnic basket and laid down on his back on the blanket. Claire May soon joined him, kissed him, and curled up next to him. It was quiet in the glade. They lay together looking up into the canopy of the trees. The late afternoon shadows danced in the leaves, while busy, black-capped nuthatches scrambled from branch to branch of the oaks, eagerly seeking out insects. A bright crimson cardinal flitted in the nearby greenbrier-infused brush, periodically calling to let his dusky brown mate know where he was. The only other sounds were the leaves quietly rustling when a welcome breeze passed by, and a rather belligerent chattering squirrel sitting in a tree some distance away. The squirrel obviously believed that the couple was encroaching on his territory.

"Isn't it beautiful here, Nathan?" asked Claire May. "It is so quiet and peaceful. I have always loved this place."

Nathan watched the cardinal move to a different feeding area, then he turned to Claire May and kissed her. "Claire May, I don't believe this beautiful spot would be near as pretty without you here. I surely do believe you are the most beautiful woman in the whole world," he said, and kissed her again.

"You had best be careful, Marshal, or you'll turn a girl's head," said Claire May as she rolled over on top of Nathan and hungrily kissed him. After a moment, Nathan gently pushed Claire May to the side and sat up. He hurriedly pulled off his boots, then stood up. Quickly, he removed his shirt and trousers until he stood in a short flannel undershirt and flannel shorts and faced Claire May who was still sitting on the blanket smiling.

"You seem to have lost your trousers, Mr. Wolf," she said and then giggled. "Just exactly what is your intent in discarding your clothing? You know, you look a bit silly standing there in your underdrawers."

Claire May was certainly not a shy flower. She was a ranch girl who had lived outdoors most of her life. She knew exactly the process required for the production of new calves and foals and had helped in the ranch's breeding process and had even assisted in the delivery of a stubborn calf or two. While still a virgin, she had fantasized about her own wedding and had looked forward to this very moment for quite some time. She knew exactly what was on her new husband's mind, because she was having the very same thoughts.

By now, Nathan's face had begun to turn red. Yet, he enjoyed a small amount of teasing from his new wife, as he knew she was perfectly aware of why he had shucked his clothing. He moved and sat down on the blanket next to her, but then stood again and went to pour himself another glass of wine from the bottle in the picnic basket. As he poured, with his back to Claire May, he said, "I thought I might be a bit more comfortable on this warm day with fewer clothes on. You might wish to try it. It is quite pleasant," he said.

Nathan turned back to move to the blanket, but as he did so he noticed articles of Claire May's clothing at the side of the blanket, and that Claire May had slipped under the blanket with only her smiling face peering at him from the top edge of the blanket.

"I don't know, Nathan. I found it a bit cool without clothing. You might want to crawl under the blanket with me to keep warm," she said.

As soon as Nathan crawled under the blanket, he was sharply pulled into an embrace with Claire May kissing him soundly. He was surprised, but in a most pleasant manner, to discover that Claire May had not one single article of clothing on her warm body. Only a few seconds passed before Nathan discarded the remainder of his clothing, and the couple was soon locked into a tender, loving embrace as they hungrily explored each other's body. As they lay on their sides facing each other, Claire May threw her leg over Nathan and pulled him even closer. In a short time, the newlywed couple moved in unison to the rhythm of blissful love.

Later, each wearing the suit they were born in, they lay on their backs looking up at the gently swaying leaf canopy. The previously chattering squirrel had moved on to other farther trees and was quiet. The birds still scrambled through the branches and bushes in their never-ending quest for food. The world appeared the same as it had some minutes previously, yet to Nathan and Claire May a new and beautiful world had opened to them, welcoming them to the peaceful and wonderful life of two people very much in love.

They talked quietly with each other, remarking on the many friends they had seen at the wedding, about life on the ranch, and any other subject that drifted across their minds. They were at peace with each other.

Claire May moved slightly to be more comfortable. Still on her back, she let her arm rest on Nathan's chest and stomach. She turned to study Nathan's face, studying his strong chin, wavy brown hair, and deep blue eyes. He had broad shoulders and strong arms yet was gentle and intelligent. But she also knew that he had gained his reputation as a no-nonsense lawman not by being timid, and she knew that when dealing with outlaws he could be ruthless. As she studied her husband, she moved her arm and hand lower on Nathan's stomach with her fingers reaching his groin.

As her hand explored further and stroked Nathan, she giggled and said, "Why, I guess that it's true that a lawman must remain ready for whatever danger may occur." They both laughed as Claire May crawled up and lay atop her husband, and their passionate recumbent dance began once more.

The couple later slept through the night, serenaded by the buzzing cicadas, katydids, and the occasional call of an owl. In the dark glade, a rare, quiet thrashing through the neighboring brush by a passing armadillo was the only other sound. As the first dim morning light filtered through the leafy canopy, Nathan awoke to find his wife staring at him as she lay on her side.

"Good morning, sleepy head," said Claire May.

"Don't you ever sleep, Mrs. Wolf?" said Nathan.

"Not now," she replied, and rolled closer to give him a long passionate kiss.

What a pleasant way to wake up in the morning, thought Nathan as his wife eagerly lay under him. After making love once more, they slowly rose to find their clothes.

"I don't know about you, Mr. Wolf, but I am very hungry," said Claire May as she hurried into her clothes. "I'm hoping Rosa made pancakes this morning, 'cause I could eat ten, I think."

"I could use some vittles myself," Nathan answered.

They packed up their gear, saddled the horses, and were soon riding back to the ranch house.

"I'll race you," said Claire May, as she spurred her horse into a lope.

Nathan knew that his wife had too much of a lead for him to catch up to her, so he only nudged the horse into a trot. As he watched the beautiful woman that he had married only the day before fly away on her horse, he chuckled at the free-spirited woman that had him enthralled.

As he rode and watched Claire May increase her lead, he thought back on how they had met nearly a year ago when he was the sheriff of the Mississippi River town of Burlington, Iowa, where he began to trail a dangerous and ruthless outlaw named Henry Vogler. It had turned out that the same outlaw had previously killed a woman employee, Lupe Vera, of the Summer Prairie Ranch and stolen some of the ranch horses. This gave cause to Virginia Summers, her children, and two ranch hands to track the outlaw in order to exact justice. Nathan and Claire May had met fortuitously, but quite by accident, on the same train in the upper Midwest as it took them ever closer to the fleeing outlaw.

During the chase of the miscreant, and while in each other's company, romance had blossomed between the two independent-thinking individuals, which finally led to Nathan Wolf's move from his home in Iowa to southeast Kansas to take the hand of his beloved Claire May Summers, and to pin on the star of the U.S. Marshal of the southeast Kansas Territory, a job in which he had been serving for the past three months. But to the Summers family, today was just another day on the ranch, a day filled with the never-ending chores of maintaining a successful cattle operation.

The couple unsaddled their horses, draped their blankets and saddles over the top rail of the corral, gave a quick brush-down to the horses, turned the animals into an adjoining corral, and headed into the ranch house. Virginia and Will had already had their breakfast and sat at the kitchen table sipping their coffee. As Nathan and Claire May came into the kitchen, Virginia and Will looked up at them.

"Good morning, Claire May," said Will as he tried to keep the knowing smile from his face, but grinned anyway.

With the death of his father some years ago, Will Summers had grown into the responsibilities of manager of the Summer Prairie Ranch. While his mother was still the principle owner of the ranch and the chief bookkeeper for the business, for all practical purposes, Will ran the ranch. His intelligence, even temper, and ability to get along well with the ranch hands were assets necessary for the success of the enterprise, and he had been very successful. Unfortunately, the long back-breaking hours to run a successful cattle operation left him little time for social interaction, especially with his primary love interest, Alice Morgan, who lived at the nearby Circle M Ranch.

"Good morning dear brother," said Claire May as she went about the task of emptying the picnic basket.

"No, no, Claire May," said Rosa, the kitchen cook. "I'll take care of that. You sit down and I will get your breakfast."

Nathan got two coffee mugs, filled them, and sat down at the table next to Claire May. Shep lazily wagged his tail from his napping place under the table, his tail making a thumping noise on the wood floor. Nathan reached down and scratched the dog's ears.

Virginia held her mug in both hands with her elbows on the table looking over the mug at her daughter. When Claire May finally looked at her mother, Virginia simply smiled and said, "It was a beautiful wedding, wasn't it?" She took another sip of her coffee.

Claire May's cheeks took on a hint of pink as she said, "It was a wonderful wedding, mother," and she also took a sip of the steaming coffee.

Rosa had, indeed, made pancakes and set a short stack on a plate in front of both Nathan and Claire May. A slice of roast beef sat on the plate next to the hotcakes. A pitcher of warm maple syrup sat near at hand on the table.

Virginia continued watching as her daughter ravenously ate her breakfast, but her mind was once again elsewhere. She was thinking of years in the past, remembering the same morning after her own wedding day. It was a wonderful memory, and she smiled slightly and looked down into her coffee mug. But those memories became clouded as she inevitably thought to herself that she would never get over missing Robert, her beloved husband who had died in the midst of a winter blizzard years ago.

With Nathan and Claire May nearly finished eating, the table conversation turned to the never-ending ranch work to be accomplished that day. Virginia, Will, and Claire May were discussing how to apportion the workload among the ranch hands and the locations on the immense ranch that needed attention. Nathan slowly ate his breakfast and only half listened to his new family. His mind was elsewhere. He was beginning to formulate a few theories about recent crime-related incidents that had occurred around the Chanute area. But his thinking and the conversation of the family was interrupted by a now-familiar sound.

Nathan rose from the table and walked to the small office off of the living room of the ranch house. This was primarily Virginia's domain, as she carefully kept the records and oversaw accounting for the ranch at her desk in this room. Looking somewhat out of place, a telegraph key sat on a small stand at the side of the desk. When Nathan had agreed to take the U.S. Marshal's job for southeastern Kansas, it was understood that his office would be in Chanute. Therefore, he arranged for the state to install a telegraph line from Chanute to the ranch so that he could be summoned if he was needed by any of the towns connected by telegraph. It had taken Nathan several days to get the hang of the Morse Code, but he, Claire May, and Will had all subsequently learned the code and could now send and receive if necessary.

Because of the wedding, Nathan had not been into Chanute for the past few days, so he was not current on events in the territory. He wondered what sort of news might be coming to him as he took a piece of paper and a pencil from the desk and sat at a chair where he could reach the telegraph key. He watched as the key tapped out the usual dot dash, dot dash, dot dash, dot dash; four A's which meant that the sender was asking the receiver to prepare to receive a message. Nathan answered with a dash dot dash, the letter 'K' which meant that he was ready to receive. The telegraph key began its dance, and Nathan wrote the letters across the paper he was holding. The sender was Bill Ward, the deputy Marshal, sending from the telegraph office in Chanute. While the key clattered on, Claire May came into the office, and looked over Nathan's shoulder as he wrote. A dot dash, dot dash dot, 'A,R' signified that Ward was done. Nathan answered with a dot dash dot 'R' meaning that he understood the message.

Nathan turned and read the full message to Claire May, even though she already had read it over Nathan's shoulder. "Bill says there is a telegram waiting for me at the office. He also says that we have a report of cattle rustling west of town. Hmm, wonder what that telegram is all about."

Claire May reached up and hugged him around his neck. "I'm sure you'll find out, Marshal, I'm sure you will." She kissed him and turned and headed back to the kitchen. "The coffee's still hot," she said over her shoulder.

*****

Thirty minutes later Nathan had brought his horse, Wander, from the corral and tied the roan gelding to a hitching stanchion next to the barn. The animal knew that he was probably going to hit the trail and stepped back and forth in anticipation of breaking the monotony of his corral. The horse's impatience only slowed down the saddling process. Nathan had to repeatedly move out of the way of the fidgety hooves of the horse as he threw the blanket over the horse's back, followed by the worn saddle. After tightening the cinch and buckling the flank cinch, Nathan brought the bridle, his pistol belt, and his Winchester 1892 from the barn. Wander took the bridle easily and stood calmly while the buckles were fastened. Nathan then examined his rifle and shoved it into its scabbard. He put on his pistol belt and removed the Colt Army 1892 .41 cal. revolver. He checked the cylinder, making sure it was fully loaded and replaced it in its holster. Finally, Nathan tied his bed roll and saddle bags to the rear of the cantle. Since he had a bunk in a corner of his office, he seldom needed the bedroll, but he was never sure if he might be called out overnight on the trail. Almost unconsciously, his hand ran over his right hip pocket, ensuring that his blackjack was in its usual place.

Out of the corner of his eye, Nathan could see his wife coming toward him from the house, carrying a package wrapped in brown paper. When she got close enough, Nathan spun around and grabbed her around the waist. Claire May laughed, kissed her husband, and handed him the package. "Some sandwiches for your trip, Nathan," she said.

"Now let me loose. You've got work to do." But Nathan only squeezed her tighter, then kissed her, and only then let her loose.

"I guess you're right," Nathan said. "I better hit the trail." He put the lunch package into his saddle bag, untied Wander, and swung himself up into the saddle. He tugged down on his hat brim so that it would not come off in the breeze, and said, "I'll see you in a few days, sweetheart."

Part Five

The Rustlers

Wander had justifiably earned his name. While walking a trail, the horse might fancy investigating anything that interested him. When that happened, his actions were taken with no thought of the rider on his back. The second way he had earned the name was the fact that Wander was simply no good as a cutting horse on the ranch. He performed well at cutting out calves, but as soon as he and the calf had an eyeball-to-eyeball confrontation, Wander would lose interest in his job, and the calf would scamper back to the safety of the herd. Will Summers thought that Wander should, therefore, earn his hay by hauling brother-in-law Nathan, the U.S. Marshal, around the territory and staying away from working cattle. And that is how Nathan and Wander had been teamed up. Predictably, Wander now began to stray from the trail toward a nearby creek.

"No, you don't, bud. Keep your pea-brain on business," Nathan said as he reined the horse back on the trail. The horse's actions were annoying but not all that important; that is, unless Nathan wanted to dismount to investigate on foot. Even though Wander was ground trained, there were times when Nathan would return to where he left Wander, only to find the horse gone, necessitating tracking Wander to where he was usually found calmly munching vegetation. But he was a strong, fast horse, and on a good day, Wander could cover the ten miles into town at a brisk walk in about an hour and three quarters. And because the weather was good, and with little distraction, horse and rider would reach town in a reasonable time.

Reaching Chanute, Nathan tied Wander to a hitch rack on the shady side of the clapboard-sided office building and took his saddle bags and Winchester from the saddle. Nodding to some passersby, he walked up the two steps and into the office where Bill Ward was in the process of making a pot of coffee on the cook top of the cantankerous, potbelly wood stove. As usual, smoke was escaping from the access door of the stove and from the stove pipe fittings, creating a cloud in the office. For some reason, the stove had never vented properly, taking a long time to achieve a proper air draw through the flume. Each time the stove was lighted anew, smoke gushed into the office. Such was the price of boiling a pot of water for coffee.

"Trying to burn the place down, Bill?" said Nathan, even though he knew perfectly well the intricacies of the old stove. Bill turned and chuckled. "Yep, been trying to burn this place down for years," he said and gave the stove a half-hearted kick with his boot, then walked over and opened a window.

"That telegram I mentioned is laying right there on your desk," said Bill. "And as soon as I get us a couple cups of mud, I need to tell you about a visit I had from Dave Morgan yesterday."

Nathan knew of Dave Morgan, as he had met the rancher at the wedding and recalled a growing relationship between Will and Morgan's daughter, Alice. Morgan owned the Circle M Ranch nearby the Summer Prairie Ranch and was a long-time rancher with the crinkled ruddy complexion indicative of days spent in the saddle nurturing a herd of ornery range cattle. He was the type of man who was completely independent of others and did not stand for any nonsense from his crew. When his ranch hands came to town, they were generally well behaved. If a cowboy got out of line, the others in the group would make sure the delinquent cowhand left town with them after they had consumed their fill of liquor and accommodating bar girls. Morgan wouldn't have it any other way. Nathan was of the opinion that Morgan was as honest as the day is long and would fight anyone who crossed him, and Nathan respected him for that.

Bill set the metal coffee mugs down, one in front of Nathan and one on the other side of the desk, then sat down across the desk from his boss. "Well, aren't you going to open that there telegram?" he asked.

"First tell me what Dave Morgan wanted," said the Marshal.

Bill stood up, walked over next to the door of the office, removed the quid of tobacco from his cheek, flipped it into the stained spittoon by the door, topped off his coffee mug, walked back to the desk, and sat down again across from the Marshal. Nathan had seen this ritual dozens of times, but never could understand Bill's affinity for his messy habit. The only time the deputy was without a tobacco chaw was when he was eating.

"Well sir, Morgan was in here a couple days ago. He was so mad, he was foaming at the mouth, ready to kill somebody."

Bill now had Nathan's undivided attention. But Bill was taking his time. After pulling a sugar lump from a small wooden box on the desk and dropping it in his coffee, he began stirring the hot coffee with his finger, a habit that must have blistered the deputy's finger a few times before he learned to let the coffee cool just enough to painlessly dunk his finger in the mug. He then sucked the sweetened coffee from his finger, scratched his two-day-old whisker growth, and looked out the window.

"Bill, what about Morgan?" Nathan had long ago learned that Bill never seemed to be in a hurry about much of anything and sometimes needed a bit of goading to continue a story.

"Oh, yeah, Morgan. Well, he was stomping around the office here claiming that he had lost some cattle."

Nathan replied, "Well, everybody loses some cattle now and then."

Bill responded, "Yeah, but not twenty or thirty head at a time. And he claims that this is the second time this has happened."

Nathan was skeptical. "You know, Bill, for the life of me I don't understand how a rancher that might have five hundred or more head of cattle would even know that he was missing twenty or thirty."

Bill chuckled. He saw his chance to needle his boss. "Yeah, I forget you're from up in farm country and not a rancher," he said. He watched as Nathan turned down a corner of his mouth, thus signaling that Bill had nettled the Marshal. But it was all in good nature as the men truly respected each other. "Believe me, when calving time, dehorning, and cutting time comes, these ranchers know pretty near just how many head they have."

"OK, OK," said Nathan with a slight grin on his face. "I reckon I ought to go talk with Morgan in the next day or so. Did he mention whether he might have any clue as to how the rustling might have happened? Or whether he might have a thought on who might be doing the rustling?"

Bill took another pull on his coffee mug and licked his lip after swallowing the coffee. "Near as I could make out, he doesn't seem to have a clue on either. But he sure was hopping mad, even accusing us of not doing our jobs."

Nathan was quiet for a moment and took a swig of his coffee. "Nothing to do about it now, I guess, other than going out to see Morgan," he said.

Bill was fidgeting in his chair so much that he appeared to have a case of Saint Vitus dance. Finally, he blurted out, "Well, when are you going to open that there telegram?"

Nathan would have preferred to keep Bill in suspense, but figured he probably needed to take a look at the wire. He picked it up and tore open the envelope, slowly reading the written words. The telegram was from Mr. Wallace Ferguson, Vice President of Security for the Union Pacific Railroad.

Nathan recognized the name. He had met Ferguson last year when he had come to Burlington to facilitate the pursuit of the outlaw Henry Vogler, who had robbed a Union Pacific train carrying a handsome amount of money. Nathan and a railroad detective named Nick Wentz subsequently began the long chase of the outlaw. Nathan and Nick had pursued the outlaw literally to his death, caused by his falling beneath the wheels of a moving railroad train. The telegram concerned the Vogler case. It read:

To: Marshal Nathan Wolf, Chanute, Kansas

This is to inform you that the Union Pacific Railroad had posted a $10,000 reward for the capture of the outlaw responsible for robbing our Army payroll train which occurred in October 1898. It is with pleasure that we have awarded $5,000 to you and $5,000 to Mr. Nick Wentz, who was your partner in ensuring the demise of Mr. Henry Vogler. A wire transfer for your share of the reward has been sent to the Prairie Bank in Chanute, Kansas, where you can claim the funds. I hope this message finds you well, and we offer our sincere thanks.

Very Truly,
Wallace Ferguson, Union Pacific Railroad
Chicago, Illinois

After seeing Nathan look up after reading, Bill blurted, "Well, ain't you going to tell me what it's all about?"

Nathan chuckled. "Now Bill, what makes you think this is any of your business?"

"Well, I ain't saying it is or it ain't my business," said Bill. "But can you at least tell me if it's good news or bad news?"

"Everything is OK, Bill. It's a bit of good news, and that's all I'm going to tell you," answered Nathan. He placed the telegram back in its envelope, folded it, and shoved it into his pocket, while a look of disappointment wrinkled Bill's face. "I suppose that I ought to make my way on out to Morgan's place. But before I go, I had better take Wander down to the livery and get him some grub."

*****

An hour and a half later on this warm Friday morning, Marshal Wolf was once again on the road, heading northwest. The Chambers farm was on the way to both Summer Prairie Ranch and Dave Morgan's place, and since he had not met the owners of that farm, he decided to make a stop. Wander needed watering anyway, so he turned into the lane to the Chambers cabin. As he neared the house, he could see a slight, black woman resting on a chair on the porch. He also noticed the empty corral at the side of the cabin and saw no one else about.

Nathan stopped Wander in front of the porch, touched his right fingers to the brim of his hat and said, "'Morning ma'am. I don't believe I've met you yet. My name is Nathan Wolf, and I'm the U.S. Marshal in Chanute." He received no response from the old woman, who simply continued watching him. She was wearing a faded, flower-patterned cotton dress that had seen better days. An apron covered her lap. Her feet were covered by a well-worn pair of brown leather booties (over-the-ankle oxfords) tied up with leather laces. Nathan could now see that her apron held a quantity of late-season green beans. She was breaking the stems off the beans and chucking the stems over the side of the porch.

"What do you want, Mr. Marshal?" said the woman.

Nathan did not quite know what to make of the reception by the older woman. "Well," he responded, "if it's all right with you, I would like to water my horse over there at your stock tank," as he nodded toward the metal tank that sat next to the corral.

The woman nodded. "Reckon that would be all right," she said as she continued to prepare the beans.

Nathan was going to respond, but thought better of it and, instead, he dismounted and led Wander to the water. He stood beside the horse as it drank, but then heard shouts and the sound of something or someone crashing through the brush. From the opposite side of the cabin, he could see a pair of mules dragging a newly felled oak tree through the scrub undergrowth. The rig was being driven by a young black man who walked beside the mules with a switch in one hand and reins in the other. He clucked to the animals and brought them to a stop at the edge of the clearing. He then disconnected the chain ring from the ropes that had been attached to the log and led the mules to the corral near where Nathan and Wander stood. Nathan moved Wander from the water tank, as he could see the man leading the mules in his direction.

The man was glistening with sweat as he brought the team to the water tank. The long-eared animals were soon drinking their fill. Unlike the elderly lady on the porch, the black man seemed to be a bit more cordial, yet cautiously addressed Nathan. "Howdy mister," he said. He had seen the metal badge pinned to Nathan's shirt. "Are you the new Marshal?"

Nathan responded, "Yes sir. My name's Nathan Wolf, and I'm the U.S. Marshal out of Chanute. I don't believe I have met you, so I thought I would stop in and introduce myself and water my horse. Are you Chambers?" he asked while he stuck out his hand to shake.

"I'm Daniel Chambers," replied the black man. "I own the place, such as it is. Old woman on the porch is my grandma Meesha.

Everybody just calls her Meezie." While the men shook hands, Daniel continued to peer intently at Nathan Wolf, as if he was trying to take a reading of the Marshal's character.

Just then, one of the mules shook himself, raising a dust cloud from its hair, and water droplets flew from the sides of its mouth. Nathan watched the animal for a few seconds, noticing the liberal sprinkling of white hairs mixed in with the darker hair on the animals. "Looks to me like your team has some age to them. How old are these big fellows?" said Nathan.

"Don't rightly know," said Daniel. "My father bought these mules a number of years ago before he died, and they've been walking my fields ever since. So I figure they have to be at least twenty years old, or so."

Out of the curious nature of a lawman more than anything else, Nathan thought for a moment and then asked, "How long ago was it when your father died, Daniel?"

Daniel did not answer right away. He was still furtively measuring up the Marshal. Finally, he answered, "My father didn't just up and die, Marshal. He and my mother were murdered about twenty years ago when I was just a kid, and nobody was ever brought to justice for their killing."

Nathan looked back at Daniel and could see that the man appeared to be absolutely sincere, so he was either telling the truth, or firmly believed a story that someone had told him regarding his parents' deaths. Nathan had learned a long time ago that an accepted story and the true facts of a matter can sometimes be far different. Still, he was intrigued and now wanted to know the details. "What makes you think that they were murdered?" he asked.

Daniel, however, was not yet certain that he could trust this lawman. Just because a man wore a tin star did not mean that he gave a whit about the plight of another man's family. For years, that had been demonstrated in his dealings with people in Chanute, as it seemed there were too many instances of a double standard between white folks and black folks, especially when it came to buying and selling merchandise and settling legal injustices, up to and including murder. As a result, Daniel was skeptical of any lawman and felt that it might be better to just stay quiet. In fact, he was not too sure that maybe he had already said too much. He turned the pair of mules, held their lead, and opened the gate to the corral. "Glad to have met you, Marshal, but I've got work to do." He closed the corral gate, turned his back to Nathan, and began to remove the harness gear from the two mules, never looking back at the Marshal.

At first, Nathan felt a bit of anger at being rebuffed in his conversation with this black man. But then a realization came to him that perhaps Daniel was just being cautious, especially if the story he had revealed was true. After all, Daniel had made no mention of the killing of his parents being a closed case with justice served. Therefore, he empathized that Daniel had no idea who might be a friend or an enemy, and possibly felt it was better to err on the side of caution. But in his mind, Nathan made the decision that one way or another, he would get to the bottom of the story.

With reins in one hand, he caught the left stirrup with the other and climbed on the saddle, wheeling Wander to face Daniel Chambers. "Good to meet you, Daniel. Maybe we can talk again some time," said Nathan. Daniel looked up at the Marshal and gave a half-hearted wave. Then went back to his chores.

Nathan turned the horse and began walking off the Chambers yard, thinking to himself that Daniel might be a tough nut to crack, but from what Daniel had said, his grandmother Meezie might know a whole lot more about the incident of Daniel's parents being murdered than her grandson. Nathan stopped Wander in front of Meezie and dismounted. He removed his hat and looked at her. "I don't believe I caught your name, ma'am. I know that you are Daniel's grandmother, but what is your name?"

Meezie was done with her work on the green beans, but she had not gone into the cabin as she was curious about the new Marshal. She had watched as her grandson had conversed with him, and then watched as the Marshal got down off his horse. Nathan did not know it, but his simple act of removing his hat before he spoke to her told Meezie a great deal about this tall white man. She could see goodness and sincerity in this man. More than anything else, he was not condescending in his words or actions, a trait that was so common from white folks, especially when she had been in servitude. However, just like Daniel, she was cautious. "My name's Meezie, Meezie Jones, Mr. Marshal," she said as she looked intently at Nathan.

"Pleasure to meet you ma'am. My name is Nathan Wolf. Your grandson told me you have lived on this place for around twenty years. Is that right?"

The old woman nodded first, then said, "Yeah, my daughter and son-in-law homesteaded this place, and I've been here ever since."

Nathan looked from side to side and said, "Well, I can see why they settled here. It's a nice place with good trees, grass, and water. It's a pretty place."

Again, the old woman nodded, but she was smiling slightly. After all, she knew how it had happened that a broken wagon axle had picked out this place to settle and her mind drifted back to that event. Then she seemed to look away, as if in a daydream thinking about her past years. She spoke no further, so Nathan took that to mean that their conversation was over. He replaced his hat, mounted Wander, and said,

"Nice to meet you ma'am. I plan to pass by here again in a couple days and maybe we could chat a bit more."

Nathan was surprised then to hear the old woman say, "Well all right, then." She then stood up, holding the corners of her apron, being careful not to drop any green beans, and slowly walked through the cabin door. Nathan glanced over and could see that Daniel Chambers was watching him from the corral. He turned Wander and trotted from the Chambers farm and followed the visible trail to the west.

*****

In less than an hour, he reached a tall post that held a metal sign, upon which was the design of an M placed within a circle, the brand of the Circle M ranch. He could see the ranch house at the end of a long lane. As his horse walked the lane, Nathan could see to the rear of the house that there was a long low building that he presumed was a bunk house. Next to that was a large corral with a few dozing horses lined up side by side and rump to head to swish flies off of each other. Nearing the house, Nathan came to a fence with a closed gate. He dismounted, untwisted the rusty wire that was holding the gate closed, led his horse through the gate, and turned and refastened the gate. After remounting, he brought Wander to a halt at a hitching rack in front of the Morgan's Circle M ranch house where he dismounted and looped his reins around the rack's cross piece. Across the wide front porch, he could see the front door opening slowly to reveal a slight, dark-haired woman carrying a shotgun in the crook of her arm.

Nathan removed his hat and addressed the woman. "No need to fear, Miz Morgan. My name's Nathan Wolf, and I'm the U.S. Marshal from Chanute. I believe we met at the Summer Prairie Ranch when Claire May and I were married. I'm looking for Dave. Is he around?"

The woman looked at the Marshal, smiled, and lowered the shotgun so that the butt rested on the porch floor while she held onto the barrel of the gun. "Of course. Now I remember you. I'm Betty Morgan. Dave isn't here right now," she said. "But I expect him any minute, 'cause he will be coming to the house for dinner."

Nathan carried no watch, but he could see from his own small shadow that the sun must be pretty near overhead, dinner time on a ranch.

"You're welcome to come up here on the porch in the shade and wait for Dave," she said as she reached out her hand.

Nathan shook hands with her. The skin on her hand was slightly calloused, the mark of a ranch woman who was not afraid of physical work. "Thank you, ma'am." He sat down on one of the porch chairs.

"I've got to get back to fixing dinner, so I'll leave you here then," said Mrs. Morgan, and she slipped back into the house.

In less than fifteen minutes, a horse and rider came from behind the house. The rider dismounted and tied his animal to the hitch rack next to Wander. He walked up the step to the porch and met Nathan, who was now standing. The two men shook hands.

"Dave Morgan, Marshal, glad to see you," said Morgan.

Nathan remembered having met Morgan at the wedding and having seen him in town. "Nathan Wolf," he said, shaking hands. "Understand you may have had a bit of trouble."

"Yeah, but let's go in the house. I've been wrestling steers all morning and I'm dirty and hungry. I'm sure the wife will have enough food for the three of us." Following Morgan's lead, the men hung their wide-brimmed hats on a hat tree just inside the door. In the house, Morgan walked over to the hand pump at the kitchen sink, cycled the pump's hand lever, splashed water on his face, soaped his hands and face, and washed up. Without asking, Nathan followed, washing his hands and drying them on the used towel that Morgan tossed to him. No sooner had the men sat down than Mrs. Morgan had platters of food on the table. She took her seat at the head of the table while the men sat at each side of her. Almost noiselessly, a very pretty young woman with curly light brown hair slid into a chair next to her father, and directly across from Nathan. Her face had a light, healthy tan that offset her blue eyes. A few freckles sat astride her nose. Nathan guessed her age to be late teens or early twenties and recalled seeing her dancing with Will at the wedding. Her tardiness to the dinner table drew a stern look from her mother, but then Betty looked down. Very quietly, Mrs. Morgan said a quick thank you to God for their food, and in unison, the men uttered, "Amen."

Morgan wasted minimal time in small talk as he stabbed a hunk of roast beef with his fork and plopped it onto his plate. "Marshal, the little lady that was a bit late to the table here is our daughter, Alice."

"Pleased to see you again, Alice," said Nathan.

"Same here," said Alice, a somewhat flippant response that drew another stern look from her mother.

"I mean, it's nice to see you too, Marshal," said Alice.

"I think I've heard your name a time or two over at Summers' place, Alice," said Nathan. A pretty shade of pink colored Alice's cheeks at that remark.

Introduction over, and between bites, Dave Morgan got down to business. "Marshal, I don't know how much Bill Ward was able to tell you, but I've had more than my share of cattle disappearing from my herd, and I'm convinced that there is a gang of rustlers operating around these parts." He paused to put a large slab of cornbread on his plate and quickly covered it with butter.

"I understood that you had another bunch of cattle go missing recently," said Nathan.

"Yeah, I figure I lost about thirty head just a few days back," said Morgan.

"How many head do you run on your place here?" asked Nathan.

Morgan swallowed, then replied, "I generally run from two hundred to three hundred depending upon the weather. In good years with plenty of rain and grass, we can maintain three hundred head. But some years aren't so good, and the herd goes down along with my profits. And I sure as hell don't need rustlers making my life any harder." Morgan then bit off a large bite of cornbread, working his jaw rapidly beneath his bushy salt-and-pepper mustache. Specks of butter and cornbread crumbs could be seen at the corners of his mouth.

Nathan swallowed the bite of roast beef in his mouth and said, "Please don't be offended, Mr. Morgan, but with that many cattle how can you tell if you are missing twenty or thirty head?"

Morgan laughed quietly, continuing to chew, then said, "Marshal, a good cattleman knows his herd. Why, I've seen damn near every one of those cows and steers being born and had to help a good number of them into this world when their mammas had trouble pushin' them out. I've branded them, inoculated them, cut the bulls, and put a bullet in the ones that got so sick that they couldn't survive. And even though they might all look the same to somebody else, they're all a little bit different." He paused to take another bite. "You always remember the cattle that have strange markings and habits, and when they start to come up missing, you start doin' some arithmetic on the herd. That's how I know I've lost them cattle. But we have also had fences torn down at about the same time we think the rustling occurred. After dinner, you and I will take a ride. I've got a few things I want to show you."

Betty Morgan had been at her stove and returned to the table with steaming mugs of coffee. After another trip to the stove, she brought plates with ample slices of warm apple pie and set them in front of the men. After getting another plate with pie for herself, she sat down. "Dave, be sure you tell the Marshal about the other missing cattle," she said.

Morgan nodded at his wife as he forked the apple pie. "Yeah, Marshal, this is not the first time we have noticed a drop in our herd. What with this latest episode, we've had three times that our fences have been cut and cattle up and disappeared. I'm telling you, there are rustlers out there."

Morgan took a long draw from his coffee mug to wash down the pie. He took one more swig, then finished off the mug. He then abruptly stood up and turned to his wife. "Betty, I'll try to get back before sundown," he said, and began walking to the front door.

Nathan rose and looked at Betty Morgan. "Mrs. Morgan, that was a fine meal, and I surely appreciate you inviting me to eat with you today."

Betty Morgan smiled. "Any time Marshal. Don't let my husband wear himself down out there. He tends to forget that he is getting older and needs to slow down a bit. We'll see you the next time you are out this way."

Morgan was already mounted when Nathan came out of the house, so Nathan quickly climbed on Wander, and the two men rode to the back of the house, past the corral, and then headed west. Nathan noticed a ranch hand walking from the corral, carrying his saddle to the bunkhouse.

"How many men have you got working here, Morgan?" asked Nathan.

"Usually only about six," Morgan replied. "I take on a couple of temporary fellas when we have to drive the big herd to a market and train terminal, but I let them go after the drive is over. The smaller drives, with just the yearlings for instance, I can handle with my permanent crew."

At the end of an hour, Morgan had led Nathan up a taller rise, where from the top, they could see several miles in all directions. Rolling hills in tan and green, interspersed with serpentine creeks and stands of cottonwoods and oaks gave the landscape a picturesque quality. Dotting the hills were single and groups of cattle, some of which were lying in the shade of small groves. The men dismounted to stretch their legs and give the horses a rest. "Marshal, I wanted to get you up here so you could get the lay of the land. If you look over yonder, you can just see a shack." Morgan was pointing in the shack's direction.

"I see it, Morgan," said Nathan.

"We keep a bunk and supplies in that shack and have a hand out here most of the time," said Morgan. "Whoever is out here rides the fence on the west and part of the south side of the ranch. He makes fence repairs and watches for strays that might have gotten out and brings them back onto my property. At the end of the day, he either sleeps in that shack or on the ground, depending how far away from the shack he's been working that day."

"How long does a hand stay out on the fences?" asked Nathan.

"The boys rotate. If you have line duty, you stay out for a week. And then another fella comes and takes your place for a week. There's another shack just like that one up on the north east corner of the spread, so there's always two hands out riding fence." Morgan continued. "Trouble is, the line riders come back to the ranch house on Friday night, and the new riders head out Sunday morning. Saturdays are the boys' day off, so they can go into town and spend their wages. I figure it's during those periods that the boundaries are not manned that the thievery takes place, 'cause the boys have told me that Monday mornings are when they find cuts in the fences."

"Stands to reason," said Nathan. "Who would know about your work schedule and how it rotates?"

"Oh, hell, Marshal. Cow hands aren't saints, and when they get a little liquor in 'em, or hangin' around with some bar floozy, they'll yak about anything that comes to mind. So, I reckon my ranch schedule is known by plenty of folks. The other ranchers have work schedules pretty much like mine," said Morgan.

Nathan reached up and grabbed his canteen and took a couple swallows of water. Morgan was mounting his horse while Nathan returned the canteen and climbed in his saddle.

"I want you to look over there at the northwest corner of the fence," said Morgan. "Can you see how that section of fence is hidden from view of the line shack by that rise over there?"

"Yes," said Nathan, and he knew what Morgan was going to say. "Is that where your fences have been cut?"

"You guessed it," said Morgan. "Of the three times we have been hit, that fence was cut twice. You can see that the grass on the other side of that fence has been bent down by a group of cattle hooves 'cause the color of the grass is different from the other grass. It gets that way when we haven't had any recent rain and the dirt shows through the grass. Let's ride on down to the line shack."

"Wait a minute, Morgan," said Nathan. "If the stolen cattle are being driven outside of your fence, which direction do they go after that?"

"Well, it looks to me like they are headed north," replied Morgan.

"All right. So, who owns that land to the west and north of you?" Nathan asked.

"You probably know that if you head over east, you'll hit the Summers place, but over on the west side, now that's a mystery. For years, I've tried to find out who owns that spread, and I keep getting stonewalled. It looks to me like the stolen cattle are being moved north across that property, whoever it belongs to."

"You mean you don't know who owns that land?" asked Nathan.

Morgan replied, "Yep, that's right. There's a county recorder in town that seems to think the county records are not to be made public. And every time I ask him about that property, he just tells me that ownership of that particular property is confidential."

Nathan paused a moment before he replied. "You ever see anybody on the property?" he asked.

"Never," said Morgan. "There is no house, no pens, no stock tank, no nothing. You can see how the grass is taller with no stock to cut it back. But there's another odd thing about that land. Take a look, farther west where I'm pointing. See anything odd out there?"

Nathan studied the area where Morgan was pointing. "I guess I can't see what you are pointing at," he said. "Only that the grass out there looks a lot darker in that one section."

"That's my point," said Morgan. "Even with the shifting light during the day, that chunk of grass always seems darker colored. I'm guessing that it is some kind of blight on that section of grass. I hope it doesn't spread to the other grass. I've seen a bit of it on my land too."

Both men continued looking at the neighboring property until Morgan finally said, "Let's head on down to the shack."

When the men reached the line shack, it was obvious that no one was about. The corral was empty, and no smoke rose from the roof chimney. They dismounted, threw their reins on the ground, and entered the shack. The bunk was made up and the place was neat. Morgan walked over to the small wood stove and laid his hand on it. He then turned around and faced Nathan. A scowl pushed his mustache up against his nose.

"Is something wrong, Morgan?" asked Nathan.

"I'm not too sure," Morgan replied. "Generally, the hands will keep a fire going in the stove to ward off the chilly nights and to brew some coffee and cook some grub. They usually don't let the fire die out completely until they are ready to leave, but this stove is cold. Let's ride down the fence a ways and see if we see anybody." The men went outside and closed the shack's door. But when they went to get their horses, only Morgan's horse was calmly standing over his reins. Wander was gone.

"That damn horse," muttered Nathan, and he began to walk to the side of the shack. Finally, he saw Wander calmly munching weeds some distance from the shack. Morgan had already mounted and rode over to Wander. He reached down and caught the reins and trotted back to Nathan. "Never seen a horse do that, Marshal," said Morgan, and he was grinning as he handed Wander's reins to Nathan.

"Yeah. He's special that way," grumbled Nathan. Morgan laughed as the two men headed down the fence line.

Riding over two ridges and following the fence line, they suddenly saw a saddled horse grazing in the distance, so they approached the horse. The circle M brand was on the horse's left hip. "Well, that's one of our horses, but where is the line rider?" asked Morgan.

Leaving the rider-less horse, the two men rode a large semi-circle around the horse. They saw no sign of the rider, so Morgan drew his revolver and fired into the air. In a few seconds they heard an answering shot that came from the north. The men rode slowly toward where the sound had come from. After a short time, they heard another gunshot nearby. Upon approaching they soon found the man. He was lying in deep grass with his pistol in his hand. His face was ashen, and a pool of rust-colored dried blood was next to his left leg. Nathan could see that the cowhand could be no older than his late teens or early twenties. "That's Billy Crawford," said Morgan.

Morgan and Nathan dismounted and kneeled next to the cowhand. "Billy, what the hell happened to you," asked Morgan.

The man was so weak that he could hardly answer. "Got bushwhacked by four riders last night. They shot up my damn leg so bad I can't even stand up; it hurts so bad. And my horse wandered too far off. So, I've been laying here all last night and today."

"Did you know those fellas that shot you?" asked Nathan as he uncapped his canteen to offer some water to the cowhand.

After taking a swig of water, the man simply shook his head indicating he did not know them. "It was too dark. I was heading back to the shack to bunk down before they ambushed me." He thirstily took two more gulps of water.

"We've got to find out where he's hit and get a tourniquet on him so we can get him on his horse. All the same, he might not make it back to the bunk house," said Nathan.

Nathan cut Billy Crawford's pant leg up the side and found the entrance wound. Blood had clotted across the wound so that it was no longer bleeding. But the ride back to the ranch would surely open the wound again, so they wrapped it tightly and put a tourniquet above the wound. Nathan used Crawford's belt as a tourniquet and managed to buckle it tightly. "I guess I've done all I can right now. Let's get him in the saddle," said Nathan. Morgan fetched the cowhand's horse.

The two men lifted the cowhand onto his horse and after using the man's lariat to tie him to the saddle so that he would not fall off, they set off for the ranch house. It was a long, slow ride with Billy swaying dangerously back and forth, but managing to hang on to the saddle horn. It was nearly eight p.m. when the two men lifted the cowhand from his horse and carried him into the bunk house. Almost immediately, Betty Morgan arrived in the bunk house, took one look at the situation and rushed back to the ranch house. She returned shortly with a basket over her arm. Nathan was pleased to see that the basket contained clean bandages and several metal medical utensils. Dave Morgan watched as his wife quickly sat down by Crawford's bunk. With scissors, she cut away the pant leg and sized up the situation. Fresh blood stained the wrappings that Morgan and Nathan had put on out in the field. Crawford's face was grayish in color, and his eyes were closed.

"Betty's mother was a nurse during the war. That's where she met Betty's dad. Fortunately for us, before her mother passed on, she did her best to teach Betty everything she could about nursing, and Betty's fixed up about every hand on the ranch at one time or another, including me," said Morgan. "If the boy can be fixed, Betty will do it."

One of the cowhands had gone to the sink in the bunkhouse and drew a mug of water and brought it over to Betty Morgan. She poured a small amount of powder from a vial that was in her basket into the water. She then managed to get the injured cowhand to drink the mixture. In less than two minutes, the young man was snoring. Betty then unwrapped the wound. She found that the bullet had entered Crawford's thigh, and may have nicked the femur and exited to the rear. She was relieved that she would not need to probe for a bullet.

"It looks to me like Billy will be OK," said Betty. "I think his source of pain was the bullet taking a notch from his thigh bone. I'm going to put some sulfa powder on this wound and sew it up. All we can do is wait and see if he heals. But he is going to be on his back for a few days, at least."

Morgan and Nathan walked outside and sat on a bench at the side of the bunkhouse.

"Dammit, Marshal. I feel bad every time something happens to one of those hands. Betty and I only have Alice, so those boys are like our kids, and except for a couple of them, they are just kids, barely twenty years old or so. I think Crawford in there is only about eighteen," said Morgan. "We sure need to find out who did this to him."

Nathan listened, but did not reply and was quiet for another full minute. "Morgan, what day is this?" he asked.

"It's Friday. I know that because three of the hands have already taken off for town," replied Morgan. "They'll spend all day Saturday there."

Again, Nathan was quiet. He was thinking.

Morgan asked, "Why do you care what day it is anyway?"

"You told me that you were pretty sure that the other times the rustlers hit your place was on a late Friday night. Is that right?" asked Nathan.

"Yeah, so what?" said Morgan.

"Well, there must be a reason those outlaws shot your cowhand. I've got a hunch they know they shot the boy, figuring that they got him out of the way, and nobody would find him for a couple days. So, here's what I'm thinking. I would bet the rustlers aim to hit your place again tonight," said Nathan.

It was Morgan's turn to be silent. Finally, he spoke up. "Hmm. Well, wouldn't the rustlers know that all they had to do was to wait another day and there wouldn't be a line rider at the fence?"

Nathan replied, "Sure they know that. But too many outlaws commit crimes just because they think they can get away with it. The temptation to have fewer Circle M hands around was too great when they were sure no one would ever know what happened to Crawford. They figured they could get off scot-free and have one less Morgan cowhand to contend with. This gang, whoever they are, has a real mean streak running through it."

"Are they really that stupid?" asked Morgan.

"Believe me, Morgan. It might be just my opinion, but I have never met a criminal who would be considered smart. Oh, they always think they are going to get away with their crimes, but in the end, they always get tripped up."

"So how do you propose that we find these characters and bring them to justice? Maybe some good old fashioned frontier justice," Morgan added.

"Oh, we'll find them all right," said Nathan. "Your cattle are the bait. If they've been successful once or twice before, you can be sure they will try again. But we need to be ready for them." Nathan paused, and then went on, "Have you got a couple hands you could spare to go with us out to the line shack tonight? I have a feeling we will have some late-night visitors."

"Sure do," answered Morgan. "I'll get them lined up. We better hurry. I figure it's already near nine o'clock."

They walked back into the bunk house. They could see that Betty was finishing up her stitching on Crawford. The young cowhand was still sleeping. Morgan pulled two of his hands aside and told them of the plan and that they would not be going into town later. They would need to go with him and the Marshal to watch over the west fence line. They didn't seem to mind very much if there was something that might turn out just as exciting as going into town.

In less than an hour, Nathan and Morgan had saddled fresh horses. Nathan had turned Wander into the corral to rest. They soon left the Circle M ranch house with the two ranch hands. All of the men carried rifles in their scabbards and wore pistol belts. It would take them a bit over an hour to reach the west boundary. The men said little as they rode, each man wondering if there would be trouble ahead.

The night was clear, with occasional groups of thin clouds marching across the sky. But because the moon was a mere sliver, it was dark, even with a blanket of stars overhead. The darkness could make their activities harder, but not impossible. Nathan and the Circle M men dismounted and left their horses in a small draw where they would be unseen from the line shack and the fence to the west of the shack. They collected their rifles and began walking rapidly toward what they believed would be the targeted fence. Suddenly, one of the cowhands tripped in the darkness. As he fell to his knees, he cursed out loud. Almost immediately, a shot rang out. The rustlers had already arrived, and when the ranch hand cried out, he had been heard. In the dim light, the outlaws had spotted Nathan and the Circle M hands. More shots followed, and Nathan and the Circle M men flattened on their bellies in the tall grass. Nathan told Morgan and the hands to fire at the muzzle flashes, and they began a rapid fire. After a short time, they held their fire. There were no answering shots from the outlaws. Instead, there was now the distinct sound of hoof beats fading into the distance. Their opportunity for apprehending the rustlers had been lost.

Nathan and the men walked over to where the muzzle flashes had come from. They found that the top strand of the fence had been cut. It was certain then, that whoever the outlaws were, they had intended to rustle more of Morgan's cattle.

"Did anyone see which way they went?" asked Nathan.

The men all agreed that it had just been too dark to plainly see the outlaws escape. But they also agreed that the sound of receding hooves had sounded like they had been moving southeast. They were probably heading into Chanute.

Morgan was disappointed in the outcome of their plan. He was hoping that they would have been able to put a stop to the rustling once and for all.

"Well, what are we going to do now, Marshal?" asked Morgan.

Nathan answered, "If it's OK with you, Morgan, I aim to stay in your line shack tonight. Those outlaws won't be back, but I want to take a look at that fence in the morning light. Never can tell what they might have left behind. You and your boys can head on back to your place. I'll stop by on my way back to town later in the morning."

"Suit yourself, Marshal. We'll get on our way," said Morgan.

The men retrieved their horses, and Nathan watched as the three Circle M men rode off. He retrieved his horse and rode to the line shack where he put the horse in the small corral and unsaddled the animal. He would try to remember to give the horse a feedbag of oats from the shack in the morning. But right now, he needed to get some sleep.

*****

Saturday morning began with light climbing from the east to meet the sky. Nathan was already up and had coaxed the old stove in the line shack to heat a pot of water and coffee grounds. He opened the door to the shack and sat on the threshold to sip his coffee. Morning was his favorite time of the day, when he had yet to take on his duties and think about the tasks ahead of him. He watched as a red-winged black bird and a meadowlark flitted after each other in a territorial game of tag. Apparently, one of the permanent mouse residents also liked the sunshine, as it had appeared from somewhere in the shack and was calmly sitting in the sunlight on the floor of the shack watching the Marshal and scratching its neck with its rear foot. Since the mouse was less afraid than normal, Nathan was convinced that someone had spoiled that mouse with handouts of food at some time or another. When Nathan finished his coffee and rose, the gray rodent scampered under the bunk.

Nathan dipped the feed bag into the box of oats and carried the partially filled bag to the corral and strapped it on the horse's head. He then finished his coffee and straightened up the line shack. After saddling the horse, he returned to the fence line that had been cut. He dismounted, crossed the fence, and began looking around on the ground where he thought the outlaws had been last night. Sure enough, he found several spent bullet casings. But another glint in the grass caught his eye, and he reached down to pick up a spent percussion cap. Looking further, he found a second cap. He knew that most rifle owners had made the transition to center-fire cartridges, but percussion rifles were still used by a few hunters because of their reliability and accuracy. Nathan now knew that he was looking for a man who carried a distinctive rifle. He spent a few more minutes searching the area and found what he was looking for. A few tell-tale, deep-red droplets of dried blood on the grass led Nathan to believe that he was now also looking for a man or a horse that may have been shot in the evening's gunfight.

After making a haphazard repair of the top fence strand, he mounted the horse and began riding back to the ranch house. He stopped only briefly at the line shack to ensure that the fire in the shack's stove was low enough to be safe. Upon reaching the bunk house, Nathan put the horse in the corral and unsaddled him. He looked across the corral and saw Wander walking toward him. He scratched the horse's neck. "You have a good night, peanut brain?" he asked. Wander blew through his lips and walked away to join the other horses.

Nathan walked into the bunk house and found Betty Morgan sitting at Billy Crawford's side. The young man was spooning soup into his mouth by himself and, although he still had not regained his full color, he looked a far sight better than the previous night.

"You doin' OK, kid?" asked Nathan.

Crawford smiled and said, "Thanks to Mrs. Morgan, I'm feeling a lot better, Marshal."

Betty jumped in, "Well, you might be feeling better, but you aren't going to be walking or riding a horse any time soon. You lost a considerable amount of blood. So just relax while you can, Billy."

"Is Dave around, Mrs. Morgan?" asked Nathan.

"It's Betty, Marshal, and yes, I think he's in the house doing some paperwork in his study," she said.

"Yes, ma'am." He turned to Billy and said, "You do everything Mrs. Morgan tells you, kid," and he left the bunk house.

As Nathan came upon Dave Morgan in the ranch house, he heard the rancher muttering to himself. "These damn bills just keep coming. I swear, if we lose many more head, we could be facing a mighty tough year." Morgan looked up when Nathan walked over to his desk. He set down his pencil and said, "You find anything interesting out there at the line shack, Marshal?"

"Yeah, I think so," said Nathan.

"Well, let's go out in the kitchen and get us a cup of coffee. I'm tired of looking at this paperwork, and we can talk over coffee," Morgan replied.

As the men sat at the kitchen table sipping their hot coffee, Nathan told Morgan about the shell casings and percussion caps he had found. He also told him that he had found traces of blood and would keep his eyes open in town for a man or a horse that may have required doctoring.

"I think I'd better be getting back to town, Dave. I also told Daniel Chambers that I was going to stop and see him on my way back." Nathan rose to leave. "For now, all we can do is keep our eyes open and see if we find any other clues along the way. But I think you need to change up your line riders' schedule and maybe put two boys out in your line shacks. Maybe that will keep those outlaws guessing."

"OK, Marshal. We'll do what we can to hang onto the cattle we've got. I don't need to have any more run off," said Morgan. He watched from the front porch as Nathan saddled Wander. In a few moments, the lawman was headed down the lane away from the ranch house.

*****

As he rode up to the Chambers' cabin, he could see the screen door slowly open. He dismounted and tied Wander to the hitch rack, taking care to take an extra turn of the reins around the hitch bar. He did not want to have to chase down his horse.

"Oh, it's you, Marshal," said Meezie Jones.

"Yes, ma'am."

"Daniel ain't here right now," she said.

Nathan, with his hat in his hand, walked up onto the porch to stand next to Meezie Jones. He replied, "Well, that's all right, 'cause I really came to see you, Miz Jones."

Meezie cocked her head to one side and looked at Nathan. "Lordy, what do you want to talk to me about?"

Nathan chuckled. "No, no, don't be alarmed. It's only that I wanted to hear a bit more about the story of you settling here and the death of your daughter and son-in-law. Could I ask you a few questions about that?"

Meezie looked down at the porch floor for a moment as if she was thinking whether or not to reveal her stories to this lawman. Then she looked up at Nathan. Her look was soft but unfaltering as she said, "Marshal, I was just going to take a little walk down by the creek. Would you like to come along?"

"Yes, ma'am, I surely would," Nathan answered.

With only a slight bit of trepidation, the wiry black woman sought one of Nathan's arms to balance her as she walked.

"It's a right pretty day, ain't it, Marshal?" said Meezie.

"That it is, ma'am, that it is," Nathan replied.

As they neared the creek, Nathan could see what he thought was just a pile of rocks. But as they got closer, he could see that those stones were carefully placed just so, arranged in the shape of a cross on the ground. The grass around the cross was short in comparison to the surrounding grass. It was obvious that someone was tending to this small area. Nathan then guessed the significance of this place.

"Is this where your daughter is buried, Miz Jones?" he asked.

"Yessir. This is where my Dehlia and her husband Jonah are resting. I come out to visit them nearly every day. We have a nice talk. Yesterday they told me they liked you, and that I should trust you. So here we are." A section of upturned tree trunk had been placed near the grave, and Meezie went to it and sat down.

Nathan was at a loss as to how to start a conversation with a woman who claimed to talk to her deceased children. Oh sure, he thought to himself, a lot of people talk to family members who have passed on, but he didn't think he had ever heard anyone claim that those who had passed talked back.

"I'm curious, Miz Jones. Did you say that your daughter speaks to you?" Nathan asked.

Meezie looked up at the Marshal. But she was hesitant to answer. She was not sure whether the lawman was truly interested, was belittling her, or if he was just humoring her. She decided to speak her mind. "Yes, Marshal, my daughter speaks to me on occasion, but mostly she just cries. It's usually just a quiet, mournful sound. She misses Daniel so much."

She looked up again at Nathan and said, "Well, then. What is it you wanted to talk about, Marshal?"

Nathan wondered whether the old woman was simply changing the subject because he had pried into a personal space in Meezie's mind. And then he thought, maybe it wasn't any of his business anyway. He decided he had better stick with what might be his business. "Miz Jones, I wondered whether you might be able to tell me more about what happened when your daughter and son-in-law were killed," said Nathan.

"Oh my, Marshal," said Meezie. That all happened nigh on twenty years ago. Nothing was done about it then, and most likely nothing will be done about it now. Ain't nobody cares about it anymore, just like back then."

But Nathan would not give in so easily. "Miz Jones. Did you ever report the death of your daughter and son-in-law to the local sheriff back then?" asked Nathan.

"Lord no, Marshal. I remember Jonah telling me all about how he had been treated in town on many occasions and how the sheriff back then seemed to be in the pocket of someone and could not give a hoot about black folks," she said. "Why, Jonah was nearly robbed and killed by a white man shortly after he settled on this place."

She went on to tell Nathan about the incident when Jonah was returning from town after filing his homestead claim. Naturally, this was the first time Nathan had heard of the incident. When she was done telling the story, she surprised Nathan by saying, "But I know a secret about the man that tried to rob and kill Jonah that day. I also know a secret about the killing of Dehlia and Jonah."

Nathan realized then that his mouth was hanging open, so he quickly closed it. He was just ready to ask Meezie more questions, but he was interrupted by the sight of Daniel running toward them, clearly agitated.

He was nearly shouting when he said, "Marshal, we've been robbed!"

"Mr. Chambers, calm down, please," said Nathan. "Tell me what happened."

"Marshal, I keep a little herd of about twenty stocker steers. I buy 'em at the end of winter and keep them on our place until the following fall. They gain weight in that time and then I go ahead and sell them."

"OK, so what happened?" asked Nathan.

"Well, when I checked on them this morning, there's only eight of the steers still on my land. And a section of my fence over on the northwest side has been cut. I figure that's where the rustlers took the cattle out."

"Daniel, can you tell which direction the cattle moved after leaving your pasture?" asked Nathan.

Daniel had calmed down since his initial outburst. "Well, it looks to me like somebody was moving them to the north. There's horses' hoof prints along with the cattle tracks."

Nathan turned to Meezie Jones. "Miz Jones, I'm going to leave you for now. I want Daniel to show me where the rustling took place. Daniel, let's you and I ride out there and take a look." Nathan walked back to the cabin where he had tied Wander. He mounted and watched as Daniel opened the corral and coaxed one of the mules through the gate. The mule stood placidly while Daniel closed the gate. Nathan was more than curious as he watched the black man leap onto the back of the mule. There was no bridle or hackamore on the mule, yet the animal moved to the side of Wander.

"Like you said, Marshal. These are old mules, and they only need a foot prod and a knee prod to know where I want to go," said Daniel.

And with that said, the mule began to fast walk, with Daniel bobbing on its back, hanging on to a fistful of mane. They rode to the northwest corner of the Chambers farm.

Later as the two men stood at the break in the fence, Nathan remarked, "Daniel, it's the same as what happened over at Dave Morgan's place. The rustlers cut the fence and made off with over 30 head of Morgan's steers," said Nathan. He went on, "What I can't figure is why these outlaws don't steal the whole damn herd. They only took a part of Morgan's herd, and a part of yours. And you are right, it looks like they moved the cattle to the north."

"Anything you can do about it, Marshal?" asked Daniel.

"I wish I could tell you that I could get your cattle back, Daniel, but even you know that those steers are probably long gone for now. What I really want to do is find out who is the ringleader of this bunch, and if I can get your cattle back I'll do it," said Nathan.

Daniel stood looking at the ground. Nathan watched as Daniel let out a long sigh and began to move his head back and forth. "Marshal, I just don't know what I'm going to do. Taking half my cattle takes away a half of my yearly income. I guess we'll have to count on the garden and the chickens to get by."

Even as Daniel was talking, Nathan was watching and sizing up Daniel Chambers. What he saw was a determined, self-reliant man who would support himself and his grandmother through thick and thin by his own hard work. Nathan admired those traits in any man. He decided that he liked Daniel Chambers and would certainly try to help him.

The two men restrung the broken fence, fixing it temporarily until Daniel could later bring more wire to the site. When they were done, Nathan mounted Wander. "I've got to get back to town, Daniel, but I will do my best to find out who did this. Tell your grandma good-bye for me." He reached down and shook hands with Daniel, then turned Wander to head for town.

He was just leaving the Chambers property when he looked off into the distance toward the west where he had left Daniel. What he saw puzzled him. It was another patch of dark grass that was interspersed with an almost black color, just like he had seen on the Morgan property and the property adjacent to Morgan's place. The only thing he could think of was that the late morning shadows on the hills made queer designs. He shrugged and nudged Wander in the ribs.

*****

Back in town, Nathan dropped Wander off at the livery stable to get a good brush-down and feed. Edwin (Ed) Mullins was busy at his forge, hammering red hot steel to make knife blades. He sold the knives to the hardware store, where they were resold. His father, Dwight, was sitting in a chair by the side door of the stable, letting the sun warm his old joints. Dwight Mullins was far from being too old to continue with blacksmith work and was usually seen working alongside his son, Ed. But little by little, he was turning the livery stable business over to his son. Dwight rose from the chair when he saw Nathan, and Ed waved from the forge area but continued to beat the hot steel.

"Where you been, Marshal? I haven't seen you for a few days," asked Dwight.

Nathan answered, "Out riding the territory, Dwight. It appears we've got some cattle rustlers roaming around these parts."

Dwight Mullins chuckled. "I thought cattle rustling had gone away with the change in times, but I guess I was wrong. Where 'bouts were they stealing cattle?"

"Out at Dave Morgan's place and the Chambers place." Nathan noticed that Ed Mullins' hammer seemed oddly quiet. "Looks like they got around forty head." Nathan looked over at Ed Mullins and caught him staring at him. Ed quickly looked back at his anvil and began hammering again.

Dwight resumed talking. "I know Dave Morgan, and I know Daniel Chambers. They're good people. Why, I knew Daniel's daddy, Jonah, when he first came to the territory some years back. He bought his mules from me, and Daniel is still using those big-eared boys. Shame what happened to Jonah, though," mused Dwight.

"I didn't want to ask too many questions when I was out at their place. What do you remember about their killing?" asked Nathan.

"Well, sir. Only thing I know is what I heard around that time. The rumor going around town was that they had been shot dead, and their house was burned to the ground with them in it. Don't know if that's true or not, 'cause it was kept pretty quiet. It's just a damn shame though."

Again, Nathan noticed that Ed Mullins' hammer was quiet, but he decided not to look over at Ed.

"Was anyone ever arrested for their murder?" asked Nathan.

"Nope," Dwight answered. "But to tell the truth, I don't think the sheriff back then put in much time trying to find the outlaws. It appeared his heart wasn't really in it. I never put much stock in that sheriff. Seemed to me that he was being paid off by somebody. He was never much of a lawman. Anyway, whoever those outlaws were, they went off scot free."

Nathan was gazing out the side door toward the pasture. It was a few seconds before he responded to Dwight. "Rustlers and a twenty-year-old murder case. Wonder what else will spring up on me," he said.

Dwight Mullins chuckled again. "Believe me, Marshal. There's a whole lot of bad boys out there that I've seen over the years. Most of the time I just kept my mouth shut so I could live to a ripe old age."

"You're not that old yet, Dwight. You got a few good years left in you," said Nathan.

"I 'spect you're right, Marshal, but I still keep my eyes open and my mouth shut. Why, right now we've got a strange fella wandering around town. He left his horse here for me to look after. Never seen one quite like that," said Dwight.

"Dwight, you've lost me. Are you talking about the strange man, or his horse?" asked Nathan.

"Well, I reckon I'm talking about both him and his horse. This fella wears a white, fringed buckskin jacket. I reckon he's an old buffalo hunter. I've seen him a few times before, but I never have seen him bring in any skins."

Nathan had started to laugh, but then quickly sobered. "What's so strange about his horse, Dwight?"

"Well, this fella said his horse got cut by a mesquite thorn as they were going through a grove, but I've looked after lots of horses and seen all kinds of injuries to mend. That fella was lying to me."

Nathan replied, "What makes you think so?"

"Like I said, I've seen every kind of wound on horses." Dwight continued, "Mesquite makes a shallow cut, if it even cuts the horse's hide. This horse has a deeper wound. I figure he's been creased by a stray bullet. I doctored him and sewed him up, but he needs another day or so to rest."

Nathan could not believe what he had heard. He knew that he was looking for either a man or horse that had been shot, and Dwight Mullins was claiming to have such a horse in the stable.

"Let's go look at this horse, Dwight." The two men turned to walk back into the stall area of the livery. As they turned, Ed's hammer resumed ringing.

The horse was dozing on three legs, with an upturned hoof on the fourth leg. It started awake as the two men opened the half door of the stall, and it put all four hooves on the floor.

"Look up there on his right haunch and you can see where my stitches are," said Dwight.

Nathan could, indeed, see where the old smithy had sewed the horse's hide back together. It would have been a fairly deep wound, as the sutures were nearly five inches from end to end. He could also see traces of dried blood on the right rear leg of the horse.

"Traces of blood go all the way down his leg," said Nathan.

Dwight chuckled. "That's nothing, you should have seen him before I cleaned him up. I can tell you for sure, he lost a good bit of blood before he got here. But he's perkin' up a bit now. He should be all right in a couple more days."

Nathan asked, "When did he come in, Dwight?"

"Well, that old hunter fella was waiting at the barn door when I got here this morning. Ed wasn't here yet, so I let the fella bring his horse on in and I worked on him. Owner wasn't a very nice fella. Didn't talk much and didn't wait around. He left the horse and went on over to the cafe for breakfast."

The word breakfast reminded Nathan that he had not eaten anything yet today and thought maybe he should get over to the cafe himself. His thought was cut short by Dwight talking again.

"Say, another strange thing about him is he wears a wide-brim slouch hat and carries some kind of big old rifle in a fringed deerskin sheath. It looks like something an Indian would carry. I'm tellin' you, he's just a bit odd."

"Take care of Wander for me, will you Dwight? I think I'm going to ride home later this afternoon," said Nathan.

Back at the Marshal's office, it took a full thirty minutes to brief Bill Ward on what had taken place at Morgan's and Chambers' places and then listen to a host of questions asked by the deputy, questions for which he had no answers. What he did have, though, were several clues, and he could now identify one of the outlaws. And he was going to act on that now.

Nathan drew his revolver, checked all chambers, and returned it to its holster. Then his hand reached his back pocket and patted it. His blackjack was in place. His badge was pinned to his shirt pocket.

"Bill, I want you to wait ten minutes and then follow me over to the Prairie Dog Tavern. I'm looking for a fellow with a white buckskin jacket, and I'll bet he's hanging out over there at the bar. I want you to load and bring your shotgun, and then come and stand inside the front door watching my back. This outlaw will probably have friends in there with him, so keep your eyes open." Nathan turned and headed for the front door.

"Good luck, Marshal," said Bill.

Nathan crossed the street and began walking on the other side. The wooden sidewalks echoed with his footsteps. He passed the Prairie Bank, and next door was the Prairie Dog Tavern. With his hand on his pistol handle, Nathan entered the bar. Quickly scanning the place, he could see that there were only seven men in the saloon. Four were playing cards at a table, two were at the bar, and the bartender was behind the bar. One of the men at the bar wore a white buckskin jacket and a slouch hat. His rifle lay across the bar next to him. Nathan was sure that the second man was an acquaintance of the outlaw. He had the same sullen, arrogant look as the outlaw.

Nathan walked up to the bar and asked for a beer. After drawing the beer, the bartender placed it in front of Nathan. He took one small sip of the beer and set it back on the bar. The deerskin sheath on the outlaw's rifle was beaded and fringed. "That's a real nice scabbard you got there, mister. Where'd you get that?" Nathan asked.

It was several seconds before the outlaw spoke. "I don't figure that's any of your business, Marshal, but I found it on a dead Indian a while back."

Nathan knew that no Indian warrior would give up such a fine rifle sheath, so it stood to reason that the outlaw probably obtained the scabbard by killing the Indian. "Well, I guess the Indian won't need it anymore," said Nathan.

"That's right," said the outlaw.

"Mind if I take a look at it?" asked Nathan.

"Go ahead," the outlaw replied.

Nathan picked up the scabbard, and in doing so, he slid the rifle out of the sheath just far enough to answer a question. The rifle was a breach-load percussion. Nathan slid the scabbard back onto the rifle. He turned slightly and could now see that Bill Ward was standing with his shotgun near the front door.

Nathan stepped back from the outlaw just enough to give him some distance and quickly drew his revolver. Instinctively, the outlaw reached for the rifle.

"Leave it be," said Nathan. "I've got a lot of questions I need to ask you about, so we're going to take a little walk over to my office."

Suddenly, Bill Ward shouted, "You there, put both your hands back up on the bar where I can see them, unless you want to eat a load of buckshot." Bill had watched the man standing next to the outlaw slowly bring his hands down to his side next to his pistol. In response to Bill's warning, the man put his hands up on the bar. Bill walked over and pulled the man's sidearm and threw it across the room.

But the outlaw in the buckskin jacket was not quite through. He had slowly bent over just far enough to reach the top of his boot. But before he could move farther, he was struck on the side of his head by Nathan's pistol barrel and fell backwards, hitting the floor. Bill had stepped back two steps so he could now cover both outlaws. Nathan stepped to the fallen outlaw and retrieved a sinister looking knife from the outlaw's boot. He thought of throwing the knife to the side, but something made him put the handle of the knife in his back pocket. He then went to where the other outlaw stood with his hands on the bar. It was then that he noticed the man's thumb on his right hand was splayed at an odd angle and had a wide scar running down the side of the thumb, through the thumb web, and up to his wrist.

"Mister, I don't know who you are, but for the moment I don't have anything to hold you for. If you know what's good for you, you might want to just get out of the territory."

Nathan walked over and picked up the other man's pistol. He looked at it briefly and opened the cylinder while he walked back to the bar. As he spun the cylinder, the cartridges from the pistol dropped harmlessly to the floor. Handing the pistol to the stranger, he said, "Now, get a move on, mister," and he watched as the man walked out of the tavern. He then picked up the buffalo hunter's rifle from the bar and said, "Let's go, mister. You and me, we've got a few things to discuss." He prodded the outlaw with the rifle barrel, and they made their way to the Marshal's office, where the outlaw was placed in a cell.

Nathan removed his own gun belt and hung it over the chair of his desk. He put the knife that had been in his back pocket in his desk drawer and entered the cell with the outlaw. With the door of the cell open, Bill stood to the side of the doorway, still holding the shotgun.

"All right, mister, this is how it's going to be. I'm going to ask you some questions and give you some instructions. I want you to listen real hard, because if you don't do what I say, you will get hurt. And if you think you can get real cute, you might find that shotgun barking at you. So, first off, what's your name, mister?"

"Clyde Morse," the outlaw replied, "and you got no right to hold me here. I ain't done nothin'."

Nathan replied, "All right Mr. Morse, now, take off your hat and give it to me."

The man did as he was told. Nathan looked at the hat both outside and inside. He found nothing out of the ordinary and threw it out of the cell. "Take off the jacket," said Nathan. Searching the jacket pockets revealed only a few percussion caps and a few dollars in bills. "If you ever get out of jail, you'll get these back," said Nathan, and he threw the jacket outside the cell.

"Now the boots, Morse."

The outlaw was biding his time. He took off one boot, the boot from which Nathan had taken the knife. But as he reached down for the other boot, his fingers went to the inside of the boot. The next thing the outlaw knew was that he was laying on his side on the cell floor with blood streaming from his nose. A blackjack was in the Marshal's right hand. Nathan reached down and took another knife from the outlaw's boot and threw it out of the cell. "Get the boot off, jackass," said Nathan. The outlaw sat up and slowly pulled off the boot, and it soon joined the pile on the office floor. "Now the shirt," said Nathan, "and wipe your damn nose with it. You're dirtying up my jail."

The outlaw removed his shirt and blew his nose in it and threw it at Nathan. This time the blackjack hit him on the side of his head, and he folded to the floor again. "While you are down there, take off the pants." The outlaw did as he was told and hauled himself up to sit on the cell bunk. He was now dressed in his union suit. Nathan searched the trouser pockets but found only a few coins and a pocketknife.

For nearly two hours, Nathan badgered the outlaw, but he could not get the buffalo hunter to talk. Finally, he said, "That rifle of yours, it's a bit rare around these parts. In fact, I've only seen one other Colt revolving percussion rifle like that one, and that was a few years back. You were using that rifle when you were attempting to rustle those cattle on Friday night, weren't you?"

"I told you before, I don't rustle cattle, and I don't know what you're talking about."

Nathan loudly slapped the outlaw on the side of his face. "Oh, yes you do, and I can prove it. You and your friends were out at the Circle M when you got interrupted stealing cattle from that ranch. You got into a gun fight with me and some of the Circle M boys."

"I don't know anything about no cattle rustling, and you're making all this up. You don't have anything on me and I want to get out of here. Let me tell you something else, Marshal. If I had been in a gun fight with you, we wouldn't be talking here. You'd be a dead man."

Nathan chuckled. "Well, as you can see, I ain't dead. But maybe this will jog your memory," said Nathan, and he retrieved two spent percussion caps from his pocket and showed them to the outlaw. "Have any idea where I got these?" Nathan asked. "They're the same type of percussion caps I found in your jacket pocket."

"No, and I don't much care," answered the outlaw.

"Yeah, I don't suppose you would care, but I found these on the ground out at the Circle M ranch where you and your buddies were trying to rustle a few cattle," said Nathan, and he opened his hand and showed the outlaw the spent caps again.

"I don't know anything about no cattle rustling. I'm a buffalo hunter and you got no right to hold me here," said the outlaw.

"You see, Mr. Morse, these percussion caps came from your rifle. You were using that rifle when you got into a fight with me and the Circle M boys. There isn't anybody in this town that's got a percussion rifle except you. So that pretty much puts you at the scene of the crime, doesn't it?" Nathan put the percussion caps back in his pocket. "Well, if you're a buffalo hunter like you say, you must have a horse. Where's your horse?" asked Nathan.

The outlaw had no idea why he was asked about his horse. He answered, "Sure I've got a horse. It's over at the livery stable."

"What's wrong with your horse? Why is it at the livery stable? Do you plan to be here in town for a while?" Nathan asked the questions very rapidly.

The outlaw clearly did not like the rapid-fire questions and showed his irritation. "My damn horse is at the livery stable because that's where you take horses when you are passing through for a couple days. There ain't nothing wrong with my horse."

This time, the blackjack hit Morse on the chin, knocking his head back. "Morse, you're lying to me again," said Nathan. "I told you that if you didn't answer my questions with the truth, you would get hurt. So, I'm going to ask you again, what's wrong with your horse?"

Morse rubbed his chin. "My horse got cut on some mesquite, so he needed some sewin' up."

"Well, you're only partly telling the truth." Nathan continued, "Your horse wasn't cut by mesquite. He was creased by a bullet in a gunfight at the Circle M Ranch, wasn't he?"

Morse looked at the blackjack in Nathan's hand and decided that he had had enough. "Marshal, it seems like you think you've got all the answers, so I don't figure I need to say anything more."

"Morse, you claim to be a buffalo hunter. Now, we both know that the buffalo herds are pretty much whittled down to nothing, and there isn't a market for buffalo hides anymore. But I'll humor you for a minute. A good buffalo hunter needs a pack horse or two to haul hides to a buyer. Tell me, Mr. Morse, where are your pack horses? Where do you keep them?"

For once, Morse could not think up an answer that might be anywhere near sounding credible, so he did not even try to answer the question. He remained silent and continued to look at the floor.

With Bill Ward still holding the shotgun, Nathan came from the cell and walked to his desk. He opened the desk drawer and took out the knife he had previously taken from Morse. He reentered the cell and held out the knife.

"This is a fine looking knife, Morse. Would you mind telling me where you got it?" Nathan asked.

Morse was tired. An ugly red welt was rising on his chin and his broken nose was giving him a great deal of pain. He was whipped and saw little reason to be evasive in answering the Marshal's question. "A man gave it to me," he said.

"This man, is he a friend of yours?" asked Nathan.

"Yeah, and once in a while he gives knives to his friends. There's no crime in that."

Nathan wasn't worried about it being a crime. When he took the knife from the outlaw, he had seen a stamped mark in the steel at the base of the knife blade, and he was concerned about something entirely different. The mark consisted of two letters, E and M. "Your friend Ed Mullins gave you this knife, didn't he?"

Morse could kick himself. The damn Marshal seemed to have all the answers. "Yeah, he gave it to me, so what. It's not a crime to give something away."

"No, that's not a crime, and it's not a crime to have Ed Mullins as a friend. But still, Morse, you're disappointing me. You're missing out on the opportunity to be a fine upstanding citizen by telling me the whole truth. But I'm going to give you one more opportunity," said Nathan. "Who are you working for, and who are the others in your group of rustlers? Talk to me Morse and tell me the truth."

When Morse looked up at Nathan, there was another look in his eyes. Nathan could see a glimmer of fear. Morse was truly afraid of something or someone. But very quickly the light of fear went out of his eyes, replaced by the same coldness he had shone earlier. Morse gutturally replied. "Go to hell, Marshal."

Nathan knew that he would get no further with Morse. The outlaw knew that he had been caught, but would not divulge the names of his leader or other members of his gang.

"Suit yourself, Morse," said Nathan. "I figure for attempted cattle rustling and shooting at a U.S. Marshal, you are going to hang, or spend a whole lot of your sorry life in the new federal prison up in Leaven-worth. That is, if you don't get killed before that." While he spoke, Nathan watched Morse and once again he saw the flicker of fear in the outlaw's eyes.

Nathan walked from the cell, closed the door, locked it, and put the knife back in his desk drawer. He looked over at Bill Ward. "Give him back his pants and shirt, Bill, but lock up his coat and boots. Then let's go outside, I need some fresh air."

By now it was late afternoon, the sun was starting to dip toward the west, and by all rights it should have been close to supper time. The two lawmen stood on the plank sidewalk outside the Marshal's office. "Bill, I'm going to head for home, but I'll be back Monday or Tuesday at the latest. There's a few more questions that I want to ask out at the Chambers place. You don't need to stay all night at the office, but I would like you to stop by periodically to check on the prisoner. You can reach me by telegraph if you need me. Also, watch your step. I've been asking a lot of questions around the territory, and that may have ruffled some feathers to the point that they want it stopped. So, stay alert."

The men walked back into the office where Nathan retrieved his gun belt, rifle, and saddle bags. He headed out the door to go to the livery stable to get Wander. "Nathan, you watch yourself too," said Bill as he watched his boss and friend walk away.

The sun's rays were now on a slant and cast shadows as they came through the occasional trees on the road north. Nathan had passed the cutoff to the Chambers and Morgan ranches, and he would soon reach the southeast corner of the Summer Prairie Ranch. It would be good to get home. His stomach was growling, and it was all he could think about. It would be so good to sit down to one of Rosa's specialties. Just as his mouth began to water, he heard the buzz and knew instinctively what it was. A bullet had passed close by, followed immediately by the sound of the shot. He quickly turned Wander into a grove of trees and dismounted. Two more bullets found their mark in the trees Nathan was crouched behind. Although he tried, Nathan could not see the shooter. By staying to the west, the shooter knew that the Marshal would have to look into the low setting sun and would be blinded. As his eyes finally adjusted to the light, Nathan could see the fuzzy outline of a man with a rifle at the top of a nearby ridge, but he had to quickly duck back to cover as two more shots hit close by. Staying in a low crouch position, Nathan reached Wander and yanked his rifle from its scabbard. When he returned to the shelter of the trees, he once more scanned the ridge. The shooter was nowhere to be seen, and the shooting had stopped. Nathan remained in cover for a few more minutes, but all indications were that the shooter had high-tailed it.

Nathan stood up and looked for Wander. He saw the horse fifty feet away, and it was plodding slowly into the grass to begin grazing.

"Damn horse," said Nathan under his breath. He slowly walked over to the horse while keeping his eyes peeled for any sign of the shooter. He figured the outlaw was long gone, so he secured his rifle, climbed in the saddle, and continued on home.

Virginia Summers and Claire May were sitting on the broad porch of the ranch house as he rode up the lane. Claire May jumped from the porch and ran to meet him. "It's my favorite lawman," she shouted. Nathan couldn't help but grin at his gorgeous wife. He slid from the saddle and grabbed Claire May around the waist as he kissed her. "Oooh," she said. "I like the kisses, but not the smell. You need a bath Mr. Wolf."

In short order, Wander had been brushed down and fed, and Nathan walked into the house. He went to the bathroom shared with Claire May, stripped down, and poured a bucket of water into the tub. He noticed that there appeared to be a tear in his shirt as he threw it on the floor. He was far too tired to bring hot water from the kitchen into the bathroom. He slid down into the cool water, letting it clear his mind. Just as he was about to reach for the soap, the bathroom door opened and quickly closed behind Claire May.

"I'm here to wash your back, Mr. Wolf," she said, smiling as she sat down next to the tub.

Nathan leaned forward as his wife began washing his back. He was so tired that he thought about just closing his eyes and taking a nap, the massage felt so good. Suddenly, Claire May cried out, "Nathan, what happened to you? Oh, no."

Nathan thought for a second he had fallen asleep as he jerked back to reality. "Whatever is the matter with you, Claire May?" But then he noticed that there were traces of blood in the bath water. "What is going on?" he said.

Claire May had seemed to recover. "You have a nasty scrape on your back that is bleeding," she said. "How did you get this?"

Nathan thought for a few seconds and remembered the tear in his shirt. There could be only one explanation. "Well," he said. "I'm not sure, but I might have been shot."

"Nathan," she screamed. "What do you mean, you might have been shot?"

He had not expected his wife to be quite so dramatic. After all, he wasn't dead and didn't even feel the scratch on his back. He replied, "Well, some joker thought he might be able to stop me from asking questions. I guess I've made a few people nervous. Anyway, he wasn't a very good shot." He could hear Claire May quietly begin crying behind him, and he turned in the tub so he could look at her.

"Doggone it, Clair Mae. There's nothing to be sniffling about. I got a little scratch, that's all," said Nathan.

Claire May was no shrinking violet. She knew the dangers inherent with Nathan's job, but she loved her husband dearly and naturally feared for his safety. "Nathan, I don't know how you can make light of this. You could have been killed!"

"But I wasn't killed, was I darlin'?" He reached out and put his wife's face between his hands and leaned up and kissed her.

Claire May was still feigning to pout, though she had cooled off. "Nathan Wolf, if somebody shoots you dead, I'll never speak to you again." At that remark, they both burst out laughing. "You know what I mean, Nathan. I just worry about you and want you to be careful."

"Claire May, I promise, that most of the time I'll be careful."

Claire May playfully slapped him. "Nathan, I'm serious."

Nathan smiled broadly. "I know you are dear, and I will try to be careful."

Claire May responded, "All right, wash your hair, get out and shave and dry off. But don't dry your back, 'cause I want to put a dressing on that cut. And hurry up because Rosa has fixed you up a plate of food."

*****

Sunday morning dawned bright and clear. Claire May had gently coaxed Nathan awake in a most pleasurable manner. The couple's lovemaking made them tardy at the breakfast table in the dining room where Virginia and Will sat sipping coffee. Will's smirking look at his sister caused Claire May to respond.

"Oh, shut up, Will," she said, but she was smiling at him.

"I didn't say anything," said Will, as he returned the smile.

"Leave your sister alone, Will," said Virginia.

Everyone laughed at that remark. They all knew that Claire May was perfectly capable of defending herself.

Rosa brought in two plates heaped with scrambled eggs, fried potatoes, and bacon and set them down in front of Nathan and Claire May. She then filled all the coffee mugs.

"*Gracias*, Rosa," said Nathan.

The conversation became more serious after breakfast was finished. While Rosa refilled their coffee mugs and cleared the table of dirty dishes, Nathan told Virginia, Will, and Claire May what had taken place over the past few days.

"Will, have any of your hands noticed anything unusual at your fence lines?" asked Nathan. "It would probably be over at your western boundary if anyone was thinking of cutting your fence and making off with some cattle."

"No one has mentioned anything about it," replied Will. "But Nathan, as you know, we have two sections of land, twelve hundred and eighty acres. And that's roughly two miles by one mile. What with cattle getting the idea that they might like the grass better outside our fences, I have to keep two men riding fence all the time. So, I guess we would see any break in fence." He paused and continued, "Do you think the rustlers might try to hit us?" he asked.

"Yeah, I do, Will. The rustlers may be just a bit more leery of hitting this place because of the number of cowhands you have. Your dozen cowboys could put up quite a fight if it came to that," said Nathan. Their conversation was interrupted by the rhythmic clacking of the telegraph key in the other room.

"Now who in the world is sending on a Sunday morning?" asked Claire May. Nathan rose and walked into the ranch house office. He acknowledged his presence by tapping the key. Bill Ward was sending. Nathan listened closely and wrote out the message. Claire May and Will came into the office and looked over his shoulder as Nathan wrote.

Ward sending: Clyde Morse shot and killed in his cell late last night. Shot through cell window. Arranging undertaker. No need for you to come in. See you Tuesday. BW

Nathan tapped the key again to acknowledge his receipt of the message.

"Who was Clyde Morse?" asked Will.

"He was a prisoner I had locked up in town," answered Nathan.

"What was he in jail for?" asked Claire May.

Already, Nathan knew where this conversation was headed and wanted to stay away from some of the details. "Let's just say he tangled with some of Dave Morgan's men. Seems he thought he might like to have a few of the Circle M steers." Nathan conveniently left out the part where he had been shot at during the rustling attempt. He did not want Claire May to get upset again.

"So, he was one of the guys you were talking about at the table a few minutes ago?" asked Will.

"Yes. We were holding him until I could get Judge Stephens to set up a grand jury for his indictment," said Nathan.

"Well, I guess you won't have to worry about a trial now," said Will.

Nathan did not respond. He was a bit disappointed, because he had wanted to make another attempt to get Morse to talk and reveal the leader and other members of the gang of rustlers.

They returned to the dining table and resumed their conversation. For several minutes, Virginia, Will, and Claire May discussed work projects, cattle prices, and cattle sale dates, topics of a general nature to a ranch operation. But Nathan's mind was elsewhere. The details of the cattle rustling gang kept spinning in his head, but he also thought again about what Meezie Jones had said. She had claimed that she knew more details about the killing of Dehlia and Jonah Chambers. He had to get back to the Chambers farm and talk with Meezie again. When Meezie had mentioned that it was a gang of men that had murdered her daughter and son-in-law and burned down the cabin twenty years ago, and now there was another gang of men rustling cattle, Nathan began to wonder if there was a connection. He thought that surely, as twenty years had passed since the killing at the Chambers place, there could not be any connection between the two incidents, or could there be?

To take his mind off of work for a time, Nathan helped Will with ranch chores for most of the rest of the day. The physical work on the ranch, and the satisfaction of completing tasks, gave him temporary relief from his concerns as a law enforcement officer. At the end of the day, he was tired, dirty, and hungry. It was a good feeling.

Later, after Rosa had cleared the dishes from the supper table, Nathan, Claire May, Virginia, and Will decided to move outdoors to the porch. Evening shadows were falling, and it would be dark in a short time. Again, the conversation turned to events of the day and the ranch work ahead in the next few days. They all idly watched as Rosa came out to the porch.

"I'm bringing you a little light out here," said Rosa. In her hands, she carried a lantern and a round metal container with a spout. They watched as she unscrewed the reservoir cap on the lantern and the cap on the metal container and began pouring kerosene into the lantern from the spouted container.

"Eeew, this stuff stinks. I wish we still used whale oil," said Rosa. "It didn't smell so bad." She continued to fill the lantern. "I don't know where this kerosene comes from, but it must be someplace really stinky." When she was done filling the lantern, she pulled a wooden match from her apron pocket and lit the lantern.

"There now, a little light for you," said Rosa, and she turned to go back into the house, carrying the kerosene container. As the screen door slammed, Nathan jumped up from his chair.

"That must be it," Nathan shouted.

"Nathan, what in the world has come over you?" asked Virginia.

Nathan looked directly at Will and said, "Will, when I was out at Morgan's and Chambers' places, they showed me some sections of their grazing areas where the grass seemed to have some dark color mixed in with it. It looked different from the normal grass color. I didn't go look at it closely at the time, and now I wish I had." He paused, but then continued. "Will, do you have any areas over on your western section where you might have some odd-looking grass like that?"

Will did not hesitate and answered, "Sure, we have an area like that over on the west pasture. And it's been that way for years. Before he died, Dad always said that the grass had some kind of blight, but it never seemed to spread, and he always said he was thankful for that. The cattle don't seem to like it. They won't eat it, and they stay away from it."

"Will, I want to go out and take a look at it tomorrow. Could you take me to it?" asked Nathan.

"Don't know why you want to see some blighted grass, but sure, I'll take you out there tomorrow."

Nathan sat back down, but now he had a smile on his face. "Oh, one more question, Will. Do you know who owns the land to the west of here?"

Will laughed a short laugh, shaking his head. "No, I don't. When Dad was alive he wanted to buy more land to the west, but could never find out who owned the property. He said that the recorder claimed that the ownership was sealed by court order, and he wouldn't tell him who owned it. I guess Dad finally figured he had enough on his plate running twelve hundred acres without getting any more and dropped the idea of more land." The conversation had brought up a sad chapter in the life of the ranch from years ago when Robert Summers died of a freak accident during a winter storm, and everyone was quiet for a minute or two.

"I wish you had known Robert, Nathan," said Virginia. She continued to speak very quietly, "He was a fine man and built up this ranch by himself. His accidental death was a blow to all of us, especially me. But with good kids, and good cow hands to help me, we have managed all right through the years. I just hope we don't have any troubles with these rustlers." She dabbed at her eyes with her handkerchief.

*****

Because it rarely happened, Will was surprised to see Nathan sitting in the kitchen chatting with Rosa early Monday morning. Nathan seldom got to the kitchen in the morning before Will.

"Well, you're up bright and early, *compadre*. Did Claire May kick you out of bed?" said Will with a smile. He reached for a mug and the coffee pot on the stove, poured himself a mug, and sat down across the table from Nathan.

Nathan replied, "Nope, I'm just in a good mood and got up early to come in and talk to Rosa. I told her she helped me with the rustling case," and he laughed along with Rosa.

"I don't know anything about no rustlers, Mr. Nathan," said Rosa. "I only know that you and Mr. Will need your breakfasts, and I have *huevos rancheros* almost ready on the stove." Barely heard by the two men were the words Rosa uttered under her breath. "*Hombres son tonto*."

Will laughed. "I heard that Rosa." He turned to Nathan, "Rosa thinks we're silly."

Nathan laughed. "Well, maybe a little silly helps get you through a tough day."

Later the two men saddled up and rode to the western side of the Summer Prairie Ranch. As they rode, Will asked, "You haven't told me why we are going out to see blighted grass. What are you thinking?"

Nathan replied, "Will, what I am thinking might make you, Virginia, and Claire May mighty wealthy. We need to just wait and see."

Will guided them to the west section of the ranch, where they came upon the strange colored grass. The men dismounted, and Nathan walked into the darkened grass. After he had gone several yards, he reached down into the grass and used both hands to part the grass so that he could reach deeper down into the soil.

"Have you got your pocketknife, Will?" asked Nathan.

Will reached into his pocket and then tossed the knife to Nathan. After opening the blade, Nathan reached down again and cut some of the grass away to more easily reach the soil. He then carefully cut out a section of the soil and lifted it up to his nose. He started laughing.

"What's so funny?" asked Will.

Still holding the piece of soil, he walked over and handed it to Will, who also held it to his nose. Will screwed up his face at the harsh smell, but still did not understand the significance of the dirt and grass bits that he held in his hand.

"I need to tell you a story, Will," said Nathan. "You know I used to work up north in a town by the Mississippi River. Well, every few days a barge would come up the river and offload barrels of kerosene. That kerosene was then taken by freight wagons to other towns to be sold for lighting the city lights and people's homes. The kerosene barges would also go on up the Illinois River to Chicago for those folks' lights."

"So, what's all this got to do with our blighted grass?" asked Will.

"Patience there, old brother-in-law. I'll get to that in a minute," said Nathan, grinning as he made that remark and continued, "I once asked a barge captain who had stopped in Burlington where that kerosene came from. He told me it came out of a refinery in St. Louis. Then he said that barges came down the Ohio River from the east, somewhere in Pennsylvania, he thought. And those barges carried what they called crude oil. The crude oil was offloaded in St. Louis at what that barge captain called a refinery, where they did something to that crude oil to make kerosene, lubricating grease, and some kind of road paving stuff called asphalt. He had used his barge for hauling both crude oil and kerosene at different times."

"What's the point of all of this?" asked Will.

"I'm getting there," said Nathan. "Well, I guess because I was so curious, that barge captain took me on board his tug and into his cabin. There, on a shelf, he had two glass bottles. Inside one of those bottles was kerosene. The other bottle had crude oil in it. Well, that crude oil was black as ink. And then the captain pulled the stopper on both the bottles and let me smell them."

Will was listening, but his facial expression said that he wasn't very interested.

"All right, I'll get to the point. Will, guess where that barge captain said that crude oil came from," said Nathan.

Will answered, "Well, I've heard tell that it comes out of ...... the ground." And as he said it, his face lit up and he smiled. "Is that what that black stuff is? Is it crude oil?" he asked.

Nathan laughed. "I don't know for a fact that this is crude oil, but that's my theory. I think you should keep this between us, your mother, and Claire May. I've got to find a way to get some kind of expert to look at this and tell us for sure what this is. I have a hunch that if this is oil, it could present some real tangled problems around the territory, but it could also make some people very wealthy. Similar dark grass areas are also on the east side of the Morgan and Chambers properties."

Nathan wiped the knife blade off in the grass, and the men wiped their hands on the grass. "Guess we can head back to the house," said Will, and the men turned their horses and rode to the east.

*****

It was only natural that the conversation at the supper table that Monday evening at the Summer Prairie Ranch centered on the speculation that there might be oil on their ranch. To Virginia Summers it was nearly inconceivable that there was any other natural resource besides the grass and water on their ranch. After all, she had grown up in a time when the petroleum industry was unknown, and just like any other new idea, she was uncertain what would transpire in the future. The truth was that all four of them, Nathan, Will, Claire May, and Virginia had the same concerns. But they knew that only time would tell what would happen to their lives if there truly was oil on their property.

With their coffee mugs in hand, they adjourned to the front porch, where Nathan gave them yet another surprise. After they gathered their chairs near to each other so that they could talk easier, Nathan retrieved the paper that he had been keeping in his shirt pocket for the past few days.

Nathan said, "Not sure you can read this in the fading light, but I've got something for you, Claire May," and he handed her the telegram. Claire May studied the telegram for a moment and let out a whoop.

"Oh, my goodness, Nathan. Five thousand dollars!" She jumped out of her chair and went over, sat on Nathan's lap, and hugged him around the neck. She then handed the telegram to her mother, who read it and handed it to Will.

"I think that it's very nice of the railroad to remember you, Nathan," said Virginia.

"What are you going to do with all that money, Nathan?" asked Will.

Claire May turned on Nathan's lap to face Will. "I bet I know what we will do with that money," she said.

Nathan laughed. "All right smarty girl. Let's see if you know. Go ahead, tell them your idea."

"I would bet that you are going to buy calves from Will. Well, aren't you?"

Nathan could not believe it. He had discussed such a plan with Claire May quite some time ago, but she had not forgotten.

"Let's just say that I'm glad we didn't put any money down and bet against you," said Nathan. He then went on to explain to Virginia and Will that he thought it might be a good idea for he and Claire May to begin their own small herd of cattle to be grazed on the ranch, but they would carry their own brand. He and Claire May would buy a season's weanlings, fatten them, and sell them to earn their own income, always keeping back a few animals to build their own herd.

Nathan paused to watch the reaction of Virginia and Will, but saw that they were looking at each other. Finally, as Will looked at his mother, Virginia smiled, but Will said, "Well, you tell him, you're the head of the family," and then they both laughed.

"Nathan and Claire May, Will, and I have been talking about a plan along the same line as Nathan mentioned. We have what we think might be a more satisfactory solution, but we never knew when would be a good time to broach the subject," said Virginia. "With this windfall of yours, I think this is the right time." She continued and outlined a plan to allow Nathan to buy a share in the ranch. With his investment, the ranch would be divided, with forty per cent owned by Will, thirty per cent owned by Virginia, and the other thirty per cent belonging to Nathan and Claire May. It was a generous offer, yet Nathan and Claire May had another concern.

"Mother, there's another thing that we have been thinking about, though," said Claire May. "We were thinking that maybe we should build a house of our own. You know, so that we wouldn't be intruding on you and Will."

"You're not intruding in the least, Claire May. I love having both my children living with me, and I certainly enjoy Nathan's company."

Will spoke up, "Claire May, I think that there might be many nights when Nathan is out in the territory. Just for safety reasons, it's a good idea to be here with mother and me."

"Maybe he's right, Claire May," said Nathan.

Claire May was surprised that Nathan was siding with Will. This discussion was not going the way she wanted, but for now, she decided, maybe they were right. She thought that now was the time to give them the biggest surprise of all. Carefully, she picked her words. "I might reconsider building a house if that is what everybody feels is best. But you must admit that Nathan and I need a little bit more privacy than what we have. I would like to propose that we put an addition onto this house. Maybe a wing that Nathan and I could call our own space. And that addition should include another bedroom. We may need the extra space."

Will guffawed. "My God, Claire May. You're talking about more room than either mother or me. Why do you need all that room?"

Virginia had been watching her daughter just now, and had, in fact, been watching her the past few days. She had seen Claire May as she ran for the bathroom periodically. She knew why Claire May would need the extra room. "How long have you known, Claire May," she said.

"Oh Mother, I can't put anything past you, can I?" said Claire May, and she laughed. It was a laugh filled with joy.

Nathan and Will just looked at each other. They had no idea what the women were talking about. Claire May and Virginia looked at the men and burst out laughing again.

"Nathan, you're going to have a little deputy Marshal. I'm pregnant," said Claire May. But her face quickly turned to concern. "Ohhh," she said, and ran for the bathroom.

"I guess we'll start building the wing on the house," said Will.

Part Six

The Bank

Chanute, Kansas

There had been a rain squall during the night, and Tuesday morning dawned bright and a bit cooler. Nathan and Claire May finished breakfast, saddled their horses, and were riding south toward town. They were going to claim the $5,000 bank draft and deposit it into the Summer Prairie Ranch account. Claire May would stay overnight in town with Nathan and ride back home the next day. Birds seemed to have liked the overnight rain. They kept up a steady, passing chorus as the couple made their way to town.

"I don't believe I have ever met this banker fella. What did you say his name was again?" asked Nathan.

"Crenshaw. Arthur Crenshaw," Claire May answered. "He's a real prissy sort of fellow, wears wire-rimmed glasses, and has a little bitty mustache. Mother never has liked him, but father opened the ranch account there when the bank opened, and we have done business there at his bank for years. There's another bank in town, a Wells Fargo National Bank I believe, but I guess if you have to use a bank, his is just as good as any other."

"What did your dad think of Crenshaw?" asked Nathan.

"Oh, kind of the same as Mother, I guess. He always said that banks were a necessary evil, although I don't really think he had much dealing with the bank, except to keep the ranch's account."

They took the horses to the livery stable so they could be grained and corralled, since they would not need them until the next morning. Later, they entered the Marshal's office. Bill Ward had the coffee pot on the stove and was sweeping the office. He paused in his sweeping, poured two mugs of coffee, and handed one to Nathan. Nathan looked to his side and could see the cell that had held Clyde Morse was cleaned up. He was thankful for that, so Claire May did not have to see the resultant mess of the killing. Bill handed the second coffee mug to Claire May.

"Thank you, Bill," said Claire May brightly and then took a sip of her coffee. She had always liked Bill Ward ever since she was a little girl, and he was a deputy sheriff. She was glad that Nathan had hired Bill as his Deputy Marshal when Bill had asked for the job, and it gave her comfort to know that Nathan was not all alone on those nights he had to remain in town.

"You're welcome, little lady," answered Bill. "Glad to see you. What brings you to town?"

"I just came to town to keep Nathan company. I'll be heading home tomorrow," replied Claire May.

"I guess you two will be staying over at the hotel tonight, then," said Bill.

"That's the plan, Bill," she answered.

"Whew, that's good," said Bill, and he resumed his sweeping.

Claire May laughed. "What do you mean 'that's good'?" she asked.

But Bill kept sweeping and was mumbling under his breath.

Claire May did not give up. "What'd you say, Bill?"

Bill stopped sweeping. "Oh, if you must know, me and the missus got into a bit of a disagreement. She keeps wanting me to paint the house a different color, but I'm plenty fine with it just as it is."

"Oh, is that all? Seems a little bit petty to me," said Claire May. But she and Nathan both knew that Bill's wife had a bit of a temper and was liable to get in a snit over some minor issues. Esparanza Ward, who everyone called Espie, was of Castilian background, a stout, pretty lady with a big heart, but she also possessed a fiery temper.

"Well, it's not quite all. Seems I forgot it was her birthday, too. So, I reckon I'm going to need one of the cells tonight." said Bill.

Both Claire May and Nathan let out a groan. "Oh, Bill. That might be two nights in here," said Claire May, and she laughed, but went over and gave Bill a hug.

"I reckon we better head over to the bank, Claire May," said Nathan, and the couple walked out onto the street. Claire May held on to Nathan's hand as they crossed the street and walked the short distance to the bank. Nathan looked up at the overhead sign on the bank. *Prairie Bank* was painted in black on a white background. The words *established 1870* were painted in smaller sized letters below. As he looked more closely, Nathan noticed that something else was painted on the sign. Very low in one corner was a red circle, and within the circle was a triangle. Under the triangle and still within the circle was printed the word *Vigilance.* The entire symbol was so small that normally it would not be noticed, but Nathan saw it as he had been looking intently at the sign. He was going to point it out to Claire May, but she had gone ahead into the bank. He quickly followed.

When Arthur Crenshaw saw Claire May enter the bank, he rose from his desk in his private office and came into the bank lobby to meet her. After all, Summer Prairie Ranch had one of the bank's largest accounts.

"Good morning, Claire May," said Crenshaw. "Always a pleasure to see you. And how is your mother getting along?" he asked.

"She's just fine, Arthur," replied Claire May. She had known Crenshaw for so long that she did not call him by his surname.

Crenshaw reached out and shook hands with Nathan. "I certainly have seen you around town, Marshal, but haven't had the pleasure of meeting you."

"Nice to meet you Mr. Crenshaw," said Nathan. He nearly smiled because Claire May's description of the man had been very accurate. Crenshaw was a slight man of slender build, nearly bald save the graying fringe from ear to ear around the back of his head. He was nearly a head shorter than Nathan. He wore wire-rimmed glasses, a gray pin-striped vest, a dark gray frock coat, and black pants. His black boots carried a polished shine. But his handshake was limp and cold. Nathan guessed his age to be in the late forties or early fifties.

Nathan was curious about the bank's outdoor sign, specifically the painted symbol on the sign. So, he asked Crenshaw, "Mr. Crenshaw, as I came into the bank, I noticed that there was a little round, red symbol painted in the lower corner of the sign. I'm curious as to what that little red circle signifies."

"Oh, Marshal, I'm sure I don't know the significance of that symbol for sure," Crenshaw replied. "You see, my father, rest his soul, started this bank and had that sign put up. I believe that he was a Mason, and that sign has something to do with the Masons, but I'm sure I don't really know. Enough of all that; come, come. Let's go into my office," said Crenshaw, as he guided them into his private office. Following Crenshaw, Nathan noticed that the man walked with a slight limp.

After the three of them were seated, Crenshaw spoke, "Well, what brings you folks into the bank today?"

Just as Nathan was about to answer, Crenshaw interrupted. "Oh, I know. I'll bet you're here about that bank draft we received for you, Marshal. My, oh my, that's quite something isn't it. And to think that it was a reward for catching an outlaw somewhere up North. Yes, sir, that's quite something."

The remark by Crenshaw seemed innocuous enough. But Nathan was always on the lookout for things that were out of the ordinary. It took him a few seconds before he made any reply, and then simply said,

"Yes, it's a very fortunate situation." In those few seconds, he knew that Crenshaw had said something that he should not have known anything about. The fact that the bank draft had come to Crenshaw's bank and was payable to Nathan was all the information that the bank would have received. The secondary fact that the reward was for the capture of an outlaw was only revealed in the personal telegram to Nathan from the Union Pacific Railroad. Only one other person, the telegraph office manager, would have read that telegram before Nathan saw it. So, there was only one explanation for Crenshaw having that knowledge. He would test Crenshaw.

First, Nathan chuckled briefly. Naturally, Crenshaw asked, "Did I say something humorous, Marshal?"

Nathan replied, "Well, Mr. Crenshaw, I'm kinda wondering how you would have known that the bank draft had anything to do with the capture of an outlaw 'up North', as you said."

Crenshaw realized his error and quickly replied. "Oh, Marshal, I believe that's common knowledge around town," and then he paused and went on. "So, what are we going to do with all that money?" asked Crenshaw. "Shall I open an account for you?"

Nathan was aware of how quickly the bank man had sloughed off his question and moved on to another subject. Nathan had his answer, and it was not the explanation voiced by Crenshaw. But he replied to Crenshaw, "I think it's best that we deposit the five thousand dollars into the Summer Prairie Ranch account, since I am now part of the ranch family." Nathan made no mention that he would soon be part owner of the ranch.

Crenshaw was caught off guard. Yes, he knew that the Marshal was married to Claire May, but he did not know that Nathan would become part of the ranch operation. Crenshaw stalled, "Well, I don't know if that would be proper. You see, you are not signatory to the ranch account, so I don't believe I can allow you to deposit to that account. You understand, of course."

What Nathan understood was that he was taking a distinct dislike to this pompous little bank man. What he did not know, was that the feeling was mutual. Crenshaw was determined to make things difficult for the Marshal.

Claire May spoke up for her husband. "Well now, Arthur. As you know, I have signatory authority for the ranch account, so why don't we just have Nathan sign over his draft to me, and I will deposit the funds to the ranch account."

Crenshaw responded slowly, and in a most condescending manner. "Well, now Claire May. I know that you have the ability to sign for the ranch, but we both know that your mother is the principal on the ranch account. I believe that you can understand that I might need her approval for such a transaction." He smiled at Claire May, and then looked at Nathan and smiled. He now had managed to anger both Nathan and Claire May.

Nathan could tell from her demeanor that Claire May was ready to give Crenshaw a piece of her mind. He thought he had better step in, and said, "Mr. Crenshaw, if you don't mind, I think that I would like to have my five thousand dollars in cash, right now. Please be so kind as to go get that for me."

"Well, I don't know for sure whether we have that kind of money on hand at this time. We might have to wait until next week when the federal bank brings us a shipment," said Crenshaw. "So, you understand, of course, that this is out of our hands. I'm sure if you come back in a week, we can have the money for you, Marshal."

It was now Nathan's turn to tell Crenshaw off, and he wasted no time.

"Crenshaw, I don't know what game you think you are playing here, but I'm going to give you one minute to get your scrawny carcass out of that chair and go get my money. If you still don't understand, I can be a bit more forceful," said Nathan.

The two men stared at each other for a part of the minute, but then Crenshaw got up and walked out of the office.

While he was gone, Claire May quietly whispered to Nathan. "What a despicable little man. Who does he think he is? I am going to talk with Mother about this. Frankly, I don't think we should do business with him anymore." She paused and then went on, "Nathan what will happen if he doesn't give you your money?"

"Claire May, you don't want to see me when I get mad," was all that Nathan said.

A short time passed until Crenshaw came back into the office. He was carrying stacks of currency and was smiling. "Well, I am quite surprised. We did have enough cash on hand to give to you, Marshal." He set the stacks on the desk and retrieved a piece of paper from his desk drawer. "I do need you to sign this paper to show that you received the cash," he said.

Nathan looked at the paper. It looked very official, but basically said that Nathan had received the five thousand dollars on this date. But then, Nathan had a thought before he signed the paper. He had noticed that the currency had bands around five small stacks of bills. Each stack contained fifty, twenty-dollar bills. The five stacks would then be a total of five thousand dollars. But Nathan had not yet cooled down, and more to just irritate Crenshaw, he decided that he would count out the money, and he tore the band off of the first stack and began counting it.

"Why Marshal," said Crenshaw. "You don't intend to count all that money, do you?" and he was smiling as he spoke.

"Yes, Crenshaw, I intend to count all this money," Nathan replied.

"Well, then, perhaps I should explain something to you, Marshal."

"And what would that be, Crenshaw?" asked Nathan, but he kept on counting the bills.

"Well, you see, Marshal, each of those packs will only have forty-nine bills in it, not fifty. So the total will actually be four thousand nine hundred dollars, not five thousand," said Crenshaw.

Nathan stopped counting and glared at Crenshaw. "Perhaps, sir, you might like to explain to me why you would attempt to give me forty-nine hundred dollars instead of five thousand," he said.

Crenshaw replied, "Oh, it is very simple to explain, Marshal. You see, a bank is just like any other business. We have to make a profit to stay in business."

Nathan did not respond. He continued to glare at Arthur Crenshaw.

Crenshaw continued, "So you see, for every transaction that the bank carries out, we have to take what we refer to as a carrying fee. It's just a small fee to cover our expenses. I'm sure you can understand that, Marshal."

Nathan deliberately stacked the bills back together and slowly pushed them across the desk. He then picked up the paper that Crenshaw had given him to sign and reread it. The printing plainly said that '*On this date, _____ received five thousand dollars from Prairie Bank, Chanute, Kansas.*' The words, 'five thousand' had been handwritten by Crenshaw when he handed the paper to Nathan. Nathan turned the paper around and shoved it across the desk. He said, "I guess this paper is not correct then, is it Mr. Crenshaw. You want me to sign this paper that says I received five thousand dollars, but you want to give me only four thousand nine hundred dollars. Isn't that right, sir?"

Crenshaw twisted slightly in his chair and said, "Yes Marshal, that's correct. But as I explained, that is our standard procedure, to deduct a carrying fee..."

Before Crenshaw could say anything further, Nathan had risen from his chair and walked around the desk. He put both his hands on the side of Crenshaw's desk and leaned into him. "Crenshaw, let me make myself clear. I don't intend to pay any of your money-grubbing fees. Frankly, I believe you are trying to swindle me, and we don't want that, now, do we? So, I'm going to give you one more minute to bring me the other one hundred dollars. If you decide not to do that, I may have to be a bit more forceful in my request." Nathan straightened up and walked back around the desk to sit down again beside Claire May. He glanced at her and saw that her eyes were wide open, and her lips were parted.

Nathan continued to glare at the banker. Then he suddenly smiled at the banker and said, "But, I figure you're a smart kind of man, Mr. Crenshaw, so I'm sure you understand what I said, don't you?"

Crenshaw stared at Nathan, with the Marshal returning the stare. Nathan saw something in the eyes of Crenshaw that had been absent in the minutes before. There was a look of cold hate on Crenshaw's face, mirrored in his eyes. It was a look of pure evil, and Nathan knew then that he would never trust this man. Slowly, Crenshaw rose from his chair and left the office. Nathan's eyes followed the banker as he walked away. He saw Crenshaw stop in the bank lobby and speak to a man. The man turned and looked back into Crenshaw's office, staring directly at Nathan. Crenshaw then walked on and entered the bank's vault, the door of which was standing open.

Nathan looked back over at Claire May, who was staring intently at Nathan. She whispered, "Well, I guess he deserved that, but my goodness, Nathan. You're full of surprises."

Nathan replied, "I'm sorry you had to see that, Claire May, although I was tempted to slap his smirking face."

Crenshaw returned to the office and sat at his desk. He counted five twenty-dollar bills as he laid them on top of the stacks of bills. His previous countenance had returned, and he smiled as he said, "I believe that you will find that the full five thousand dollars is there, if you would like to count it out." He held his smile.

Nathan retrieved the paper that had previously been given to him by Crenshaw and signed and dated the document. He shoved it back across the desk.

"Now then," said Crenshaw as he picked up the paper. "I'll go ahead and get the papers together to open your new account here, Marshal." Crenshaw began to rise from his chair.

"That won't be necessary, Crenshaw," said Nathan. "Claire May can simply deposit the money in the Summer Prairie Ranch account."

Crenshaw sat back down. The smile on his face seemed permanently affixed as he said, "I believe that I mentioned that I would not feel comfortable doing that without Mrs. Summers' approval. Perhaps she could come into the bank next week with the money." His eyebrows raised, as if he was expecting an immediate approval from Nathan and Claire May.

Instead, Nathan rose from his chair and slowly placed the five stacks of currency, along with the five loose bills into his trouser pockets. "Mr. Crenshaw, I believe I will take my money with me. Maybe another bank would appreciate my deposit without charging any extra fees or insulting my wife." Nathan knew that Claire May was absolutely fuming, and added, "I believe that you have underestimated my wife, Mr. Crenshaw. She is just as much a part of her family's ranch as her mother, and I would not be surprised if the family moved their account from your bank." Nathan glared at the pompous little banker.

"Nathan," said Claire May as she rose from her chair, "that same thought occurred to me. Arthur, rest assured that I will be discussing the future of our account with my mother and brother. However, in the meantime, I believe that we will be examining our accounts at home, and then returning here to the bank to compare our figures with those of the bank. If there is any kind of discrepancy between the accounts, you can rest assured that our account will need to be made whole before we move it from your bank. I believe that we can go now, Nathan."

Crenshaw had stood, and said, "I don't believe I would advise you to do that, Claire May," smiling as he said it, but then receiving no reply, he watched as Nathan and Claire May walked out of the bank. In a moment, he walked back into the lobby and resumed a quiet conversation with the man he had previously spoken with. The man departed the bank and stood on the sidewalk watching Nathan and Claire May as they walked away.

In the short span of thirty minutes, Nathan and Claire May had opened a new account at the Wells Fargo Bank down the street from the Prairie Bank. The bank manager at Wells Fargo was happy to receive the couple. After leaving the bank, they went to the cafe for lunch, where Claire May sat idly stirring her cup of coffee. "Nathan, I was afraid you were going to hit Arthur Crenshaw, not that he didn't deserve it," she said.

"The thought crossed my mind, dear, but I wouldn't do that in front of you," said Nathan.

As Nathan laid some coins on the cafe table to pay for their lunch, he said, "I have a couple more stops to make. Would you like to tag along, or would you rather go shopping?"

Claire May's face lit up. "Why, of course, I would rather go with you. She stood up from the table. "Where are we going, Marshal?"

They walked to the *Wheatfield Hotel* and entered the lobby. For the area, the hotel was considered to be somewhat fancy, catering to the wealthy, but willing to accept money from cowboys and working men as well. An ornately carved, maroon-carpeted stairway rose to the side of the clerk's counter. A sparkling glass chandelier hung high over the lobby area. It was on a pulley system so that its lantern array could be lowered, cleaned, and refilled with oil before lighting it each evening. The reservation counter was also ornately carved and gleamed from oiling and polishing. A man stood behind the counter, and behind him were rows of pigeonholes holding keys and guests' mail. They walked to the counter where the clerk greeted them. "Good day, folks. How can I help you?" he asked.

Nathan replied, "My wife and I would like a room for the night."

"Yes, we have a very nice room on the second floor. It is at the back of the building, so there is no street noise." The clerk pulled a key from the row of boxes and handed it to Nathan. "That will be three dollars for the night, payable in advance, please."

Nathan slid the money across the counter to the clerk. Then he leaned on the counter and pulled his vest aside so that his badge was visible. "My name is Nathan Wolf, and I am the U.S. Marshal for the southeast Kansas territory. I am investigating a crime, and I need to know if you have a guest registered by the name of Clyde Morse."

The clerk hesitated a few seconds. "Marshal, was he the poor unfortunate man that was killed in the jail a couple nights ago?"

"Yes, he is the one," answered Nathan.

"Why yes, he was a guest here," said the clerk. "We are still trying to decide what to do about his room. We don't believe that he has any family around these parts."

"Mister, I need the key to his room," said Nathan.

"Oh, I don't know if that would be permissible. Don't you need a search warrant or something."

"Look, mister. Morse is dead. I don't need a search warrant to look at the room of a dead man," said Nathan. "Please, just give me the key."

The clerk turned, scanned the pigeonholes behind him, and retrieved a key from one of the boxes. He turned and handed the key to Nathan. "Please bring the key back to me when you finish," said the clerk who looked down and feigned reading some papers that lay behind the counter.

Nathan and Claire May climbed the stairway to the second floor, found their room, and opened the door. "Oh, this is very nice," said Claire May. "It's very pretty, don't you think, Nathan."

"Yes, my dear, it is very nice," he answered.

Claire May reached up and kissed her husband. He grabbed her around the waist and returned the kiss. Then he said, "We don't have time, Claire May. Let's go and finish my errands."

Claire May puffed up her lower lip. "Marshal, you're just no fun." She quickly smiled and said, "Where are we going?"

Nathan looked at the second key in his hand. "We're going over to room 204," he said.

The couple walked down the hall to 204, and Nathan opened the door with the key the clerk had given him. The room emitted a musty, dirty smell and was unkempt, to say the least. Soiled clothing was strewn about the room, and a half empty bottle of whisky sat atop the dresser. The bed was unmade, and dirt was evident in the bed clothes.

"A pig lived here, Nathan," said Claire May.

"No, my dear. The late Clyde Morse, outlaw rustler lived here, and I need to search through this mess to see if it can tell me any more about the deceased buffalo man."

For the next twenty minutes, Nathan rummaged through the room searching through clothing, bedding, and the dresser. True to form, he lifted the sagging mattress and found over two hundred dollars in a leather pouch. Nathan pocketed the money. He knew exactly what he would do with it later. But then, as he searched in the drawer of the small lamp stand next to the bed, he found an item of interest. Hidden among some clothing, he found a medallion. It was metal and about one and a half inches in diameter. In the middle of the medallion was an imprinted image of a triangle. Beneath the triangle was the word *Vigilance.* But when Nathan turned the medallion over, a larger imprint was evident. The imprint was just three letters: K K K. And at the bottom of the medallion, under the three K's, was a much smaller imprint of the letters E M. Thoughts swirled through Nathan's head as he looked at the medallion.

"What did you find, sweetheart?" asked Claire May.

"Nothing but bad news, I'm afraid, Claire May. Nothing but bad news."

He handed the medallion to his wife, while he continued searching the room. He found nothing more of interest.

"What does it mean, Nathan?" asked Claire May. She turned the medallion over in her hand. "What does KKK mean? Is it somebody's initials?"

Nathan knew of the Klan. He had run across a few members in the upper Midwest, but they did not belong to any particular chapter and had posed no threat. "It stands for Ku Klux Klan, Claire May. The Ku Klux Klan is known to be a nasty, hate organization. They hate Negroes, or anyone who doesn't have the same ugly beliefs that they have. They are a dangerous group, and now I find that there may be a group of them here in Chanute," Nathan said, as he shook his head.

"What is this, Nathan." Claire May had been on her hands and knees looking into the bottom drawer of the dresser. She held up a white tunic, on the front of which was a drawing of a red circle with a yellow triangle within the circle. Nathan took it from her hands and looked closely at it.

"Do you remember the symbol that was drawn on the sign at the bank?" he asked.

"Oh, it looked like this, didn't it?" she answered. She then held up another article she had found in the same drawer. "Does this thing go with it," she asked. She was holding a conical hood with holes for eyes, nose and mouth cut into the cloth.

"I'm afraid so, Claire May. This is the garb that the Ku Klux Klan members wear when they are up to no good. It appears that our deceased outlaw, Mr. Morse was a member of that gang," said Nathan.

"Let's go, Claire May. I have another stop I want to make," said Nathan.

They folded the tunic and hood and took them with them when they left the room, and soon left the hotel after returning Morse's room key to the front desk. Claire May tucked her arm into Nathan's as they walked down the street.

"Where to now, Marshal Wolf?" she asked, grinning up at her husband.

"Well, we're going to see another sidewinder," said Nathan. In a few minutes, he held the door open for his wife, as they entered the Continental Telegraph Office. Homer Green, the office manager sat at his desk, his telegraph key within easy reach. He looked up from reading a newspaper.

"Oh, afternoon Marshal. Beautiful day today, isn't it," said Green. "And good day to you, Mrs. Wolf. What can I do for you folks?"

"Homer, you keep a copy of all your telegrams, don't you?" asked Nathan.

"I sure do. Never know when someone might need to see a copy," answered Green.

"Homer, I need to go through your file for the past couple weeks."

Green looked at the Marshal, and hesitated. Yet, he couldn't think of any reason why the Marshal should not see the file. "Well, it's a bit out of the ordinary, but I guess you can see the file. Sure, I'll get it," he said as he stood and moved to a shelf where he pulled a large cardboard-sided folder and brought it over to the counter. He pushed it across the counter to Nathan and returned to his desk, casually watching as the Marshal leafed through the wires.

The telegram copies looked just like the originals and appeared to be second prints from the teleprinter machine. They had been two-hole punched and filed by date. It took only minutes for Nathan to find the telegraph he was searching for. It was a telegram addressed to Arthur Crenshaw at the Prairie Bank. The telegram stated that a transfer of funds in the amount of five thousand dollars was being made to the Prairie Bank. The registered owner to whom the funds should be given was Nathan Wolf. Questions should be addressed to the sender, Union Pacific Railroad. Nathan also briefly reviewed the telegram he had received from the railroad and closed the folder.

Nathan looked directly at Henry Green and said, "Henry, I just left a meeting with Arthur Crenshaw."

Green's eyebrows lifted and he smiled. "Fine gentleman, Arthur Crenshaw," he said. Nathan ignored the remark.

"Henry, I would like to know how Mr. Crenshaw might have found out that the funds that I received from the railroad were a reward for capturing an outlaw up in the northern Midwest. How would he have known that, Henry?"

Green's response was exactly what Nathan had expected. "Oh, I think that is rather common knowledge around town, isn't it Marshal?" It was an echo to Crenshaw's answer.

"Well, you see, Henry, it's not common knowledge. In fact, only the Union Pacific Railroad and I know the circumstances associated with those funds." Nathan paused and continued staring at Henry Green. He then picked up the folder of telegrams, walked around the counter, went to Green's desk, and slammed the folder down on Green's desk with a loud bang.

"I misspoke, Henry." Nathan continued, "Besides me and the railroad knowing the details of the reward, you also knew, because you saw both of the Union Pacific telegrams. Isn't that correct, Henry?"

At last, Henry Green knew why the Marshal had been interested in seeing the telegram file. He became panicky and out of nervousness, grabbed the telegram file and replaced it on the shelf so that he would not have to look directly at the lawman. He knew where the conversation was headed. He then attempted to be bold. "Oh, look at the time, Marshal. I have some telegrams that I have yet to deliver. So, if there are no further questions, I should probably go ahead and lock up and deliver them."

Nathan took two steps, grabbed Henry Green by the front of his shirt, and literally threw the man back down into his chair, which very nearly tipped over backwards.

"We're not done yet, Henry," said Nathan. "It appears that the Continental Telegram Company has a stool pigeon, leaking confidential information," said Nathan. "And Henry, you're that leak. The only way Crenshaw would have known the details of my business is if you told him, and you told him, didn't you, Henry."

Green's panic now turned to fear. Sweat broke out on his forehead. He answered, "I honestly don't remember. It may...it may have come out in a conversation with Crenshaw, I suppose, but I just don't remember."

Nathan leaned on Crenshaw's desk and drew closer to Green. "Oh, you remember, all right. You're a weasel, Henry. You ran right down and showed the telegram to Crenshaw when you got it, didn't you?" Then Nathan lightly slapped Green on the face. "Didn't you, Henry?"

Green had no excuse and no place to run. He had been revealed to be the source of Crenshaw's knowledge. "I suppose I did," he said, "but I meant no harm."

"Maybe you didn't, and maybe you did. In either case, you're still a no-count weasel, and I don't tolerate weasels." Nathan continued, "So here is what we are going to do. Get yourself a piece of paper and pen and write out what you just told me, that you revealed to Arthur Crenshaw personal information that you were entrusted to safeguard. You broke the trust of the Continental Telegraph Company, and I'm sure they would like to know how you did that. Start writing."

Henry Green did as he was told. He took paper and pen from his desk drawer, and with Nathan looking over his shoulder, he wrote out a confession, retelling the fact that he had revealed private information to Crenshaw.

"Sign it and date it, Henry," said Nathan when the paper met Nathan's satisfaction. Green complied, and Nathan folded the paper and put it in his pocket. Green then opened the desk drawer to put the pen back in it, but as he went to close the drawer, he was blocked by Nathan's fist resting in the drawer's opening.

"Pull the drawer back, Henry," said Nathan.

Green pulled the drawer open wider, and Nathan reached in and retrieved an object he had seen earlier when Green opened the drawer. It was another KKK medallion.

"Tell me, Henry," said Nathan, as he showed the medallion to Green. "Are you a member of the Klan?"

Fear caused Green to stutter. "Oh, m-my, Marshal. Certainly not. I don't know where I found that thing, but when I found it, I just threw it in the desk drawer. I don't know anything about the Klan," he said in what he thought was his most convincing voice.

Nathan was not convinced. He was certain that he knew the truth. He reached back to the counter where he had left Morse's folded Klan tunic. He unfolded it and held it up to Green. "Henry, do you have one of these nasty outfits hidden over at your house, or is it hidden here in the telegraph office? Maybe I ought to look around the place to see if I can find one, what do you think?"

Green was now sputtering, clearly rattled. "No...no, Marshal. I don't even know what that is. Why would I have one of those shirts?" he stammered.

Nathan was sure he knew the truth, but figured any further conversation with Henry Green could wait. "All right, Henry. I'll just hang on to this medallion for the time being, if you don't mind."

Green nodded his head, mumbling, "OK."

"I'm also going to give you some advice, Henry. I would advise that you go ahead and resign your position with the telegraph company, because I will be contacting them to tell them about your poor performance of your duties." In the meantime, I want you to pick up your own belongings and clear out of the telegraph office. I don't want you back in this office unless I tell you. Do you understand?"

Green did not respond. He held his head down, looking at the floor. Nathan and Claire May left the telegraph office, walked up the street, and entered the Marshal's office where Bill Ward was sitting at his desk leafing through a new batch of wanted posters.

Nathan briefed Bill Ward on what had transpired that morning: the search of Morse's hotel room, the conversation with Arthur Crenshaw, and the meeting with Henry Green. Then he showed Bill the KKK medallions he had found and the Klan uniform that had been in Morse's room.

"Bill, I feel quite certain that there are a number of men in this town that belong to the Klan. I also believe that Henry Green is a snitch for them, and that is extremely dangerous for us because he has access to every wire coming into Chanute." Nathan continued. "It might not have been in my authority to do so, but I have kicked Henry Green out of the telegraph office."

"Probably a good thing," said Bill. "Never liked that fella very much."

"Well, you might not think so when I tell you the rest," said Nathan. "Bill, I want you to sit in at the telegraph office for a while. In other words, I want you to run the place until Continental Telegraph can put a new manager in here. So, the very first wire you need to send is to the Continental Telegraph Company and tell them they need to immediately replace Henry Green, who suddenly resigned."

Bill's reaction was immediate. "Aww, Nathan. I don't want to be any old telegraph man. I'm a law man, you know that."

"Yeah, Bill. I know that, and you are one of the best," said Nathan. "But, to get to the bottom of this cattle rustling and the killing of Morse and the Chambers murders, I need to make sure that we don't have a snitch in that telegraph office. I know it isn't what you signed up for, but would you please do this for both of us? I also feel certain that Continental Telegraph won't want to leave the position open. They don't make any money without a man in the office."

Bill Ward hung his head for a second, but then looked up and said, "Sure, if that's what it takes to solve these crimes, I'll do it."

Nathan added, "One more thing Bill. Wear your handgun and keep your shotgun handy behind the counter down there. You need to protect yourself and be alert. No telling right now who is a friend and who is a member of this gang."

*****

As the afternoon shadows lengthened into evening, the waitresses at the Hereford Steak House moved through the dining room, lighting the wall sconce lanterns that cast dancing shadows on the walls next to them. Nathan and Claire May were seated at a table near the back of the dining room. A glass with two fingers of bourbon in it sat next to Nathan's plate. A glass of wine was at the side of Claire May's plate. They had each ordered the house special, a medium rare T-bone and were enjoying the juicy steak.

"Who knows, Nathan. These could have come from one of our steers," said Claire May.

"Well, we'll do our part to keep the beef prices up," said Nathan as he put another morsel of steak in his mouth. "Changing the subject, I haven't even asked you how you are feeling, and what you are thinking about having a baby. Are you excited? Are you feeling OK?"

Claire May laughed. She reached over and put her hand on top of Nathan's. "Silly man. Of course, I'm excited. I've always wanted to have a little girl, or boy, of my own. And now that the morning sickness has gone away, I actually feel better than I have ever felt. I'm kinda scared about actually having the baby, I mean giving birth and all, but still, I'm looking forward to it."

Nathan looked across at Claire May. He couldn't help but think to himself how pretty she was, and how lucky he was to have her. "I love you," he said. Claire May smiled and replied, "I love you too, Nathan."

Later, as they rose from the table to retire to their room, Nathan was sure that he saw the same man who had been in Crenshaw's bank stick his head in the door to the restaurant and quickly back out again. Nathan now knew for sure that they were being watched, probably on orders from Crenshaw.

It was already light when Nathan woke the next morning. He lay still, remembering where he was. One arm was under Claire May's neck and the other arm and hand were on Claire May's bare stomach. Neither he nor his wife wore bed clothes. As he tried to shift positions, Claire May suddenly rolled over and faced him. "Finally awake, sleepyhead?" she asked.

He chuckled. "How long have you been laying there awake?"

"Just long enough, mister, waiting to do this," she said as she rolled on top of her husband.

"What a way to wake up," said Nathan.

*****

Later as they sat eating breakfast at the cafe, they discussed what had transpired yesterday. "Nathan, I swear I'm going to talk to Mother and Will about moving the ranch account out of that despicable little man's bank."

"I don't blame you. I would do the same thing. Oh wait, I already did," he said, smiling. But he quickly became sober again.

"Claire May, I'm a bit worried about you and your family. It looks like I may have stepped into a hornet's nest asking a lot of questions of folks hereabouts. I'm afraid this outlaw group may take it out on you or your family."

Claire May paused as she dipped her piece of toast in the sunny-side-up egg on her plate. "Well, remember sweetheart, you are family too. And I'm worried about you."

"We will need to be extra alert until I get to the bottom of all of this and it finally blows over," he said. "Anyway, I need to go back out to the Chambers place. I would like to talk again with Meezie Jones. You and I can ride that far together, and after we talk to Miz Jones, you can head on home while I go back to town."

Early Wednesday morning, Nathan and Claire May checked out of the hotel. Claire May had changed back into her riding pants and carried her saddlebags containing her other clothes and essentials. Later they sat on a hay bale at the livery stable and watched Ed Mullins saddle up their horses. Nathan was amused to see that Wander danced on Ed's feet much the same as the horse did to him.

The couple left town riding slowly without much conversation but enjoying each other's company and the crisp fresh air. They turned at the fork in the road that led to both Morgan's and Chambers' places, and eventually turned into the lane leading to the Chambers' cabin. They were dismounting and tying their horses to the hitch rack when Meezie Jones emerged from the cabin.

"Good morning, Miz Jones," said Nathan as he removed his hat.

"Marshal," was the only reply from Meezie Jones.

"Miz Jones, this is my wife, Claire May," said Nathan. "Claire May, this is Meezie Jones."

"Pleased to meet you, Miz Jones," said Claire May.

"Yes, ma'am," said Meezie. "I see the Marshal got himself a real pretty wife."

Claire May blushed slightly. "Thank you, ma'am."

"Is Daniel about, Miz Jones?" asked Nathan.

"I believe he's out doing a repair on the chicken shed," she answered. "But I expect you're here to talk with me. Seems we got interrupted the last time you were here. I'll get my hat, and we'll take a little walk," said Meezie.

Shortly, she stepped from the porch, and once again took Nathan's arm as they walked to the burial site of her daughter and son-in-law. "They was talking to me yesterday, Marshal."

Gently and quietly, Nathan asked, even though he thought he already knew the answer, "Who was talking to you, Miz Jones?" Meezie did not answer and kept walking.

As they turned slightly to go toward the edge of the creek, Nathan glanced at Claire May. Her face reflected that she was paying close attention to the older woman. They reached the grave site, and Meezie took her seat on the upturned section of log. "Dehlia and Jonah told me you would come back. They told me again that I should trust you," said Meezie.

Again, Nathan glanced at Claire May. She was watching and listening in rapt attention to hear the older woman speak. She seemed fascinated with Meezie. "Claire May, Miz Jones was a slave before the war," said Nathan. "After the war, she and her daughter and son-in-law came and settled here, but her daughter and her husband were killed about twenty years ago. This is where the couple is buried. Miz Jones has raised their son, Daniel, who lives here with her."

"I recall mother and father talking about this place being burned down when I was a child," said Claire May. "It must have been horrible. What kind of people do such things?"

"Claire May, there are a lot of good people in the world, but there are also a whole lot of bad people, and it's those horrible people who do such things. I guess that's why I have a job," said Nathan.

Suddenly, Nathan and Claire May looked at Meezie. She was making a strange sound.

"Shhhh," voiced Meezie. So quiet that they could barely hear her, she said, "Do you hear? Dehlia is happy."

A breeze had come up and was rustling the leaves of the cottonwoods and willows by the creek. That was all that Nathan and Claire May heard. Meezie then appeared to have been startled. Then she began to laugh and looked at Claire May. "Why, child, you are going to have a baby, aren't you?" she said.

Claire May was shocked. She stared at Meezie with her mouth open. She had told no one that she was pregnant except her immediate family. To her, the old woman was certainly eerie. How could she possibly know? She stammered, "Ho... How did you know?"

Meezie just smiled. "Dehlia knows," she said.

Claire May walked to her and placed her hand on Meezie's shoulder. Then she sat down on the ground next to Meezie's log seat and said, "Miz Jones, could you tell me a little bit about your life before you settled here?"

Nathan moved and sat on the ground on the other side of Meezie, and for the next hour, they asked Meezie Jones about her life and her time spent in bondage before the Civil War. The couple was fascinated listening to the sharp details remembered by the older woman about the time when she had been enslaved and the succinct answers to their questions. At last, Meezie had talked about the subject long enough. She paused for over a minute, and finally said, "But Marshal, that story is not why you came to see me today."

Nathan was taken aback somewhat. He had been enthralled by Meezie's narrative of her past life, but he soon resumed his work-related questions. "Miz Jones, when you and I last talked, you mentioned that you might know something about the man who attacked your son-in-law when you first settled here. I know that's been a long time ago, but what do you remember about that?"

The breeze stirred again and made the tree leaves rustle. The sound was almost like a person whispering. Meezie looked up, then nodded her head as if she was in a conversation. Nathan and Claire May glanced at each other with blank looks on their faces.

"Like you said, Marshal," she began. "It was a long time ago, but I remember it like it was yesterday. It was when we first settled here. We had barely begun to build our soddie. Jonah took our savings and went into town to buy our mules and our supplies. He said he met several good people in town, but some of the other folk weren't so nice. He talked about the blacksmith, a Mr. Murrin, or Miggins..."

Nathan interrupted, "Mr. Mullins?"

"Yes, that's it, Mullins," said Meezie. "Jonah said he was a good man. Anyway, it was on his way back home here that Jonah had some trouble." She paused.

"What kind of trouble, Miz Jones?" asked Nathan.

"Well, when Jonah told the story about it later, he said that a man had followed him around town while he was buying his supplies. The same man watched him every place that he bought something. When Jonah was done buying supplies, he walked out of town. He had the mules so loaded down with supplies that he had to walk and lead them." She paused again.

"Marshal, do you see that tin cup hanging on the pump handle over by the cabin?" Meezie asked.

Nathan looked toward the cabin. "Yes, I see it. Would you like for me to bring you a cup of water?" asked Nathan.

"Yes sir, I'm a bit parched," she answered. Nathan stood up and walked back to the cabin.

While Nathan was gone, Meezie turned to Claire May. "I don't 'spect your husband to understand about me talking with my late daughter and her husband. He may even think I'm a bit daft. But Miz Wolf, I surely do hear them speak to me, and they were so happy that your husband was taking an interest in getting to the bottom of their killing."

Claire May did not know how to answer. She simply said, "I'm glad."

Meezie Jones then chuckled to herself.

"What's funny, Miz Jones?" asked Claire May.

Meezie replied, "Dehlia done told me what you were going to have, a boy or a girl. But I ain't going to tell you that. It's my little secret."

It was Claire May's turn to laugh. Still, she wondered what Meezie Jones was thinking.

Nathan returned with the cup of water and handed it to Meezie, who took two sips of the cold water.

"What happened when Jonah walked out of town, Miz Jones?" asked Nathan.

Before speaking, Meezie took another sip of water. "Jonah had left town and was walking back here. He needed to camp for the night 'cause he left town in the afternoon. When it was dark, the mules woke him up and he hid, because he knew it was trouble. Sure enough, a man came into the camp with a gun, yelling for Jonah to come out where he could see him. But Jonah sneaked right up on the man and hit him with an axe. He told me it was the same man that had followed him around and watched him when he was in town."

"Did he kill the outlaw, Miz Jones?" asked Nathan.

"Oh Lord, no, Marshal. Jonah said he hit the man's hand where was holding the gun." Meezie went on, "Then he took the man's gun and shooed him on out of camp. He didn't kill him."

"Was the man hurt?" Nathan asked.

"Well, I only know what Jonah told me. He said he sliced that man's hand wide open from the wrist to the end of his thumb. I'm surprised it didn't cut the man's thumb clean off," she said. "And I know that man is still around, because I saw him again when he was following the will of Satan. He helped kill my daughter, my Dehlia," said Meezie.

"What do you mean, he helped kill your daughter?" asked Nathan. "Did you see him?"

"Well, not exactly. You see, Marshal, the men that killed Dehlia and Jonah were Klansmen. When they came to the cabin that night twenty years ago, they were all dressed in their coward suits with their faces covered."

Even though he was pretty sure he knew the answer already, Nathan asked, "I still don't understand, Miz Jones. Do you mean they were wearing some kind of suits?"

"Oh Marshal. They was Klansmen," she said. "You know, Ku Klux Klan. They all had white suits and white hoods over their heads."

It was the answer Nathan had expected. "I guess I'm still a bit confused," said Nathan. "How do you know it was the same man that attacked Jonah?" Nathan asked.

"Well, when those men came, this fellow was closest to the creek, where I was hiding with Daniel. He was one of the men carrying a torch. They used those torches to burn down the cabin. Well, when he raised his right hand, he had the torch in that hand, and I could plainly see that his thumb was not quite right even though he could still hang onto the torch, and there was a big ugly scar on that hand that was shiny in the light of that torch. And I would bet the last few years of my life that he was the same man that attacked Jonah some years prior to that night."

With no one speaking, it was serenely quiet. The breeze was still. The three of them sat and watched the slow flow of water over the rocks in the creek. Nathan churned Meezie's stories over in his head. He knew she had no reason to make up such a story. He also knew he had recently seen the same man with the mangled right hand. The outlaw had been standing at the bar in the tavern when Nathan arrested the buffalo hunter, Clyde Morse. And Nathan had allowed the outlaw to walk away, not knowing the extent of the man's history. If only he had known, he thought.

"The water makes a real pleasant sound, doesn't it Miz Wolf," said Meezie.

"It surely does, Miz Jones. It surely does. I think I need to get down to our creek at Summer Prairie more often," said Claire May. "It seems like the sound washes away some of life's hurts, doesn't it."

Meezie Jones nodded her head in agreement.

True to his lawman psyche, Nathan interrupted the reverie and asked Meezie another question. "Miz Jones, do you remember anything else about that night when the Ku Klux Klan men came to your cabin?"

"Yes sir, I remember a couple more things about that night," she answered. She seemed to be gathering her thoughts as she paused and then began. "Jonah was such a hard worker. He built our cabin the second year we were here. Oh sure, me and Dehlia helped him, but he pretty much did everything himself. And on that night, those cowardly devils came to destroy everything we had, and kill us at the same time. They was come to do Satan's work."

She paused and went on. "But Jonah was a strong man. He was determined not to let those men tear down what he had built. So, he met those men with his shotgun. But Lord, before he could defend himself, they done killed him and Dehlia. But Jonah tried. He fired that shotgun, and it hit one of the horses and the leg of the man riding that horse. That horse screamed and nearly threw the rider, but he hung on. But, I know that man was hurt, 'cause the horse had acted up so when it was hit by that buck shot. It was the right side of the horse, and the man's right leg that was hit."

Tears appeared on the old woman's cheeks, and she stopped talking for a moment. Then she nodded her head and began to speak again.

"There was one other thing, Marshal," said Meezie.

"Yes, ma'am," said Nathan.

"It was sprinkling rain when those men came to the house. But it stopped before they left." Meezie went on. "The next morning, when I took care of my daughter and Jonah, there were hoof prints all over where the front of the cabin had been."

Nathan was looking at the old woman as she spoke. He nodded as she paused, as if to encourage her to continue.

"Well, one of those horses had an odd hoof print. That horse was wearing a strange shoe that I had only seen once before in my life on one of the plantation animals. The horse had a barred shoe," said Meezie.

Nathan's brow furrowed. "A barred shoe? I don't believe I know what that is," he said.

"I don't rightly know what it's for," said Meezie, "but the horseshoe has a metal bar that goes across it between the two ends of the shoe. Well, that horse had that kind of shoe. And I'm pretty sure it was the horse that got shot by Jonah's shotgun."

"What makes you think that the barred shoe was on the injured horse?" asked Nathan.

"Marshal, I don't know for certain, only what I seen. You see, beside each of the hoof prints with the barred shoe was a drop or two of dried blood. That's why I think it was the injured horse that had that barred shoe," said Meezie.

Nathan was truly surprised. Meezie might be old, he thought, but she certainly had a head for details and seemed to remember them so clearly. Frankly, he had never heard of a barred horseshoe. He also wasn't sure how this information could be of any use in identifying the killers of Meezie's daughter and son-in-law.

After more small talk, it appeared that Meezie had finished with any details that she might have remembered from the night her daughter was killed. Nathan stood and took her hand, saying, "Miz Jones. I want to thank you for sharing your memories with us. Right now, I don't hardly know what to make of everything you told me, but I want you to know that I'm going to keep looking into what happened that night. We might be able to get justice for your daughter and son-in-law if I can put all the pieces of the puzzle together."

Meezie surprised him again, and said, "Oh, I know you will, Marshal. I truly know you will."

"Do you want us to take you back to the house, Miz Jones?" asked Claire May.

Meezie smiled. "No child. I'm going to sit here a bit longer. You've wasted enough of your time talking to an old woman," she said.

"It certainly was not a waste of time," said Claire May. "I enjoyed our talk, and I enjoyed meeting you so much." She had taken one of Meezie's hands in both of hers and held it for several seconds before she turned to Nathan. "Are you ready to go, Nathan?"

Back at the cabin, they mounted their horses and began walking them out the lane. As they neared the road, Claire May said, "Nathan, you are going to think I'm crazy. But I'm telling you that I also heard her daughter speaking. She called me by name and said thank you to me. Do you think I might be crazy?"

Nathan laughed. "No, I don't think you're crazy. Sometimes there just isn't an answer to some things we witness in life. And I certainly don't know anything about talking spirits, but Dehlia sure seems to be a spirit that Meezie is on close terms with."

When they reached the main road, Nathan drew up beside Claire May and leaned out of his saddle and kissed his wife. With a free hand, Claire May hugged him around his neck. "Be very careful, Nathan. I love you, and I'm afraid for you," she said and kissed him again.

"I'll be home in a couple days," said Nathan, and he watched as Claire May turned her horse for home; she still had two miles to go. Nathan turned Wander and headed south toward town. Just at the edge of town, he turned into the lane of a stately, white clapboard house. It was a two-story house with gray shutters and flower boxes at two of the windows with a yard that was neatly maintained. At the corners of the house were flowering bushes, which had lost most of their color as summer was nearly at an end. Behind the house was a stable, also clad in white board siding. It was the home of Federal District Judge Rodney Stephens. The judge and Nathan had become friends through the processing of several minor cases. Nathan had grown to admire Judge Stephens for his honesty and ability to see through the lies of deceptive criminals to get at the truth, then mete out justice accordingly. He was also a knowledgeable man and had given Nathan sage advice on more than one occasion. He was a good friend to the lawman.

After tying Wander to the hitch rack near the front porch, Nathan walked up the porch steps. He was just lifting the light green patinated brass door knocker when the door opened. A no-nonsense, thin middle-aged woman stood in the doorway. She was Millie, the judge's housekeeper who had worked for Stephens for several years. She spoke as she faced Nathan with a feather duster in her hand and wearing her apron.

"Hello, Marshal. What brings you out today?"

Nathan removed his hat. "Hello, Millie. Is the judge in?"

"Come in, Marshal. He's in his study. I think you know the way. I've got to get back to my dusting," she said as she walked away.

*****

Rodney Stephens had practiced law for more than twenty years and had held his judgeship for nearly as long. He had lived in Chanute all of his life, so he knew nearly everyone in town. His head was covered in a tangle of gray-white hair. He was single, as his wife had died many years ago during a miscarried attempt at childbirth, leaving him a child-less widower. He had never bothered to remarry, as the death of his wife left him melancholy at times and unable to think about another spouse in his life. He was serious in nature, and if he was not in the court room, he could be found in his study perusing several large city newspapers or digesting new case law. As a general rule, he usually had a pipe either hanging from his mouth, or in his hand, tamping it or installing a new plug of tobacco. True to form, he was tamping down the tobacco in the bowl of his pipe, looking at it intently as Nathan entered his home office. He looked up and smiled when he saw Nathan.

"Well, well, Nathan. How's the Marshal business this fine day?" he asked.

Nathan found the strong smell of pipe smoke comforting even though it was permanently infused in all the furnishings in the judge's office. It was an aroma that brought back memories of Nathan's child-hood, as his father had also been an avid pipe smoker. In addition to the aroma, the judge's office reflected the home base of an occupant who did not rest on pretenses. Sure, there was the usual array of framed certificates attesting to his occupation, but nothing fancy was in evidence. Except for one important item. Because of his position as a Federal District Judge, behind the judge's chair on a shelf that ran the width of the room, amidst the jumble of papers and books, rested a telephone. It was the first and only telephone in Chanute and was wired directly to a switchboard in Topeka.

The judge rose from his chair, and the men shook hands. "I reckon you aren't here on a social call," said the judge. "Only time I see you is when you're on official business." He chuckled and put the pipe stem in his teeth.

"Yeah, I reckon that's right," said Nathan. "Judge, I've got some strange business I need your help with."

"Well, I'll do what I can," said the judge, as he held a match over the top of the pipe's bowl. "What's going on?"

For the next half hour, the two men talked, with Nathan telling the judge every detail of the recent cattle rustling incidents, and then going on to discuss the twenty-year-old murder case of Jonah and Dehlia Chambers. They were interrupted only briefly after noon when Millie brought coffee and ham sandwiches to the two men and slipped quietly out of the room, not saying a word. She knew better than to make small talk when the judge was talking business.

After eating his sandwich, the judge took a series of long draws on his pipe and then set it down on his desk and took a swallow of his nearly cold coffee. "Okay, you've given me the details of what you know so far. Looks to me like you're making progress. So, what do you need from me?"

Nathan then began to tell Judge Rodney Stephens his plans. In the course of his discussion, he asked, "What do you know about oil companies? I would like to get a person from one of those companies to come down here and do some work for me. How would I go about making that happen?"

"OK, I think that's easy," said the judge. "From what I've read, you need a geologist, a man of science, to come down and do the testing for you. The biggest, and only oil company I know of is called the Standard Oil Company. And it so happens that one of their attorneys is a friend of mine, so I will give him a call and see what I can find out."

"That's fine. Thank you, Rodney," said Nathan. Nathan had been told many times that he could call the judge by his given name, as long as they were not in court.

"That's OK. But why do you need their help?" asked the judge.

"I think there is oil on the properties that have been bothered by the cattle rustlers, but I want to find out for sure," said Nathan. "I think there must be some sort of link between that oil and the cattle rustling."

The judge's eyebrows raised. "I guess I don't see the connection between the two," he said.

Nathan chuckled. "Well, to tell you the truth, neither do I. But I don't think it's just coincidence that those ranches were hit by rustlers just to steal cattle. For the life of me, I haven't nailed down the connection."

"Hmmm." The judge pondered what Nathan had said and moved on. "What else is eating at you, Nathan," asked the judge.

"Well, I need a couple of search warrants," answered Nathan, and he told the judge the reason and the subject of the search. When he was finished, he watched the judge scratching his whiskers and sucking on his pipe.

"The first warrant you want is easy enough, but I sure wonder what Dwight Mullins is going to think. The second one, why, you may want to bring Bill Ward with you when you serve it. Jack Willis, the recorder, isn't one to be pushed around," said the judge, and he began filling out the warrants.

"I have one more question, judge," said Nathan.

The judge kept writing, but answered, "Fire away."

"Do you know of a fellow who hangs around town here, always wearing a side arm. Kind of a skinny fella, but he has something wrong with his right hand; like an old injury that left a scar and made his thumb all whopper-jawed."

The judge stopped writing and looked at Nathan. He set his pen on the desk and picked up his pipe and relit it. "Oh yeah, I know that fellow. His name is Malvern Owens. He's stood across the bench from me several times. He is one of the meanest, most evil men I ever ran across. He's liable to do anything for money, and I mean anything. I've had him on trial for everything from petty theft to murder. But all the cases get thrown out by hung juries. I've only been able to put him behind bars on one occasion for thirty days. Frankly, I think the jury members are either afraid of him or are getting paid off. After that one jail sentence, the former sheriff stopped arresting him for anything, no matter what happened."

"Well, what's he do for a living? Who does he work for?" asked Nathan.

"I don't rightly know." The judge continued, "As far as a job, he doesn't seem to have one. I figure he's doing some sort of criminal activity and getting paid that way. Rumor has always been that he has a boss in crime, but nobody knows for sure who it is."

Nathan mulled over what the judge had said. Then he stood up and reached in his pocket. He laid the medallion that he had taken from the dead buffalo hunter's hotel room on the judge's desk. "I got this off of the buffalo hunter who was killed in our jail. Have you ever seen one of those before?" he asked.

Stephens picked up the medallion and turned it over in his hand. "My god," he said. "I thought this nonsense had ended years back. You say this fella had this medallion on him?"

"No, I actually found it in his hotel room when I searched it after he was killed," said Nathan.

"Well, many years ago, I saw some of these medallions," said Stephens. "As you probably already know, the KKK stands for Ku Klux Klan. Several fellows around town at that time were members of a Klan chapter around these parts. They were pretty brazen in telling others about their membership and trying to get other men to join. And when they were recruiting folks, they would show them a medallion something similar to this one, but the designs may not have been quite the same. This one has some letters on it I never saw on the old medallions. Nathan, I've got to tell you, I thought those Klan fellows had given it all up. I haven't heard anything about them for years." The judge continued to eye the medallion.

"Do you know what this little 'em' stands for on the bottom of the medallion?" asked the judge.

"Yes, I'm pretty sure I know what it means. But I've got to look into it further," answered Nathan.

"Well, Nathan. You need to be very careful and watch your back. Those old Klanners carried out some nasty work in the old days," said the judge. "Who knows what these fellows are capable of. If you're ruffling their feathers, they may decide that they need to get you out of the way."

"Good advice, Rodney," said Nathan. He was thinking back to the bullet hole in his shirt and the bushwhacker who had shot at him out on the trail. "I think they've already tried once. I'll keep my eyes open."

Ten minutes later, Nathan rode Wander to the Marshal's office. When he walked in, he could see that the office was clean and neat.

Bill had obviously spent some clean-up time while he was gone. He had just put down his gear next to his desk when he heard the shot. Checking to make sure his pistol was loaded, and patting his back pocket to make sure his blackjack was in place, he hurried out the door toward where he saw a number of people beginning to assemble.

Part Seven

The Kidnapping

Three Hours Earlier

Caire May had stopped her horse and was watching the red fox trot across the trail. It was followed quickly by two kits, probably born this past spring. She continued watching as one young fox chased its sibling's tail while they ran to follow the vixen. Claire May unconsciously placed her hand on her stomach. "You won't be the only mama around these parts pretty soon, missus fox," she said to herself.

She saw them out of the corner of her eye. Two horsemen had burst from tall shrubbery and were heading straight for her. At first, she thought that it was probably a couple of Summer Prairie cowhands, because she was getting closer to home. But then, suddenly, she could see that they were strangers. A bolt of cold fear shot down her back and a sour taste formed at the base of her throat. She was unarmed and knew she had to flee, but before she could spur her horse, the men were on her. One of the men grabbed her horse's reins, while the other raised his fist and crashed it to the side of Claire May's face. Just before she was struck and passed out, she saw a glimpse of the hand of the man holding her reins. His hand had an ugly red scar that ran from his thumb to his wrist, with the thumb taking an odd angle from the hand. When she woke up, she was laying on a dirty floor in a small, locked closet. Her head ached painfully, and her hands had been bound behind her. She had no idea where she was.

*****

The two men were standing, holding their respective horse's reins. They had arranged to meet away from town where no one would see or hear them. The peaceful quiet of the location was broken by their loud shouting at one another.

"I don't want to hear any more of your excuses, Malvern. I told you a long time ago that we are getting along just fine, and I didn't want any of your damn hair-brained schemes to foul things up. I told you that cattle rustling plan of yours would only bring the ranchers and the Marshal down on us, and by god, it has. That damn Marshal is nosing all over the territory and sooner or later the trail is going to lead to you and probably me. Damn it, how do you get us into these messes? For being my half-brother, you don't have Mama's brains, that's for sure."

"All right, all right, calm down boss. We've got about fifty head at the corral, and there is a train coming first thing Friday morning," said Owens. "We'll get rid of this batch, and we won't do any more rustling. But you have to admit, we've made some nice money on those cattle. And I think if we stayed at it long enough that Chambers fella and maybe Dave Morgan might just want to sell out. We could then pick up their ranches when they go up for sale."

The other outlaw could see the reasoning in this, but he had not cooled off. "Of course, there's money in it." Veins stood out on the outlaw's neck as he continued to shout, "But ranchers don't take kindly to rustlers. They tend to hang rustlers and ask questions later. And to top it off, you now go and tell me you've got the Summers woman. What the hell were you thinking?"

"She ain't a Summers anymore, boss. She's the Marshal's wife," said Owens.

"Yeah, yeah, yeah, I know all that. I don't know what got into you, Malvern. Kidnapping a U.S. Marshal's wife has to be one of the most hare-brained ideas you ever had. Just exactly what did you think you were going to do with her?" asked the outlaw leader. "Where do you have her locked up?"

Owens turned his head away from the leader. "She's up at the depot. Jeb is looking after her. We ain't gonna let her die. I figured that maybe we could hold her for ransom. Maybe get the Marshal to pay us, oh say, ten thousand to get his wife back. And then when we get the money, we high-tail it out of Kansas. Maybe go to California or someplace like that," he said.

The leader still had not calmed down. "Damn it, Malvern. Do you know how much money a Marshal makes? It's pocket change. He doesn't have any ten thousand dollars. He's lucky to have three dollars in his pocket."

"Yeah, boss. But don't forget, she's a Summers. Them folks has got plenty of money."

"Well, they don't have enough to set us up for life in some other place. You need to either let her go or get rid of her." He paused, then said, "Hmmm. Maybe if she just disappeared with no clues, kidnapping her could never get traced back to us. That's it, Malvern. Just get rid of her," said the outlaw. "I have a feeling that the Marshal might just calm down when he finds out that his wife has disappeared. Maybe he'll want to play along with us like the old sheriff did."

"You mean that we ain't going to get any money out of this," said Owens.

"That's exactly what I mean. I still don't want my neck stretched by a damn rope. So, here's what I want you to do. When your cattle buyer and train come in on Friday, you need to kill the woman and while the train men aren't looking, you put her dead body in one of the cattle cars with the steers. By the time that train gets to Kansas City, she will be so trampled by those cattle that no one will recognize her. They'll just figure she was some hobo's girlfriend that hopped the train at one of its stops. The Kansas City police will probably think her boyfriend killed her."

Reluctantly, Owens answered, "OK, I'll take care of it."

Part Eight

Continuing Clues

There was the distinct and irresistible aroma of freshly fried chicken and warm baked biscuits emanating from the picnic basket that Espie Ward had placed on the counter. Espie was watching as her husband Bill continued talking with the new Continental Telegraph operator. The new operator was a young man, barely into his twenties, and was still considered a trainee with the company. He had been under instruction at the Topeka office and had, for the most part, completed his training. Continental had rushed him to the Chanute office to take the place of Henry Green, who, at the urging of U.S. Marshal Wolf, had suddenly submitted his resignation and had left town in the darkness of night. If the truth were known, Henry Green was deathly afraid of being another statistic as a result of actions by "the enforcer," the man who did most of the dirty work for the "boss" of the local KKK, of which Green was a member. Wisely, perhaps, Green had decided that he could not get away from those men quickly enough.

"Now then son, I think I have shown you everything you need to know about the office." Bill was being a bit condescending to what he considered to be a mere kid. Indeed, the new operator had a boyish face and did not yet appear to shave on a regular basis. Espie made the remark that he was a "darling young man," a remark that Bill did not take kindly.

When the men were finished discussing the intricacies of the telegraph office, Espie began opening the picnic basket and laying its contents on the back counter that stretched across the rear of the office. In addition to the fried chicken, she had brought biscuits, baked beans, and a frosted cake. Bill's mouth watered as he watched his wife lay out the spread.

Bill loved Espie more than he could ever express. She was a fine-looking woman, stout with an ample bosom and ink-black wavy hair. She was so tall, that she could look at Bill eye to eye. She was also a proud woman who could trace her heritage back to early Spanish settlers.

Espie treated Bill with a great deal of tenderness and understanding, and wore her love for him on her sleeve. Bill would do anything for her, but he also knew that Espie had a flashy temper that sometimes took a day or so to cool off, just as it had a couple days ago when he forgot her birthday. For her part, Espie adored her "little Bill." She might let her temper flare against him occasionally, but never so much that it would jeopardize their solid marriage. And she worried about him a great deal. Being a Deputy Marshal was a good solid job, she thought, but it carried inherent danger. She had often thought that she did not know how she could get along if something bad were to happen to her "little Bill." And she would protect him any time that she could.

Just as Espie had placed all the food on the back counter and began to lift the plates and silverware from the basket, the door to the telegraph office opened. A stranger, a man that neither Bill nor Espie knew, entered the office. His slouch hat, kerchief tied around his neck, and drooping mustache gave him the look of a cowboy. But the gun belt that he wore low on his right hip indicated that punching cattle was not his occupation. Bill was immediately on alert, but because he knew his day was going to be training the new telegraph operator, he had ignored Marshal Wolf's advice to remain armed at all times and was not wearing his side arm.

The stranger spoke as he looked at Bill and the telegraph operator. "Which one of you is Bill Ward?"

"I'm Ward," said Bill. "What can I do for you, stranger?"

The gunman laughed. "It's not what you can do for me, Ward. It's what I can do for you." The man slowly drew his revolver and pointed it across the counter.

"You see," said the outlaw, "I've got a job to do. I have a bullet in this gun that has your name on it. The boss doesn't want you around town anymore, so I'm gonna have to kill you," he said.

Espie had slowly moved closer to the man across the counter. She was terrified, but her outward countenance would not reveal her fear. She was determined that this stranger would not be allowed to gun down her husband, and the internal fire was beginning to rise in her. Now, standing closer to the counter she said, "OK, OK, mister. You're the only one with a gun. But you wouldn't gun down my husband without letting him have a last meal, would you?"

The gunman laughed out loud. "Lady, I don't give a damn about any last meal for your husband. Bill Ward is going to be killed. So why don't you just back away so you don't get hurt."

Espie was not backing down. Wasting no time, she quickly turned around and brought the plate of fried chicken and set it on the counter in front of the outlaw. She did the same with the beans, biscuits, and the cake. She did not know it yet, but she had the gunman hooked. He hadn't had anything decent to eat yet that day. The smell rising from the chicken was more than he could resist. He was torn between carrying out his evil assignment and his gnawing hunger. Hunger won him over. He turned slightly, locked the office door, and turned back to face Espie.

"All right then, lady. Fix me up a plate of that chicken and cut me a piece of that cake." He then looked at Bill Ward. "Don't you even think about doing anything stupid, Ward. You're about to have your last meal."

Espie did as she was told. She fixed the outlaw a plate of food and placed it on the counter. As she did so, the outlaw laid his pistol right next to the plate so he could reach it quickly if necessary. Espie now laid a knife next to the plate and was in the process of placing a fork next to the plate, but she dropped the fork on the floor behind the counter.

"Oh, dear," said Espie, and she bent over to get the fork. As she was bent over behind the counter, she was out of the direct sight of the outlaw. While still bent over, she reached beneath her full skirt and located the leg holster which held her small .32 revolver, a gun she had been carrying ever since Bill had been named Deputy Marshal, a job that often times left her at home alone while he attended to his duties. She then stood up and placed the fork next to the outlaw's plate. When the outlaw picked up the fork and the knife to begin forking up the beans, Espie raised her other hand, took quick aim, and with an unwavering hand, shot the outlaw in the forehead. With the fork and knife still in his hands, the outlaw fell backwards to the floor.

The noise of the gunshot had been extremely loud within the confines of the small office. Bill's ears rang momentarily from the loud report. A wisp of white-gray smoke rose slowly from the barrel of Espie's revolver. After she was sure the outlaw was not going to get up, Espie lowered the pistol. Release of tension, relief that neither she nor Bill was hurt, and the sheer shock of the shooting took hold of Espie, and she began to cry. She stood with her head lowered, sobbing uncontrollably. Bill rushed to his wife and folded his arms around her.

"There, there, sweetheart," cooed Bill. "You really did a good thing. We're both here to see another day, and the outlaw will never hurt anyone again."

"Well, I was not about to let that outlaw take you away from me. He was going to kill you, Bill," said Espie, continuing to sob. "Will I have to go to jail?" she wailed.

Bill continued to hold his wife. He chuckled, "No dear, you're not going to jail. It was self-defense. Instead of going to jail, you are a hero. You saved my worthless life," he said, and laughed as he said it.

Espie looked up. With the pistol still in her hand, she reached up and hugged Bill around his neck and kissed him. "Your life is certainly not worthless. Don't you ever go and get yourself killed," she said.

"I don't plan to, dear. Nope, I don't plan to," said Bill as he kissed Espie.

Standing behind them, the new telegraph operator's face was ashen. "Does this sort of thing happen often?" he asked.

*****

There were a dozen people milling about in front of the telegraph office as Nathan made his way through them and into the office to investigate the gun shot that he had heard. He had to wait a few seconds for Bill to come around the counter and unlock the door. Upon entering, he saw a man lying face up on the rough wooden floor with a bullet hole in his forehead. The man was still holding a fork in his right hand, and a knife lay next to his left hand. He looked peaceful, as if he was sleeping, but the bright red hole in his forehead indicated that the nap was permanent. Nathan looked at the dead man but did not know him. He then turned his attention to Bill Ward and the two other people behind the counter who were staring at him. Espie's small revolver was still in her hand. Another larger revolver lay on the counter next to a plate of food. A third man stood with his mouth agape behind Bill and Espie.

171

As he faced Espie, the first words from Nathan were, "Are you and Bill all right?"

He received the couple's grateful reply that they were fine.

Nathan then asked, "Who's he?" as he pointed to the new telegraph operator.

Bill grinned. "He's the new telegraph man. I'm breaking him in right."

Nathan just shook his head, but smiled slightly. "OK, so who's the gent on the floor with the hole decorating his noggin?" asked Nathan.

"Don't rightly know," said Bill. "But he came in here aiming to kill me, and Espie put a stop to that right quick."

Nathan turned to the new telegraph man. "Do you know where the undertaker's place is?" he asked.

"I-I-I think so," the man stammered.

"Well, go get him," said Nathan, and watched as the young man rushed out the door.

"Let's look at this fella, Bill," said Nathan, and he and Bill began to go through the dead man's pockets. Sure enough, Nathan soon stood up, holding a metal medallion in his hand. The letters KKK were stamped into the medallion along with an imprint of a triangle and the small letters, EM. Nathan was not at all surprised. Instead, he was disheartened that now, in addition Clyde Morse and Henry Green, he had found a third man with one of the medallions. It appeared that the Klan's reach was more widespread than he had first thought. He could only ask himself, how many more local men belonged to this organization? Of course, the other question remained; who and where was the leader of this band of outlaws?

While they waited for the undertaker to come and get the body, Nathan realized that the smell of the chicken was making him hungry. He had not eaten for several hours. From the dead man's plate, he grabbed a drumstick and hungrily bit into it. "Great chicken, Espie," he said.

*****

Later, after Espie had repacked her picnic basket and gone home, and the undertaker had come and removed the outlaw's body, Nathan and Bill left the telegraph office and headed back to their office. Before they left, they turned to see the new telegraph operator still standing behind the counter with his mouth open. Color had returned to his face, but he was having difficulty digesting what he had just witnessed. His lunch plate on the back counter showed little sign of activity.

When they got to the office, Nathan said, "I want you to get your gun belt on, Bill. And load your shotgun and bring it along. We've got another stop to make." In minutes, they left the office and walked down the street. Their destination was the county recorder's office.

Jack Willis had held the county recorder's position for as long as anyone could remember there being a county recorder. He had just reached his sixtieth birthday. He was a hulk of a man. At nearly three hundred pounds and close to six feet tall, he was a man that no one crossed or picked a fight with. His permanently etched scowl and close-set eyes gave off a persona as deadly as a grizzly bear. He had obtained the recorder's job when he had been owed a favor many years ago. Willard Crenshaw, the former president of Prairie Bank and the the father of Arthur Crenshaw, had owed him. It seems that Willard Crenshaw owed a great deal of money in gambling debts to an itinerant professional cardsharp gambler who had been passing through town and who had cleanly fileted Willard Crenshaw in a crooked game of seven card stud. Willard didn't have the money to pay off his debt, even if he had embezzled the cash from the bank. With a warning from the gambler that his debt would be collected in cash or by the death of Willard, the former bank president was in a pit of quicksand. He had no way to produce the money to pay the debt, and much as he preferred not to, he was on the verge of embezzling bank funds to pay off the gambler. He felt that his day of reckoning was anon. It was at this same time that grifter Jack Willis came to town. Somehow, Willis learned of the former bank president's plight and saw an opportunity for self-gain. Three days after meeting with Willard Crenshaw, Willis carried out his plan. As a result, the professional gambler was never seen again, and Jack Willis assumed the position of County Recorder. Until he died, Willard Crenshaw was in debt to Jack Willis. Over the years, Willis kept up the facade that he was a law-abiding citizen, but in fact, he was capable of doing anything for personal gain or to retain his job as recorder. Although there was no written record of such activity, a thorough examination of land recording deeds and purchase transactions might prove that Willis was not always on the up and up in his dealings as county recorder.

Willis looked up when he heard the door open. What he saw was Nathan and Bill entering the office. Willis quickly glanced beneath the front counter and then back to the two lawmen and tried to keep his composure. "Well, well, I must really be in trouble," he said. "Two lawmen paying me a visit. What do you want, Marshal?"

"Mr. Willis, I've come to take a look at your plat drawings," replied Nathan.

"Well, you're going to need to be a bit more specific, Marshal. Every one of those books you see on the shelves contains plat drawings and deeds."

"All right, I'll be more specific. I would like to see the plat records for the Summers ranch," said Nathan.

Strangely, Willis did not object to the request. He turned and re-trieved a book from the shelves and put it on the counter in front of Nathan, but he did not offer to help find the specific map for the Summer Prairie Ranch.

After searching through several pages, though, Nathan found what he was looking for; the plat drawing for the 1,280 acre Summer Prairie Ranch. The deed on the facing page showed the signatures of Robert Summers and Virginia Summers. Turning several more pages both for-ward and backward in the book revealed the plat and deed for Dave and Betty Morgan, and Jonah and Dehlia Chambers. Nathan turned several more pages but did not find any reference to the property to the west of the three properties. Nathan slowly closed the book and shoved it back across the counter.

"Willis, I don't find reference to the property to the west of Summer Prairie Ranch. I would like to look at the book that contains the records of that plat," said Nathan.

Willis grabbed the book that was on the counter and slowly re-placed it on the shelf from which it had been taken. He then approached Nathan and laid his meaty hands on the counter. "Well," he said. "I'd like to oblige you, Marshal. But you see, that particular book is sealed, and no one is allowed to look at it."

"Who says so?" asked Nathan.

Unnoticed by Willis, Bill had stepped slowly back and to the side of Nathan, where he had a clear view of Willis.

"Why, I believe that is a court order, Marshal," said Willis with a smirk.

Nathan knew that Willis was bluffing. In this case, there was no reason that a court order would have been used to seal a county record, a record that was open for viewing by the public. "You wouldn't mind showing me that court order then, would you, Willis?"

Bill slowly moved his free hand to the hand grip on the forward part of the shotgun but did not raise it.

"Marshal, like I told you, I would like to help you, but you see, I don't know what ever happened to that court order. Probably lost over the years," said Willis. "But, maybe Judge Stephens has a copy of it."

"Willis, let's presume that there is a court order like you say," said Nathan. "Wouldn't a copy of that order be filed in the recorder's office?"

Willis answered, "Well, yeah. Normally it would, but I'm telling you I don't have that particular one."

"All right, Willis," said Nathan. "We're going to try to do this the easy way." Nathan reached into his vest pocket and retrieved a folded paper. He opened it and placed it on the counter. "This is a search warrant, Willis. I'm sure you know what that is. You will see it is signed by Judge Stephens. It gives me the right to tear this office apart, one piece of paper at a time. But rather than make that kind of mess, I'll ask you just one more time. Get me the book that contains the plat for the property west of Summer Prairie Ranch. Do it now, Willis."

The slight smile had reappeared on Willis's face. "Now, Marshal, I told you I can't do that. That record......."

Before Willis could go any further in his objection, Nathans blackjack had struck the big man on the side of his cheek and nose. Willis was unprepared for the blow and stumbled backwards. Blood quickly began flowing from his nose. But the look on Willis's face had also changed and was now covered with a mask of rage streaked with blood. He shook his head and cautiously approached the counter. Just as fast as Nathan had hit him, Willis lashed out with his fist, striking Nathan on the side of his head. Nathan reeled back. The thought occurred to him that he had never been hit this hard by anyone else. But he, too, came back to the counter, and both men struck simultaneously.

Nathan's blackjack struck Willis in the left temple area, while Willis's fist hit Nathan on the left side of his face, but Nathan had turned his head slightly, so the blow was glancing rather than having full impact. This time, Willis staggered back and fell into a sitting position. He slowly got up but did not move to the counter yet.

"Are you going to give me that book, Willis, or do we have to go a few more rounds of patty-cake?" said Nathan.

Willis glared at Nathan, then slowly moved over to the shelves and brought down another book and shoved it across the counter to Nathan. Nathan opened it and slowly leafed through the pages. He was intently looking at the contents of the book and had not noticed Willis remove his hand from the counter. Suddenly the recorder's office exploded in sound. There was one extremely loud blast followed quickly by another explosion slightly less intense.

The noise startled Nathan so much that he literally jumped backwards and began to draw his revolver. He then could see that his intervention was unnecessary. Jack Willis sat on the floor in an upright position against the back wall of the office. A large bloody hole was open on his chest. The shotgun blast from Bill's shotgun had killed him almost instantly. Still in his hand was the revolver that he had taken from under the counter. Willis's finger had pulled the trigger on the pistol as he fell back, accounting for the second ear-popping blast.

"Geez, Bill. I never even saw him move," said Nathan.

"I figured as much," said Bill. "As soon as I saw him drop his hand, I knew he was going to come up with a gun."

"I owe you one, Bill," said Nathan.

"Yeah, you do, but I don't necessarily want to collect," chuckled Bill, who walked over to the door and told one of the gathering crowd to go get the undertaker. When he came back, he looked closely at his boss. "Looks to me like you're going to need a new hat."

Nathan removed his hat and looked at it. A bullet hole was through the brim on the left side of the hat. Only two inches had spared Nathan's life from the last shot by Jack Willis before he died. "Uh, oh," said Nathan. "Better not let Claire May see this. Don't want her to worry over me."

While they waited, the two lawmen looked at the book that Willis had set on the counter. Nathan turned the book and walked around the counter to study it. He did not want someone to come in the door while his back was turned.

"Bill, look at this," said Nathan. He was pointing to a page that contained the plat of land next to the Chambers, Morgan, and Summers ranches. The deed was registered, and the registered owner was recorded as *Prairie Trust*.

"What the hell does that mean?" asked Bill.

"Your guess is as good as mine," answered Nathan. "I'm not sure I even know what a trust is."

Just then, the undertaker came in the door. "Oooowee," he said. "Marshal, you need to take a few hours off. They're starting to stack up down at my place," he said. "And every damn one of 'em is a county funeral. I won't be making any money on these outlaws."

Nathan and Bill chuckled. "Sorry," said Nathan, "we'll try to find a higher class of criminal for you." They laughed again.

Nathan closed the deed book and tucked it under his arm. "Let's go, Bill."

Back at the Marshal's office, the two lawmen got their horses, and with the record book under Nathan's arm, they rode north until they reached Judge Stephens' place, where they tied their mounts and walked up onto the porch. Nathan began to believe that Millie, the ever-present housekeeper must keep a vigil out the front window of the house. Before the lawmen could knock at the door, Millie opened it from within.

"Twice in one day. My, my," said Millie. "Must be something mighty important going on. Did I hear some gunfire earlier?" she asked.

"That you did, Millie; that you did. Is the judge available?" Nathan asked.

"We're just going to have to install a side door to the judge's office for you so I don't have to keep opening the front door," replied Millie, but she was smiling when she said it. "Sure, he's in his office. Go on through."

Judge Stephens had overheard a bit of the conversation at the front door and had risen from his desk to meet Nathan. The judge shook hands with both Bill and Nathan and instructed the lawmen to have a chair.

"You're back to see me kinda quick like, Nathan. But I do have some news for you," said the judge.

"That's good," replied Nathan. "But Judge, as I keep digging into this rat's nest of criminals, I keep stumbling into more questions that need answering."

"I guess that's normal," said the judge. "That is, until you finally get to the bottom of that rat's nest and root all of them out of it. What's your latest question?"

Nathan stood up and waited while the judge cleared some of the many papers to the side of his desk to make room for the recorder's book that Nathan was trying to place on his desk. Nathan turned the book around in the cleared space so the judge could read the page where Nathan had opened the book.

"The plat map that I have open is the property to the west of Summer Prairie Ranch, Dave Morgan's Circle M Ranch, and the Chambers

179

farm. But as you can see, the owner of the property is listed simply as '*Prairie Trust*,'" said Nathan. "Rodney, I'm not a very sophisticated fellow, so maybe you can help me with this. What in the world does it mean that the owner of that property is a trust?"

For the next several minutes, the judge explained how a trust can be set up as a legal instrument to preserve ownership of a property for a family or group of individuals so that the property remains the ownership of the group in case a member of the group dies.

"But isn't there somebody who acts as the head of the trust, someone who is responsible for running this trust?" Nathan asked.

"Absolutely," said the judge. "Every trust has what is known as a trustee. It is the responsibility of that trustee to carry out the wishes of the majority of the members of the trust." He continued, "Jack Willis, down at the recorder's office ought to be able to tell you who initiated the trust. Did you ask him about it?"

Nathan and Bill looked at each other, then Nathan spoke, "Yeah, Rodney, we asked him about it. But for some reason, even with your search warrant, he wouldn't tell us and went on to say that if there ever was a trust agreement it was not in his possession."

"Well, do you want me to go down and visit with him? Maybe I can convince him to tell me who the trustee is," said the judge.

Once again, Bill and Nathan looked at each other. "Well, you see, Rodney, it won't do much good to go down and see him. He's not talking anymore. He's laying down at the undertaker's place. Pulling a gun on us while we were in his office was not a healthy thing for him to do," said Nathan. He picked up his hat from the floor and showed Rodney the bullet hole in the hat's rim. He set the hat back on the floor next to his chair.

"My, oh my. You boys sure do disturb the peace and quiet around these parts. Millie told me that she thought she had heard gunfire in town," said the judge.

"Oh, Rodney. When we came in, you said you had some news for us," said Nathan.

"Oh my, I almost forgot." The judge went on, "You remember I told you I had an attorney friend on the staff at Standard Oil?"

"Sure, I remember," answered Nathan.

"Well, I called him and told him about your hunch. He checked into it and called me right back. And he had a real surprise for me. He told me that a geologist from their company had already been down here about a year and a half ago."

Nathan began to laugh. "The plot continues to thicken, doesn't it, Judge."

"The geologist's report stated that there was definitely oil in the area of those ranches," said the judge. "I guess that explains the strange looking grass you saw."

Nathan did not respond right away. Finally, he said, "That geologist report might explain a few more things."

"Oh? What do you mean?" asked the judge.

"Well, for instance, did your friend say who requested that survey? Or who paid them to do the survey?"

Judge Stephens responded. "Standard Oil said that the request to do the survey of that area was made by somebody representing the Prairie Trust. When they were paid for the survey, it came to them by wire transfer from Prairie Trust."

"There's that same trust again," said Nathan, "and we can't figure out who's running that scheme."

The men sat in silence for a couple minutes thinking. Nathan broke the silence.

"Well, I'm thinking that there might be a motive in here some-where. From what I have heard, having oil discovered on your property can result in the landowner becoming very wealthy," said Nathan. "So, what would happen if those ranch owners were put into such a financial bind that they had to sell out? If that would happen, then this trust thing would be able to buy up the properties."

"Oh, Nathan. I think that idea may be a bit of a stretch. After all, your family's ranch isn't in any danger of being put out of business, is it?" asked Stephens.

"No. But you just never know. Why, Dave Morgan told me that if he continued to have cattle rustled from him, that he might have trouble keeping his place going," said Nathan. "Summer Prairie Ranch could also be hurt if they started losing cattle. And I think that the only reason they haven't been hit by the rustlers is because they have more cow-hands to contend with. And poor Daniel Chambers has lost over half of his small herd. That has really hurt him."

Bill Ward had been very quiet as he listened to the discussion be-tween his boss and the judge. But now he spoke up, "Judge, you and I are old enough to remember a bunch of years ago. And if you think back on it, this same scheme happened many years back. I recall that several small black farmers around the territory were forced off their land by the Klan. Those no-good Klan members wanted to increase the size of their own land holdings while getting rid of all the black folks in the territory." Bill went on, "This cattle rustling scheme may be sort of along the same lines as those old methods they used."

The judge answered, "You fellas could be right. Like I said, you better watch your backs." The judge swiveled around in his chair, picked up the telephone and put it on his desk, taking care not to tangle the wires attached to the instrument and wall.

"I'm going to make a call to Topeka, Nathan, and it could take a few minutes. They have a state recorder's office up there, and they ought to have a copy of the trust agreement on file for that property west of Summer Prairie. I'll find out the details of that trust. In the meantime, why don't you and Bill wander out to the kitchen and tell Millie that I would like a sandwich for all of us, with a good mug of hot coffee.

Nathan and Bill followed the judge's suggestion and spent the next twenty minutes watching Millie in the kitchen as she carefully put together three sandwiches and poured coffee into three mugs. She had to good-naturedly slap Bill's hand twice when he attempted to pick up a slice of roast beef and pop it in his mouth. When she was done, Bill carried the tray for her, and they all went into the judge's office.

Judge Stephens was smiling when they came into the room.

"Is there anything else you need, Judge?" Millie said.

"No, nothing more right now, Millie. Thank you," said Stephens, and he watched as Millie left the room.

"You're smiling like a man that just got dealt a full house," said Bill.

The judge already had a bite of sandwich in his mouth, but he smiled and nodded in agreement. He soon swallowed and spoke up. "The Prairie Trust has a principle trustee and a co-trustee, with a bunch of other men named as members of the trust group. And guess who they are," he said grinning.

*****

It was already near-dark as the two lawmen rode back to the livery stable. Ed Mullins was just getting ready to lock the stable doors when Nathan and Bill rode up.

183

"You don't need to brush 'em down, Ed," said Nathan. "Just throw a few oats at them and plenty of hay. We'll see you tomorrow."

"Sure thing, Marshal," said Ed. "See you then."

Nathan and Bill watched as Ed led the two horses into the livery stable and turned around and closed the Dutch door behind him.

Quietly, Bill remarked, "It's a shame what we gotta do tomorrow, ain't it."

"Yeah, I'm not looking forward to that. I feel bad for Dwight," said Nathan. "You go on and go home, Bill. Espie's gonna wonder where you are. It's been a long day, and I'm going over to the cafe for supper and then go to bed. I'll see you in the morning."

Bill waved as he walked away.

Later, as Nathan stabbed at the piece of apple pie and sipped his coffee to complete his supper at the cafe, he was mulling over all that had happened that day. Two outlaws had been killed, and several clues had turned up. He was pretty sure where the rest of the rustling and murder cases would lead him. But, even though he thought he knew, he still did not have conclusive proof. Therefore, he did not want to get ahead of himself and jump to a conclusion quite yet. He still needed to clear up some questions. What bothered him most was that it seemed that every time he turned around, he came face to face with another outlaw who seemed to have ties to the KKK. Just how many men in town were affiliated with that gang was an unknown. And what sort of terrible deeds would the perpetrators of serial violence carry out to protect their hold on weaker men?

As he lay on the lumpy mattress on the jail's cot in his office that night, the possible scenarios and conclusions rolled through Nathan's thoughts and kept him from a sound sleep on that Wednesday night.

*****

Thursday Morning

Nathan had arranged to meet Bill Ward for breakfast at the cafe, and he had arrived early. He desperately needed a cup of coffee to offset a restless night with little sleep. He gazed out the cafe window and watched as the town began to come to life. Merchants were sweeping off the wooden sidewalks in front of their stores and a few horsemen began tying up to hitch rails along the street. It was not long before he saw Bill cross the street and come through the door to the cafe.

"Morning, Bill," said Nathan.

"Morning, Boss," was the groggy response from the deputy. He could see by the empty plate in front of Nathan that the Marshal had already eaten. He could also see by his puffy eyes that the Marshal had spent a night with little sleep.

"I sure could use a cup of mud," said Bill. He smiled when the waitress, who knew Bill quite well, read his thoughts and arrived with a steaming mug of coffee. "Can you scramble up a couple of those hen fruits, with bacon and a slab of bread?" he asked the waitress.

"Sure, Bill," she replied. "Be back in a jiffy."

Watching Bill attack his scrambled eggs and bacon brought a smile to Nathan's face. "Those eggs aren't going to crawl off the plate, Bill," said Nathan.

Knowing he was being jibed by his boss at the rapid rate he was eating, Bill replied, "Yep, I'm making damn sure of it, too." He, too, grinned as he used his bread to soak up the last of the bacon grease on his plate.

The waitress came back to the table, refilled the men's coffee mugs, and picked up their plates. Bill couldn't resist teasing the waitress. "I don't know why I keep comin' to this cafe. I swear, the bacon slices keep getting shorter all the time."

She replied, "Tell it to the pig farmers, Bill. They keep selling us shorter pigs." The men laughed as she walked away from the table.

"Well, I suppose we need to head down to the livery stable. Do you think Dwight is at work yet?" asked Nathan.

"Long as I've known him, he always gets to work when the sun comes up," replied Bill. "Let me finish off this coffee, and we can head out."

True to habit, Dwight Mullins was getting the forge fired up and other chores necessary to get the livery stable ready for business. Ed was standing in the open doorway tying his leather apron around his waist.

As the lawmen approached the livery stable and were passing by the corral at the side of the building, Nathan stopped in his tracks and was looking just inside the corral. Bill was curious to know why Nathan had stopped, but didn't say anything.

"Bill, could you please go get Dwight and tell him I want to talk with him out here?" said Nathan.

"Sure thing," answered Bill.

In a moment, with Dwight at his side, Bill walked back to Nathan.

"Morning Dwight," said Nathan.

"Morning, Marshal. Bill said you wanted to talk to me," said Dwight. The three men then turned and stood leaning on the corral rails, with their backs to the corral.

Nathan took the piece of paper from his shirt pocket and handed it to Dwight. "I wanted you to see this, Dwight, before I show it to Ed."

Dwight read the search warrant that specified that U.S. Marshal Nathan Wolf had authority to conduct a search of the home of Edwin Mullins, and a search of the *Mullins and Son Livery Stable*. After he had read the paper, he looked at Nathan. "What does this mean, Nathan?"

"Dwight, I consider you a friend. And doggone it, I hate to have to tell you this, but I'm pretty sure that Ed is mixed up with a gang of Ku Klux Klan outlaws."

Dwight's mouth dropped open. "Now wait just a damn minute, Marshal. There's no way that Ed could get himself mixed up with outlaws. I thought the Klan had been gone from these parts for years. I think you've got the wrong man, Nathan." He handed the search warrant back to Nathan. "I think I told you a few days ago that the way to survive in this town is to lay low, keep your ears open, your mouth shut, and stay out of other people's business. By god, Nathan, you're messing into my business. Ed's no more a criminal than you are." Dwight took a step forward as if to return to the livery stable.

Nathan reached in his pocket and then withdrew his hand. "Dwight, I want to show you something." He handed the KKK medallion to Dwight. "Look closely at it, Dwight. I think you'll see who made it."

Dwight could not take his eyes off of the medallion. He looked up at Nathan, then looked back at the medallion. Then, he shuddered, sending a tremor through his body as he shook. This time, when he looked back at Nathan, he handed the medallion back, and his eyes were on the verge of tears. He wiped them with the back of his hand, then on his trousers.

"I had suspected Ed of acting sort of strange sometimes when I would walk over to the anvil to see what he was working on, but he always claimed he was forging knives to sell at the hardware store. I was afraid there was more to it, because sometimes he wouldn't show me what he was making." Dwight paused. "But the KKK. Are you sure, Nathan?"

"Dwight, those knives that Ed was making; he sold them to the hardware store, that's for sure. But he was also giving them away to his KKK friends. This medallion came from Clyde Morse, the buffalo hunter that was killed in our jail. You will recollect that you sewed up a bullet crease on his horse."

Dwight nodded his agreement.

"He was a Klan member," said Nathan, "and he also had two of Ed's knives on him when we arrested him. He told us that Ed had given him the knives."

Dwight could not look up. He kept his face down, turning it from side to side. A muffled sob came from him.

Nathan placed a hand on his friend's shoulder. "I'm sorry, Dwight. But I've got a job to do," he said.

Finally, Dwight faced Nathan. "I wish it wasn't this way, Nathan. Thanks for letting me know."

The men said nothing for a moment. Then Nathan broke the silence. "Dwight, Bill and I are going to go over to Ed's place. In the meantime, I would appreciate it if you didn't tell Ed what we are up to. We'll be back shortly."

Edwin Mullins was unmarried and lived in a small house that he rented two blocks from the livery stable. His life would, by most standards, be considered rather mundane. He had few interests other than companionship with his father and the physical labor involved in the work that he loved at the livery stable. Ed would probably be considered a decent, honest, but not very exciting individual. But then, livery stable customers did not grade the business by its proprietors' exuberance; instead, they wanted the best service for their horses and riding gear. Both Dwight Mullins and his son, Ed, were held in high regard by the public.

It took Nathan and Bill only a few minutes to cross the threshold of Ed Mullins' house. In less than twenty more minutes, the lawmen found what they were looking for. Ed Mullins had a cache of KKK medallions in a cabinet drawer, along with several of his signature knives. Most damning, though, was the KKK garb they found at the back of a closet in Ed's sleeping room. Nathan folded it up and put a small handful of the medallions in his pocket.

"Let's go, Bill. I think we have what we need here," said Nathan. He folded the KKK clothing up into a small white bundle that was unrecognizable to anyone seeing it under the arm of the Marshal as the men left Ed Mullins' house and walked back to the livery stable. They met Dwight at the door.

"Dwight, can we use your office for a little while?" asked Nathan.

"Sure, Marshal," Dwight Mullins answered.

"Bill, can you go close and lock the doors to the livery stable. I don't want any of the public coming in here while we are talking," said Nathan.

As Bill was closing and locking the livery's doors, Nathan watched Ed Mullins. Ed had laid down the shoe he was working on and set down the tongs. He dipped his hands in the water bucket near the anvil and wiped them on his trousers. Nathan felt certain that Ed knew that the presence of the lawmen concerned him.

Nathan shouted over to Ed. "Let's go in the office, Ed. You can come, too, Dwight."

The four men entered the ramshackle office of the livery and cleared debris from a rickety table and chairs where they took a seat.

Ed Mullins sat across from Nathan. His face was ashen, and fear showed in his eyes. He dreaded this conversation and was not sure the direction the conversation would go. He did not have to wait long.

Wasting words was not something that Nathan Wolf practiced. Instead, he went to the heart of the matter. "How long have you been a member of the Ku Klux Klan, Ed?"

Ed's fears were confirmed, but he answered, "Whatever gave you that idea, Marshal? There isn't any Klan around these parts. They were gone a long time ago."

"Well, you see, Ed. That's not exactly the truth, is it?" stated Nathan.

Ed Mullins squirmed in his seat, but still was not going to give up. "Far as I know, there used to be a few men around that belonged to the Klan, but that was years ago, and they're all dead and gone."

"I'm going to ask you again, Ed, and I would appreciate you telling me the truth. How long have you been a Klan member?"

Ed was building his confidence. Maybe he could escape culpability if he just continued to lie. He answered the Marshal's question. "I told you, Marshal, I'm not a member of the Klan, and there isn't any KKK in these parts that I know of."

Fast as a rattlesnake bite, Nathan reached across the table and open-handedly slapped Ed Mullins. When Nathan again regained his seat, Dwight Mullins looked at his son and then at Nathan. He almost opened his mouth to protest, but decided to wait for a few more minutes.

"How long, Ed?" repeated Nathan.

This time, Ed Mullins did not answer. Instead, he remained looking down at the table, his hands in his lap.

"Stand up, Ed," said Nathan, and he stood as Ed Mullins stood up.

"Now empty your pockets, Ed," said Nathan.

Ed looked up at Nathan. "What the hell do you want me to empty my pockets for?" he asked.

Outwardly, Nathan remained calm. "Ed, I'm going to warn you now. I don't want you to question me when I give you instructions. I want you to simply do as I say. And if you don't do what I ask, or answer my questions with the truth, it will become very painful to you. Do you understand?" asked Nathan.

Ed Mullins nodded his head in assent.

"Now, go on and empty your pockets," said Nathan.

Ed appeared to fumble in his pockets, but soon threw a few coins, a pocketknife, and other small articles on the table. Nathan pushed the items around to separate them, then looked back at Ed. He now had to play a hunch, and he feared that it could backfire. But he went ahead.

"Ed, I asked you to empty your pockets and you have not done it. Empty your pockets."

"Marshal, it's all there on the table, everything in my pockets," said Ed.

Again, Nathan's right hand flew, resulting in a loud smack to the side of Ed's face. "Empty them, Ed."

The side of Ed's face was scarlet. He slowly reached his hand into his pocket and retrieved its contents. He held something in his closed hand.

"On the table, Ed," said Nathan.

Slowly, Ed Mullins opened his hand and dropped the KKK medallion on the table. Nathan picked it up, looked at it, and dropped it back on the table. Dwight Mullins picked up the medallion and turned it over in his hand. His eyes were moist as he then looked at his son. Still, he remained quiet and dropped the medallion back on the table.

In a rather quiet voice, Nathan asked again, "How long have you been a member, Ed?"

Ed Mullins did not look up, and though he knew there might be consequences to his silence, he did not answer.

Nathan then reached into his pocket and brought his hand up and dropped the handful of KKK medallions on the table. The sound of the many coins hitting the table filled the small office. Then the room was quiet for a moment before Nathan spoke.

"I like your craftsmanship, Ed. Those are nice medallions that you make for the KKK. And you even put your initials on the bottom of each medallion to show who made it. I found all those medallions in a drawer over at your house this morning," said Nathan.

Ed instantly looked up. "You can't go snooping around in my house. I think there's a law against that."

"You're right, Ed. There is a law against that, unless, of course, I have a search warrant, like this one," said Nathan as he laid the piece of paper on the table in front of Ed Mullins.

Ed made no move to pick up and read the paper. He knew the Marshal would not be so stupid to put a false document in front of him.

"So, what. I made some medallions. That doesn't mean I'm a member of any Klan group," said Ed.

"Well, maybe not," said Nathan. "But you also gave away a knife or two to your Klan friends, didn't you?"

"I don't have any idea what you are talking about. If somebody had a knife of mine, he probably bought it at the hardware store. They sell my knives over there," said Ed.

This time, it was not an open hand. Nathan reached over and slugged Ed Mullins in the face, bringing blood from Mullins' nose. At this, Dwight Mullins finally spoke. "Marshal, you didn't have to do that. Ed gave you a perfectly good reason that somebody might have one of his knives." Nathan ignored Dwight initially.

"You see, Ed. You just told me a lie, said Nathan. "And I told you that you need to tell me the truth. Clyde Morse, your KKK buddy who was killed in the jail, told me before he died that you gave knives to a few of the Klan members with whom you are friends. So, consider yourself warned again. I will not tolerate you telling me lies. You're a member of the Klan, aren't you Ed?"

In a barely audible whisper, Ed replied, "No."

Nathan sat back in his chair and said nothing. The room was quiet. After a moment or two, Nathan reached down to the floor next to his chair and picked up the white bundle that he had placed there.

"Well, Ed. You lied to me again. While we were over at your place, we found something else," said Nathan, and he unfolded the cloth bundle, spreading it out on the table until the entire Klan uniform was revealed, with its painted medallion on the tunic, and the mouth and eyes cut out of the conical hat.

Dwight was heard letting out a groan as he looked at the clothing on the table.

Nathan continued. "Ed, you are not a stupid man. You've got a father who thinks the world of you, you have a good job, and you are self-reliant. I think people have always thought that you were a good man. For the life of me, I can't figure out how a good man like you goes wrong and joins the Klan. What would make you do that, Ed?"

The room was silent. Dwight, Bill, and Nathan all watched as Ed Mullins continued to look down. But then they noticed that Ed's shoulders began to move. Then they heard the quiet crying of a man in deep distress. He was beaten. Ed had realized that there was no more room for lying. So lowly at first, they barely heard him say as he looked up at his father with tears in his eyes, "They were going to kill you, Dad."

Nathan had not clearly heard Ed, and asked, "What did you say, Ed?"

Louder now, Ed said, "They were going to kill my Dad."

"Who was going to kill your Dad?" asked Nathan.

"Marshal, you know very well who was going to kill him; the Klan," said Ed.

Quietly, in a reassuring voice, Nathan said, "Tell me about it, Ed."

For the next two hours, Ed Mullins told of the evil hold that the Klan chapter had on him. His dealings with Klan members started out innocent enough. Men that he did not know had come into the livery stable asking him to make knives for them. The men had claimed that the knives were going to be given as gifts to friends of theirs. Ed had been paid handsomely for his work. As time passed, the men had become more friendly to him, and Ed was asked to begin making the medallions for the men. At first, Ed had resisted. He had a hunch that the KKK on the medallions might have indicated the Ku Klux Klan, but when the men offered him a lucrative fee for making the medallions, he could not resist. As more time passed, the men would come in the livery, and while waiting for knives or medallions, they began to ask Ed his thoughts on a variety of topics, including politics and the outcome of the Civil War. At first, Ed thought that they were just making conversation. But later, the men invited Ed to come to a meeting with them and some other men. The men alleged that the meetings were just a way for men to get together to talk politics and other news events. It seemed harmless enough, so Ed agreed to meet with the men and their friends.

When Ed Mullins attended that first meeting, the real purpose of the group was quickly made known. The leader of the group, whom Ed had known for years, came up to Ed and said, "Welcome to the Klan, Ed." Ed wanted no part of the Ku Klux Klan, and before the meeting had formally begun, he had walked out and gone home. But in a few days, the men whom he had done work for returned, and this time, they had a third man with them. They called that man "The Enforcer," and the man had an odd, large scar on his right hand. The enforcer was Malvern Owens.

On the day of their visit to the livery, the three Klan members asked Ed to come outdoors with them. When they were out of range of Dwight's ability to hear them, Owens told Ed that he needed to be a member of their Klan chapter. Ed had told the three men that he had no interest in joining the group. After much discussion, Owens made his intentions clear. Ed was told that if he did not join the Klan that his father would be financially ruined. Ed still resisted, but the statement that finally forced Ed to join was then uttered by Malvern Owens. With his face covered in a mask of hate and grotesque evil, Owens had told Ed that if he did not join the group, Dwight Mullins would be killed. Ed had looked into Owens' eyes when he had made the threat, and what he saw was pure evil. He knew then that the Klan, and its enforcer, Malvern Owens, would stop at nothing to carry out their evil plans. With a sheriff at the time who seemed to take no interest in enforcing the law and was probably on the payroll of the Klan, Ed had no choice. He was one man against a dozen outlaws. He joined the Klan.

After Ed had told the story to the two lawmen and his father, it seemed an eternity before anyone spoke.

"I believe you, Ed," said Nathan. "But I have a question for you. Have you ever heard anyone in the Klan talk about the killing of a black couple out north of town? Do you know who might have done that?"

"Sure," said Ed. "Malvern Owens and a gang of other guys did that. He still talks about it. Even though it was twenty years ago, Owens seems real proud that he killed that couple and burned them out."

"One more question, Ed. Who is the leader of the Klan chapter?" asked Nathan.

A look of terror came over Ed Mullins' face, and the color drained from his cheeks. "No. No Marshal. You can't make me tell you who that is. I would be dead in minutes. I swear, Marshal. Do what you want with me, but I can't tell you his name. I'd be a walking dead man . . ." Once again, tears came to Ed's eyes.

Nathan watched Ed for a moment, then spoke. "All right, Ed. I don't need his name right now. But I want you to write down the names of every other man you know in that group." While Ed wrote the names, Nathan said, "Ed, even though you helped me solve a couple of crimes, that does not absolve you of all guilt. Failure to report a crime is a crime in itself. And by not informing me about the cattle rustling, it makes you an accessory to a crime. I could lock you up right now."

Dwight spoke up then. "Please don't do that Marshal. He ain't going anywhere. I'll look after him so he doesn't leave."

Nathan thought for a few minutes. "Like you said, Ed. You might very well be a dead man walking right now. You might be safer in jail. But that's what I thought about Clyde Morse, and he's pushing up daisies."

Nathan looked over at Dwight, then knew his answer. "All right, I haven't decided what I'm going to do yet in the long run. For now, Ed, I'll leave you with your Dad. But if I were you, I'd keep a mighty low profile."

As if on cue the side window of the office exploded from a gunshot. Glass shards flew in all directions. All four men hit the floor. When there were no follow-up shots, Nathan rose and ran to the locked doors. He quickly drew his revolver and opened the door. Seeing no one about, he ran to the side of the building near the window. He cautiously looked about but saw no one. Whoever had fired into the window was long gone. Nathan walked back into the livery.

Bill was digging a slug out of the wall next to where Ed had been sitting. "An inch or so to the right, and he would have got you, Ed," said Bill.

"I don't think it's safe for either of you to be here tonight," said Nathan as he looked at Dwight and Ed. "Maybe you ought to get out of town."

"Naw, that won't be necessary, Nathan. We'll just sit tight up in the hay loft. Nobody can see us up there, and one of us will stand guard all night," said Dwight.

"Dwight, I need you to come outside with me. I've got something I want to show you," said Nathan.

The two men went outside. Bill and Ed watched them from the doorway while Nathan led Dwight next to the small corral where he showed Dwight the hoof print. The impression was of a horseshoe with a bar across the opening of the two ends of the shoe. It was the print of a barred horseshoe.

"Is that what they call a barred shoe, Dwight?" asked Nathan.

"Yep," said Dwight. "Sure is."

"Do you know who's horse made that print, Dwight?"

"Sure," said Dwight. "It's that horse over yonder." He was pointing to a horse out in the pasture by the corral where there were two horses. "It's the one with the spots on its side. I had to bring him in from the pasture yesterday to file his teeth. He's a real old timer and just living out his days here."

"Could we go out in the pasture and bring him in here?" asked Nathan.

"No need to," said Dwight. "Just hang on a minute," he said as he walked away. A minute later, he reappeared with a bucket in his hand. He walked over and opened the corral gate and banged the bucket on the rail of the corral. Out in the pasture, the two horses lifted their heads out of the grass. Dwight banged the bucket again, and the two horses began walking toward the livery owner. When they got to him, he led them into the corral and dumped the bucket of oats into a feeding trough. The horses hungrily ate the oats.

"Can you show me his hoof, Dwight?" asked Nathan.

Dwight walked over and let the animal know he was behind him, patting him on the rump. The horse that Dwight had gone to had a strange pattern of white hairs in the form of dots mixed in with his brown hair on his right side. The white dots were in a more or less three quarters of a circle shape. Moving to the horse's right side, Dwight lifted the horse's right hind foot, exposing the odd, crossed shoe. After Nathan had seen it, Dwight let the foot drop, patted the horse again and joined Nathan.

"Do you have any idea how that horse got that strange white dot pattern on its side. Was it born that way?" asked Nathan.

Dwight laughed. "No, he didn't come with those white dots. That white hair is the result of some sort of trauma. At least that's what a horse doc told me once. But I know how they got there. Everywhere you see one of those white dots, I dug out a piece of buckshot near twenty years ago. Owner told me that the horse got shot when he was out bird shooting. Had no reason to doubt him, I guess," said Dwight.

"A twenty-plus year-old horse. He is on his last legs, isn't he," said Nathan.

Dwight then said, "Yep, I'm just letting the owner park him in my pasture until the old boy dies. And that could be any time, but he still keeps kicking, and the owner didn't want to put him down. So, here he is."

Nathan turned and looked directly at Dwight. "Has the same owner had that horse all these years?"

"Yep. Over twenty years," said Dwight.

Still looking intently at Dwight, Nathan finally asked, "Who owns that horse, Dwight?"

"Oh, I thought you knew, Marshal. That's Arthur Crenshaw's horse," said Dwight.

Nathan did not say a word. He just nodded. "Guess I'll go get Bill. Time we were going. You and Ed be careful tonight. I may stop by in the morning."

The two lawmen walked back to the office. Bill voiced his sentiment again, saying, "I feel pretty sorry for old Dwight. He had no idea what Ed had gotten himself into."

Nathan agreed. "I don't think I'd want to be on the receiving end of Dwight's tongue tonight," he said. "That boy has learned a hard lesson, and it's not over yet. Bill, you can head for home, but I want you to come by early in the morning, say seven o'clock or so. I think it's time that we cut the head off of a snake. I'm going down and get a little supper and hit the hay."

*****

Friday Morning

Nathan had slept well Thursday night. All the pieces in the puzzle of the crimes were coming together. It was now a matter of rounding up the players. Friday morning dawned with a cloud cover. There was a chance that they could get a shower during the day. Just as Nathan was making up the bunk in the jail, he heard someone pounding on the office door. He rubbed his eyes, looked up at the clock to see it was six a.m., and thought, Geez, Bill, not this early. But when he went to the door, he saw that it was the new, baby-faced telegraph operator.

"Glad I caught you, Marshal. This telegram came in late last night. He handed it to Nathan and turned to walk away.

"Hey, you, wait a minute," said Nathan. He tore open the envelope. The telegram was from Will. It read:

Is Claire May with you in town? She hasn't been home since you left on Tuesday. Advise Please. Will

Nathan suddenly felt a wave of fear. It was as if his whole life was staring at him from the page of the telegram. His knees felt weak, and his breath was suddenly labored. Where could Claire May possibly be, he asked himself. He immediately blamed himself for not being more cautious. If he had accompanied her all the way home, this would not have happened. He did not know what the world would be like without his wonderful wife. He knew he had to take some sort of action, but what?

"Hey, you," Nathan said to the telegraph operator.

"Yes, sir," the young man answered.

"Send this reply," said Nathan.

Claire May not here. I'm headed home.

"Have you got that?" he asked the operator. "Repeat it back to me."

The operator repeated it verbatim.

"Send it now," snarled Nathan.

"Y-y - yes sir," said the operator and took off running back to the telegraph office.

Nathan looked again at the telegram and shoved it in his pocket. He hurriedly went back into the office and grabbed up his bedroll, gun belt, and rifle. At the same time, Bill came into the office and saw the activity.

"What's up, boss?" asked Bill.

"Bill, grab your bedroll from the closet, bring your pistol and a rifle from the rack. We've got to make tracks, now," said Nathan. "I'll meet you at the livery stable, and I'll get the horses ready," he said rushing out the door.

Uh, oh, something big is up, thought Bill as he grabbed his bedroll.

Nathan trotted down the street to the livery stable and pounded on the door. He heard Dwight's voice, "Who's there?"

"It's Marshal Wolf, Dwight. Open the door."

As the door to the livery stable opened, Dwight said, "Mornin' Marshal. You're up early." Dwight watched as Nathan hurried to Wander's stall.

"Dwight, can you please saddle Bill Ward's horse? He'll be along shortly," said Nathan. Dwight hurried off to get Bill's horse ready.

Before Nathan had finished saddling Wander, Ed Mullins came to the door of Wander's stall. Nathan looked up at the man, but then turned back to his task.

"Marshal, there's something that I forgot to tell you yesterday," said Ed.

Nathan turned back to face Ed Mullins. "Well, what is it, Ed? Make it quick 'cause I need to get on the road."

Ed blurted out, "I forgot to tell you that the Klan has plans to burn out Summer Prairie Ranch tonight."

"What?" Nathan was shouting, "And you are just now telling me this?"

"I-I-I'm sorry, Marshal. But yesterday was so confusing that I forgot it altogether. I'm really sorry."

Dwight had finished with Bill's horse and had walked over to where he overheard his son and the Marshal.

"My god, son," said Dwight.

"I know, I know," said Ed. "I'm sorry."

Nathan finished with Wander and stood looking at Dwight and Ed. "All right, Ed. Here's the deal. We are going to need every gun we can get hold of out at Summer Prairie. I need you and Dwight to ride out to Summer Prairie as soon as you can. I have a feeling we're going to have a final showdown with the Klan. Ed, if you want to prove that you were forced into joining them, you now have the chance to even the score and fight on the side of Prairie Summer Ranch. If you do it, I'll give that weight when we are trying to determine whether or not to arrest you. What do you say?"

Ed's face had brightened. "You bet, Marshal. I surely would like to get in a lick or two against all those buzzards." He turned to Dwight. "OK with you, Dad?" he asked.

"We'll be there, Nathan, with plenty of ammunition," said Dwight.

"Good," said Nathan, and he began to lead Wander out of the barn.

Bill had already taken his horse outdoors and was waiting for Nathan.

Nathan turned and faced Dwight and Ed. "You boys better be careful here today. I would suggest that one of you stay on guard until you ride out to Summer Prairie."

Nathan and Bill mounted their horses and loped out of town. They rode to the cutoff to the Chambers and Morgan farms, and for the next hour they walked and rode all over the area, moving north toward Summer Prairie's turnoff. They found no clues.

Finally, Nathan turned to Bill. "Bill, I want you to ride on ahead to Summer Prairie. Tell Virginia and Will why you are there, and that they need to bring the cowhands in from the pastures. We will need every gun we can get. I want to double back and go over to the Chambers place."

"All right, Nathan," said Bill. He wheeled his horse and resumed riding to the north.

*****

Old Tioga Train Station

Claire May was stiff and sore all over. She had now spent three fitful nights on the floor of the closet in the abandoned depot. Sleeping on the hard floor was taking its toll on her joints. The outlaws had taken her from the closet twice a day so that she could use the outhouse at the side of the station. So, she knew where she was. A faded sign on the side of the building contained the letters, *Tioga.* When they were younger, she and Will had ridden up to the old decrepit Tioga depot to explore it. Tioga was the name of the settlement that would later be moved and become Chanute, Kansas.

Claire May's hands were also untied so that she could eat, but then retied when she finished. Her wrists gave evidence of the rope's constant chaffing. The outlaws had just finished feeding her breakfast; toasted bread soaked in bacon grease. It had been a new outlaw who had fed her this morning, and he had made a mistake. Instead of tying Claire May's hands behind her back as they had done for three days, the new outlaw tied her hands in front of her. Making sure they were tightly tied, he had picked up the tin plate and fork and left the closet, locking it behind him. But he was not familiar with the door lock, and unbeknownst to him the dead bolt had not moved completely into the latch opening. The door was not locked. For three days, Claire May had heard that dead bolt click as it fell home. But this time, she knew there had been no telltale click. She knew the door had not locked properly.

With nothing else to do for three days, Claire May had passed time by squinting through the broken and shrunken clapboard siding. Thus, she knew that the large corral at the side of the depot contained approximately fifty head of cattle. At the rear side of the corral there was a three-sided loafing shed. For three days, there had been only her horse and the horse of the outlaw who had been watching her. But this morning, there were nearly a dozen horses tied to the corral rails. She did not know why so many men were at the depot, but the question was soon answered. She could hear the sound of an approaching train. Its short, shrill whistle pierced the air, and four cattle cars soon came into view, pushed by a steam engine. The train stopped next to a wooden chute that was attached to the rails of the corral.

She heard the voice of a second outlaw who had entered the depot.

"Sam, we need you out by the chute. It's gonna take all of us to get the cattle loaded. Then we'll come back and deal with the woman. We'll kill her and put her on one of the cattle cars. Let's go," he said.

Claire May could hear the sound of the two men's footfalls and the screech of the depot's main door opening and closing as they left. She knew that this was the chance she had been waiting for. It took her little time to use her teeth to untie the ropes on her wrists. She could now try the door. She was afraid that moving the knob or the door might send the dead bolt home, so she looked carefully at the knob and lock before gently turning the knob. The door opened, and sure enough, as the lock passed the slot in the door frame, the dead bolt fell. But the door was already open. Claire May breathed a sigh of relief. Looking all around, she quickly made her way to the outer door at the rear of the depot. After exiting the building, she looked down the side of the building toward the corral. The attention of all the men was locked on the process of loading the cattle into the rail cars. She ran to the loafing shed, but before she climbed on her horse, she took the rifle from the scabbard on an outlaw's horse. She checked to see that it was loaded, then untied her horse. She climbed onto the horse and slowly backed him from the stall. Wheeling the horse, she tore down the path to the south.

Claire May was seen leaving. Two outlaws sprinted for their horses. They had been given instructions by the leader of the loading crew to kill the woman as she was of no use to the Klan leader. Claire May's lead was no more than a few minutes, and she knew that her horse could not keep a full gallop all the way to Summer Prairie Ranch. She had to find an ideal place to take cover. She passed such a spot and did a quick turnaround. Next to some oaks there was a drop off to a creek. She would make a stand there. She coaxed her horse down the steep bank and into the creek where she dismounted. The roots of two of the trees were exposed by the erosion of the creek bank. After tying the reins to the protruding tree roots, she retrieved the rifle, climbed the creek bank, and took position in the cover of the trees. The grass-packed trail she had been following had been made by the stolen cattle as they had been driven north to the depot by the outlaws. Claire May knew that the men following her would be on the same path, and as they passed, they would be no more than twenty yards away from her hiding place. Now she only had to wait.

The outlaws following Claire May had slowed their horses to a fast walk as they kept their eyes on the tracks. But they talked as they rode.

"Frank, I'm not real keen on killing this woman. We've done some loco things in the Klan, but killing women was never on my list, and I hate to have that on my conscience."

The second outlaw answered. "Yeah, I don't know what got into Owens. I never have figured out that hombre. All I know is I don't want to get on Owens' bad side, and the boss wants her dead. So I reckon we keep going. Not sure we're going to catch her though," he said.

He was answered by the first outlaw. "This raid tonight has me worried, too. That Summers place has a fair number of cowhands. We might find ourselves in a bad situation."

"I've been thinking about that too," said the second outlaw. I reckon we can hope that half of them boys are out on the range. Maybe we'll get lucky."

The outlaws' approach and their voices were heard by Claire May, as she hunkered down behind a tree. It would now only be seconds before she had a clear shot.

Claire May's first rifle shot caught one outlaw in the neck. He fell from his horse, writhing on the ground as he clutched his neck. He would be dead shortly. Her second shot caught the side of the other outlaw. She quickly rechambered a shell and shot again before the outlaw could make a run for it. Her next shot caught the man in the chest. He too, fell from his horse and would die in a moment. Soon, the only movement was the outlaws' horses as they walked to where the grass was full and began grazing. Cautiously, Claire May moved from cover and keeping her rifle at the ready, she approached the fallen men. She recognized one of them as a man who had guarded her during the past three days. She then looked at the second man and was surprised to see a man she recognized as being a clerk in the hardware store in town. She turned and walked back to the creek, slid down the creek bank, stowed the rifle, and remounted her horse. Prodding the animal, they climbed a low area on the creek bank and turned south. She figured she would be home in less than an hour.

*****

Chambers Farm

Nathan rode down the lane to the Chambers' cabin at a trot. At the sound of an approaching rider, Daniel emerged from behind the cabin where he had been working in his vegetable patch. Nathan dismounted and shook hands with the black man.

"What can I do for you, Marshal?" Daniel asked.

"Good to see you, Daniel," said Nathan. "I have some news for you. I found out who the men were that killed your mother and father. Your grandma Meezie told me it was the Ku Klux Klan that killed them. She was right."

"We sort of knew that all along, didn't we, Marshal?" Daniel replied.

"I guess so, Daniel. But I could not quite believe that there was still a KKK gang operating in these parts twenty years after the death of your parents. Guess I was a little slow on the uptake," said Nathan.

Daniel just nodded his head.

"Your grandma also mentioned that she remembered a couple of other clues in their murder. It seems that one of the men who came and killed your parents and burned down the cabin had a distinguishing scar on his hand, and that was the same man who tried to kill your father when he first homesteaded. Your father fought the man off at that time and gave the man that scar on his hand."

Daniel answered, "Yeah, my grandma has told me that story."

"Well, we know the name of that man. He is Malvern Owens," said Nathan. "We also know the leader of that gang of cowards. Do you know Arthur Crenshaw, the president of the Prairie Bank?"

"Oh yeah, I know him. He has sent some of his friends to see me a couple times. They want me to sell our farm to them. They keep telling me that Mr. Crenshaw will pay good money for it. But their offer is so low that it is an insult. Besides, I have no interest in selling out," said Daniel. He continued, "Hmm. Don't know that Mr. Owens, but I might like to meet him and Crenshaw," said Daniel. His face revealed a burning ambition, a need to set things right.

Nathan paused for a moment, then made up his mind. "Daniel, how would you like the chance to avenge the wrong that took your parents' lives?"

Daniel looked intently at Nathan. "What do you have in mind, Marshal?"

"Daniel, Crenshaw and his KKK band of outlaws are going to pay us a visit at Summer Prairie tonight. I intend to give them a welcome that they will never forget and put a stop to their terror once and for all. Would you like to come up to the ranch and help us out?"

Daniel did not hesitate. "You bet I would, Marshal. What can I do?"

"I know you are a crack shot with your rifle, keeping meat on the table for you and your grandma all these years. All I want you to do is bring your rifle and some ammunition and be part of our defense force to meet the KKK."

"OK, Marshal. I'll be there," said Daniel.

"I've got to leave you now, Daniel. My wife is missing, and I have a feeling that this gang is holding her somewhere. Come on up to Summer Prairie as soon as you can. I'll see you there," said Nathan. He then climbed up on Wander and trotted back down the lane and out to the road, where he prodded Wander into a lope.

For the past several hours, Nathan's foremost thoughts had been on the welfare of his wife. He continually had to force the thought of losing Claire May out of his mind. He loved Claire May more than anything in the world. The morose thought of life without her would mean a life with no more meaning. Not only would he lose his wonderful wife, but the child she was carrying. Tears came to his eyes just thinking about it. The tears flew from the corners of his eyes in the wind caused by his swift ride. A raging anger was growing inside him, and he looked forward to a show down with Crenshaw and his gang of thugs. It might not bring Claire May back to him, but he wanted the satisfaction of taking the life of Crenshaw. Yet, in the remote corner of Nathan's thoughts, he was aware that there had been no report of finding Claire May, whether dead or alive. That small part of Nathan's mind still held a remote hope that she might still be all right.

Nathan turned Wander into the lane to the Summer Prairie Ranch house, dismounted, and tied Wander to the hitching rack. He was not sure how he would face Virginia and Will, and paused on the porch step to catch his breath. This was going to be very difficult, he thought. Pulling himself together, he walked across the porch and opened the front door. He could hear voices from the kitchen, so he hung his hat on the hat rack and walked toward the sound. As he crossed into the kitchen, he saw Rosa at the stove and Virginia and Will sitting at the table. In addition, Dave Morgan, Betty, and Alice and Bill Ward also sat at the table, with Alice curled up on her chair and leaning into Will. They all turned to look at Nathan. Seeing them looking his way threw a lump into his throat, and he began tearing up again. He could not speak. His mouth moved, but no sound came out. He then looked down at the floor and sobbed.

Nathan had not heard her. Claire May had sneaked up behind him from the front room and now jumped up on her husband's back, nearly knocking Nathan over. Nathan's immediate reaction had been to fight, and he turned quickly to free himself. But he could not shake the person on his back, and just then he heard her laughter. She was laughing as she kissed him on the neck. She let go and the two people turned to face each other. Nathan was crying. He could not talk. Claire May wiped his tears with her fingers and reached up to kiss him. They remained in a tight embrace with their lips together.

Finally, Will said, "All right you two love birds, unlock. We don't want you dying from lack of oxygen." Alice giggled.

Between kisses, the couple went over the events of Claire May's capture and her daring escape from the outlaws. When she was talked out, Nathan kissed her again.

"I was so worried about you. I never should have let you head for home on Tuesday without me. I'm so sorry," said Nathan.

This brought on another session of hugs and kisses. At last, the couple calmed down. Nathan looked over at the table. "Good to see you, Dave and Betty. How did you happen to be here?" he asked.

"Well, Alice wanted to come over and see Will. It seems your brother-in-law has it in his mind to marry our Alice, so we wanted to talk to Virginia about it," said Dave.

"Really? Really? Will's going to get married?" said Nathan.

"Oh, come on, Nathan. It wasn't like I was never going to get hitched," laughed Will.

"Congratulations, you two. That's great news," said Nathan. "Two pieces of good news. You can't imagine how relieved I am." He grabbed Claire May and kissed her again.

Nathan then looked over at the stove. "I am so hungry."

Everyone laughed then, and Rosa scolded Nathan, "You go wash your hands. Dinner will be on the table in a few minutes."

After they had eaten, they all sat at the table talking. Bill spoke up and said, "Will's got his cowhands all coming into the bunk house."

"They should be here by now," said Will.

They were interrupted by a knock on the front door. Claire May went and found Daniel Chambers at the door. Meezie Jones sat in the seat on a buckboard parked at the foot of the walkway to the door. One of the two mules pulling the buckboard brayed with impatience.

"Oh Daniel. So good to see you. You come on in and go into the kitchen. I think you are just in time for dinner."

"We didn't come here for dinner, Miz Claire May. We are here because the Marshal asked us to come up here."

"That's OK, Daniel, but you need to have dinner before things get ugly. Now go on out to the kitchen, and I'm going out to fetch Meezie." And with that, Claire May hurried out to the buckboard where she helped Meezie step down.

Nathan looked up and saw Daniel making his way to the kitchen. "Ah, Daniel. I'm glad you got here. Come in here. I'm sure Rosa has another plate. Is your grandma with you?"

"She's coming with Miz Claire May. We didn't come for no dinner, Marshal. We just came to help with the outlaws," said Daniel. But he could not help but smell the results of Rosa's ministrations at the stove.

Virginia had stood and reached out to Daniel. "Nonsense, Daniel, have a seat and a bit of food. Here comes your grandma. She can sit right here."

"I guess I should not presume that you know everyone, Daniel and Miz Jones," said Virginia. She then proceeded to introduce Daniel and Meezie to everyone. The small talk continued while Daniel and Meezie ate dinner. But when they finished, Nathan began speaking to the group.

Part Nine

As the group sat around the kitchen table, Nathan said, "I believe Bill briefed everyone on what is about to happen." Around the table people were nodding.

"The Ku Klux Klan is determined to get us three landowners off of our property. Arthur Crenshaw is the leader of those outlaws," said Nathan.

This was news to Dave and Betty Morgan. "Well, I'll be," said Dave. "I never have liked that little skinflint s.o.b. Beg your pardon, ma'am," he said turning to Virginia. "Every dealing I've had with him soured my stomach. Never thought he was man enough to be an outlaw, let alone recruit a whole gang of them."

"I have a feeling that this whole KKK chapter started when Arthur's father was running the bank," said Nathan. "Arthur probably just took over after his old man died."

Nathan then changed the subject. "I have some other good news. It was confirmed that those dark patches of grass on our lands are signs of oil seeping from the ground. In other words, all of our properties have oil deposits on them, and Art Crenshaw knew it. I'm convinced that's the reason he wanted to buy you out, Daniel, and force you out, Dave. He wanted that oil property. He wanted it bad enough that killing people to get it was on his agenda."

Will spoke up. "Why in the world would they want to kidnap Claire May?" he asked.

"Your guess is as good as mine," said Nathan. "I can only think that a couple of Crenshaw's goons thought they might be able to get ransom money for her."

"Well, I know her well. She ain't worth five bucks," he said teasingly and smiled at his sister.

Claire May stuck her tongue out at her brother.

The room then became noisy as the folks talked among themselves and continued to ask questions.

Nathan raised his hands and asked for attention. Just as he was ready to speak, there was another knock on the door. Virginia left the table to answer the door and returned with Dwight and Ed Mullins.

Nathan shook hands with Dwight and Ed. "Good to see you." He turned to the others in the kitchen. "I asked Dwight and Ed to help us out tonight," said Nathan.

He continued. "Folks, the reason we have brought all the ranch hands in and asked you to join us is because the KKK boys intend to pay us a visit tonight. My sources told me that they want to kill us and burn us out, just like they did to Daniel's mother and father years ago. We aim to stop them." Nathan did not tell the group where he had received his information.

"So, here is what we need to do," said Nathan.

For the next forty-five minutes, the Marshal told them of his plan to defend Summer Prairie Ranch. Following that, instructions were given to the cowboys, who were sent scurrying around the ranch house, the bunk house, and the barn. One of the Summer Prairie ranch hands had already left to notify the Circle M crew to come to Summer Prairie Ranch to help. They would arrive soon. All of the horses were taken from the corral and moved into the woods and tied down to keep them out of gunfire. All buckets and containers that could hold water were filled and placed strategically around the buildings. Brush was cleared and pushed together for hiding places for the cowhands to take firing positions. Nathan explained that they would set up a pincer movement by having men stationed on each side of the lane and the corners of the house. When the Klansmen moved into the lane, they would be caught in a crossfire from three sides. Then the hidden ranch hands would squeeze the pincer, closing it from behind, and catching the outlaws in a web of deadly bullets. Other men would be positioned near the bunk house and the barn to defend them against Klansmen firing at the buildings. Nathan ensured that every man had plenty of ammunition and warned everyone that the men attacking them had every intention of killing them. In this situation, he told them, it was best to shoot first to save your life. He also told them not to fire until he fired the first shot. He wanted to make sure that the outlaws were within the trap before shooting. He did not want any of them to escape.

*****

Dusk arrived. The shadows lengthened and the men all took their places behind cover. There was nothing to do now but wait for the outlaws. But Crenshaw and his men were in no hurry. They had done all this before and knew that it was best to wait until 1 a.m., when it was felt that everyone would be asleep.

The outlaws talked quietly among themselves. Several of them had misgivings about attacking such a large ranch operation. After all, there were at least a dozen cowhands on that ranch who all knew how to shoot straight. But it was too late to back out. Blindly, they followed their deranged leader, Arthur Crenshaw, in his quest to make himself powerfully wealthy by acquiring the oil-rich land north of town. They moved forward after taking the turnoff to the Summers' place. It was nearly 1:30 a.m. as they turned in the lane to the ranch house. They paused while a half dozen torches were soaked in kerosene and lit. The group could now plainly be seen by the cowboys who lay in waiting.

The horsemen moved forward to where they could throw their torches. Four men with torches split off from the group, with two of them moving toward the bunk house and two toward the barn. As those four horsemen moved close to the bunkhouse and barn, the first shot was fired by Nathan. It caught a man carrying a torch, and he rolled from the saddle to the ground. His torch sent sparks flying as it hit the ground. What ensued was a deafening roar of small arms as the Summer Prairie defenders let fly with vengeance. The outlaws began falling from their horses. The rest began firing back, but because they were on horseback, their aim was not precise. In addition, they were far outgunned.

Daniel Chambers was lying under the front porch of the ranch house. From where he was, he had clear shooting, and the outlaws could not fire at him well from horseback. As a result, he methodically hit two of the outlaws, but then paused. In the torchlight, he saw the outlaw who was often in his thoughts. The light from the torch that he held aloft revealed the outlaw's right hand. The scar was plainly evident. Malvern Owens held a revolver in his left hand and the torch in his right. His reins were in his teeth. He was wildly shooting at the house, but hitting no one. Daniel breathed slowly watching the man who had attempted to kill his father, and who had been part of the gang that later killed both his mother and father. He drew a small breath, held it, and slowly squeezed the trigger of his rifle. The bullet entered Owens' chest, breaking the sternum, and moving further to enter his heart. The shock from the lead bullet breaking into the heart stopped it immediately. Malvern Owens fell from his horse, dead from a shot fired by the son of the black couple he had helped kill twenty years before. The torch he had been holding fell harmlessly to the ground, sending sparks flying to the side of it.

So many guns were being fired at the same time that the noise had reached a staccato roar. In the midst of the din, Nathan had seen two of the riders move toward the bunk house. One of the men held a torch while they both dismounted, firing on the Summer Prairie ranch hand pinned down next to the building. In another minute, Nathan had reached a position that was close to the ranch hand's location and began firing upon the two outlaws. Shots were returned from both sides. But unseen by Nathan, another outlaw had dismounted behind the bunk house and was approaching Nathan from the rear. The outlaw raised his gun hand and began to take aim when a rifle shot rang out behind Nathan. Nathan turned in time to see the outlaw who had been behind him, drop in the dirt only six feet behind him. He looked farther back to see Will give him a wave after saving his life. Will hurried to join Nathan, and the two men made short work of the two outlaws who had pinned down one of the ranch hands. Will then grabbed one of the water buckets next to the bunkhouse and extinguished the torch that the two men had been carrying.

As suddenly as it had begun, the sound of gunfire stopped. It was eerily quiet. The smell of burnt gunpowder permeated the entire area, carried on the gray-white smoke. Several torches still burned where they had fallen on the ground, lending eerie light and shadows to the killing area. Ranch hands began dousing them with water. Three horses lay among the fourteen men scattered on the ground from the lane to the ranch house and to the bunk house. Other horses had bolted away from their fallen riders and could be seen standing in the shadows. Nathan scanned the front yard of the ranch house, then his eyes drifted to the lane leading from the house to the road. At the far end of the lane, he could dimly see him, a sole rider astride his horse in the lane. Nathan knew then that Crenshaw had ordered and cowardly watched the massacre of his entire Klan chapter without participating. Still

217

watching Crenshaw, Nathan saw him turn and gallop away. Nathan was not concerned. He would eventually find Crenshaw.

Miraculously, no one defending Summer Prairie had been injured. In the darkness, they had been well hidden in their firing positions, so that the outlaws did not have clear shots at any of the defenders. Almost as if they were in a daze, the ranch hands began slowly walking toward and gathering at the front porch of the ranch house. Nathan made his way through the men, making sure that each of them was all right and thanking them for defending the ranch. He then stepped across the porch and into the house. Will was right behind him. They found the women on the floor of the kitchen. Virginia, Claire May, Betty, and Alice Morgan, Meezie, and Rosa were huddled together in a corner that offered the most protection from stray bullets. Still, bullet holes pock-marked areas of the kitchen walls. It was the front of the house, though, that had suffered the most. The windows were all shattered or gone, and bullet holes adorned the walls of the front rooms and adjoining dining room. If anyone had been in those two rooms during the gunfire, they would most likely have suffered injury. The women stood, looking at the damage, muttering and shaking their heads. Nathan turned to Will and put a hand on his shoulder.

"Thank you, Will, for saving my skin out there," he said.

"You would have done the same for me. Besides, that baby Claire May is carrying needs his daddy," said Will. "I'm just darn glad we still have a home, and that none of our boys got hurt."

The men walked outside and joined the other men on the porch. Dave Morgan joined them. Several of them had broken out their tobacco and papers and were enjoying a smoke.

Will shouted, "I think the Summer Prairie Ranch has the best cowboys in Kansas. Thank you, boys."

Dave Morgan took up the challenge. "Nah, the Circle M boys can outshoot all of your boys."

A whooping and hollering followed with the men teasing and shouting at one another. The din soon died down though, as the men looked at the sobering scene of bodies littering the front yard of the ranch house, at the bunk house, and the corral.

Will turned to Dave Morgan. "Dave, I would really appreciate it if your boys could stay over tonight and help my boys bury those three horses in the morning. There may be others that are wounded and have to be put down. We probably need all the hands to help load the bodies on one of my hay wagons and haul them into town to the undertaker in the morning. My boys will let your men have the bunk house, and my boys will grab a few hours of sleep up in the hay loft of the barn. Can they do that?"

"Sure," said Morgan. "You hear that boys. We'll look for you back at Circle M about noon tomorrow." Betty had come out of the house to join Dave. Turning around, Dave said to Will and Nathan, "Betty and I will be going on home. We'll talk again soon."

Bill Ward came up and shook his boss's hand. "I'm heading out, too, Nathan. I'll probably see you tomorrow," he said and followed the Morgans to go get his horse.

As Dave Morgan walked away to get their buckboard from among the trees, Alice came out of the house to join her mother who was waiting for Dave to bring the buckboard, but she stopped to kiss Will. This drew a few hoots and whistles from the cowboys. Will didn't mind.

"I sure do thank you, Dave and Bill," said both Nathan and Will to Dave Morgan and Bill Ward as they watched them going to get the Morgan buckboard and Bill's horse.

Their departure was immediately followed by Daniel Chambers who had gone into the house to get Meezie.

"We'll be going on home too, Marshal," said Daniel.

Nathan leaned in close to Daniel. "You got him, didn't you Daniel?"

Daniel answered quietly, "Yes sir."

Nathan looked at Meezie. She smiled at Nathan and crooked her finger at him to lean down closer. When Nathan got close, she kissed him on the cheek. "Thank you, Marshal. Come and see me when you can," she said before taking Daniel's arm and walking down the porch step.

Finally, Dwight and Ed Mullins came over and both shook Nathan's hand. Dwight was smiling. "You know, Nathan, I was fifteen years old when I joined the Union Army just before the shooting started in the war between the states. Don't think I ever told you that. Anyway, damned if last night didn't bring back a whole lot of memories I've tried to forget, some good, but mostly bad. I am mighty glad we won't see any of those no-counts anymore."

"I appreciate the help that you and Ed gave us, Dwight. I was sure I could count on you."

Nathan watched as Ed uncomfortably shuffled his feet. "Ed, I saw what you did tonight. You took out at least one of the Klan, maybe two. So, I've been thinking. If you had the guts to risk your life last night to make things right.... Well, I think you've paid your debt to the law. I'm not going to press any charges against you."

Ed looked up at Nathan. "That's mighty good news, Marshal. And I want you to know that my dad and I thank you, for sure," said Ed, as he stuck out his hand again to shake with Nathan. Dwight did the same, and his smile was even broader. The two blacksmiths then turned and walked away to get their horses.

Will had gone into the house, but soon returned. In his hands he held four bottles of bourbon. He handed them to the ranch hands. "I want to thank all of you boys, and maybe a good shot of bourbon will help you all sleep a little better. Another whoop or two and whistles answered Will, and the Summer Prairie and Circle M hands began to wander toward the bunk house. Chances were that the cowboys would begin playing a bit of poker and having a drink or two before they finally bedded down.

Later, when the house had quieted, Will and Nathan sat on the top step of the porch, sharing another bottle of bourbon. In the dim natural light, the men could see the bodies of the outlaws lying in a row where the ranch hands had dragged them.

"Nathan, I never want to see something like that again," said Will. I didn't realize there were people in this world who were that damn evil."

"Most of 'em aren't, Will. But, I know for darn sure that I'll run across a whole bunch more outlaws in my lifetime. I think they call that job security," said Nathan.

Will chuckled. "Well, even though I like you, brother-in-law, I wouldn't want your job. Let's go in. I need a couple hours of sleep," said Will.

Part Ten

Capture

Saturday Morning

At five a.m. on Saturday morning, Nathan bolted up in bed. Hurriedly, he put on his clothes. Claire May sat up in bed. "Where are you going?" she asked.

"Gotta go to town," Nathan answered. "I'll see you later today."

He grabbed his gun belt and rifle where he had left them in the front room the night before and left the house. He trotted over to the grove where the horses were still tethered. He found Wander and led him by his halter back to the barn where he saddled and bridled him. His stomach growled as horse and rider trotted out the lane.

At seven a.m., Nathan entered town and headed directly to the railroad station, where he tied Wander to the hitching rack. Striding purposefully, he went directly to the ticket window. The ticket clerk was not at his window. Nathan looked around and saw the man sweeping the floor under the benches in the waiting room. There were no passengers waiting when he walked over to the man who was sweeping.

The man looked up and stopped his broom. He could see the badge pinned to Nathan's vest. "Morning Marshal. You're sure up early, ain't you."

"Yeah, I guess I am," Nathan answered. "Tell me something. Was there a passenger train that left here during the night or this morning?"

"Well sure, Marshal. We have the same train every Saturday morning. You just missed it." The man pulled a pocket watch from his pocket. "It left about thirty minutes ago."

"Where was it going?" asked Nathan.

"That train goes all the way to Chicago," said the clerk. "'Course it makes a few stops along the way."

"What are the stops?" asked Nathan.

"Well, there are several, you see."

"Yeah, yeah, never mind. Does it stop in Topeka?" asked Nathan.

"Oh, sure. It will get to Topeka..." He paused to look again at his watch. "I'd say another two hours, if the engineer can maintain a steady forty to forty-five miles an hour."

"One more question, mister."

"Sure, sure," said the clerk.

"Did you sell a ticket for that train to Arthur Crenshaw?" asked Nathan.

"Yep, he was in here just as soon as I opened the depot door this morning. He bought a one-way ticket to Chicago. He wanted a compartment by himself, so I had to charge a little extra for that service," said the clerk.

"And you're sure the train will stop in Topeka?" asked Nathan.

"Oh sure, I'm positive it'll stop there. Say, what's all this about, anyway?" asked the clerk.

Nathan answered, "I don't have time to explain, but thanks for your help, mister," said Nathan, and he hurried for the door.

Nathan's next stop was going to be the telegraph office, but as he rode past the Prairie Bank, he could see that the door of the bank was standing ajar. He stopped Wander, dismounted, and tied the horse. He only had to cross the threshold of the bank to see that the main vault door was also open. He walked to the vault and looked inside. It was a mess, with various drawers and cabinets open, but Nathan could see no sign of any cash. He turned and walked back out of the bank. He then mounted and prodded Wander toward the telegraph office. After tying the horse, Nathan entered the telegraph office. The operator had just opened the door and was rubbing his eyes and yawning as he looked out the office window.

"Oh, hello, Marshal. Kinda early, isn't it?" he said.

Nathan thought to himself, *apparently a couple people think I should be working shorter hours.* "Yeah, I guess it is," he answered. "I need to get a wire off to the U.S. Marshal at Topeka. Can you do that?"

"Sure Marshal. Just tell me what you want to send, and I'll do it," said the operator.

Nathan and the operator then spent several minutes drafting the telegram. It was to go to the Marshal who had jurisdiction for northeast Kansas. When the wire was finished, the wording stated that the Marshal in Topeka should muster as many men as he could and hold the passenger train that was headed there from Chanute. He was also to apprehend a fugitive named Arthur Crenshaw who was thought to be travelling alone. The fugitive would be in possession of several thousand dollars and papers stolen from the Prairie Bank in Chanute. In addition, he was wanted in Chanute for kidnapping, extortion, robbery, bribery, and murder. Instructions to the Topeka-based Marshal were that the fugitive and the stolen money should be returned to Chanute accompanied by at least two reliable lawmen as soon as possible. The receiver was to acknowledge receipt of the wire, and to send confirmation to the sender of the apprehension of Crenshaw.

Then Nathan had the operator send another wire, this time to the state bank examiner's office in Topeka. In the wire, he explained that the Prairie Bank in Chanute had been robbed. The suspect in the robbery was the president of the bank. Therefore, Nathan was requesting an immediate bank examination to determine the scope of the robbery and the losses to the bank and its customers.

After sending the wire to the bank examiners, Nathan sent a final wire to Claire May Wolf, Summer Prairie Ranch.

The brief message simply said:

I love you. See you tonight. Nathan

Nathan watched as the operator sent the wires. Within thirty minutes the telegraph key began to chatter. The Marshal in Topeka had received his wire and would take appropriate action. Now there was nothing further to do but wait, so Nathan headed for the cafe to have breakfast. No sooner had he sat down, than Bill Ward joined him. Nathan and Bill discussed the escape of Crenshaw and the telegram that he had sent to Topeka. Espie had fed Bill before he left for work, so he ordered a coffee and watched his boss hungrily eat his breakfast.

The lawmen made small talk over their coffee. After leaving coins on the table, Nathan said, "Let's take a walk, Bill."

Nathan needed to get Wander fed, so he led the horse and walked to the livery stable, where Dwight Mullins was already standing in the doorway. "Morning, Nathan," said Dwight.

"Morning, Dwight."

"Hell of a night, wasn't it Marshal," said Dwight.

"Indeed, it was, Dwight, indeed it was. Can you get Wander fed and watered, and I'll pick him up around four or five o'clock?" asked Nathan.

"Sure can. Say, Nathan. I just want to thank you again for what you did for Ed," said Dwight.

"I figure he earned it," said Nathan. "But I would prefer you keep that between us for now. Nobody in town needs to know the details."

"You bet, Nathan," answered Dwight.

Nathan turned and walked out of the livery stable to join Bill, who was standing outside.

"Where we headed, boss?" asked Bill.

"Crenshaw's place," said Nathan. "I want to talk to his house-keeper."

The lawmen walked the three blocks to Arthur Crenshaw's house, climbed the two steps to the porch, and used the knocker to rap on the door. The door was soon opened by a thin, attractive woman with a sprinkling of gray in her hair. Her reaction to seeing the lawmen at the door was immediate.

"Oh, no," she said. "You must be here about Art."

"What do you mean, ma'am?" asked Nathan.

"Well, Art came in before dawn this morning and changed clothes. Then he grabbed a bag and went out again. I thought that was very unusual for him. And the only explanation I had was that he must be in some kind of trouble." She paused, then asked, "Well, is he in trouble?"

"Yes, ma'am. I think he is. But we are trying to get to the bottom of it. Would you mind if we came in and had a look around?" asked Nathan.

"Well, I 'spect that would be all right," said the housekeeper, and she opened the door wider to let the men inside.

"Does Mr. Crenshaw have a study, or work room, ma'am?" asked Nathan.

"Why yes. It's through the dining room there and then to the back of the house. But wait," she said. "Could you please tell me what this is about?"

Nathan turned to face the woman. "Right now, I can't tell you much. But I can tell you that Mr. Crenshaw left town this morning, and we believe that he robbed the bank before he left."

"Art. Robbed the bank? How could that happen?" asked the housekeeper. "He was the president of the bank. Why, we were planning......"

Nathan looked intently at the woman. "What were you planning, Ma'am?"

In a low voice, the woman responded. "We were planning to get married one of these days," she said. Then, she looked up quickly at Nathan. Tears filled her eyes, and she said, "Do you think he is coming back?"

Nathan hesitated, and then said, "Yes, ma'am. I believe he will be coming back to Chanute."

"Oh, that's nice," said the housekeeper, and she smiled. "Maybe then I can talk to him and help him if I can. There's got to be an explanation for this accusation, and I'm sure Art will know what to do."

Nathan and Bill left the housekeeper standing in the foyer mumbling to herself and walked back through the house to find Crenshaw's study.

"Nathan, what are we looking for?" asked Bill.

"To tell you the truth, Bill, I don't rightly know," said Nathan. "But I'm guessing that Crenshaw must have kept some kind of records for the KKK, since he was their head honcho. Plus, maybe we can find any other thing that would link him to the cattle rustling, or my wife's kidnapping, or any other damn thing he was mixed up in. Anyway, we'll take it slow and see what we find."

The two lawmen spent the next hour carefully sifting through the contents of Arthur Crenshaw's study. They even went so far as to pull a great portion of the man's library books from their shelves, but they found no incriminating evidence. Finally, Bill said, "I don't think there is anything here, Nathan. Have you found anything interesting?"

"No, I'm with you, Bill. But I still think there must be something substantial to link Crenshaw to the Klan activities," said Nathan. He moved over to and sat down on an upholstered chair by a window. As he sat down, he thought he had heard a squeaking noise, the sound of floorboards rubbing together. He thought little of it. His feet were resting on a throw rug in front of the chair. Out of frustration and impatience, he was slightly tapping one of his booted feet on the rug and floor. He then heard a different sound and immediately became alert. He then tapped his foot more forcefully. What he was hearing was a muffled, yet hollow sound in addition to the squeak he had heard earlier. His interest was piqued. Standing, he turned to look at the chair and the throw rug. After going down on his hands and knees, he pushed the throw rug aside. At first, he saw nothing out of the ordinary and ran his fingers over the exposed wood floor. As he did so, he noticed a slight movement of a knot in the wood. Upon closer examination, he was able to wiggle and lift the knot from the knot hole. He now had Bill's attention, and he came to look over Nathan's shoulder.

"You gonna stick your finger in that hole, or am I?" asked Bill.

Nathan answered by putting a finger in the knot hole. He felt nothing, but then tried to lift the board. To his surprise, the board lifted from skillfully crafted joints to reveal a hidden space beneath the board. The space contained a thick, leather-bound book and a locked metal box. Nathan carefully lifted them out, then replaced the board, the wood knot, and the rug.

The lawmen moved to Crenshaw's desk and examined the book. On its leather cover was the triangle they had seen on the KKK medallions and the symbol on the corner of the Prairie Bank sign. Inside the front cover were the letters KKK over the word "*Vigilance.*" The men leafed through the pages of the book. It was readily apparent that it was a diary, with entries that began in 1870 and came forward to the present. The entries were signed and dated, with the earliest entries signed by Arthur Crenshaw's father, Willard, and the more recent ones signed by Arthur himself. The entries recorded the significant events in which the local chapter of the KKK had participated over the years.

The book amounted to a signed confession to every evil and unlawful act ever carried out by the men in Chanute who had fallen under the vile ideology of the Klan. Nathan leafed to the last entry in the book. It read:

Intend to eliminate the Summer Prairie Ranch tonight.

Nathan sighed, and thought, it was a good thing we were able to thwart Crenshaw on that action. He turned and smiled at Bill. "We hit the jackpot, Bill."

"Oooh boy, I reckon we did, boss," answered Bill. "But what kind of outlaw makes a diary of his misdeeds?"

"An outlaw who thinks he is above the law and will never be caught," answered Nathan. "Let's see if we can find out what's in that box."

Nathan was not wearing his gun belt. He said, "Let me borrow your pistol, Bill."

Bill handed over the pistol. Nathan opened the cylinder and emptied out the cartridges into Bill's hand. Then he grabbed the pistol by the barrel and used the handle as a hammer. Three sharp blows broke the surrounding bezel of the lock, allowing the lock to fall into the box. Nathan opened the lid and saw a small amount of cash and a few KKK medallions. But the most interesting item was a roster of all the men who were members of the Chanute Klan chapter. Next to each name was a record of their submissions of yearly dues to the chapter.

Then Nathan saw another smaller ledger book with a green cloth cover. He lifted the book and opened it. In the front cover were written these words, *Prairie Trust*. As he leafed through the pages, he could see that they contained names and dates along with another column of cash amounts. It was a ledger of all the monies placed into the *Prairie Trust* by Arthur Crenshaw.

"I think we have everything we need here, Bill." Nathan continued, "But I do want to go around back of the house to the stable and look around."

"You're not going anywhere, Marshal." Crenshaw's housekeeper had come into the room, and she was holding a pistol in her hand. The gun barrel was pointed between the two lawmen.

"What's this all about, ma'am?" asked Nathan.

"You see, Marshal. I guess it was not in Art's plans to marry and take me with him. But that doesn't mean that I don't love him. And when he comes back, I'll talk him into taking me with him. Unfortunately, that means I am going to have to kill both of you," said the housekeeper.

Bill spoke up, "Listen lady. When Crenshaw comes back to town he will be in handcuffs and will be tried for murder, kidnapping, and robbery. He won't be going anywhere except to the hangman."

"Oh dear, Mr. Ward," said the housekeeper. "I believe you underestimate my Art. He's a very smart man, certainly smarter than the two of you. Now, just set that book and box on the desk and step away."

The men did as they were told, but when Bill stepped back from the desk, he tossed one of the bullets he was holding. It clattered at the feet of the housekeeper. When she looked down to see what made the racket, Bill threw the rest of the bullets directly at the woman. As the small projectiles hit her, she became flustered, brushing at them with her free hand. Nathan quickly covered the distance between him and the woman and easily grabbed her gun hand. He wrenched the gun out of her hand and continued to hold her by the wrist. She attempted to hit Nathan in the face, but he easily fended off the blow. He then told the woman, "I am arresting you for obstruction of justice. I hope you find our jail up to your housekeeping standards."

"You have no right to do this," said the housekeeper. "When Art comes back you are going to be very sorry. He is a powerful man."

"Yeah, well, we'll see about that," said Bill.

Nathan kept a firm grip on the housekeeper's upper arm, and with Bill carrying the ledger books and metal box, the two lawmen left Crenshaw's house and made their way back to the office. With the housekeeper safely tucked away into a cell, Bill put on the coffeepot and then locked the housekeeper's pistol and the ledger books in a storage locker.

"There sure are a lot of people who get turned around on the right road of life, aren't there?" said Bill. He was about to pour two mugs of coffee.

"Yep. For the life of me I can't figure out why that housekeeper would think that Crenshaw was going to marry her," said Nathan. "There's not a warm bone in Crenshaw's body. He's only looking out for himself."

Bill added, "I sure hope we get hold of that sidewinder. He's one man I would like to see swing by a rope."

The two lawmen blew across their coffee mugs in a feeble attempt to cool the hot coffee, and then took careful sips. When they were nearly finished with their coffee, Nathan said, "Bill, would you please go back over to Crenshaw's place and go around back to his stable and have a look around. There may not be anything of interest, but sometimes an outlaw will keep some things he doesn't want seen in someplace other than his house."

"Sure," said Bill. He took the final gulp from his coffee mug, set it on the table and got up to go. "I'll be back in a few minutes." Nathan watched his deputy walk out the door and cross the street.

To pass the time, Nathan picked up the worn broom in the corner of the office and began sweeping the office floor. He thought that the task would take his mind off of the events of the past few days. Even as he began the rhythmic sweep of the broom, he could not help but remember how close he had come to losing Claire May at the hands of the Klan outlaws. When he thought of it, it only made him more angry, and he took his anger out on the broom. Dust was flying and was reflected in the sun's rays coming through the front window. He only stopped sweeping when the telegraph operator came breathlessly through the front door.

"Marshal, I've got a wire for you from Topeka," he said as he waved the envelope above his head. Then he handed it to Nathan.

Nathan tore the envelope open and unfolded the telegram. It was from the U.S. Marshal in Topeka, and read:

Per your instructions, suspect Arthur Crenshaw apprehended and removed from train. Suspect held in our jail. Suspect in possession of firearm and bag containing approx. $18 thousand. Two of my deputies will escort subject to Chanute on Tuesday.

U.S. Marshal, Topeka sends.

"Is there anything else you need, Marshal?" asked the telegraph operator.

Nathan was smiling when he answered, "No, that's all right now. Let me know if you hear anything from the state bank examiner's office, but I figure we won't hear from them until Monday. Thanks."

"Anytime, Marshal. See you later," said the operator as he went out the office door.

Nathan refilled his coffee mug and sat down. He read the telegram again, and thought to himself, they had been lucky to catch Crenshaw. If he had gotten past Topeka and gotten to Chicago, or even Kansas

City, the odds of catching him would not have been good. He smiled again, then thought to himself, got you, you weasel.

In a few minutes, Bill returned to the office. He was carrying a folded white cloth bundle. Nathan did not have to be told what it was as Bill began to unfold it and spread it out on the desk. It was Crenshaw's KKK robe and mask.

"Guess he kept his Klan suit where he could get to it when he was going to ride to the next Klan gathering," said Bill. "I found it in his saddlebag in the stable."

Very quietly, so he could not be overheard by the prisoner, Nathan told Bill to fold the uniform up and to lock it away in an evidence locker along with the ledger book and the metal box. After Bill did that, he came back to the desk.

"You want Espie to cook for the prisoner?" Bill asked. Espie usually did the cooking for the jail prisoners and was paid a small stipend for her labor.

"Sure, Bill. That will be good," said Nathan. "Let's go over to the cafe and get a bit of dinner. I'm hungry again. After dinner, I'm leaving you in charge. I've got to ride up and see Judge Stephens on my way out of town. Then I'm going on home. I'll be back early on Monday morning. Crenshaw's train will be coming in on Tuesday. That'll be the high point of the day, won't it?"

Bill chuckled as he locked the door to the office behind them. "I agree. Can't wait to see the face on that jackass outlaw."

After eating dinner, the two lawmen parted company. Bill was going home to tell Espie that she would need to feed the prisoner, and Nathan went to the livery stable to get Wander. He saw Dwight Mullins in the doorway of the livery stable, sitting on a chair and idly watching the day go by. He shouted into the livery stable, "Hey Ed. Marshal's here. Get his horse ready, please."

By now, the whole town knew that the Prairie bank had been robbed, and the rumor was that it was Arthur Crenshaw who had taken the money. Nathan also knew that when he told Dwight Mullins anything, it was sure to make its way around town as customers came and went at the Mullins and Son Livery Stable.

"Thought you might like to know, Dwight, said Nathan. "The U.S. Marshal in Topeka grabbed Art Crenshaw off of his train. They have him in jail up there, and the money from the bank was with him. So, Crenshaw and the money will be coming back to town."

"Oh, that's good news, Marshal. Folks will be happy to hear that their money is being returned," said Dwight.

Nathan laughed to himself. *Yep, he thought, that won't take long to get around town.*

In a few minutes, Ed Mullins brought Wander out to the Marshal. Nathan slipped his rifle in its scabbard and climbed into the saddle. "I'll see you boys on Monday," he said as he rode north.

Part Eleven

Justice Served

It was only a few minutes before he was tying Wander to Judge Rodney Stephens' hitching post, then removing his hat as he walked up the porch steps.

I don't know how she knows I'm here, thought Nathan as the front door slowly opened with Millie holding it. She was smiling. "Afternoon, Marshal. The Judge is in his study."

"Afternoon, Millie. Thanks, I'll head on back there," said Nathan.

As Nathan entered the room, the judge looked up from his work at his desk. "Always glad to see my favorite Marshal," said Stephens. "Especially good to know that none of the Summer Prairie crew was hurt last night, and you're still in one piece."

Nathan had to laugh. "Now, how in the world would you know about what happened last night?"

"I have my sources, Marshal. They're as good as any military spies," said the judge.

Nathan had to think for a few seconds. Hmm, he thought. Espie Ward and Millie. That had to be it. He chuckled again. "Bill Ward must talk in his sleep."

The judge laughed out loud, shaking his head. He reached out and grabbed his pipe and began loading the bowl with tobacco. "I also heard that Crenshaw slipped out last night and left town with the bank's money. Is that right?"

"I believe, Judge, that I'm going to have to deputize Millie. She knows too much," said Nathan, and the two men laughed.

"He only thought he got away," said Nathan. "Deputies from Topeka will be bringing him back to Chanute on Tuesday."

"That's good news, Nathan. Now, what can I do for you?" asked the judge.

For the next half hour, Nathan briefed Judge Stephens on events of the past couple days, and also told him about finding the KKK logbook and roster of the chapter members.

"I don't want to lose this case, Rodney. So, I wanted to check in with you," said Nathan. "From what I've told you, what do you think our chances are in convicting Crenshaw?"

"You can never tell what a jury will do, Nathan, as you know. But, for crying out loud, I think you've got Crenshaw on a serving platter for a jury," said the judge. "Stealing folks' hard-earned money from his bank probably sealed the case. I would also like to be around to hear what the bank examiners find next week. It wouldn't surprise me if we find out that he had been robbing the bank by embezzlement for a long time."

"Wouldn't surprise me either," said Nathan.

"Speaking of juries, and I was, about a minute ago, I would bet that potential jurists will be lined up around the block to serve on that jury. Good guess that there isn't a man in this town who wouldn't like to see Crenshaw strung up."

True to form, Millie entered the room and sat two steaming mugs of coffee in front of the two men.

"Hey Millie. Did Espie tell you what time Crenshaw's train comes in on Tuesday?" asked Nathan.

Millie's face got red, but in her firmest voice, she replied, "Marshal, I just don't know what you're talking about." Just as quickly as she came in, Millie left the room to the sound of the two men laughing.

"Now, now, Nathan. You need to let Millie alone," said the judge. "After all, she's better than my telephone about giving me the latest information."

"Rodney, I need to ask you another question. Do you remember about that Prairie Trust we talked about?" asked Nathan.

"Sure, I remember. That trust will probably become null and void if Crenshaw gets put to death."

"Well, that's what I wanted to know about. If Crenshaw has no relatives and both trustees are dead, what happens to that land that he owned in the trust?" asked Nathan.

"Well, if we assume that he hasn't named a beneficiary in a will someplace, the land would probably go into probate. And if there are no heirs, or beneficiaries, that land would probably go to the state of Kansas," said the judge.

"What does the state of Kansas want with ranch land?" asked Nathan.

"Well, actually, they don't really want it. So most likely after it is determined that there are no living relatives, the land would go up for sale. We won't know for sure until the estate is settled. Why do you ask, Nathan?"

"I was thinking that maybe that property could be purchased and then be split up between the Summers, Morgans, and Chambers families. Seems fair to me since Crenshaw caused grief to all of those families," said Nathan.

"Well, that could happen, Marshal, and it would be a good use of the land. But, we won't know for certain what will happen until the will is read, or not found. Time will tell," said the judge.

Nathan stood up, leaned over and shook the judge's hand. "Always good to talk to you, Rodney. I'm mighty glad to have someone to hash over ideas with. I need to be heading home. It's been a mighty long day. I'll probably see you Monday. I 'spect the whole town will turn out to see Crenshaw get off the train on Tuesday."

"You may be right, Nathan. And a whole bunch of those folks will want to string Crenshaw up right then and there. You might want to take some extra precautions to keep that from happening. I'll look for you on Monday," said the judge.

As Nathan kept Wander at a fast walk toward Summer Prairie Ranch, he went over the past few days' events in his mind. They had been long days, but justice was much closer to being served. He hoped that the outcome would relieve Meezie and Daniel Chambers of a long-standing burden. And then his thoughts were interrupted by a gnawing in his stomach, and he thought of Rosa's cooking, wondering what she would have for supper, and then thinking how nice it would be to sleep in his own bed. Unfortunately, with his daydreams, he was not paying close enough attention to the whims of Wander, and the horse strayed from the road. Nathan pulled him back on course, but as he did so, Wander stepped in an unseen ground hog hole, and as the horse quickly brought his leg out of the hole, he caught the edge of the shoe on the opening of the burrow and pulled the already-loose shoe off of the hoof. It flew in the air and landed on the road with a thud.

Dammit, thought Nathan. That shoe must have been loose, but this stupid horse has done it to me again. He quickly recovered and realized that it was not the horse's fault necessarily that he dropped a shoe.

Nathan dismounted and picked up Wander's hoof. He then saw the crack in the hoof wall. He cursed aloud. He was now hesitant to put his weight on the horse and risk further damaging the hoof. Looks like I'm walking, he thought, and he started out striding to cover the two miles remaining to get home.

Later, Nathan walked up to the corral at the Summer Prairie Ranch and led Wander into the corral. He unsaddled the horse and stowed all of his gear in the barn. The ranch foreman was in the barn, and Nathan asked him to tend to Wander's hoof and re-shoe the hoof.

"Might as well check the other three feet, and make sure that the others aren't loose," said Nathan.

"I'll get one of the hands on it right away, Nathan," said the foreman.

Nathan was hungry and bone tired as he walked through the door of the ranch house.

Claire May saw him come in, and squealed in delight, ran to him, and kissed him. Nathan suddenly felt better.

"How soon 'til supper?" he asked.

Claire May faux pouted. "Always thinking of your stomach instead of me," she teased.

Nathan kissed her again. "Well, not always, sweetheart. But right now, I'm really hungry."

"Go get yourself cleaned up," she said. "Supper will be in about an hour."

Later, after filling the bathtub with warm water, Nathan sank into the bliss of a bath. He was unwinding, letting his mind wander and thinking that maybe he could just stay in the warm water and take a nap, but he was interrupted in his thoughts by Claire May coming into the bathroom. She was carrying his shaving mug, soap, and razor.

"Soap up your face, sweetie, and I'll give you a shave," said Claire May.

"Are you any good with that razor?" Nathan asked teasingly.

"Oh, you'll find out, Marshal, you'll find out," she answered. "I might let you keep the mustache, but the beard has to go. It makes you look too old."

Nathan lathered his face and held it close to the side of the tub so that Claire May could work on the stubble. It turned out that she was fast and did a good job on the shave. When she was done, she kissed him long and passionately. "I do like a man with a smooth face," she cooed. "I'm not sure yet about the mustache, but I'll leave it for now. She got up from the floor by the tub and was going to leave. She turned and said, "Hurry up and get dressed, so we can talk while you have a bourbon with Will before supper." She quickly walked out the door.

Later, Virginia, Will, Claire May, and Nathan sat on the front porch talking as they waited for Rosa to finish preparing supper. In that time, Nathan told them everything that had happened in town. As he finished talking, the bourbon worked its effect on a very tired man. Nathan fell asleep in his chair. The others let him sleep until Rosa came and summoned them. Claire May roused him, saying, "Come on sleepyhead. It's time for supper."

*****

Sunday

Repeating a thought that he had had several times before, Nathan knew it was a great way to wake up. Claire May lay on his stomach in the suit she was born in. She rolled off of him and sighed, snuggling up against him. He ran his hand slowly up and down on her tummy, feeling the small expansion in its size. The baby was growing, and Nathan could not help but wonder about the miracle of another human being growing inside Claire May. He thought it was going to be a wondrous thing to be a father. He reached his head down and kissed his wife.

"I'm hungry," he said.

Claire May raised up on her elbow and slapped him playfully. "Always thinking about your stomach," she said.

Nathan chuckled and pulled her on top of him again. "Not always, Claire May. Not always," he said as he pulled her even closer.

After breakfast and three hot mugs of coffee, Nathan went with Will to finish some chores. With the help of several ranch hands, they made repairs to the damage to the house, the barn, and the bunk house as a result of Friday night's gun battle. The holes in the clapboard siding of the house would need to be sealed with daubing, a mixture of soil, sand, and lime. One of the ranch hands would be sent to town in the next couple days to purchase the lime, along with new glass panes for the windows, and some lumber.

"I guess we've done all the repairs we can for the time being," said Will. "Let's head to the pump and wash up for dinner. I'm thinking we'll take the afternoon off and go fishing. What do you say?"

Nathan was thinking that a nap would be better, but he was also curious about where Will was going to fish. "Sounds good to me," he said.

Alice Morgan had ridden over from the Circle M to see Will, and the women were chattering in the kitchen when the men came into the house. Later, after dinner, the two couples broke out fishing poles, stringer, and a half loaf of bread, and walked to the closest ranch water tank. The pond was a bit low with the lack of recent rain.

"This is my favorite tank," said Will. "It's the largest one on the ranch and has some great catfish and a few bass in it." He showed Nathan how to make a dough ball from the bread and thread it on the hook.

"The bass are a bit finicky and won't bite on the bread very often. But the catfish love it, and when we catch the first cat, we'll cut it up for bait. The bass will bite on the fish bits."

Nathan was not a fisherman by any stretch of the imagination. And though he only caught one keeper, he enjoyed the day immensely. Just being around Will, Alice, and Claire May made him happy. Later, tired and a bit sun burned, the couples walked back to the house with Will carrying the stringer of catfish and bass. Rosa would fry them up for supper with cornbread, grits, and canned green beans.

After supper, Nathan pulled Will aside, and they went out on the front porch.

"What's on your mind, Nathan?"

"Will, I'm worried about what the town's folks are going to want to do with Crenshaw when he gets here on Tuesday."

"Yeah, I'm sure some of them have a bone to pick with him. Hell, even I would like to beat the stuffing out of him," said Will. "After all, he made off with our ranch's money when he robbed the bank."

"Well, if you take your attitude and figure that maybe a hundred folks in town feel the same way, I am afraid that they might decide that they can take the law into their own hands and even the score by stringing Crenshaw up," said Nathan.

Will sat thinking about that scenario for a moment. "You know, Nathan, you could get yourself killed in the middle of that mess. What are you going to do about it?"

"I've got a plan, Will. The trouble is, I need your help along with Dave Morgan's to carry it out. I can't help you when the time comes, and I'll explain why in a minute," said Nathan. At the end of an hour, the two men had worked out a way to keep peace in Chanute upon the arrival of the outlaw, Arthur Crenshaw.

*****

Monday Morning

At six thirty a.m., Nathan had kissed Claire May good-bye and was heading back to town. Light cumulus clouds scudded across a brightening blue sky. Nathan was feeling good after a bacon and egg breakfast and the review with Will at breakfast on his role in bringing

Crenshaw to trial. As he neared town, he had to stop at Judge Stephens' house. He would bring the judge into the plan in preparation for Crenshaw's return.

How in the hell does she do that, thought Nathan as Millie stood holding the door open for him. "Morning, Marshal," she said, smiling.

"Morning yourself, Millie. I guess the judge is up?"

"He's up and had his breakfast. You know where to find him," said Millie.

Nathan entered Rodney Stephens' office and shook hands with the judge. "I swear that Millie must have some kind of homing pigeon flying around following me. She seems to know ahead of time when I am coming up the front walk."

The judge laughed. "No, she's not magic. If you look in the kitchen, she has a window that looks out at the road. She can see anybody coming into or leaving town. That's how she keeps me posted on the comings and goings of Chanute," he said. "Speaking of comings and goings, when is your prisoner coming to town?"

"Well, that's what I came to talk to you about. Remember when you told me that I might want to think about a bit more security when that sidewinder comes back?"

"Sure, I remember," said the judge.

"I've given this some thought, and I have a plan. But I'm going to need your help with some of the details," said Nathan.

Nathan then went on to tell the judge his plan and received approval for his help in keeping the peace when the outlaw arrived.

"I think that will work, Nathan. Once the trial gets underway, the crowd will lose its lust for blood and let the law work the case. I don't think there's much doubt that Crenshaw will see the hangman, but I'm with you in wanting the law to take care of that gruesome detail rather than an angry crowd."

"In that case, I need to use your telephone. I need to talk to the U.S. Marshal in Topeka," said Nathan.

The judge put the call through, and Nathan talked to his counterpart in Topeka. After explaining the plan twice to the other Marshal, Nathan was sure that the Topeka lawman knew his role. He agreed to take part.

After Nathan hung up the phone, Judge Stephens said, "I will start to get a jury pool together and have the attorneys work on whittling the jury down to twelve. That will all have to be done by tomorrow evening. Guess I had better get to work," said the judge. He wrote down two names on a piece of paper and handed it to Nathan. Nathan looked at the names. He knew both of the attorneys.

"Do me a favor on your way to the office. Stop by those fellas' offices and tell them to hot-foot it up here to see me right now," said Stephens.

"Will do," said Nathan. "The bank examiner is coming into town today at eleven a.m. It will be interesting to find out how Crenshaw managed the Prairie Bank. I'll probably get hung up with him for most of the afternoon. I'll talk with you later." Nathan grabbed his hat and left Stephens' house. He trotted Wander to the Livery Stable and handed the reins to Ed Mullins.

"Morning Marshal. Will you need your horse this afternoon?" asked Ed.

"I don't think so, Ed. I'll be staying in town tonight," said Nathan.

Surprisingly, Ed Mullins did not ask about Crenshaw, but as Nathan walked back to his office, several of the town folks asked him if Crenshaw was coming back to town. Nathan gave the same answer to all of them. "Yes, he's coming back to stand trial, but I don't know when that will be." He figured he was telling them the truth, since he did not know for certain the exact time when Crenshaw would make an appearance.

Nathan stopped at the two attorneys' offices on his way to his office. He had to chuckle as he watched the two men immediately drop what they were doing, grab their coats, and begin trotting up the street toward Rodney Stephens' house. Normally, an attorney would not be summoned to a judge's house unless there was something big in the wind. Therefore, in all likelihood, both of the men knew they were being summoned to serve as attorneys in the Crenshaw case, the biggest case that the city would hear in years. One of the two attorneys would serve as prosecutor and the other as Crenshaw's defense attorney. Unless he was clambering for the limelight's notoriety, there was not a lawyer in the city who would want to defend Crenshaw, so Judge Stephens figured that he would appoint an attorney and pay him from county funds, thereby ensuring that Crenshaw had adequate representation. Judge Stephens, of course, would be hearing the case with a twelve-person jury panel.

Later that morning, Judge Stephens could be seen walking down the street with the two attorneys. As they passed their respective offices, the attorneys stopped to pick up the necessary paperwork, supplies, and applicable law books, then quickly entered the courthouse where the judge was waiting. They were making all preparations for picking a jury. Oddly, by word of mouth, news was soon circulated that Judge Stephens was going to pick a jury for the Crenshaw trial. Stephens' words to Nathan were prophetic, as very soon a line of hopeful jurors wound around the base of the courthouse. Nathan and Bill were both armed as they stood in the shade of an oak tree, watching the potential jurors file in and out of the courthouse. The difficulty in picking a jury, of course, was the notoriety of Crenshaw and his misdeeds, and the fact that he was known by everyone in town, making it difficult for the defense attorney to find the appropriate number of open-minded jurors. As a result, it would take nearly four hours before the jury and alternates were selected. When the judge and the attorneys had completed their work, a bailiff came to the door of the courthouse and advised the crowd that they could go home. A jury had been selected.

After jury selection was completed, Nathan and Bill entered the courthouse and went into the court room where the judge and the attorneys were gathering up their belongings to leave.

"Is there anything you need from us, Judge?" asked Nathan.

"No, I guess not, Marshal. Keep me posted on the disposition of the accused so that I can set the court date," said Stephens. "For you two attorneys, I will tell you that this trial will take place before the week is over. I figure that you have ample time to prepare. For the defense, you will have access to the accused for a full twenty-four hours. That is all I will say at this time." The two attorneys looked at each other. A look of worry and concern crossed their faces. They were wondering what they had gotten themselves into.

"We will talk with you later, Judge," said Nathan, and the two lawmen left the room.

In truth, if all went according to plan, Judge Stephens knew exactly when the trial would be held. But neither he nor Nathan wanted to tell the two attorneys. The fewer people who knew the details of the upcoming trial, the easier it would be to carry out their plan. The prosecuting attorney would start immediately to gather witnesses for the prosecution. With Crenshaw's nefarious KKK cohorts all deceased, the defending attorney had only Crenshaw, and possibly his housekeeper, to testify for his defense. He knew he had been asked to defend a lost cause, but he would still attempt to do his best to remain professional under the circumstances.

*****

In typical railroad fashion, the eleven o'clock train from Kansas City via Topeka was right on time. Nathan could not help noticing that there were an unusually large number of folks standing on the platform. He was sure that there were curious people among them who hoped that Crenshaw might be on the arriving train. Nathan paid no attention to them, and instead, was carefully looking at each passenger as they stepped to the platform. He dismissed all the passengers until he saw a somewhat portly man wearing a derby hat, dark suit, glasses, and carrying a rather large leather satchel. Nathan figured this was the bank examiner and walked over to introduce himself. After he told the man his name, the man responded.

"Warren Franks, Marshal. I'm a Federal Bank Examiner from Kansas City. I'm certain you know why I'm here," he said.

"I'll take you over to the bank, Franks," said Nathan.

"Wait just a minute, Marshal. I've got to go back on the train. I have another bag to retrieve," said Franks.

Nathan watched as the bank man climbed back up into the passenger car. But his eyes wandered when he saw two more men step to the platform. They were dressed in cheap suits. Frayed collars and scuffed shoes revealed that the men were not gentlemen. They were stockily built and had vacant stares as they looked around the small crowd. Seemingly satisfied, they walked through the depot and out onto the street. Nathan knew as soon as he saw them that they were criminals of some sort. The hair on his neck tickled. Those two would bear further investigation.

No sooner had they disappeared than another man came out of the rail car. He was taller and thinner than the first two and wore a gray suit, a bowler hat, and carried a small suitcase. He, too, looked around the crowd, then looked through the doorway of the depot to see the previous two men as they walked out onto the street. He was walking slowly toward the depot as if to follow the two men, but then looked over at Nathan. He changed course and walked slowly toward Nathan, looking intently at Nathan's badge as he walked. When he got to Nathan, he said, "Are you Marshal Wolf?"

"I am, sir," Nathan answered. "But I believe you have me at a disadvantage."

The stranger stuck out his hand. "Sorry. My name's Rath, Charles Rath." He pulled a badge and identification wallet from his pocket and showed them to Nathan.

"Pinkerton man, eh," said Nathan.

"Yes sir," Rath answered. "I need to go with you to somewhere we can talk."

"We can go over to my office, Rath, but I need to wait here for a federal bank examiner and take him over to one of our banks." As Nathan finished speaking, Warren Franks stepped to the platform and walked toward Nathan.

"Hmm, I understand," said Rath. "I'll go on over to your office and wait for you." Rath then turned and walked through the depot.

The second bag that Warren Franks had brought over to Nathan was as big as the first one that he had. Nathan could not help but wonder why a bank examiner would need so much luggage.

"Can I help you carry one of those?" Nathan asked.

"I have a rather unpleasant back, Marshal. Would you mind picking both of these up for me?"

"You want me to carry both your bags?" Nathan asked incredulously.

"If you would be so kind, sir," said Franks. He turned slightly as if to walk away.

Nathan bent and lifted the two bags, and then quickly set them back down due to their surprising weight. "Franks, which of these two bags do you need at the bank?" Nathan asked.

Franks turned back. "Oh, the lighter colored one I will need at the bank. The other bag can go to the Wheatfield Hotel, if you would be so kind."

Nathan was ready to slap the pompous bank man but decided that he would walk away without giving the man a piece of his mind. What an arrogant twit, thought Nathan.

Nathan looked around the train platform, saw who he was looking for, and whistled. The black porter came quickly. "Yes sir. What can I do for you?"

"This fella here, is Mr. Franks. He needs you to take this bag to the Wheatfield Hotel, and this bag to the Prairie Bank. He will walk along with you and pay you for your services. Isn't that right, Mr. Franks?" asked Nathan.

"Hmmph. I suppose so," said Franks, who was relegated to having to pay for having his bags toted by the porter.

Nathan watched the man walk away with the straining porter carrying his two bags. Nathan thought that he would check in with Franks at the bank later. But now, he walked out of the depot and headed to his office. As he arrived, he could see that Bill and the Pinkerton man were getting along well. When Bill saw Nathan coming in the door, he poured a third mug of coffee and sat back down at the small table.

"I suppose you wonder why I'm here, Marshal," said Rath.

"To tell you the truth, Mr. Rath, I figure it has something to do with the two hooligans that got off the train about the same time you did. But I am wondering how you knew my name," said Nathan.

"And you would be correct, Marshal. Those two thugs, or hooligans as you called them, are Ku Klux Klan heavies out of Kansas City," said Rath. "Those two men have been involved in all sorts of crimes, but we just can't seem to catch them in the act or get enough evidence together to put them away. The only reason I know your name is that we check ahead of time to see who the lawmen are in the location we are going to when following a case."

Rath continued, "Anyway, it seems that our state attorney general is a buddy of the Federal Attorney General, and the Washington fellow wants to put a lid on the KKK and all their crimes once and for all. So, Pinkerton has a contract to assist in making that happen, and that's why I've been following those two characters for nearly a month up in Kansas City. Now, they've up and come down here. We don't know why, but that's what I'm going to find out. Have you got any idea why they might be here, Marshal?"

Nathan looked at Bill, and both men smiled slightly. "Oh, yeah," said Nathan, "We've got an idea."

Nathan went on to tell the Pinkerton man the whole story of Arthur Crenshaw and the local KKK chapter, the members who had all been killed in a gun battle with local ranchers and the lawmen, except for Arthur Crenshaw. He also let the Pinkerton man know that Crenshaw was charged with several major crimes and would be returning to Chanute for trial in the near future.

"Ooowee," said Rath. "Sounds like you boys have been mighty busy down here. Wonder how come all of that didn't make it to the Kansas City papers."

Bill laughed aloud. "Probably because we have been without a paper for several days. It seems that our local newspaper man was also a member of the Klan. Kinda hard to run a newspaper and wire service when you're pushing up daisies."

"Hmm," said Rath. "Guess that would explain it. Marshal, you said you might have an idea about why..." Rath stopped in mid-sentence and paused. "Only two reasons why those thugs would come here, isn't there?" he said.

"You got it, Rath. They are here to either kill Crenshaw for fouling up the whole KKK operation in these parts, and they don't want him to talk, or they are going to try to spring him from jail and drag him up to Kansas City to face his KKK bosses," said Nathan.

Just then, the men were interrupted by the office door opening quickly. In the doorway stood the heavy breathing, portly, Mr. Warren Franks, the bank examiner, who blurted out, "Marshal, you've got to do something. I can't complete my work under these conditions." His face was florid, and he continued to breath heavily.

"What's your problem, Mr. Franks?" asked Nathan.

"Why, Marshal, there are people standing around in the bank asking me questions, there are papers strewn all over the bank, the place is so dirty it's just a mess, and I could barely find the ledger books in all the upheaval," said Franks.

"Franks, what do you want me to do about all of that?" asked Nathan.

"Why, I want you to come down to the bank and help me. I need you to stand guard and pick up the trash and help me find things, and shoo all those people out of the building," said Franks. "I simply cannot work under these conditions."

Both Bill and Rath sat staring at the bank examiner with their mouths open. Nathan had reached the end of his patience with this petulant, pompous man. "Mr. Franks, what is your job?" asked Nathan.

Puffing himself up, Franks answered, "Why, I'm a Federal Bank Examiner, Marshal. You know that."

"And what does a bank examiner do, Mr. Franks?" asked Nathan.

"I think you know what a bank examiner does, Marshal. I'm here to look at the books of a failed bank, find out why the bank failed, and make restitution to the depositors if it can be done."

Nathan stood up and walked over to face Franks. "Sounds to me like you know what a bank examiner is supposed to do, Mr. Franks. Therefore, I would suggest that you go back down to Prairie Bank and do your job. Take charge of the situation. Shoo those people out of the bank, pick up all the papers, and get on with the business of examining the books." Nathan continued, "Mr. Franks, I don't want to send a wire to your office and tell your boss that you are incompetent, now, do I?"

"Incompetent? I am most certainly not incompetent, Marshal. I think you are being extremely rude, and I may report you to my supervisor," said Franks.

"Mr. Franks, you report me to whomever you want to. In the meantime, get the hell out of my office and go do your job." Nathan then grabbed Franks by his shoulders, spun him around, and shoved him out the door.

Nathan sat back down at the table and took a gulp of his coffee. "As if I don't have enough problems," he said.

After taking a sip of his own coffee, the Pinkerton man asked, "Are you at liberty to tell me when this Crenshaw fella is going to be back in town?"

Nathan was not quite ready to reveal that answer to Rath. "It's still a little bit of an unknown," said Nathan, "but I figure he'll be here in time for his trial."

The men finished their coffee. "I don't know about you boys, but I'm hungry," said Nathan, "and I'm going to the cafe for dinner if you want to come along."

As the lawmen sat down at the cafe, Nathan looked around and saw the two KKK men sitting in the corner of the dining room. They were looking back at the three lawmen, but quickly looked down at their plates in front of them. The lawmen finished their dinners and were preparing to leave. But Nathan quietly told Bill and Rath to stay seated.

Quietly, Nathan said to Bill and Rath, "Don't you think it's a bit odd that those two haven't left yet? I have a strange feeling that they might just be waiting for us to step outside. What do you think?"

"Knowing those two like I do, I have to agree with you Marshal," said Rath.

Both Bill and Nathan were wearing side arms. Nathan asked, "Rath, are you armed?"

Rath tapped his suit coat on its left front side. "Yes, sir, always," he answered.

Nathan turned to Bill. "Go on and slip out the back door, Bill, like you are heading to the outhouse in the alley. Rath and I will wait here for another ten minutes before we come out. You come around the side of the building and cover me and Rath as we come out and head back to the office. I'm betting those two snakes are going to make a move on us when we get outside."

"OK, boss," said Bill. He stood, laid some coins on the table and made a point to say loudly enough to be overheard, "I'll see you back at the office." He then walked back to the rear of the cafe and slipped out the back door. In a few minutes, both Rath and Nathan stood, paid their bills, and walked out of the cafe. Nathan could see out of the corner of his eye that the two outlaws were now standing at their table.

Nathan and Rath began walking slowly toward the office. "You've got a lot of faith in your deputy, Marshal. Sure hope we don't get a slug in the back," said Rath.

No sooner had he spoken than they heard Bill's voice, "Don't try it mister unless you have a death wish."

Nathan and Rath both spun around drawing their pistols as they turned and saw one of the outlaws with his hand inside his coat.

"Pull that hand out real slow, mister," said Nathan. The outlaw did as he was told. "Now put your hands up on top of your head."

Both outlaws now had their hands clasped on top of their hats. "Go get their guns, Rath," said Nathan.

"Glad to, Marshal."

Rath put his gun back in its shoulder holster and walked toward the two men. He was savvy enough that he walked to the outlaws, staying out of Nathan's line of fire. But as he began to reach into the coat of the first outlaw, the man grabbed Rath, turning him and holding him in front of himself. He had drawn his gun and held it up against Rath's head. "Call off your deputy, Marshal, or I plug this Pinkerton cop."

Nathan's mind was racing. The other outlaw had also drawn his gun from beneath his coat. How could he tell Bill what to do without having Rath get shot and probably get himself shot as well? He hoped Bill understood when he called out, "Bill, this looks like another telegraph office problem. Guess we better do what the man asks."

Bill knew exactly what Nathan meant. It was another of those 'shoot first, ask questions later' situations. He took a breath, held it, and took careful aim. The shot from Bill's gun ran true and entered the back of the head of the outlaw holding Rath. The man's head jerked forward, and he began to slump to the ground.

The shot startled the second outlaw, and he looked at his cohort. When he did that, Nathan raised his pistol and held it aimed at the outlaw. When the man turned back to face Nathan, he could see the black hole of Nathan's gun barrel pointing directly at him.

Nathan shouted, "Don't try it mister. If I don't get you, my deputy will. You don't want to look like your friend. Now drop your gun and put your hands back up."

The outlaw looked down at the gruesome remains of his fellow enforcer. Deciding that he, indeed, did not want to suffer the same fate as his partner, he slowly dropped the gun and put his hands on his head.

Rath had drawn his pistol again and cautiously kicked the outlaw's pistol away from the feet of the outlaw, then reached down and picked it up.

"Bill, guess you better go down and get the undertaker while Rath and I take this fella over to the jail," said Nathan.

"All right," said Bill. "I'll be back in a few minutes."

At the office, Rath kept the outlaw covered.

"Take your hat and coat off, mister," said Nathan. The outlaw complied. "Now your shoes." Again, the outlaw kicked off his shoes. "Now the trousers," said Nathan.

"What? I ain't taking off my pants for you, clod buster," said the outlaw.

Nathan took one step closer to the man and slammed his blackjack into the side of the man's head. The outlaw reeled backwards.

"If you want some more of that, just keep yapping. Now get the pants off," said Nathan. After he had the outlaw's trousers, he went through the pockets. He threw the contents on the table, but held the medallion in his hand. Then he spun it on the table where it turned for a few seconds and then fell flat to reveal the triangle symbol of the Ku Klux Klan.

The outlaw was now in his union suit, socks, and a shirt. "Shirt off, mister," said Nathan.

The outlaw hesitated, but then thought better of it and removed his shirt. "Now lay down on the floor on your belly. Rath, just keep your pistol aimed at this sidewinder's head."

The outlaw laid on his stomach, while Nathan thoroughly frisked him. Rath did not understand why the Marshal was being so thorough, but soon saw Nathan push up the ankle cuff of the union suit to reveal a stiletto in a thin leather sheath on the man's ankle. Nathan removed the knife in its sheath and finished frisking the man.

"Sit down at that table, mister," said Nathan. "We're all going to have a little talk."

Bill came in the office door then and Nathan said, "Bill, keep your eye on the door. I don't want any visitors."

Bill knew what that meant and moved one of the chairs to where he could watch the door and at the same time make sure that the outlaw didn't try anything stupid.

"All right, mister. We can do this the easy way or the hard way," said Nathan.

The outlaw was pretty sure he knew what the hard way was, as the side of his head was burning with hot pain. But he had to test Nathan again.

Nathan began questioning the man. "Tell me what a big tough guy like you from Kansas City is doing down here in my territory."

"I ain't telling you nothing. You might be a big man in your little town, but you don't mean diddly to me," said the outlaw.

"All right, I asked you nice. Now I'm asking you again. What are you doing here, tough guy?" asked Nathan.

With a sneer on his face the outlaw said, "Go to ......" He did not finish the sentence as Nathan's blackjack struck him across the mouth and nose. Blood began flowing from the man's nose, and he reached up to his mouth and gingerly wiggled a front tooth.

"You want more? Or are you going to talk to us?" asked Nathan.

The outlaw put both his hands on the table and glared at Nathan, but said nothing.

Nathan turned to Rath, "Mr. Rath, I don't think this man wants to talk to us. And we've been very nice to him up to now. What do you think we should do?"

"I say we put a bullet in him and hand him to the undertaker," said Rath.

The outlaw had turned to look at Rath, but said nothing.

Nathan's blackjack went to work again, this time breaking two of the man's fingers that had been on the table as it slapped the top of them. The outlaw screamed in pain, holding his maimed hand with his other hand.

"Mister, I am losing my patience with you," said Nathan. "Now tell me why you are here."

The outlaw held his hand as he looked down at the table. Blood from his nose dripped into his lap. In a very quiet voice, he said, "I was sent to kill Crenshaw."

"Now, that wasn't all that difficult was it?" said Nathan. "You see, I already knew that, but I wanted to hear it from you. Now I only have one more question. What is the name of the man in Kansas City who sent you?"

The outlaw physically lurched, as if he had received a jolt of lightning. Nathan's question was obviously one that the outlaw held in great significance. Nathan may not have known it, but he had just asked the outlaw whether he wanted to die at the hands of the law, or at the hands of the KKK. The outlaw knew that if he gave up the name of his handler, he would be killed by the KKK.

Before either the outlaw or Nathan could speak again, Rath spoke up. "Marshal, this fella doesn't need to tell us who sent him. I already know that. You see, we have been watching an esteemed judge up in Kansas City for months. We know that he is the head of the KKK up there. And, we have seen this fellow and his dead cohort almost living at the judge's house in Kansas City. Judge Epperson sent you, didn't he, boy."

Again, it was as if the outlaw had received a jolt. His eyes grew wide and he blurted out to Rath. "I didn't tell you that. You've got to make them understand that I didn't blab."

"I don't have to do a damn thing you want me to do, mister," said Rath. "And after Crenshaw's trial, you're going back up to Kansas City to have your own trial for attempted murder. Maybe we can even arrange to have Judge Epperson preside at your trial. Wouldn't that be something. You'd be a dead man walking, wouldn't you?"

"You're a regular funny man, aren't you Pinkerton," sneered the outlaw.

Nathan grabbed the man by the upper arm and began walking him back to the cells. "I've got a surprise for you. A couple cells down is Crenshaw's girlfriend. You two should have a lot to talk about."

When Nathan returned, Rath said, "I think I'd better go down to your telegraph office and let my boss know what happened here today. I figure I can bunk in your jail with you tonight if that's all right."

"Fine with me, Rath. Somebody to play Hearts with," said Nathan. "Penny a point if you can afford it."

Bill had watched the jail as Nathan and Charles Rath went to supper. He went home when they returned. Later, the two men sat at the table and played cards, chatting about nothing in particular. Two short glasses were in front of them, and the bourbon bottle sat at the side. The men goaded each other as they played.

"I'm real sorry about that, Marshal," said Rath as he totaled up the score. "Looks like you're gonna owe me fifty cents."

"OK, OK, smart guy. One more hand and then I've got to get some sleep."

*****

Tuesday Morning

Nathan was trying to fully wake up as he looked at his image in the cloudy mirror at the back of the office, working the shaving brush in the shaving mug. He lathered his face and then heard the front door open. He recognized Bill and Espie's voices. He hurried and finished his shave and put on his shirt. He could smell the coffee steaming on the stove. He glanced into the cells of Crenshaw's housekeeper and the KKK enforcer. They both looked fine as they gloomily watched him pass.

"I thought you could use some biscuits and gravy this morning, Nathan," said Espie. She was setting plates at the table. Rath was watching with rapt attention as she set biscuits on his and Nathan's plates. Apparently, Bill had already eaten at home, as he was content to sit back and watch while sipping his coffee. She had brought biscuits and gravy to the office on other mornings, so Nathan knew he was in for a treat as he watched Espie ladle on the sausage cream gravy. She finished preparing the plates and watched as Nathan and Rath forked up the covered biscuits.

"I have to get back home," said Espie. "I have chores to do." She turned to her husband. "Bill, there's bread and jam in the basket for your prisoners. After everyone is fed, I need you to bring the plates and silverware home in the basket when you come home later. Don't forget," she said. They watched as she hurried out the door.

"Don't forget, Bill," teased Nathan.

"Lord help me if I do," laughed Bill.

After Nathan cleaned his plate, he shoved it away and lifted his coffee mug. "Well, gents, let's hope this is a quiet day. I'm going to go up the street to see Judge Stephens. I'll be back pretty quick. Just want to make sure everything is going all right with him. I would appreciate it if at least one of you stayed here at all times. Never know who might want to pay us a visit. Bill, after you feed the prisoners, why don't you and Charles have a seat on the sidewalk bench outdoors, and you can fill him in on the details of what is going to happen in the next couple days, while I check in with the judge."

As Nathan walked up the street to Judge Stephens' place, he had a plan. He was going to fool Millie this morning. He would sneak around the back of the house and go in the back door. As he neared the judge's house, he kept to the side of the road and then slipped around the back. Got her this time, he thought. But as he was about to turn the knob on the back door, it opened, and there stood Millie.

"You really should use the front door, Marshal. It seems to be a bit demeaning for a U.S. Marshal to be coming to the back door," she said. She shoved a mug of coffee at Nathan. "Here's your coffee. The judge has his in the study," she said, smiling.

He couldn't let her see it, but Nathan was laughing on the inside. Millie had fooled him again. He simply said, "Morning, Millie," and walked to the judge's study.

Rodney Stephens looked away from the paper he was reading, a one-week-old *Kansas City Star*. "Morning Marshal."

"Morning Rodney. I thought I better check in with you and make sure everything was all right," said Nathan.

"As a matter of fact, you missed the phone call I just got from the Marshal up in Topeka. He said he just loaded two of his deputies and Crenshaw on the train. He wanted to let me know they were on their way."

"Everything set in back?" asked Nathan.

"Sure thing," said Stephens. "The tack room is all cleaned out."

Nathan finished his coffee while he briefed the judge on the two outlaws and Pinkerton man, as well as the shooting of the one outlaw.

"Does your life ever slow down, my friend?" asked Stephens.

"I sure as heck hope so, after Crenshaw's trial," replied Nathan. "Guess I'd better get back to the office." The two men shook hands. "See you tonight, Judge."

At a quarter to eleven a.m., Nathan and Charles Rath walked to the rail station. They were not meeting anyone, but the crowd that had gathered did not know that. A couple of folks in the crowd shouted at Nathan.

"Is Crenshaw on this train, Marshal?" Nathan made no attempt to answer and kept quiet. With mild amusement, the two lawmen watched as the steaming, bell-clanging locomotive crawled past them on its track. In a few seconds, a loud screech signaled the application of the train's brakes.

The two lawmen watched as the passengers stepped to the platform. Thankfully, no one caught their attention. But they watched as the crowd craned their necks hoping to get a look at Arthur Crenshaw. The bystanders were disappointed that the train cars had emptied, with no sign of Crenshaw. Nathan and Charles Rath began walking back to the office. At their back, they heard shouts. "Where is he, Marshal? We're going to string him up." There were other shouts, but the lawmen kept walking.

Back in the office, Nathan asked Bill to go to the telegraph office and send a wire. He also asked that Bill send it personally and get the telegraph operator to stand outside while it was sent. In a few minutes, Bill sent the wire. It was addressed to Will Summers at Summer Prairie Ranch. The text was:

Your visitors are coming.

The afternoon at the Marshal's office was spent preparing for the evening. The lawmen were expecting trouble. Shotguns were loaded, as well as their revolvers. Any buckets and containers were filled with water and placed where they could be reached if they were needed. The men waited.

*****

Old Tioga Depot
Tuesday, Late Afternoon

The train had slowed to a crawl, which was followed by the shriek of brakes as the train stopped. A brakeman jumped to the ground and ran to a nearby switch, which he unlocked. He then shoved the switching bar to move the rails. He did not bother to relock the switch, as he knew that he would come back in less than an hour. He waved at the engineer and watched as the train began backing up and approaching him. As the rear cars turned and entered the side spur, the train neared the brakeman, who swung himself back aboard the train. The train, now running in reverse, began to pick up speed.

Aboard the train, a couple of passengers had watched with interest as the train made the change in direction. Two of the passengers confronted the conductor.

"What is the meaning of this? Why have we left the main line?" they asked.

"I can't really tell you, mister," said the conductor. "All I know is that we are taking a short run down this spur, and then we will come back and proceed on down to Chanute. It should not take that long, so please be patient."

The conductor's words, while reassuring, did not completely satisfy the tempers of all the passengers, as several of them continued to grumble. But, they were also curious to see what this was all about. However, not everyone was curious. The two stoic men wearing badges and sitting on each side of Arthur Crenshaw were not curious. They knew exactly what was happening.

Several minutes passed before the train began to slow again. It finally stopped when the last two cars came abreast of a dilapidated building with a worn and weathered sign that read, *Tioga Depot*. Passengers now were able to look out the windows to see seven men dressed in the clothes of ranch hands standing on the platform of the old depot. A group of horses was tied to the hitch rack at the side of the building. Passengers continued to watch as the two Deputy Marshals led their handcuffed charge from the train to join the group of men on the platform. The train engineer gave a short whistle, and the train began moving forward again to reach the main line.

Will watched as the deputies brought Crenshaw over to his group. He thought that Crenshaw's appearance had changed. He no longer looked as if he was in charge of his surroundings. In fact, Crenshaw's face was wan, and he continued to look down at the ground. His demeanor was that of a disheartened man.

Will introduced himself to the deputies, and then introduced his ranch hands, all of whom were armed. "Good of you to meet us, Mr. Summers," said a deputy. "Looks like we will be with you for a while. Our instructions are that at least one of us has to remain with this turkey at all times. Are your boys willing to help us out?"

Will confirmed that his hands would also be watching Crenshaw along with the deputies. He and Nathan had decided that four ranch hands would stay with the outlaw, as he was going to be held temporarily at the Summer Prairie bunk house. Will pointed out the extra horses he and the hands had brought with them, and all the men were soon mounted. It was a long ride from the depot to the ranch, but Will knew the route well. By late afternoon, Crenshaw was safely hand-cuffed to a steel framed bunk in the bunkhouse of the ranch with round-the-clock guards watching him. He wasn't going anywhere.

*****

Tuesday Night in Chanute

At midnight, Charles Rath, the Pinkerton man, was awake and keeping watch. Bill and Nathan were in cell bunks trying to get some sleep over the snoring of the KKK enforcer prisoner. His smashed nose was obviously making his breathing difficult. Rath yawned. Another hour and he would trade places with Bill. He was having trouble keeping his eyes open, but a flash of light in an otherwise inky dark night caught his eye. It did not go away, and instead seemed to dance in the night. Rath got up from the table and went to the door. He could then see what the light signified. There were several lights, and they were coming down the street toward the Marshal's office. Rath ran back to the cells and shook Bill and then Nathan. "They're coming," was all he said.

It was all he needed to say. Both Bill and Nathan quickly rose and moved to the gun rack. They each picked up a shotgun and broke them to load the 12-gauge shells into the breach. Raft was already back at the front door waiting for Bill and Nathan. The three lawmen went out onto the sidewalk to wait for the mob. They could hear men yelling even before the crowd reached them.

"Lynch him," and "Hang Crenshaw" were repeated over and over. The faces in the crowd now became clearer. Nathan knew several of the participants. Like every lynch mob, this one soon identified a leader from within the group. Nathan thought to himself, look for the loudest and most angry sounding individual, and that will be the chief inciter.

Nathan watched as the red-bearded, burly man came to the front of the crowd and began shouting.

"Get out of the way, Marshal. We aim to get Crenshaw and send him to his grave," said the man.

"I don't believe I know you, mister, but no one is taking Crenshaw anywhere. He isn't here," said Nathan.

"Don't give us that, Marshal. Crenshaw took the last penny I had, and now wants to take my farm away from me," said the man. "Nothing he does is honest, and we're going to see that justice is served."

"Mister, you need to calm down. I've told you Crenshaw isn't here," said Nathan.

The angry man turned back to the crowd. "Are we going to stand here and listen to the lies of the Marshal?" he asked. "Hell no, let's go get Crenshaw." As the man took a step forward, he raised his torch as if to throw it through the front window of the office. But before he could throw, Bill's shotgun blasted buckshot into the flames of the torch the man was carrying. The result was that flaming sparks of cloth and fire went in all directions. The crowd parted and many were seen rapidly dusting the flaming bits from their clothing. The loud shotgun blast and the shower of hot sparks had a sobering effect on the crowd. They became quieter.

"Now you listen to me, mister," said Nathan. "I've told you that Crenshaw is not here. But you won't believe me. So, I want you to go on in my office there and go back to the cells and see if you can find Crenshaw. The rest of us will wait right here."

The man hesitated, as if he was wondering if this was some kind of trick. But then, as if to demonstrate his bluster, he replied, "Damn right I will." He then went into the office. He returned in a few minutes. "He ain't here," he shouted to the crowd, which resulted in the sound of mumbling and quiet talking.

"Where is he?" asked the leader. "We'll go get him."

Nathan pulled his watch from his pocket. "Well, let's see. It's about 1 a.m. I figure he's fast asleep someplace safe from lynch mobs."

Replacing his watch, Nathan said, "So you're not going to get Crenshaw. He is going to stand trial in accordance with the law. Some of your fellow citizens have already been chosen to sit on the jury. It will only be a few days before it starts. So, I suggest that you all just go on home."

Nathan then pointed at the mob's leader. "And as for you, mister, unless you like the looks of our luxurious cells, and before I decide to arrest you for attempting to incite a riot, I would suggest you hot foot it out of here, too. Let the court do its duty. You're not a one-man judge and jury. Now get on out of here before we throw you in a cell to cool down for a couple days."

The crowd slowly and grudgingly dispersed, leaving only a handful of men in the street still talking among themselves. One of the men was seen to throw up his hands and walk away. Soon, the remaining men also left. The mob's leader was with them, and he looked back at the Marshal's office twice as he walked away. The crisis had passed for the time being, and the street was quiet again. Nathan set his shotgun on its butt end on the sidewalk and watched the last of the crowd disappear.

"I don't know about you fellas, but I'm going back and get a couple more hours of sleep," said Nathan, and he turned and walked back into the office. "Your turn to stand watch, Bill."

******

Wednesday

As it happened, the three lawmen would have a chance to catch up on their sleep during the day on Wednesday. It would not get hectic again until late that evening. But the morning found them in the cafe eating breakfast. From where they sat, they could see out the front window with a view of anyone approaching the Marshal's Office. Apparently, having learned that Crenshaw was not being held in the Marshal's jail, the townsfolk were content to wait for further developments.

While they finished their breakfast, they found humor in watching the two appointed attorneys for the Crenshaw trial trotting up the street more than once to Judge Stephens' house and back again to their respective offices.

"Ever think you might like to be a lawyer, Charles?" Nathan asked of the Pinkerton man.

"Not so much, Marshal. I prefer to be on the prosecutorial side of the law. I've seen some real nasty criminals go off scot-free because of crafty lawyers who could convince a jury to jump off a bridge to feel a pleasant breeze in their face as they were falling. That's not for me. At least I've got a steady paycheck, and I like my job," said Rath.

"Not me," said Nathan. "I'm only doing this job because I like Bill's coffee every morning." The men laughed.

"Oh no," Nathan said suddenly. "Trouble is knocking on our door."

Nathan had seen Warren Franks, the bank examiner crossing the street and heading for the Marshal's office.

"Guess I'd better go and see what Franks wants," said Nathan. The lawmen paid their checks and left the cafe. They could see that Franks had entered the office, but then saw him come back out and look both ways up and down the street. He spied Nathan walking toward him and waited on the sidewalk. A ledger book was tucked under his arm.

"Morning, Franks. To what do we owe such a pleasure?" said Nathan facetiously.

The irony was lost completely on Franks. He even smiled, taking the remark as a compliment.

"Good morning Marshal. I have come to tell you that I stayed quite late last night to finish my work," said Franks. "But with all the excitement in the street last night, I thought it best to take a candle and hide in the bank vault until all those people went away. I must say, it was quite frightening, and I will have to report such a disturbing situation to my supervisor."

It was all the three lawmen could do to keep from laughing out loud. After composing himself, Nathan said, "Well, did you finish your examination or not?"

"Oh yes, Marshal. I finished, and I think you will see that my findings are quite extraordinary. Shall we go into your office?" asked Franks.

"Indeed, we shall," answered Nathan. He watched as Franks went back into the office, and while Franks could not see him, Nathan turned, showing a wide grin as he looked at Bill and Charles. They burst out laughing, but Nathan turned back to enter the office with a straight face.

The lawmen filled their coffee mugs from the coffee pot.

"You want a cup of coffee, Mr. Franks?" asked Bill.

"Oh dear, no," answered Franks. "Coffee seems to get my stomach in a whirl, so I must refrain."

"Suit yourself," said Bill, while he filled three mugs.

Warren Franks sat at the table and opened his ledger book. But he hesitated when he looked toward the back of the office and saw the two prisoners in their cells.

"Oh, dear, Marshal. Should those people be allowed to overhear our conversation?" he asked.

"Mr. Franks, it really doesn't matter what those two people hear. They are already charged with other crimes. Therefore, they aren't getting out any time soon. I'm sure what you have to say won't affect them in the least," said Nathan.

"Hmm. Well, I guess I can proceed then," said Franks. "It seems that your bank manager, Mr. Crenshaw was not very honest in his dealings."

"Hang on a second there, Mr. Franks. Arthur Crenshaw was not 'my bank manager.' As far as we're concerned, Crenshaw is just another outlaw that we are going to bring to justice. So, no, he is not 'my manager.'"

"Oh, I beg your pardon. Of course, he's not your manager," said Franks. "It was just a figure of speech. I'll rephrase it; The previous bank manager was not very honest in his dealings."

"Um, hmm," muttered Nathan.

Franks then proceeded to explain to the lawmen that for every transaction that the Prairie Bank carried out, Crenshaw was taking an administrative fee charged to the individual customers. He attempted to hide those fees by placing all the proceeds into the Prairie Trust.

"I was unable to find a ledger book for the Prairie Trust, however," said Franks.

"I believe we have that trust book, Mr. Franks," said Nathan.

"Oh, that's wonderful," said Franks. "May I see it?"

Bill left the table and returned with the green-covered ledger, which he handed to Franks. Franks then compared his ledger book with the trust's book.

"Yes, indeed, the entries match. That certainly is the ledger book for the Prairie Trust." Franks handed the book back to Bill.

"But, just as troubling," said Franks, "was that Mr. Crenshaw was violating federal usury law. He was charging at least one to ten per cent higher interest rates than either the maximum allowed federal or Kansas rate. I believe the term is 'bilking' his customers. For such a small bank, Mr. Crenshaw was making a great deal of money by being less than ethical with his customers. A great many folks owed every-thing they had to that scoundrel."

"It seems that he had a set of financial handcuffs on a whole lot of folks around these parts. I guess that was the source of his control of the members of his KKK group," said Bill.

"That explains how a little runt weasel like Crenshaw could main-tain control. After gaining financial control, all he has to have are a couple of ruthless enforcers to keep everyone in line, and he can run the operation for years without fear of the law," said Nathan.

"Can any of these people get their money back?" asked Rath.

"Oh, yes," said Franks. "Depending upon how much cash he has with him when you catch him, we can adjust the books, return the over-charges and excess interest in an equitable manner that will allow de-positors to establish new accounts with another bank. But, of course, that all hinges on catching Mr. Crenshaw, and whether he has any cash with him."

"Mr. Crenshaw has been caught and is in custody, Mr. Franks," said Nathan. "He had a great deal of money with him when he was caught, and both Crenshaw and the money are being returned to Chanute."

"Oh, that's wonderful," said Franks. "Most of the time when I find a large bank discrepancy, the depositors are never reimbursed because any ill-gotten monies are already gone. And Mr. Crenshaw can be ar-rested for embezzlement and violation of usury law."

"OK, Mr. Franks. We can add those charges to the laundry list we already have on him, and I will inform the prosecuting attorney to plan accordingly. I want to thank you for all your work," said Nathan.

Nathan thought for a moment and then said, "Can you also write up a list of the customers and the money owed to them by the bank so that we can make restitution to the customers as soon as the money is re-turned?"

"Certainly, Marshal. Do you think it would be possible to use the services of Mr. Rath? I know that investigating bank crimes is right up Pinkerton's alley. If I could have him help me write up the list, it would go much faster, and I could have the list ready by the end of the day," he said.

"Charles. You think you could help Franks? I won't need you again until this evening," said Nathan.

"Sure, I reckon," said Rath. "Not sure how much help I will be, but if it means having everything ready for the customers, I'll do what I can."

"Oh, wonderful. Come along, Mr. Rath," said Franks. "We have work to do."

As Franks walked away, Rath quickly turned to Nathan and muttered, "You owe me."

Nathan nodded his head and smiled.

*****

Summer Prairie Ranch
Wednesday, 10 P.M.

The Deputy U.S. Marshal kicked the steel-framed bed in the bunk house at the Summer Prairie Ranch. "Wake up, manure breath," he shouted. "We're going to take you for a little ride."

Crenshaw was suddenly awake. He had been dreaming the same dream again. In the dream, he was at a bawdy house in Kansas City. He had bought the gentlemen's sporting house with the proceeds of his criminal activities. But at the end of the dream, he could hear the voices of all the Chanute citizens that he had swindled. They were shouting, "Lynch him, string him up!" It was always at that point in the dream that he woke up.

Crenshaw had developed a real hatred for the two deputy Marshals. It seemed to him that the two men took every opportunity to belittle him with their constant harassment, not that it wasn't well deserved. But he was now wondering what the meaning was in the deputy's remark about taking a trip. A cold fear swept over him. He feared that this trip would culminate in much the same manner as his dream. He wondered, was he going to be lynched?

Begrudgingly, he rose from the bunk.

"I need to go out back," said Crenshaw.

The deputy followed Crenshaw to the outhouse at the back of the bunk house. With a full moon casting down its light, they could see their way quite clearly. The lawman watched as Crenshaw entered the outhouse and closed the door.

After a few minutes, the deputy called out, "You've been in there long enough, Crenshaw." There was no answer.

"If you don't come out by the time I count to five, I'm coming in to get your sorry carcass," said the lawman. Still, there was no reply.

The deputy pulled the door open, but when he leaned his head through the door, Crenshaw used his full strength to smash his hand-cuffed wrists and hands down on the back of the deputy's neck. Luckily, the Deputy's hat brim had caught a part of the impact, but still, the dazed deputy fell onto the ground. Crenshaw quickly stepped on the deputy's back as he was lying in the open doorway, then jumped onto the ground and began running. His intent was to steal one of the saddled horses he had seen in the corral and make a run for it. As he climbed up on the first rail of the corral, a shot rang out. The bullet struck with a loud thunk sound into the heel of Crenshaw's right boot, tearing the heel from the boot. The force of the bullet striking his boot knocked Crenshaw's leg to the side, and he fell in a heap to the ground outside the corral. He lay on the ground for a moment as the second deputy walked over to the prostrate outlaw. Crenshaw lay in pain on the ground. The impact of the bullet had jarred his right leg; the leg that had been injured many years ago.

"Get up, Crenshaw, before I accidentally miss on my next shot and put you out of your misery for good," said the second deputy. The four ranch hands who had been in the bunk house came running at the sound of the shot, and Will Summers came running from the house. A revolver was in one of his hands. The other held a large carpetbag. When he saw that the deputies had Crenshaw, he holstered the gun and continued walking toward the corral, where he waited for the rest of the group.

The deputy shouted to his partner, who had gotten up from the doorway of the outhouse and was walking up toward them. "This little jackass get the jump on you?" He then laughed.

When the first deputy reached Crenshaw, he threw his fist into Crenshaw's jaw, knocking the outlaw to the ground. "Guess we're even now," said the lawman. Crenshaw remained where he fell, his handcuffed hand rubbing his cheek and jaw.

"Get up, bank man," said the deputy.

Crenshaw got groggily to his feet, and the men entered the corral. The lack of a heel on his right boot gave Crenshaw a lop-sided gait. Crenshaw, who had walked with a slight limp before, now had a pronounced limp as he moved forward. The men's horses had been saddled ahead of time, waiting for their travel. With the help of a deputy, Crenshaw climbed into the saddle of one of the horses. When the rest of the men were mounted, Will opened the corral gate and swung up onto his horse. He put the handle of the carpetbag over his saddle horn.

"Remember men, you can yak on the way to town, but when we get close to town, nobody talks," said Will. "Understood?" A few mumbled "yeses" followed, and the men rode out, a deputy on each side of Crenshaw.

Even before they got close to town, the group stopped. One of the deputies dismounted, walked to the side of Crenshaw's horse, and literally pulled Crenshaw to the ground. He then removed a bandana from his pocket and wrapped it across Crenshaw's eyes and nose. When he was done, he helped Crenshaw back into the saddle.

The deputy then said to Crenshaw, "If you even think about touching that blindfold, I'll knock you clean out of the saddle." He then remounted his horse, and the group went on. Just outside of town, the group stopped again. It was nearly one-thirty a.m. Thursday morning. This time, Will left the group at a fast trot. Within thirty minutes, he returned, having made two stops; first to the Marshal's office, where he rapped on the office door until the door was answered, and then to Judge Stephens' house, where he also rapped on the door until it was answered. Then, he remounted and rode back to the waiting group.

"Everything is ready," said Will. "Let's go." The men then rode at a slow walk so that noise would be kept at a minimum. An hour later, Will and two of his ranch hands rode back out of town to return to the Summer Prairie Ranch. The carpetbag, full of Crenshaw's ill-gotten monies, had been given to Nathan.

Nathan and Charles Rath joined the deputies, the two ranch hands, and Crenshaw who was still blindfolded. They led some of the horses into Judge Stephens' stable. The others were staked out of sight behind the stable. Crenshaw was led to and shoved into the dark, emptied tack room of the stable. Then the lawmen closed and locked the door. The tack room had no other door and no windows. Crenshaw would remain in this darkened room until the start of the trial. He would only see daylight when the defense attorney came to interview him.

When the door slammed on the tack room, Crenshaw cried out, "Can I take the blindfold off?"

Nathan replied, "Yeah, you can take it off."

Crenshaw pulled the bandana down his face, but was dismayed to find that the only light coming into the room was a dim bit of moonlight which came from around the door. He did not know where he was.

"How about taking these handcuffs off," shouted Crenshaw.

"Sorry, Crenshaw. Those bracelets are never coming off except when we're watching you. And you'll be happy to know that you will be nice and safe with four of us here at all times. Get used to the handcuffs," said Nathan.

The lawmen made up a schedule for the men watching the stable. Four men would be there at all times, and all of them would be armed with shotguns or rifles, and pistols. For each shift, a Deputy Marshal or Charles Raft would be with the Summer Prairie ranch hands. Their orders were to not allow anyone except the defense attorney near the stable.

As dawn arrived, Millie was in a dither. Both she and the judge were up, and Millie had just given a mug of coffee to the judge who was sitting at his desk. She now knew that not only would she be looking after the judge, but an extra five men would require feeding. She was standing in front of the judge's desk as she said, "Now Judge, you know I'm not one to complain, but feeding all those men in the back yard is going to be a great deal of extra work. I'm sure you understand that."

She wanted to go on, but before she could continue, Judge Stephens raised his hand, palm out. "Now, now, Millie. Of course, I know that those men require more work. But, I am willing to bet that you will get some help. Now, go on and get my breakfast, please."

Millie stood with her hands on her hips and glared at the judge. *Sometimes he can be so infuriating*, thought Millie. *Where does he think we are going to get the help?* But she also knew that most of the time it was useless to argue with the judge.

She responded, "Hmmph. I swear," she said while shaking her head. "I'll get your breakfast, but I don't know how soon that gang in the back yard can get their vittles," she said as she walked out of the room.

Judge Stephens was still looking up and glanced out the front window. He saw the shadow move across the porch and toward the front door. The judge smiled and quickly jumped up and hurried to the door before anyone could knock. He opened the door to see Espie Ward with her hand raised to rap on the door. The judge signaled silence with his finger to his lips. Espie came into the house, and the judge quietly closed the door. Then he leaned over and whispered in Espie's ear. "Sneak up on Millie in the kitchen. She is going to be so happy to see you," he said.

Espie gave the judge a look of wonderment, but then walked toward the kitchen. The judge stood still, waiting for it, and soon heard Millie's squeal of delight.

"Love it when a plan works," muttered the judge as he went back to his desk to read his papers. Espie would be helping Millie keep up with the demands of the men at the stable.

*****

Thursday, 9 a.m.

The spoon clinked against the porcelain coffee mug as Nathan stirred his coffee at the cafe. An empty plate with streaks of yellow egg-yolk sat in front of him. Ten minutes ago, he and Bill had watched the defense attorney trudge up the street to the judge's house.

"He doesn't look too happy, does he," remarked Bill.

"Hard to be happy when you know you have a losing case," mused Nathan, as he continued stirring his coffee to cool it down. "Wonder how Rodney convinced him to act as defense attorney. I suppose he sold him on how it would be great experience for him."

The two men finished their coffees. Bill rose from the table and said, "I reckon I'd better get up to the judge's and relieve the Pinkerton man. He's gonna need some sleep."

Nathan stopped when he got outside the cafe and said to Bill, "Look up the street there, Bill. See anything unusual?"

Bill studied the view. After a few seconds, he said, "I believe I do. What do you suppose they're up to?"

The lawmen had seen several men standing in a cluster about a block away. The men appeared to be in animated conversation, gesturing with their hands. All the men wore side arms, and at least three carried shotguns.

"I think we both know what they're talking about," said Nathan. "Let's head on up to the Stephens place. Better grab your shotgun as we pass the office, Bill."

In a small town, it is difficult to keep a secret. Apparently, the multiple trips by the attorneys to the judge's home, the fact that Crenshaw had not been at the jail, and the fact that Nathan and Bill remained in town, indicated to interested townsfolk that Crenshaw was being held somewhere nearby. Judge Stephens' place was the likely spot.

When Nathan and Bill reached the stable, they let the other lawmen know what was happening. Nathan then asked everyone except one of the Summer Prairie hands to come with him. The man remaining behind would keep watch on Crenshaw.

After alerting the men guarding Crenshaw, Nathan and the other lawmen walked to the front of the Stephens house and spread

themselves across the road. With one ranch hand remaining at the stable, there were eight lawmen straddling the road. Every man except
Nathan held a shotgun. They all wore side arms.

The crowd of twenty men spoke loudly with each other as they
neared the Stephens' house. Perhaps he had paid a visit to one of the
taverns to boost his courage, or maybe had his own liquor supply, but
the burly man with the red beard appeared to be leading the lynch mob
again as they approached the lawmen. One of the men in the group was
carrying a coiled length of rope. Shouts of "String him up," and "Lynch
him" reached the lawmen.

When the group of men got close enough, Nathan shouted out,
"That's far enough, men. I thought I made it clear to you that Mr.
Crenshaw, as much as you want to string him up, is going to have a fair
trial. Now get on out of here and go back home."

The red-bearded man turned to face his cohorts. "We've heard
enough talk out of this Marshal. Let's go get Crenshaw," he said. His
speech was slightly slurred. While his back was turned to the lawmen,
the man drew a revolver from his waistband, an action that was unseen
by any of the lawmen. The man turned swiftly and drew a bead on
Nathan. "Sorry it had to be this way, Marshal, but we're going in to
get Crenshaw."

As the red-bearded man took aim, a shot rang out. The burly inciter
crumpled to the ground, howling in pain and grasping at his bleeding
thigh. The lawmen looked all around them, and then saw the Summer
Prairie ranch hand waving his rifle in the air as he stood behind some
bushes. Nathan waved back at him, and then quickly walked forward
to pick up the red-bearded man's revolver.

Addressing the crowd, Nathan said, "You men are facing seven
shotguns and my pistol and that fella over there with the rifle. None of
us wants to get killed over some hot head like this trying to get you to

carry out his agenda. Our shotguns won't kill all of you, perhaps, but I guarantee that several of you will die if you keep this up."

Just then, Judge Stephens walked up to join the lawmen. Looking at the lynch mob, he addressed them. "I know most of you men. None of you are criminals, but if you keep this up, you are all going to get badly hurt or spend time in prison. Now do what the Marshal is telling you."

The men in the mob quietly mumbled to each other.

Stephens continued, "Does anybody know who this man is?" he asked, pointing to the man on the ground who was still moaning.

One of the men in the mob spoke up. "Oh, that's Lester Mills. Only time he comes to town is when he wants to get drunk or cause trouble. Otherwise, he lives by himself in a shack out in the woods by the Neosho River. He's not such a bad guy, unless he's been drinking."

"Well, I suggest you boys take him over to the doc's to get that bullet dug out of his leg and get him patched up. Then he needs to get on his horse and get out of town. I don't want to see him back here again," said Nathan.

The judge then spoke up. "Just so you know, it looks like the trial for Crenshaw is going to be tomorrow. The law will set things straight."

The judge's remarks caused a mumbling among the remainder of the mob. They began to break up as six men in the mob got around Lester Mills, lifted him, and began carrying him toward the doctor's office. Mills was still groaning as they walked away.

Nathan and Bill walked over to the ranch hand who was still standing by his bushes. "Much obliged," said Nathan.

The ranch hand replied, "I figured you could use another gun, so I kicked Crenshaw's attorney out of the stable and locked it up so I could come up here.

"Well, I appreciate it, but you probably need to get back and look after Crenshaw." But Nathan noticed that the other hands had already returned to stand by the stable, so there was no need to hurry.

The ranch hand spoke up, "Marshal, I gotta tell you that I really feel sorry for that young attorney. I can't help but overhear him talking to Crenshaw."

Nathan was only mildly interested, but asked anyway, "So what do they talk about?"

The ranch hand chuckled. "Crenshaw keeps telling the lawyer that he is innocent, and that he needs to plead him not guilty. The attorney keeps telling him that the evidence is overwhelming, and that the best they could do is to ask the court to be allowed to plead guilty to a lesser charge." The ranch hand laughed again. "But old Crenshaw won't hear of it. The lawyer keeps telling him that he has no witnesses to speak for his defense, but Crenshaw seems to think he won't need anyone. He will get on the stand and set things straight. Does he really believe that he can get himself off, Marshal?"

"Yep, he sure does," said Nathan. "Crenshaw thinks that laws are made for other people, and that he has every right to break the law for his own benefit. He's a damn fool for thinking he's above the law."

Charles Rath had joined the group. "You wouldn't believe how many truly vile men are behind bars, but still contend they are innocent."

"Yeah, I would believe it," said Nathan. "Almost every outlaw I've ever put in jail tells me he's innocent, even with enough evidence to convict him twice over. Our jobs will always be needed, Charles."

Just then, Crenshaw's court-appointed attorney bustled past the lawmen and headed back to his office. "Poor fella," said Bill. In less than thirty minutes, the attorney hurried back to the stable. It was apparent that he was doing all he could to give Crenshaw a defense.

At three o'clock on that Thursday afternoon, Nathan walked to the telegraph office, where he sent a wire to Summer Prairie Ranch. The wording on the telegram was addressed to Will Summers and said:

Please escort Daniel Chambers and grandmother Meezie Jones to town to arrive 9 a.m. Fri. They will be prosecution witnesses. Claire May to come with you. She will be witness. Ensure they are well protected. NW sends.

At four o'clock, Judge Stephens summoned both the prosecuting and defense attorneys to his home. His conversation with them was brief.

"Are you gents ready to go to court?" asked the judge.

"Yes, sir," said the prosecutor.

The defense attorney did not answer.

"I take it your silence means you are not so sure. Is that right?" asked Stephens.

After hesitating, the defense attorney said, "Your honor. I'm sure you are aware that I have found nothing to hang my hat on in Crenshaw's defense. I can't even find a character witness outside of that loony woman sitting in the Marshal's jail. In short, I would probably never be ready for court in this case."

"I understand," said the judge. "But son, you were dealt a loser from the start. Why, if Crenshaw was walking out of a church on Easter Sunday, everybody he passed would still want to hang him. All I can ask is that you do your best."

"Yes, sir," said the defense attorney.

"Well," said Stephens. "If there are no extenuating circumstances, I intend to hold trial tomorrow morning. I will inform the jury panel and seat them at 8:30. Trial will begin at 9 a.m. Anything else, gentle-men?"

Neither attorney had an objection, and they left the judge's study. The prosecuting attorney returned to his office, and the defense lawyer, with his head hanging down, trod slowly back to the stable.

*****

Friday Morning

An overnight drizzle left water droplets on the grass. The rising sunlight caught the moisture, making the grass sparkle. The air smelled fresh on this cool morning. Crenshaw's guards had been rotated again, and breakfast at the cafe was being served at 6:30 a.m. to Nathan; Bill; Charles Rath; a deputy U.S. Marshal; Warren Franks, the bank exam-iner; and a Summer Prairie Ranch hand.

"Ought to be an interesting day," remarked Bill.

Surprisingly, no one answered. Apparently, they were all trying to wake up, or they all had their own thoughts on what might transpire that day. But they all held one mutual thought. They would be mighty glad to see this case closed.

But then Warren Franks spoke up. "I don't mind telling you, Mar-shal, I'm a bit nervous about testifying. Are you sure it will be safe?"

"As safe as we can make it, Mister Franks," said Nathan.

Thirty minutes later, the door of the cafe opened to reveal Will Summers and Claire May coming through the door. Nathan rose and hugged and kissed his wife. Several cat calls were heard from the old-timer regulars sitting in a corner nursing their coffee. Two more chairs were pulled up to the long table. Claire May and Will were introduced to the unfamiliar faces at the table. The group watched as Will and Claire May ordered their breakfast.

Bill was the first to rise from the table, as he had already eaten breakfast at home.

"I figure I better go down to the courthouse and make sure the crowd doesn't beat each other up to get a seat in the court room. I'll see you fellas down there," said Bill. Sure enough, as Bill made his way to the courthouse, he could see a line of people winding around the corner of the building. He thought to himself, I hope everybody stays nice and peaceful.

At 8:30, the jury was seated, and then a portion of the crowd was allowed to enter the court room, but Judge Stephens' bailiff and Bill kept others out when all seats were taken. Will found a chair in the court room, while Claire May made her way to the witness room. A single row of people were allowed to stand at the back wall of the court room to observe the proceedings. After Judge Stephens entered the room, his bailiff called the trial to order.

Nervous as he might be, Federal Bank Examiner Warren Franks was the first witness to testify. His testimony reiterated the recent bank robbery and embezzlement, crimes for which many folks in town had suffered financially at the hands of Crenshaw. Franks carefully went through the events that had led to the indictment of Crenshaw for embezzlement, extortion, robbery, breaking usury law, and money laundering into the Prairie Trust. At the end of his testimony, the court room was silent. The townsfolk had not realized the extent of Crenshaw's financial crimes.

A low murmuring arose from the crowd, but that was soon interrupted by Crenshaw himself. He stood and shouted, "That money is all mine. I earned it, and you have no right to take it away from me. I demand that this slanderous trial be stopped at once."

Crenshaw's defense attorney quickly stood and pulled Crenshaw's arm to force him back into his chair. The court room then erupted with catcalls and cries for hanging the outlaw. It was a full two minutes before Judge Stephens could restore order.

"You folks who are here observing the trial are to remain silent. If I have another outburst, you will all be escorted from the room," said the Judge. "As for you, Mr. Crenshaw, you will have your turn to testify. If you insist on interrupting this court room, I will have you bound and gagged. Does everyone understand?"

There was a low murmuring from the observers as they watched Crenshaw retake his seat next to his attorney.

At the end of Franks' testimony, he was asked whether there would be any restitution for the bank depositors. He answered that repayment would be made to all depositors who had lost monies in the robbery of the bank. He also told the court that distribution of the funds would be made when the trial was over, and this brought another low murmur from the observers, who now knew that they were going to receive the money that had been stolen from them.

The second witness of the day was Claire May Wolf. Her testimony led the jury through her kidnapping step by step, who her kidnappers were, and the operation of the cattle buying and shipping at the old Tioga rail station. She revealed that she had overheard gang members say that they intended to kill her and load her onto a cattle car. She then told how she escaped and her ambush of her outlaw pursuers. This brought on a quiet murmuring from the audience. When she had completed her testimony, she looked over at Nathan, who winked at her and smiled.

At the end of Claire May's testimony, Crenshaw once again leaped up, stating, "You can't pin that kidnapping on me. I didn't do it, and I wasn't there."

Judge Stephens rapped his gavel. "Sit down, Mr. Crenshaw. I warned you about such behavior. And by the way, sir, you have not been charged with kidnapping. You have been charged with being an accessory to kidnapping. Now sit down."

"Under his breath, but still audible to the court, Crenshaw said, "I'd like to see you prove that." This remark brought a fierce glower from Judge Stephens.

After the court room had calmed and quieted, Judge Stephens turned to the defense counsel. "Your witness, counselor."

The defense attorney rose. "I only have one question, your honor." Facing Claire May, he asked, "Mrs. Wolf, you don't know whether Mr. Crenshaw was involved in your kidnapping, do you?"

"No, I don't," answered Claire May. "But I know that he was the leader of the men that carried out my kidnapping."

"I object, your honor," said the defense attorney.

"Yes, yes," said Stephens. "Mrs. Wolf, please answer only the question as it is asked by the attorneys. Don't add your own commentary. The jury will disregard Mrs. Wolf's final comment." He then turned back to the attorney. "Does the defense wish to continue?"

"No, your honor, I have no further questions," said the defense attorney.

Judge Stephens turned again to Claire May. "Mrs. Wolf, you may step down."

The prosecutor was now ready to move on to another line of questioning. Your honor, as you know, I have charged Mr. Crenshaw as an accessory to murder."

Stephens answered, "Yes, I'm aware of that." The judge turned to the jury and continued. "For the benefit of the jury, a murder was committed some twenty years ago for which no one was ever charged. New evidence has come forward, which gave the prosecution reason to indict Mr. Crenshaw for being implicated as an accessory to that murder."

Judge Stephens went on, "You may proceed Mr. Prosecutor."

"Thank you, Judge. I would like to call Miz Meesha Jones to the stand."

A buzz ensued in the court room. Almost no one knew who Meesha Jones was. The judge rapped his gavel again for silence. All eyes in the court room turned to observe the thin black woman as she came from the witness room, and slowly took her place on the witness stand.

The prosecuting attorney had spent only an hour with Meezie at their farm the previous day. He had left the farm knowing that he did not need to spend any more time with Meezie. In his opinion, the elderly woman was sharp as a tack and remembered the essential details surrounding the murder of her daughter and son-in-law twenty years prior. He walked Meezie through her testimony, praising her when she hit upon each of the points needing to be made. With her words, she painted a picture of how the gang of KKK men had come to attack her family, killing her daughter and son-in-law, and how she had hidden from them, but had seen the grisly murder. The prosecutor gave her plenty of time to testify, as Meezie paused several times to wipe away her tears and gently blow her nose. Meezie went on to describe the sounds, the smell, and the evil flames as the men burned down their cabin. Of the men she saw clearly, she described the men's characteristics, including the enforcer with the scarred hand. She told the jury how that man had gotten the scar while attempting to kill Jonah when they had first settled on their land. She also mentioned the set of hoof prints that she had examined the morning following the murder, and how one horse had been wearing a barred shoe. Finally, she discussed the shotgun blast from her son-in-law, and how it had hit a horse and rider on the right side of the horse and on the rider's right leg. The prosecutor then turned the witness over to the defense.

Meezie's testimony had taken the defense attorney somewhat by surprise. Since her testimony was that of an eyewitness to the crime of murder, he was at a loss to find holes in her account. He rose from his chair, vainly searched his notes, and finally shook his head. "I have no questions for the witness, your honor."

Judge Stephens smiled slightly and turned to Meezie. "Thank you for your testimony, Miz Jones. Bailiff, please help Miz Jones to her seat."

All eyes were again on the small black woman who had the courage to come to court and describe the cowardly murder of her daughter and son-in-law that she had witnessed. Seeing no empty chairs, the bailiff was going to escort Meezie back to the witness room, but a man who had been sitting next to Daniel in the court room stood up and gave his chair to Meezie. After she was seated, Daniel took her hand and held it.

Judge Stephens looked at the prosecuting attorney. "Mr. Prosecutor?"

The prosecutor stood, turned to face the back of the court room, raised his hand, and waved to the back of the court room. He was signaling someone.

The prosecutor's wave was immediately followed by a great commotion at the rear of the room. The court room doors had opened to reveal Dwight Mullins, who was leading a saddled horse into the court room. This brought a rap of the gavel from Judge Stephens, who shouted, "What is the meaning of this. You can't bring a horse into my court room." He continued pounding his gavel. "Mr. Prosecutor, you had better have an explanation for this," as he glared at the young prosecuting attorney.

"Please, your honor. I know this is highly irregular, but this will only take a minute, and we can send the horse on its way."

"This better be good," said the judge.

"Yes, sir. Let me explain. If I could get the assistance of the bailiff and a deputy, please," said the prosecutor.

The bailiff walked over to stand by the attorney, who had now taken his place on the right side of the horse, the same side that now faced the jury.

"Your honor, we are going to put Mr. Crenshaw on the back of this animal, and while the bailiff and deputy do that, could we please swear Mr. Mullins in as a witness for the prosecution?" asked the attorney. "But I need him to stay here and help me with the horse."

"Mr. Prosecutor, you are trying my patience," said the Judge, but he turned to address Dwight. "Mr. Mullins, raise your right hand and swear that you will be telling the truth."

Following the judge's instructions, Dwight Mullins raised his hand and swore to tell the truth.

Crenshaw had not moved from his chair. The bailiff signaled to one of the Federal deputies who had been standing at the side of the room, and who now came over to assist the bailiff. Together, the two men carried Crenshaw and placed him up on the back of the horse.

The prosecuting attorney turned to address the jury. "Members of the jury will recall the testimony of Miz Jones, who witnessed the cold-blooded murder of her daughter and son-in-law twenty years ago. If you remember, she stated that her son-in-law, Jonah Chambers fired his shotgun on that fateful night. Miz Jones said that the buckshot hit one of the horses and the right leg of its rider."

The prosecutor turned to Dwight Mullins. "Now, Mr. Mullins, I draw your attention to these patterned white spots on the side of this horse. Why does this horse have such a distinctive group of white spots?"

"I believe those white-haired spots are caused by trauma to the horse's skin where buckshot pellets hit the horse years ago," said Dwight. "The hair regrew, but it came out white."

"How do you know that, Mr. Mullins?" asked the prosecutor.

"Because I dug each of those pieces of buckshot out of this horse, myself," said Dwight.

"Mr. Mullins, how long ago did this happen?"

"Mmm, it's got to be a little over twenty years ago," answered Dwight.

"Mr. Mullins, do you recall any other injuries that happened at the same time as the injury to this horse?"

"You mean, like to Crenshaw?" asked Dwight.

"Yes, OK, what about Crenshaw?" asked the attorney.

"Well, when he brought the horse in to have it looked at, his pant leg was all bloody. He told me that he had been shot in a hunting accident and had to get over to the doc's to get his leg looked at," said Dwight.

"That's fine," said the attorney. The horse had fidgeted and turned slightly so that the attorney said to Dwight, "Could we turn the horse again, so his side is facing the jury."

Dwight turned the horse so the jury could view the horse's right side. "Thank you, that's good. Now, Mr. Crenshaw, please put your foot in the right stirrup." Crenshaw refused. The deputy reached up and jammed Crenshaw's boot into the stirrup.

"I want to draw the jury's attention to the pattern of the spots on this horse's side. See how they are in a circular pattern, as if they were hit by a shotgun blast," said the attorney. He drew his hand around the circular shape of the white spots. "Remember what Miz Jones said. She said that the buckshot hit the horse and also its rider," said the attorney.

The deputy and the bailiff had been briefed ahead of time, and the bailiff put his foot in the left stirrup and mounted the horse, sitting behind Crenshaw. He then put Crenshaw in a bear hug, leaned over and grabbed the saddle horn in front of Crenshaw, so that the outlaw could not move. After that was done, the deputy reached up again and grabbed Crenshaw's right leg. He wrestled Crenshaw's boot off, and his sock. He then held Crenshaw's foot with one hand and shoved Crenshaw's pant leg up to his knee. Then he jammed Crenshaw's bare foot back into the stirrup and held it there.

"Gentlemen of the jury. I would like to draw your attention to Mr. Crenshaw's leg. The old scars are quite evident. Not only was a portion of his calf excised by the shotgun blast, but you can also see the smaller scars where buckshot was removed from his leg." The jury then appeared to whisper quietly to one another until Judge Stephens rapped his gavel and asked for quiet.

"Notice that Mr. Crenshaw's leg covers a portion of the side of the horse and that there are no white-haired spots behind his leg."

The prosecutor asked Dwight Mullins to turn the horse a bit so that the horse's rump was facing the jury.

The prosecutor then said, "Members of the jury will recall Miz. Jones describing the hoof prints in the dirt the morning after her daughter and son-in-law were killed. You will recall that she said that one of the horses had been wearing a barred shoe."

"Mr. Mullins, I will hold the horse's halter. I would like you to lift the horse's right rear leg so that the jury can see the shoe on that hoof."

Dwight moved to the right side of the horse and attempted to lift the horse's leg. With two men seated on the horse, the animal was reluctant to lift its leg. But after several attempts, Dwight was able to lift the horse's right rear leg to reveal the barred shoe. He then dropped the leg and patted the horse on its rump.

The prosecutor then turned back to Dwight Mullins. "Mr. Mullins, are you familiar with this horse from your livery business?"

Dwight answered, "Sure. I've been taking care of this horse near all of its life."

Has this horse always worn a barred shoe on its right hind hoof?" asked the attorney.

"Yeah. He's got a problem with his pastern on that foot, and the barred shoe helps distribute the weight on that hoof. He gets along just fine with that shoe," said Dwight.

"Do any of your other customers have a horse with a barred shoe?" asked the prosecutor.

"No sir," said Dwight.

"Mr. Mullins, who owns this horse?" asked the prosecutor.

"Why, it's Arthur Crenshaw's horse. He's owned this old boy since he was foaled over twenty years ago," said Dwight.

A steady, dull mumbling rose from the audience and the jury after Dwight's remark.

The prosecutor continued, "Members of the jury, I contend that it was Mr. Crenshaw riding this very horse twenty years ago participating in the bloody murder of Mr. Jonah Chambers and his wife Dehlia Chambers."

No sooner had the words come from the attorney's mouth than Crenshaw shouted out. "You're not going to frame me for any murder. I never even knew those Chambers people, and I've never met that Miz Jones in my life. You can't get away with this."

Crenshaw then kicked the horse with both of his feet and yelled for the animal in an attempt to make it charge out the door. But Dwight Mullins and the lawmen had expected something like this to happen. Dwight Mullins kept a firm hand on the horse's halter. The animal skittered around in a circle, knocking over the prosecutor's table. What the lawmen did not foresee was that somehow, Crenshaw was able to reach behind him and wrench the bailiff's handgun from its holster. He drew it forward and pulled back the hammer. He was going to take aim at Judge Stephens. But the bailiff recovered and pushed Crenshaw's arm upward. The pistol went off with a reverberating blast. The bullet flew toward the ceiling and struck the supporting bar that was attached to a bracket which held three kerosene-filled lamps. The bracket teetered for a second or two and then detached completely, sending the three oil lamps crashing down onto Judge Stephens' bench. Kerosene and glass flew in all directions. Judge Stephens sprang from his chair. The oil had splashed all over his robe. His face was crimson, as he hammered his gavel so forcefully that the head of the gavel flew off and landed on the defense attorney's table.

"Recess. Recess for thirty minutes," shouted Stephens.

At this point, the horse decided that it was only fitting in all of this excitement to spread its rear legs and urinate a prodigious amount of liquid on the floor of the court room.

Stephens continued, "And get that goddam horse out of my court room!"

*****

After a time, decorum was restored, Crenshaw was placed back at the defense table, and the horse was removed from the court room. The bailiff and the deputy produced a bucket and rags to clean up the puddle of horse urine and removed the oil lamps, broken glass, and the light bracket from the judge's table. Court resumed.

There were only two more witnesses, Nathan Wolf and Edwin Mullins. Ed Mullins emotionally described how he was forced to join the local KKK chapter under threat that his father would be harmed if he did not join. He went on to describe the inner workings of the KKK chapter of which Arthur Crenshaw was the leader, named all of the dead members, and detailed how enforcement was carried out on people who crossed the KKK. He also testified that the Klan had vowed to kill his father if he did not join their group, testimony that brought murmurs from the crowd and the jury. Judge Stephens quickly returned the room to quiet order.

The prosecutor asked, "How did the local KKK get involved in cattle rustling?"

Ed Mullins answered that the cattle rustling was the idea of Malvern Owens, the stepbrother of Arthur Crenshaw, and that Owens had been the man with the badly scarred hand, and who was also the enforcer for the chapter. Ed told how he had made special knives and medallions for Arthur Crenshaw.

"Did anyone in the KKK chapter ever talk about the killing of Jonah and Dehlia Chambers?" asked the prosecutor.

"Yes, it was common knowledge in the chapter," said Ed. "Mr. Crenshaw and Malvern Owens spoke about it many times, as if they were proud that they had burned down the black folks' cabin and killed the couple that lived there."

"No further questions, your honor," said the prosecutor.

"Very well," said Judge Stephens. "Does the defense have any questions of the witness?"

The attorney rose. "Just a couple questions, your honor. Mr. Mullins, are you being paid for your testimony here today?"

"Being paid? No one is paying me for what I'm saying today," said Ed.

"Did someone force you to come here today and testify?" asked the attorney.

"No one forced me to be a witness. I guess you might say that the Ku Klux Klan forced me to come here, since they threatened to kill my dad," said Ed. "I figured it was about time to let people know what is going on and make some of these men pay for their crimes."

The defense attorney was clearly flummoxed. Everyone in the court room knew Ed Mullins, and his testimony was too credible to question. "No further questions, your honor," said the defense attorney.

But then, Arthur Crenshaw quickly stood up and began shouting. "I wouldn't ask that Judas anything. He is a traitor and has dishonored the Ku Klux Klan by his lies and by testifying against the righteous cause of the Klan. He is not to be believed. This is all part of a plan to railroad me. I have done nothing wrong." At the end, Crenshaw was shouting at the top of his voice and continued gesturing with his hands in the air.

"Bailiff, cuff and gag Mr. Crenshaw, please," said Judge Stephens. "I have heard enough of his outbursts. He has nothing constructive to add in his defense."

In short order, Crenshaw was handcuffed, and a gag was tied around his mouth.

"Mr. Mullins, you may step down," said the Judge.

"Your honor, I would like to call Marshal Nathan Wolf to the stand," said the prosecutor.

The damning testimony of the previous witnesses had already sealed the fate of Arthur Crenshaw, but the prosecuting attorney wanted to bring out one more piece of evidence.

"Marshal Wolf, did Arthur Crenshaw and his gang of outlaws attempt to take your life and the lives of the Summers family at Summer Prairie Ranch?" asked the attorney.

"Yes," said Nathan.

"For the court, would you please describe those events?"

Nathan then went into detail concerning the events that occurred the previous week, and how they had all led up to the gunfight at the ranch.

"How many men were killed in that fight, Marshal?" asked the prosecutor.

"We believe that fourteen men were killed. Every one of those men had a KKK medallion in his pocket, proving that they were all members of Arthur Crenshaw's Klan chapter. They had come to the ranch with the intent to kill everyone at Summer Prairie and burn down all of its buildings. What they did not know was that we were ready for them," said Nathan.

"Marshal, how did you know that Crenshaw and his men were going to attack the Summer Prairie Ranch?"

Nathan replied, "We would not have known about it had it not been for Ed Mullins. When we found out that Ed was being blackmailed into joining Crenshaw's gang, he volunteered to help us put an end to Crenshaw's KKK gang. He let us know the details of the upcoming raid on Summer Prairie Ranch. That's how we were able to be ready for the attack and wipe out the KKK group without any of our people being injured. We owe a lot to Ed Mullins for his help."

"During that fight, did any of Crenshaw's men escape?" asked the prosecutor.

"Only one," said Nathan. "Crenshaw, himself. He had stayed back to let his gang do the killing. I saw him watching from a safe distance. When the fight was over, he rode away to plan his escape."

"Was Crenshaw able to escape?" asked the attorney.

"For only a short time," said Nathan. "Crenshaw came back to town after the raid on Summer Prairie. It was then that he robbed the bank and left town by train. Luckily, we were able to apprehend him in Topeka, as the train made a stop there. When he was picked up by the U.S. Marshal there, Crenshaw had all of the bank's money with him. That was a blessing for us, and we intend to give the money back to the bank depositors."

The prosecutor said, "Well, Marshal, I think the town owes you a debt of gratitude for your work."

Immediately, the court room burst forth with applause and shouts of gratitude, quickly squelched by the pounding of Judge Stephens' hammer. He had replaced his broken gavel with a ball peen hammer and was rapping it loudly on his desk.

After the room quieted, Judge Stephens looked at the defense table. "Does the defense counsel have any questions for the witness?"

The defense attorney rose from his chair and looked down at Crenshaw. The outlaw did not even raise his head and continued looking down. "Your honor, I don't believe we have any questions," said the defense attorney, who then slowly sat down.

"Marshal Wolf, you may step down," said Judge Stephens. "Mr. Prosecutor, are we done with witnesses?"

"Yes, your honor. The state rests its case," said the prosecutor.

Judge Stephens responded by asking the defense attorney, "Does the defense have any witnesses or last questions. Any final comments? Does Mr. Crenshaw intend to testify on his own behalf?"

The defense attorney stood again and looked at Crenshaw for a few seconds. In spite of his pompous bluster and claim that he would exonerate himself on the witness stand, Crenshaw had finally come to the realization that he could not win. He was a beaten man and continued to look down at the floor. The defense attorney finally answered, "No, your honor."

Judge Stephens responded, "In that case, I would like the court room cleared. I am going to give the jury their charge, and only the court officials may remain. Please clear the court room."

As the last of the spectators left the court room, Judge Stephens addressed the jury. "Members of the jury, you have been asked to make a decision on the following charges that are pending against Arthur Crenshaw. He has been charged with being an accessory to murder, an accessory to attempted murder, accessory to kidnapping, accessory to arson, embezzlement of bank funds, blackmail, extortion, violation of Federal and state usury laws, and accessory to cattle rustling. You are to find Mr. Crenshaw either guilty or not guilty to each of these charges. Please raise your hands if you understand my instructions."

Each member of the jury raised his hand.

"All right then. I would ask that you all file into the jury room to discuss your opinions amongst yourselves. You will also see a bell on the table in that room. If you wish to summon the bailiff to ask for help on something, just ring the bell, and the bailiff will come. Any questions? If not, then you can head on out to the jury room."

The jury had no questions, and they filed out of the court room. Judge Stephens stood up and stretched.

"Bailiff, do we have any coffee in the back room?" asked the judge.

"Yes sir, your clerk just made a pot," answered the bailiff.

"It has been a long day, gentlemen, but at least we got through all the testimony," said the judge. "There should be enough mugs back in the back for all of us. Let's go get a bit of coffee."

The lawmen and the judge stood around the judge's chambers drinking their coffee. It had been thirty minutes since the jury left the court room when the coffee drinkers heard the bell.

"Uh, oh," said the judge.

The bailiff quickly left the room to go to the jury room. He was back in only a few minutes and spoke to the judge.

"They want a definition of the word accessory. They want to make sure they understand it properly," said the bailiff.

"Oh, lord," said Stephens. "I'll go talk with them, but I want both attorneys with me, so I don't get accused of collusion. C'mon gentlemen."

The judge, the bailiff, and the two attorneys left the room. In only ten minutes the men returned.

"Damndest thing I ever saw," said the judge. "No sooner had I explained what an accessory means, than they all raised their hands. They have made a unanimous decision."

"Well, what is it, Judge?" asked the prosecutor.

"In the court room, gents. In the court room." said Stephens.

When the lawmen and the jury had all reassembled in the court room, the judge told the bailiff to allow the spectators back into the room. This time though, after the spectators had been seated, an additional row of spectators had been allowed to stand at the back of the room. The bailiff called the court to order once again.

Judge Stephens turned to the jury and said, "Mr. Foreman, has the jury reached a decision?"

The foreman stood up and answered. "Yes, your honor. We find the defendant, Arthur Crenshaw, guilty of every dang one of those charges."

There was no point in Judge Stephens trying to calm down the court room for at least a few minutes. He let the shouting and loud talk continue for a while. Then, he rapped his ball peen hammer on the desk and shouted for order. Slowly, the court room got quieter, until all eyes were on the judge.

"Will the defendant please rise," said the judge.

Crenshaw's attorney rose, but Crenshaw remained slouched in his chair, his bare foot poking out from under the table. Judge Stephens nodded at the bailiff, who then walked over and jerked Crenshaw to his feet.

"Arthur Crenshaw, the jury in your case has found you guilty of each of the charges against you," said Stephens.

Before Judge Stephens could continue, Crenshaw blurted out, "To hell with your jury and you too. I am innocent. I am a vigilant warrior, and I am not subject to your frivolous laws." With that, he picked his boot off of the table and threw it at the judge's bench.

Crenshaw kept shouting nonsense and obscenities as the bailiff walked over to him and placed the gag back on Crenshaw's head.

Judge Stephens continued. "Arthur Crenshaw, I am sentencing you to be hanged by the neck until dead. Justice will be served. Your hanging will take place at ten a.m. this coming Monday morning. May God have mercy on your soul." With those words, the judge rapped his hammer.

"This court is adjourned," said Stephens.

*****

Saturday Morning

Millie set the three mugs of coffee on the corner of Judge Stephens' desk. "Now that Crenshaw's trial is over, what are you two boys going to do to keep busy?" she teased.

Nathan picked up his mug and blew across the top to cool the hot coffee. He and Rodney Stephens had been discussing the trial on a drizzly morning at the Judge's home. Claire May sat next to Nathan, sipping her coffee. They all watched as Millie left the room.

"Kinda sassy, ain't she," remarked the judge.

Nathan laughed. "Yeah, but somebody needs to keep you in line, Rodney," said Nathan.

The two men and Claire May sat in silence for a moment sipping their coffee.

"That's the damndest thing I ever saw. A horse in my courtroom," said the judge. "But that young attorney has guts and is going to go places. I'm wondering whether I should reprimand him or make him the county prosecutor on a full-time basis."

The judge sipped his coffee and continued. "All right. Down to business and the reason you folks are here. I called my attorney friend in Topeka last night to discuss that trust again. He assured me that I could let the land that Crenshaw owned go into probate. Then, owner-ship would roll over to the state. And since the state doesn't want to own farm and ranch land, the land will go up for auction. And when it does, you can legitimately carry out your plan. In the meantime, I understand that you have arranged to have the Federal Bank Examiner set up shop at the old bank this afternoon and make distribution of funds to the Prairie Bank depositors. Is that right?"

"Yes, sir. I plan to have a couple of lawmen sitting with him so we don't have any problems from anybody, but I think folks will be so glad to get some of their money back, that everything will go smoothly," said Nathan. "I'm figuring everyone will be paid back, and Dave Morgan and Daniel Chambers will get the proceeds from the cattle rustling so they can replace their cattle. I also have another two hundred dollars that came from the now-deceased Clyde Morse, and I'm using that to have a proper gravestone made for Meezie Jones' daughter and son-in-law. At least that's the plan."

"I hope it all goes smoothly," said Stephens. "I'll have to get in line with everybody else. I had money in that bank, too. Are you going to make sure everything is set for Monday?"

"Yes, sir. The deputies from Topeka are going to stick around until after the hanging, and Charles Rath, the Pinkerton fellow, is also staying. So, I think we will be all right. I can't imagine anyone wanting to stop Crenshaw's execution. The whole town wants to watch him die." Nathan paused for a moment.

"Kinda sad when a fella doesn't have even one friend in the world, ain't it," said Nathan.

"Well, we both know that outlaws bring their problems on themselves," said Stephens. "Which reminds me, we will need to set trial dates for that KKK fellow, and Crenshaw's housekeeper in the next few days. But they can wait a few days to let the town calm down."

Nathan answered the judge. "We won't have to try the KKK henchman. Charles Rath and the deputies are going to take him up to Kansas City to stand trial. I'm not sure what they've got on him, other than trying to knock off Crenshaw and drawing a gun on Rath and me," said Nathan. "But at least we won't have to deal with him."

Nathan and Claire May stood up to leave. "Guess I'll see you at the bank. After that, Claire May, Will, and I are heading for home. I'll be back early Monday morning. Crenshaw will be safe in the jail for the next couple of days. Bill, the two Topeka deputies, and Charles Rath will be keeping an eye on him."

The judge stood, and the men shook hands.

"Get on home and take care of this little wife of yours," said the judge. "By the way, when is that baby due?" he asked, looking at Claire May. Nathan had previously told him the news that Claire May was expecting.

"I think it will be in another six months or so," said Claire May. The couple waved as they left Stephens' house.

Nathan was right about the redistribution of the funds from the Prairie Bank. Most depositors were just happy to be getting their hard-earned money back. The majority of the people walked down the street and opened new accounts at the Wells Fargo Bank. Will, Nathan, and Claire May walked to the Wells Fargo Bank after receiving the money owed to Summer Prairie Ranch and opened their own new account. When they walked back to the Marshal's office, Warren Franks, the Federal Bank Examiner was waiting for them.

"Marshal, all distributions have been made to the bank depositors. There was two thousand dollars left in the funds that Crenshaw had in his bag, and I'm turning that over to you. I trust you will find a proper use for that money. Perhaps it will defray some of the extra costs you have had due to Crenshaw's misdeeds and his trial. I'm going to leave town on the five o'clock train. But I wanted to thank you for helping me get to the bottom of the Prairie Bank problems," said Franks.

"Glad we could help," Nathan responded, "and we're mighty grateful you were able to help us."

Franks puffed up on hearing the compliment. He then said, "I sort of wish I could stay to see Crenshaw get what is coming to him, but I fear the spectacle might be a bit too much for me. So, I will bid all of you gentlemen *adieu*, and also to you, Mrs. Wolf. I'm going down to the depot."

After Franks shook hands with everyone, he walked out of the office and headed for the train depot. Apparently, he had gotten someone to carry his large, heavy bags to the rail station.

"What is an *adieu*?" asked Bill.

"I think it's a fancy way to say good-bye," said Charles Rath. "He certainly was an odd fellow, wasn't he?"

Those same sentiments were voiced by Claire May as she, Will, and Nathan rode home early in the evening. Nathan was getting drowsy as he was lulled by the horses' steady rhythm in their walk. Claire May teasingly reached over and pinched her husband. He smiled but did not open his eyes. Hmm, she thought. Maybe I'll just drop back a bit and watch him. She signaled to Will, who dropped back with Claire May.

Sure enough, after they dropped back, Wander lived up to his name and drifted off the road and began munching grass in the shade of a tree. Claire May rode slowly up to her husband, then shouted, "Hey, Marshal!"

Nathan lurched awake, turned to the side and saw Claire May laughing at him and Will grinning. "Damn horse," muttered Nathan, and jerked Wander into a lope down the road, leaving Claire May and Will still laughing behind him. But then Nathan began laughing too and slowed to wait for Claire May and Will.

"You're not very nice," Nathan said to Claire May.

"Oh, you're wrong, Marshal. I can be very nice," she responded and laughed, while she prodded her horse into a gallop. "See you at home."

Will was chuckling next to Nathan.

But Nathan was smiling as he said, "Can't you keep that sister of yours in line?"

The men prodded their horses into a lope and rode the rest of the way home.

That evening at supper, Nathan told the family what he intended to do with the remaining money from Crenshaw's funds. The money would benefit Daniel Chambers and his grandmother. Using part of the funds, Will was to go to Dave Morgan and buy a dozen stocker steers and get them over to the Chambers farm to replace the stock that was stolen by Crenshaw's rustlers. In addition, Dave Morgan would be paid for the cattle that had been rustled from him. The remaining money would be made available to Daniel to pay for his share of the land held in the old Crenshaw Prairie Trust. The land would be purchased by the three ranches when the state put it up for auction, and then would be divided between the Summer Prairie Ranch, the Circle M Ranch, and the Chambers farm. Because there would be future revenue from oil production, the mineral rights for the property would be divided equitably between the three families. The Standard Oil Company had already notified Virginia Summers and Dave Morgan that they would like to send a representative to Chanute to discuss drilling contracts.

"Sounds like a good plan," said Will. "I'll take care of buying the calves from Dave Morgan on Monday morning. I don't intend to go into town to watch Crenshaw swing," said Will. "Alice Morgan has been wanting me to come over and talk with her anyway. I guess I'm going to have to set a date for the wedding."

"Well, it's about time," said Claire May. "You've been stringing Alice along, and she doesn't like it one bit. If you don't take care of business, dear brother, little Alice will up and marry somebody else, and then where would you be?"

"Happy?" said Will, completely in jest. Claire May made a face at him in response.

Later, after dinner, Nathan and Claire May sat on the front porch listening to the crickets sing.

"I suppose you need to be in town Monday morning," said Claire May.

"Townsfolk would probably think it was strange if their Marshal didn't show up for Crenshaw's final day," said Nathan. "Do you want to come to town with me?"

"I'll go with you," said Claire May. "But I don't want to watch a hanging. I'll just wait for you in the office. Then I need to head back, because I want to stop and see Meezie Jones on my way home."

"Oh, that's good. I need to go to see Daniel, myself. So, we can go out there together," said Nathan. "I want to let him know what we are doing to replace his cattle, and then talk with him about the trust ranch. I hope he is all right with us doing that. I figure Crenshaw caused more pain to him and his grandmother than to anyone else. I can't imagine what it would be like to have your mother and father killed before your eyes by a bunch of ignorant KKK outlaws."

*****

Monday Morning

Claire May kissed Nathan and said, "I'll wait for you here." They were in the Marshal's Office, and Nathan was about to leave to walk over to where the gallows had been erected on Saturday. Bill Ward had left the office earlier and was already at the execution site. Claire May watched as Nathan walked out the office door.

It appeared that nearly the whole town had turned out for the hanging of the notorious outlaw. Most of the stores on Main Street were closed, with the owners joining the crowd. The townsfolk talked among themselves, biding their time until the moment of execution.

At fifteen minutes until ten, the two deputy U.S. Marshals, who had been waiting in Nathan's office, opened Crenshaw's cell door and walked with him to the gallows. They escorted him up the steps of the gallows where Nathan, Bill, Judge Stephens, and a church pastor waited. The hangman, who wore a black hood, helped the deputies place Crenshaw on the trap door, covered Crenshaw's head with a hood, then placed the rope around his neck. The minister said a few words while standing next to Crenshaw, then moved to the side with the lawmen. At ten o'clock, the hangman took his place next to the lever for the trap door, and with a quick motion of the lever, the execution of Arthur Crenshaw was finished. He would never hurt anyone again.

Surprisingly, the crowd was quiet as they slowly dispersed. The lawmen and the hangman watched Crenshaw's body sway slightly in the breeze. After the crowd was mostly gone, the men walked down the steps, moved toward Crenshaw's body, and cut the rope. Then they carried the body to the undertaker's waiting wagon. The undertaker took his seat on the wagon, and slowly drove away.

Over dinner at the cafe, Claire May asked Nathan, "Was it horrible, Nathan?"

Nathan paused before answering. "I guess it's horrible to see a person throw away his life, believing that he is above the law. But it's not so horrible to see justice served to an outlaw whose crimes affected so many people. He got what he deserved. But I don't really think that the execution of outlaws should be cause for a public display, or a cause for celebration. Anyway, it's over and that's good."

Epilogue

Chambers Farm
Monday Afternoon

Claire May stood to the side and watched while the two men talked. Meezie Jones sat in her chair on the front porch and also watched her grandson and the Marshal as they talked.

"Daniel, I am hoping you will understand the intent of this," said Nathan. He had explained more than once to Daniel that the stocker steers that Will had delivered that morning were to replace those that Daniel had lost to rustlers, and that they were paid for out of Crenshaw's ill-gotten monies. In addition, he had explained that the neighboring property, which had belonged to Crenshaw was going to be divided between Daniel, the Morgans, and the Summers.

"I understand the replacement of my steers, Marshal," said Daniel. "That seems to be the right thing to do. But I'm bothered by this land business. I've never taken any charity, and that's what this seems. I didn't do anything to have claim to that land, so I ain't so sure of it."

"I understand," said Nathan. "But I believe that you have every right to receive restitution for the deaths of your mother and father."

The men continued to talk, but Daniel still was not completely convinced.

Out of the corner of her eye, Claire May saw Meezie Jones rise from her chair and walk down the porch steps. Claire May caught up with her as she walked to the creek. Meezie sat down on her upturned log, and Claire May sat on the ground next to the small black woman. After a few minutes, they were joined by Nathan and Daniel. Daniel walked to where his grandmother sat and placed his hand on her shoulder. Meezie turned her head and looked up at Daniel.

"Dehlia says it will be all right, Daniel," said Meezie.

No one said anything for a moment. Then very quietly, Daniel said, "All right, Grandma. If you say it's all right, we will take the extra land."

Meezie smiled. "That's good," she said.

Again, everyone was quiet for a few moments.

Then, almost as if talking to herself, Meezie said, "Marshal Wolf tells me that a fine stone marker is going to be delivered for you, Dehlia."

After a moment, Meezie looked at Claire May and said, "You hear them, don't you, Claire May? They are singing. Dehlia has a fine voice, doesn't she?" She continued to look at Claire May, whose eyes had opened wide, and her mouth was parted. Ever so quietly, she answered Meezie. "Yes. I hear them singing," she said. Then she and Meezie quietly sang along to the words.

I've got peace like a river,
I've got peace like a river,
I've got peace like a river
in my soul.
I've got peace like a river,
I've got peace like a river,
I've got peace like a river
in my soul.

Author's Notes

For those of you who have read my previous book, *Trail of the Outlaw,* you will recognize the main characters in *Singing Creek.* Marshal Nathan Wolf and Claire May Summers began their romance in the pages of *Trail of the Outlaw*, and have now married in Kansas. He traded his life as a local sheriff on the Mississippi River in Iowa to become the U.S. Marshal for Southeast Kansas and began new adventures in a time when Kansas still remembered how it earned its reputation as "Bleeding Kansas."

I thank all of you who continue to read my works. Watch for more adventures of Marshal Nathan Wolf. Comments from readers continue to inspire and encourage me.

A special thank you to my wife, Janet, who continues to provide support and guidance for my work.

About the Author

Award winning author James Duermeyer is a versatile writer who has written in nonfiction, historical fiction, and the Western genre. James holds a B.A. degree from William Penn University in Iowa, and an M.A. in U.S. History from the University of Texas at Arlington. He and his family live near Fort Worth, Texas.

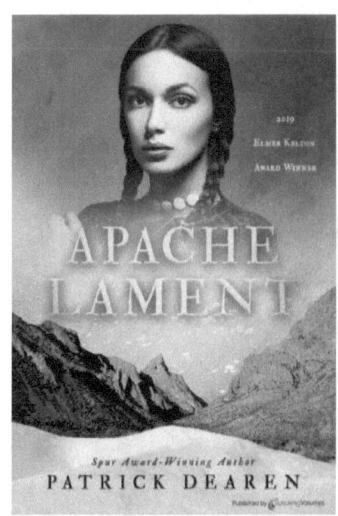 

On Sale Now!

JIM JONES
JARED DELANEY SERIES

For more information
visit: www.SpeakingVolumes.us

www.ingramcontent.com/pod-product-compliance
Lightning Source LLC
Chambersburg PA
CBHW020223260626
47156CB00002B/512